The LAST TESTAMENT

ALSO BY SAM BOURNE

The Righteous Men

The LAST TESTAMENT

N
W E
S

SAM BOURNE

HarperCollins Publishers Ltd

The Last Testament

Published by HarperCollins Publishers Ltd.

Originally published in Great Britain in 2007 by HarperCollins Publishers.
First published in Canada by HarperCollins Publishers Ltd in 2009.

First Canadian edition

HarperCollins Publishers Ltd
2 Bloor Street East, 20th Floor
Toronto, Ontario, Canada
M4W 1A8

www.harpercollins.ca

Library and Archives Canada Cataloguing in Publication
information is available

ISBN: 978-1-55468-074-0

Printed and bound in the United States
RRD 9 8 7 6 5 4 3 2 1

For my father, a testament to my love
and enduring admiration

The
LAST TESTAMENT

PROLOGUE

BAGHDAD, APRIL 2003

The crowd were pushing harder now, as if they scented blood. They charged through the archway and their combined weight pressed against the tall oak doors until they went crashing to the ground. As they rushed through, Salam moved with them. It was not a decision. He was simply a part of a moving beast made up of men, women and children, some even younger than him. They were a collective animal and now they gave a mighty roar.

They burst into the first vast hall, the glass of the display cases glinting in the silver moonlight that spilled through the ceiling-high windows. There was a brief pause, as if the beast were drawing breath. Salam and his fellow Baghdadis contemplated the scene before them. The National Museum of Antiquities, once Saddam's treasure house, bursting with the jewels of Mesopotamia, now laid wide open. There was not a guard in sight. The last of the museum staff had abandoned their posts hours earlier; and the few remaining security men had fled at the sight of this horde.

The brief moment of silence was ruptured by a sledgehammer

crashing through glass. On that cue, the room was instantly filled with thunderous noise, as one after another they started wielding pistols, axes, knives, clubs, even heavy strips of metal torn from wrecked cars – anything to spring these precious, ancient objects from their cases.

Pane after pane of glass shattered. Ivory statues tumbled; ancient ceramic plates smashed to powder as they hit the floor. The room, usually blanketed in museum quiet, echoed now with a mighty din: the breaking of stone and glass, even gunshots as the most impatient shot out locks that refused to surrender to a crowbar. Salam noticed two well-dressed men setting to work methodically with professional glass-cutting equipment.

The ground trembled as wave after wave of people stampeded into the museum, ignoring this first exhibition hall, looking for fresh pickings elsewhere. They collided with those anxious to get out, hauling their priceless booty on handcarts, wheelbarrows and bicycles, or struggling under heavy plastic crates and cardboard boxes. Salam recognized a friend of his father striding out, his face flushed and his pockets bulging.

Salam's pulse was throbbing. In all his fifteen years he had never seen anybody behave like this. Until a few days ago everyone he knew had moved slowly, heads down, eyes averted. In Saddam's Iraq you knew better than to break the rules or draw attention to yourself. Now these same people – his neighbours – were wild in their desire, stealing anything they could lay their hands on and destroying the rest.

Salam reached into a broken case for a necklace made of pale orange and amber stones. But someone grabbed his wrist before he could grasp it: a middle-aged woman, eyes ablaze, blocking Salam with her left hand, stealing the necklace for herself with her right. He backed away.

It was like a scene from the sacking of an ancient city, Salam thought: an orgy driven not by lust, but by greed, the participants writhing with avarice, slaking an appetite that had been pent up for decades. Suddenly he was pushed forward again: a new group of looters had arrived and they were making for the stairwell.

Salam was swept along as they headed down a flight of stairs: a rumour had spread that the museum staff had stashed all the best stuff in the storerooms. He saw a knot of men standing around a door which they had clearly just lifted off its hinges. Behind it stood a freshly-constructed wall of cinder blocks, the cement barely set. First one man, then two, began hacking away at the bricks with hammers; others joined them using bars, even their shoulders. They turned to Salam.

'Come on!'

They passed him a metal table leg.

Soon the hastily-assembled wall gave way, a sandcastle crumbling in the waves. The leader of the group stepped through the hole and at once began to laugh. Others quickly joined him. Salam could soon see the source of their joy: the room was packed with treasure – stone carvings of princesses and kings; etchings of rams and oxen; statues of buxom goddesses and Nubian women; ceramic jars, urns and bowls. There were copper shoes, fragments of tapestry and, on the wall, a frieze of soldiers fighting some long-forgotten war.

Salam's eye caught a few of the museum labels, still stuck to these hidden treasures. One identified a 'lyre from the Sumerian city of Ur, bearing the gold-encased head of a bull, dated 2400 BC'. That was soon carted off. Next was a 'white limestone votive bowl from Warka, dated 3000 BC': Salam watched as it disappeared inside a football kit bag. A 'statue representing King Entemena from Ur, dated 2430 BC' took two men to lift and a third to navigate through the newly-opened hole in the wall. Salam remembered what they had taught him at school: that the Baghdad Museum contained treasures that were five thousand years old. 'Inside that museum lies not just the history of Iraq,' his teacher had intoned, 'but the history of all mankind.'

Now it resembled nothing grander than a vegetable market, the customers scrapping over the produce. Except these were not squashed tomatoes or bruised peppers, but artwork and tools that had survived since the birth of civilization.

Salam could hear raised voices: two of the ringleaders were arguing. One slapped the other and the pair began to fight, bringing a metal bookcase stacked with pots crashing to the ground. Someone produced a knife. A man gave Salam a hard push in the back, shoving him towards the violence. Instinctively, he wheeled around, dived out of the hole in the cinder-block wall and ran.

He rushed down the stairs, hearing a new clamour at each landing. Every one of the eighteen galleries in the museum was now undergoing the same plunder. The noise scared him.

Salam kept heading down, flight after flight, until he had left the crowds behind: no one was bothering to come this far down now with such easy pickings higher up. He would be safely away from them here.

Salam pushed open a door and it moved easily. In the gloom he could see a few boxes of papers overturned, their contents carpeting the floor. Whoever was responsible had been right not to linger: this was merely an office. He noticed a few decapitated wires, dangling like the roots of an upended tree: someone had stolen the phones and fax machine and left the rest.

Maybe they had missed something, Salam thought. He tugged at the desk drawers, hoping to find a gold pen or even a cash-box. But all he found were a few old sheets of paper.

There was a larger drawer underneath; he'd give that one last pull and then he'd go. Locked.

He headed for the door only to catch his foot on a ridge by the desk. Salam looked down to find a loose stone square. His bad luck: all the others were flat and perfectly even. Hardly thinking, Salam wedged his fingers into the gap between the squares and prized out the loose one. It being too murky to see, he felt for the ground below – but his hand just sank into a narrow but deep hole.

Now he felt something solid; cool to the touch. It was a tin box. At last: money!

He had to lie on the ground, his cheek against the stone, in order to reach down far enough. His fingers struggled to grasp their target. The box was difficult to lift, but at last he got it out. It was locked; but its contents seemed too silent for coins and too heavy for notes.

He stood up, peering through the darkness until he found what he assumed was a letter opener lying on the desk. He slid it under the thin tin of the lid, leaning on the blade to lever up the metal. He did that all the way along one side, opening the box like a can of beans. By tipping it to one side, he could make the object inside slide out. His heart was pounding.

The second he saw it, he was disappointed. It was a clay tablet, engraved with a few random squiggles, like so many of the others he had seen tonight, many of them just smashed to the ground. Salam was about to discard it, but he hesitated. If some museum guy had gone to such lengths to hide this lump of clay, maybe it was worth something.

Salam sprinted up the stairs until he could see moonlight. He had come out at the back of the museum, where he could see a fresh horde of looters breaking their way in. He waited for a gap in the line, then stepped through the broken-down exit doors. Running flat out, he slipped into the Baghdad night – carrying a treasure whose true value he would never know.

CHAPTER ONE

Tel Aviv, Saturday night, several years later

The usual crowd was there. The hardcore leftists, the men with their hair grown long after a year travelling in India, the girls with diamond studs in their noses, the people who always turned up for these Saturday night get-togethers. They would sing the familiar songs – *Shir l'shalom,* the Song for Peace – and hold the trusted props: the candles cupped in their hands, or the portraits of the man himself, Yitzhak Rabin, the slain hero who had given his name to this piece of hallowed ground so many years earlier. They would form the inner circle at Rabin Square, whether handing out leaflets and bumper stickers or softly strumming guitars, letting the tunes drift into the warm, Mediterranean night air.

Beyond the core there were newer, less familiar, faces. To veterans of these peace rallies, the most surprising sight was the ranks of *Mizrachim,* working-class North African Jews who had trekked here from some of Israel's poorest towns. They had long been among Israel's most hawkish voters: 'We know the Arabs,' they would say, referring to their roots in Morocco, Tunisia or Iraq. 'We know what they're really like.' Tough and permanently wary of Israel's Palestinian neighbours, most had long scorned the leftists who showed up at rallies like this. Yet here they were.

The television cameras – from Israeli TV, the BBC, CNN and all the major international networks – swept over the crowd, picking out more unexpected faces. Banners in Russian, held aloft by immigrants to Israel from the old Soviet Union – another traditionally hardline constituency. An NBC cameraman framed a shot which made his director coo with excitement: a man wearing a kippa, the skullcap worn by religious Jews, next to a black Ethiopian-born woman, their faces bathed by the light of the candle in her hands.

A few rows behind them, unnoticed by the camera, was an older man: unsmiling, his face taut with determination. He checked under his jacket: it was still there.

Standing on the platform temporarily constructed for the purpose was a line of reporters, describing the scene for audiences across the globe. One American correspondent was louder than all the others.

'You join us in Tel Aviv for what's billed as an historic night for both Israelis and Palestinians. In just a few days' time the leaders of these two peoples are due to meet in Washington – on the lawn of the White House – to sign an agreement which will, at long last, end more than a century of conflict. The two sides are negotiating even now, in closed-door talks less than an hour from here in Jerusalem. They're trying to hammer out the fine print of a peace deal. And the location for those talks? Well, it couldn't be more symbolic, Katie. It's Government House, the former headquarters of the British when they ruled here, and it sits on the border that separates mainly Arab East Jerusalem from the predominantly Jewish West of the city.

'But tonight the action moves here, to Tel Aviv. The Israeli premier has called for this rally to say "Ken l'Shalom", or "Yes to Peace" –

a political move designed to show the world, and doubters among his own people, that he has the support to conclude a deal with Israel's historic enemy.

'Now, there are angry and militant opponents who say he has no right to make the compromises rumoured to be on the table – no right to give back land on the West Bank, no right to tear down Jewish settlements in those occupied territories and, above all, no right to divide Jerusalem. That's the biggest stumbling block, Katie. Israel has, until now, insisted that Jerusalem must remain its capital, a single city, for all eternity. For the Prime Minister's enemies that's holy writ, and he's about to break it. But hold on, I think the Israeli leader has just arrived . . .'

A current of energy rippled through the crowd as thousands turned to face the stage. Bounding towards the microphone was the Deputy Prime Minister, who received a polite round of applause. Though nominally a party colleague of the PM, this crowd also knew he had long been his bitterest rival.

He spoke too long, winning cheers only when he uttered the words, 'In conclusion . . .' Finally he introduced the leader, rattling through his achievements, hailing him as a man of peace, then sticking out his right arm, to beckon him on stage. And when he appeared, this vast mass of humanity erupted. Perhaps three hundred thousand of them, clapping, stamping and whooping their approval. It was not love for him they were expressing, but love for what he was about to do – what, by common consent, only he could do. No one else had the credibility to make the sacrifices required. In just a matter of days he would, they hoped, end the conflict that had marked the lives of every single one of them.

He was close to seventy, a hero of four Israeli wars. If he had worn them, his chest would have been weighed down with medals. Instead, his sole badge of military service was a pronounced limp in his right leg. He had been in politics for nearly twenty years, but he thought like a soldier even now. The press had always described him as a hawk, perennially sceptical of the peaceniks and their schemes. But things were different now, he told himself. There was a chance.

'We're tired,' he began, hushing the crowd. 'We're tired of fighting every day, tired of wearing the soldier's uniform, tired of sending our children, boys and girls, to carry guns and drive tanks when they are barely out of school. We fight and we fight and we fight, but we are tired. We're tired of ruling over another people who never wanted to be ruled by us.'

As he spoke, the unsmiling man was pushing through the crowd, breathing heavily. '*Slicha,*' he said again and again, each time firmly pushing a shoulder or an arm out of his way. *Excuse me.*

His hair was silver grey, his chest barrelled; he was no younger than the Prime Minister. This wade through the throng was exhausting him; his shirt collar was darkening with sweat. He looked as if he was trying to catch a train.

He was getting nearer to the front now and was still pushing. The plain clothes guard in the third row of the crowd was the first to notice him, immediately whispering a message into the microphone in his sleeve. That alerted the security detail cordoning the stage, who began scoping the faces before them. It took them no time to spot him. He was making no attempt to be subtle.

By now the plain clothes officer was just a couple of yards away. '*Adoni, adoni,*' he called. *Sir, sir.* Then he recognized him. 'Mr Guttman,' he called. 'Mr Guttman, please.' At that, people in the crowd turned around. They recognized him too. Professor Shimon Guttman, scholar and visionary, or windbag and right-wing rabble-rouser, depending on your point of view; never off the TV and the radio talk shows. He had made his name several summers ago, when Israel pulled out of Gaza: he camped out on the roof of a Jewish settlement, protesting that it was a crime for Israeli soldiers to be giving back land to 'Arab terrorists, thieves and murderers'.

He was marching on, squeezing past a mother with a child on her shoulders.

'Sir, stop right there!' the guard called out.

Guttman ignored him.

Now the agent began making his own journey through the crowd, breaking through a small cluster of teenagers. He considered pulling out his weapon, but decided against it: it would start a panic. He called out again, his voice was instantly drowned out by sustained applause.

'We do not love the Palestinians and they do not love us,' the Prime Minister was saying. 'We never will and they never will . . .'

The agent was still three rows away from Guttman, now advancing towards the podium. He was directly behind the older man; one long stretch and he could grab him. But the crowd was more tightly packed here; it was harder to push through. The agent stood on tiptoes and leaned over, just lightly brushing his shoulder.

By now Guttman was within shouting distance of the stage. He looked up towards the Prime Minister, who was coming to the climax of the speech.

'Kobi!' he yelled, calling him by a long-forgotten nickname. 'Kobi!' His eyes were bulging, his face flushed.

Security agents from all sides were now closing in, two on each side, as well as the first man advancing from behind. They were ready to pounce, to smother him to the ground as they had been taught, when a sixth agent, standing to the right of the stage, spotted a sudden movement. Perhaps it was just a wave, it was impossible to tell for sure, but Guttman, still staring maniacally at the Prime Minister, seemed to be reaching into his jacket.

The first shot was straight to the head, just as it had been rehearsed a hundred times. It had to be the head, to ensure instant paralysis. No muscular reflex that might set off a suicide bomb; no final seconds of life in which the suspect might pull a trigger. The bodyguards watched as the silver-haired skull of Shimon Guttman blew open like a watermelon, brains and blood spattering the people all around.

Within seconds, the PM had been bundled off the stage and was at the centre of a scrum of security personnel shoving him towards a car. The crowd, cheering and clapping thirty seconds earlier, was now quaking with panic. There were screams as those at the front tried to run away from the horrible sight of the dead man. Police used their arms to form a cordon around the corpse, but the pressure of the crowd was almost impossible. People were screaming, stampeding, desperate to get away.

Pushing in the opposite direction were two senior military officers from the Prime Minister's detail, determined to break the impromptu cordon and get to the would-be assassin. One of them flashed a badge at a police officer and somehow ducked under his arms and inside the small, human clearing formed around the body.

There was too little of the dead man's head to make out, but the rest of him was almost intact. He had fallen face down and now the officer rolled the lifeless body over. What he saw made him blanch.

It was not the shattered bone or hollowed eye sockets; he had seen those before. It was the man's hands, or rather his right hand. Still clenched, the fingers were not wrapped around a gun – but gripping a piece of paper, now sodden with blood. This man had not been reaching for a revolver – but for a note. Shimon Guttman hadn't wanted to kill the Prime Minister. He had wanted to tell him something.

CHAPTER TWO

WASHINGTON, SUNDAY, 9.00AM

'Big day today, honey.'

'Uh?'

'Come on, sweetheart, time to wake up.'

'Nrrghh.'

'OK. One, two, three. And the covers are off—'

'Hey!'

Maggie Costello bolted upright, grabbed at the duvet and pulled it back over her, making sure to cover her head as well as her body this time. She hated the mornings and regarded the Sunday lie-in as a constitutionally protected right.

Not Edward. He'd probably been up for two hours already. He wasn't like that when they met: back in Africa, in the Congo, he could pull the all-nighters just like her. But once they had come here, he had adapted pretty fast. Now he was Washington Man, out of the house just after six am. Through a squinted eye jammed up against the pillow, Maggie could see he was in shorts and a running vest, both sweaty. She was still unconscious, but he'd already been for his run through Rock Creek Park.

'Come on!' he said, shouting from the bathroom. 'I've cleared the whole day for furnishing this apartment. Crate and Barrel; then Bed Bath & Beyond; and finally Macy's. I have a complete plan.'

'Not the whole day,' Maggie muttered, knowing she was inaudible. She had a morning appointment, an overspill slot for clients who could never make weekdays.

'Actually not the whole day,' Edward shouted, the sound of the shower not quite drowning him out. 'You've got that morning appointment first. Remember?'

Maggie played deaf and, still horizontal, reached for the TV remote. If she was going to be up at this hideous hour, she might as well get something out of it. The Sunday talk shows. By the time she clicked onto ABC, they'd already started the news summary.

'Nerves on edge in Jerusalem this hour, after violence at a peace rally last night, where Israel's prime minister seemed to be the target of a failed assassination attempt. Concern high over the impact of the latest events on the Middle East peace process, which had been hoped to yield a breakthrough as early as—'

'Honey, seriously. They'll be here in twenty.'

She reached for the remote and turned up the volume. The show was hopping back and forth between correspondents in Jerusalem and the White House, explaining that the US administration was taking steps to ensure all the parties kept calm and carried on talking. *What a nightmare,* thought Maggie. The last minute external event, threatening to undo all the trust you've built, all the patient progress you've made. She imagined the mediators who had brought the Israelis and Palestinians to this point. Not the big name politicians, the secretaries of state and foreign ministers who stepped into the spotlight at the last moment, but the backroom negotiators, the ones who did all the hard graft for months, even years before. She imagined their frustration and angst. *Poor bastards.*

'The time coming up to 9.15 on the east coast—'

'Hey, I was watching that!'

'You haven't got time.' As if to underline his point, Edward was towelling himself in front of the TV set, blocking her view of the blank screen.

'Why do you suddenly care so much about my schedule?'

He held the towel still and faced Maggie. 'Because I care about you, honey, and I don't want your day getting off on the wrong note. If you start late, you stay late. You should be thanking me.'

'OK,' Maggie said, finally hauling herself upright. 'Thank you.'

'Besides, you don't need to follow all that stuff any more. It's not your problem now, is it?'

She looked at him, so different from the man in chinos and grubby polo shirt she had met three years ago. He was still attractive, his features straight and strong. But he had, as she would have said back in her school days in Dublin, 'scrubbed up' since they'd moved to Washington. Now an official at the Commerce Department, dealing with international trade, he was always clean-shaven, his Brooks Brothers shirts neatly pressed. His shoes were polished. He was a creature of DC, not too different from any of the other juiceless white males they would see at the suburban brunches and cocktail parties they went to, now that he was part of official Washington. These days only she would know that somewhere under that button-down exterior was the stubbled, unkempt do-gooder, working for an aid organization, distributing food, she had fallen for.

They hadn't got together straight away. He had been transferred to South America soon after they first met. By the time he came back to Africa, she had moved on to the Balkans. That was how it was for people like them, an occupational hazard. So it remained no more than a spark, a maybe-one-day, until they met again just over a year ago, back in Africa. She was falling through the air after the episode they almost never spoke about these days – and he caught her. For that, she would never stop being grateful.

She stumbled into the shower and was still drying off when the intercom sounded: the clients, down at the entrance to the apartment building. She buzzed them in. Allowing for the lift journey, she would have about a minute to get dressed. She scraped her hair back into a rapid ponytail and reached for a loose grey top, which fell low over her jeans. She flung open a cupboard and grabbed the first pair of low-heeled shoes she could see.

Just time for a quick glance at herself in the mirror by the front door. Nothing too badly out of place; nothing anyone would notice. This had been her habit since she had come to Washington. 'Dressing to disappear,' Liz, her younger sister, had called it, when she was over on a visit. 'Look at you. All greys and blacks and sweaters that a family could camp in. You dress like a really *fat* person, do you know that, Maggie? You've got this drop-dead gorgeous figure and no one would know it. It's like your body's working undercover.' Liz, blogger and would-be novelist, laughed enthusiastically at her own joke.

Maggie told her to get away, though she knew Liz had a point. 'It's better for the work,' she explained. 'In a couples situation, the mediator needs to be a pane of glass that the man and woman themselves can look through, so that they see each other rather than you.'

Liz was not convinced. She guessed that Maggie had got that bullshit out of some textbook. And she was right.

Nor did Maggie dare let on that this new look was also the preference of her boyfriend. With gentle hints at first, then more overtly, Edward had encouraged Maggie to start tying her hair back, or to put away the fitted tops, tight trousers or knee-length skirts that constituted her previous urban wardrobe. He always had a specific argument for each item: 'That colour just suits you better'; 'I think this will be more appropriate' – and he seemed sincere. Still, she couldn't help but notice that all his interventions tended to point her in the same direction: more modest, less sexy.

She wouldn't breathe a word of that to Liz. Her sister had taken an instant, irrational dislike to Edward and she didn't need any more ammunition. Besides, it wouldn't be fair on him. If Maggie dressed differently now, that was her own decision, made in part for a reason that she had never shared with Liz and never would. Maggie had once dressed sexily, there was no denying it. But look where that had led. She wouldn't make that mistake again.

She opened the door to Kathy and Brett George, ushering them towards the spare room reserved for this purpose. They were in the couples' programme devised by the state authorities in Virginia, a new 'cooling off' scheme, in which husbands and wives were obliged to undergo mediation before they were granted a divorce. Normally, six sessions did it, the couple working out the terms of their break-up without any need to call a lawyer, thereby saving on heartache and money. That was the idea anyway.

She gestured to them to sit down, reminded them where they had got to the previous week and what issues remained outstanding. And then, as if she had fired a starting gun, the pair began laying into each other with a ferocity that had not let up since the day they had first walked in.

'Sweetheart, I'm happy to give you the house. And the car for that matter. I just have certain conditions—'

'Which is that I stay home and look after your kids.'

'Our kids, Kathy. Ours.'

They were in their early forties, maybe seven or eight years older than Maggie, but they might as well have come from another generation, if not another planet. She had listened with incomprehension to the rows about who got to use the summer house in New Hampshire, which in turn triggered an almighty clash over whether Kathy had been a good daughter-in-law to Brett's father when the old man was sick, while Kathy insisted that Brett had been consistently rude whenever her parents came to stay.

She had just about had it with the Georges. The two of them had sat there on that couch, slugging it out for four consecutive weeks without taking a blind bit of notice of a word she said. She had tried it soft, saying little, offering a gentle nod here and there. She had tried it hands-on, intervening in every twist and turn of the conversation, directing and channelling it like a stream running through the middle of the room. She preferred it this second way, firing off questions, chipping in with her opinions, no matter if Little Missy over there turned up her nose or if Mr Rod-Up-His-Arse squirmed in his seat. But that didn't seem to work either. They still came back in as much of a mess as when they first started.

'Maggie, do you see what he did there? Do you see that thing he does?'

Listening to the pair of them made Maggie despair that she'd ever made this move in the first place. It had made sense at the time. 'Mediator' the job spec said and that's what she was. OK, this was not quite the area she was used to, but mediation was mediation, right? How different could it be? And, after all, she couldn't face going back to the work she had done before. She had become frightened of it, ever since she had seen what could happen when you failed.

But Jesus Christ, if these two weren't convincing her she'd made a terrible mistake.

'Look, Maggie, I hope this is already firmly on the record. I am more than happy to pay whatever maintenance budget we all decide is reasonable. I'm no miser: I will write that cheque. I just have one condition—'

'He wants to control me!'

'My condition, Maggie, is very, very simple. If Kathy wants

to receive my money for the upbringing of our children, in other words, if she wants me to effectively *pay* her to bring them up, then I would expect her to do no other job at the same time.'

'He won't pay child support unless I give up my career! Do you hear this, Maggie?'

Maggie could detect something in Kathy's voice she hadn't noticed before. Like a rambler spotting a new path, she decided to follow it, see where it led.

'And why would he want you to give up your career, Kathy?'

'Oh, this is ridiculous.'

'Brett, the question was directed at Kathy.'

'I don't know. He says it's better for the kids.'

'But you think it's about something else.'

'Yes.'

'Oh, for Christ's sake—'

'Go on, Kathy.'

'I wonder sometimes if, if . . . I wonder if Brett kind of likes me being dependent.'

'I see.' Maggie saw that Brett was silent. 'And why might that be?'

'I don't know. Like, maybe he likes it when I'm weak or something. You know his first wife was an alcoholic, right? Well, did you also know that as soon as she got better, Brett left her?'

'This is outrageous, to bring Julie into this.'

Maggie was scribbling notes, all the while maintaining eye contact with the couple. It was a trick she had learned during negotiations of a different kind, long ago.

'Edward, what do you say to all this?'

'Excuse me?'

'I'm sorry. Brett. Forgive me. Brett. What do you make of all this, this suggestion that you are somehow trying to keep Kathy weak? I think that was the word she used. Weak.'

Brett spoke for a while, refuting the charge and insisting that he had wanted to leave Julie for at least two years but didn't feel it was right until she had recovered. Maggie nodded throughout, but she was distracted. First, the intercom had sounded while Brett was speaking, followed by the sound of several male voices, Edward's and two or three she did not recognize. And, worse, by her ridiculous slip of the tongue. She wondered if Kathy and Brett had noticed.

Regretting that she had opened up this theme – more therapist territory than mediator's – Maggie decided on a radical change of tack. OK, she thought, we need to move to final status. 'Brett, what are your red lines?'

'I'm sorry?'

'Your red lines. Those things on which you absolutely, positively will not compromise. Here.' She tossed over a pad of paper, followed by a pencil, thrown a tad too sharply for Brett's taste. 'And you too, Kathy. Red lines. Go on. Write them down.'

Within a few seconds, the two were scratching away with their pencils. Maggie felt as if she was back at school in Dublin: the summer, exam season, the nuns prowling around to check that she wasn't copying her answers off Mairead Breen. Except this time she was one of the nuns. *At last,* she thought. *A moment of peace.*

She looked at this couple in front of her, two people who had once been so in love they had decided to share everything, even to create three new lives. When she had met up with Edward again after, after . . . everything that had happened, she had dreamed of a similar future for herself. No more war zones, no more anonymous hotel conference rooms, no more twenty-hour days fuelled by coffee and cigarettes. On the wrong side of thirty-five, she would settle down and have a family life. Fifteen years later than the girls she had gone to school with, admittedly, but she would have a family and a life.

'You finished, Brett? What about you, Kathy?'

'There's a lot to get down here.'

'Remember, not everything's a red line. You've got to be selective. All right, Kathy. Give us your three red lines.'

'Three? You kidding?'

'Selective, remember.'

'All right.' Kathy began chewing the top of her pencil, before she realized it wasn't a pen and pulled it out of her mouth. 'Child support. My kids have to have financial security.'

'OK.'

'And the house. I have to have the house, so that the kids can have continuity.'

'And one more.'

'Full custody of the children, obviously. I'm having them. There's no shifting on that.'

'For Chrissake, Kathy—'

'Not yet, Brett. First you gotta give me your red lines.'

'We've been over this like a thousand times—'

'Not this way we haven't. I need three.'

'I want the children with me at Thanksgiving, so that they have dinner with my parents. I want that.'

'All right.'

'And spontaneous access. So that I can call up and say, I dunno, "Hey Joey, the Redskins are playing, wanna come?" I need to be able to do that without giving, like, three weeks' notice. Access whenever I want.'

'No way—'

'Kathy, not now. What's number three?'

'I have others—'

'We're doing three.'

'It's the same one I said before. No child support unless Kathy is a full-time mom.'

'Are you sure that's not just saying no to Kathy's first red line? You can't just block hers.'

'OK. I'll put it this way. I'll pay for child support only if I'm getting a five-star service for my money. And that means the kids get looked after by their mom.'

'That is not fair! You're using our kids to blackmail me into giving up my career.'

And they were off again, back to shouting at each other and ignoring Maggie. Just like old times, she thought to herself with a smile. After all, this was what she was used to. Negotiating a divorce between people who couldn't stand the sight of each other, who were tearing each other's throats out. An image flashed into her mind, which she quickly pushed out.

But it helped. It gave her an idea, or rather it made her see something she had not realized until that moment.

'OK, Brett and Kathy, I've made a decision. These sessions have become useless. They're a waste of time, yours and mine. We're going to end it here.' Maggie snapped shut the file on her lap.

The two people on the couch opposite suddenly turned their attention away from each other and stared at her. She could feel their eyes on her, but she ignored them, busying herself with her papers instead.

'You don't need to worry about the paperwork. I'll get all that to the Virginia authorities tomorrow. You've both got lawyers, haven't you? Course you have. Well, they'll take it from here.' She stood up, as if to usher them out.

Brett seemed fixed to the spot; Kathy's mouth hung wide open. At last, Brett forced himself to speak. 'You can't, you can't do this.'

'Do what, exactly?' Maggie had her back to him, as she put the file back on the shelf behind her.

'You can't just *abandon* us!'

Now Kathy joined in. 'We need you, Maggie. There is no way we can get through this without you.'

'Oh, don't you worry about that. The lawyers will get it sorted.' Maggie kept moving around the room, avoiding eye contact.

Outside she heard the buzzer go again, and the sound of another person or people moving in and out of the apartment. What was going on?

'They'll kill us,' said Brett. 'They'll take all our money and make this whole thing even more of a nightmare than it already is!'

This was working.

'Look,' he said. 'We'll sort this out, we promise. Don't we, Kathy?'

'We do.'

'OK? We're promising. We'll get this done. Right here.'

'I think it's too late for that. We set aside a period of time to resolve everything—'

'Oh, please don't say that, Maggie.' It was Kathy, now imploring. 'There's not such a lot of work to do here. You heard those red lines. We're not so far apart.'

Maggie turned around. 'I'll give you ten minutes.'

In fact it took fifteen. But when they left Maggie's office and walked into the sunshine of a Washington September morning, Kathy and Brett George had resolved to share the costs of child support proportionate to their income, Brett paying more because he earned more, Kathy's financial contribution shrinking to zero if she gave up paid work to look after the kids. From now on, he would pay his way even if she carried on working, though she would have a genuine incentive to stay home. The children would live in their own house with their mother, except for alternate weekends and whenever either the kids or their father fancied seeing each other. The rule would be no hard and fast rules. Before they left they hugged Maggie and, to their surprise as much as hers, each other.

Maggie fell into a chair, allowing herself a small smile of satisfaction. Was this how she would make up for what she had done more than a year ago? Bit by bit, one couple at a time, reducing the amount of pain in the world? The thought was comforting for a moment or two – until she contemplated how long it would take. To balance all the lives lost because of her and that damned, damned mistake, she would be here, in this room, for all eternity. And still it wouldn't be enough.

She looked at her watch. She should be getting on. Edward would be waiting for her outside, ready to hit the full range of Washington's domestic retail outlets in a bid to equip their not-quite-marital home.

She opened the door to a surprise. Flicking through one of Maggie's back numbers of *Vogue*, in the tiny area that served as Maggie's waiting room, was a man who oozed Washington. Like Edward, he had the full DC garb: button-down shirt, blue blazer, loafers, even now, on a Sunday. Maggie didn't recognize him, which didn't mean she hadn't met him. One of the troubles with these Washington men: they all looked the same.

'Hello? Do you have an appointment?'

'I don't. It's kind of an emergency. It won't take long.'

An emergency? What the hell was this? She headed down the corridor, opening the door onto the kitchen. There she saw Edward, signing on one of those electronic devices held out by a man wearing delivery overalls.

'Edward, what's going on?'

He seemed to pale. 'Ah, honey. I can explain. They just had to go. They were taking up too much space, they messed up the whole place. So I've done it. They've gone.'

'What on earth are you talking about?'

'Those boxes which you've had sitting in the study for nearly a year. You said you would unpack them, but you never did. So this kind gentleman has loaded them onto his truck and now they're going to the trash.'

Maggie looked at the man in overalls, who stared at his feet. Now she understood what had happened. But she could not believe it. She stormed past Edward, flung open the door to the study and, sure enough, the space in the corner was now empty, the carpet on which those two cartons had once sat more compacted, a different shade from the rest. She flew back to the kitchen.

'You bastard! Those boxes had my, my . . . letters and photographs and, and . . . whole fucking life and you just THREW THEM OUT?'

Maggie rushed to the front door. But, doubtless sensing trouble, the trash guy had made his getaway. Swearing, she pressed the lift button again and again. 'Come on, come on,' she muttered, tensing her jaw. When the lift came, she willed it down faster. As soon as it arrived on the ground floor and the door opened a crack, she squeezed through it, running through the main doors of the building and out onto the street. She looked left and right and left again before she saw it, a green truck pulling out. She ran hard to catch up, coming within a few yards. She was waving wildly, like someone flagging down traffic after a road accident. But it was too late. The van picked up speed and vanished. All she had was half a phone number and what she thought was the name: National Removals.

She rushed back upstairs, frantically grabbing the telephone, her fingers trembling over the buttons. She called directory information, asking for a number. They found it and offered to put her through. Three rings, then four, then five. A recorded message: *We're sorry, but all our offices are closed on Sunday. Our regular opening hours are Monday to Friday* . . . If she waited till tomorrow it would be too late: they would have destroyed the boxes and everything they contained.

She went back into the kitchen to find Edward standing, defiant. She began quietly. 'You just threw them out.'

'You're damn right I threw them out. They made this place look like a student shithole. All that junk, all that sentimental crap. You need to drop it, Maggie. You need to move on.'

'But, but . . .' Maggie wasn't looking at him. She was looking at the ground, trying to digest what had just happened. Not just the letters from her parents, the photographs from Ireland, but the notes she had taken during crucial negotiations, private, scribbled memos from rebel leaders and UN officials. Those boxes contained her life's work. And now they were in a dumpster.

'I did it for you, Maggie. That world is not your world any more. It's moved on without you. You've got to do the same. You need to adjust to your life now, as it is. Our life.'

So that's why he had been so keen to get her locked away in the consulting room this morning. And she thought he just wanted her to get a punctual start to the day. She had even thanked him! The truth was that he just wanted the garbage men in and out before she had a chance to stop them. For the first time, she met his gaze. Quietly, as if unable to believe her own words, she said, 'You want to destroy who I am.'

He looked back at her blankly, before finally nodding towards the other end of the apartment. In a voice that was ice cold, he said, 'I think someone's waiting for you.'

She almost staggered out of the room, unable to absorb what had happened. How could he have done such a thing, without her permission, without even talking to her? Did he really hate the Maggie Costello he had once known so much that he wanted to erase every last trace of her, replacing her with someone, different, bland and subservient?

She stood in the landing that served as the waiting area, her head spinning. The man in blue was still there, now turning the pages of *Atlantic Monthly*.

'Bad time? I'm sorry.'

'No, no,' Maggie said, barely out loud. On auto-pilot, she added. 'Is your wife coming?'

He made a curious smirk. 'She should be along soon.'

Maggie gestured him into the consulting room. 'You said it was some kind of emergency.' She was struggling to remember his case, to remember if he was one of the handful of clients she said could contact her out of hours.

'Yes. My problem is that I'm finding it hard to adjust.'

'To what?'

'To life here. Normality.'

'Where were you before?'

'I was all over. Travelling from one screwed-up place to another. Always meant to be doing good, always trying to make the world a better place and all that bullshit.'

'Are you a doctor?'

'You could say that. I try to save lives.'

Maggie could feel her muscles tensing. 'And now you're finding it hard to adjust to being back home.'

'Home! That's a joke. I don't know what home is any more. I'm not from DC; I haven't lived in my hometown for nearly twenty years. Always on the road, on planes, in hotel rooms, sleeping in dumps.'

'But that's not why you're finding it hard to adjust.'

'No. It's the adrenaline I miss, I guess. The drama. Sounds terrible, doesn't it?'

'Go on.' Maggie was remembering everything that was in those boxes. A handwritten letter of thanks she had received from the British prime minister, following the talks over Kosovo. A treasured photo with the man she had loved through her mid-twenties.

'Before, everything I did seemed to matter so much. The stakes were high. Now nothing even comes close. It's all so banal.'

Maggie stared hard at the man. The words were coming out of him but his eyes were flat and cold. She began to feel uneasy at his presence here. 'Can you say more about the work you were doing?'

'I started with an aid organization in Africa, working with

people there during a particularly vicious civil war. Somehow – it was a fluke really – I ended up being one of the few people who could talk to both sides. The UN started using me as a go-between. And I got results.'

Maggie shivered. Her mind was racing, wondering whether she should call for Edward, though that was truly the last thing she wanted to do.

'Eventually I became known as a sort of un-official diplomat, a professional mediator. The US government hired me for a peace process that had stalled. And one thing led to another. Eventually they were sending me around the world, to peace talks that had hit the buffers. They called me "the Closer". I was the one who could close the deal.'

Could she make a run for it? But something told her not even to glance at the door: she did not want to provoke this man. 'Then what happened?' Her voice betrayed nothing: years of practice.

'I was the best in my field. Sent everywhere. Belgrade, Baghdad. Back to Africa.'

Maggie swallowed hard.

'And then I made a mistake.'

'Where?'

'In Africa.'

Maggie's voice stayed low, even as she said, 'Who the hell are you?'

'I think you know who I am.'

'No, I don't. So tell me, who are you and what are you playing at? Tell me now or I'll call the police.'

'You know who I am, Maggie. You know very well. I'm you.'

CHAPTER THREE

WASHINGTON, SUNDAY, 10.43AM

It wasn't a surprise. She had known that much the moment he had mentioned Africa and the UN. He had been telling her own life story back to her, pretending it was his own. It was a nasty little trick.

Still, that wasn't why she had grown agitated: she was used to dealing with creeps. This man seemed to know everything about her. Including her – what had he called it? – 'mistake'.

'I'm not here to taunt you.'

'But you're not here for bloody divorce mediation either, are you?'

'There's no wife for me to divorce. I'm like you used to be. Married to the job.'

'And what job is that exactly?'

'I work for the same people you used to work for. The United States government. My name is Judd Bonham.' He extended a hand.

Maggie ignored it, heading slowly backwards towards her chair. She was reeling. First Edward and the boxes and now this. Initially, she had him down as some psycho stalker, a jilted husband who blamed her for his divorce. It wouldn't be too difficult to Google her whole life story, then trick his way in to scare her, to freak her out. But she had read him wrong. He was here on official business. But what on earth could it be? She hadn't done anything for the Agency or State Department since . . . then. That had been well over a year ago and she had cut all her ties instantly. Not a phone call, not a letter. Nothing. If she had had it her way, she wouldn't even be living in bloody America. She couldn't have gone back to Ireland, couldn't face that; but she had thought about following Liz to London. Instead she had ended up in sodding Washington, inside the belly of the beast. To be with Edward.

'Gotta hand it to you though. You haven't lost your touch.'

She looked up at him.

'You're still good. The old jet-on-the-runway trick. Engines revving up, ready to fly any moment. Love it.'

'What?'

'Your last appointment, Kathy and Brett. Threatening to walk out on the parties: they should teach that at negotiator school. Didn't Clinton do it at Camp David? Get the chopper all fired up, blades spinning. The mediator says he – or she – will walk and the parties get scared. Realize how much they need you and how much they need the talks. They suddenly see that any deal they'd make outside the room would be worse. And it brings them together, both sides desperate to keep the talks going. You mediation guys call it a "shared project", don't you? Something like that. Even unites them against a common enemy: you. Genius.'

'You were listening.'

'It's the training, what can I say?'

'You arsehole.'

'I like how you say that. *Ahhhrse*-hole. Sounds sexy in your accent.'

'Get out.'

'Though I see you don't really do sexy so much these days. No more of the hair-tumbling-down-in-front-of-the-eyes routine. Is that Edward's influence?'

'Go.'

'Oh, I'll go. But first I have a little proposal to make.'

Maggie stared at him.

'Don't worry, not that kind of proposal. Not that I couldn't be tempted, should you ever get tired of Edward—'

'I'm going to call the police.' She reached for the phone.

'No you're not. And we both know why.'

That stopped her; she put the phone down. He knew about her 'mistake'. And he would tell. The *Washington Post*, some blog, it didn't matter. The true reason for her exile, currently known only to a few diplomatic insiders, would become public. What was left of her reputation would be ruined.

'What do you want?' Almost a whisper.

'We want you to come out of retirement.'

'No.'

'Come on, first rule of any negotiation: you have to listen.'

'I am not having a negotiation with you. I want you to piss off.'

'The people I work for tend not to take no for an answer.'

'And who is it you work for exactly? "The United States government" is a bit vague.'

'Let's say this has come from as close to the top as you can get in this town. You have a reputation, you know. Miss Costello.'

'Well,' you can tell them I'm flattered. But the answer is no.

'You're not even curious?'

'No, I am not. I don't do that work any more. I work here now. I mediate between husbands and wives. And I don't take emergency cases. Which means you have about one minute to get up and leave.'

'I won't insult your intelligence, Maggie. You read the papers. You know what's happening in Jerusalem. We're this close to a deal.' He held his thumb and forefinger half an inch apart. 'We've never been so close before.'

Maggie ignored him.

'And you also know what happened yesterday. An attack on the Israeli Prime Minister. Or what looked like an attack. Israeli security ended up killing some internal critic of the peace process. Could screw the whole thing.'

'The answer's no.'

'The powers that be have decided that this is too important an opportunity to be lost. They need you to go in there and do your thing. Work your magic. Come on, you've still got it. I could hear that just now. And this is something that really matters. Middle East peace, for Christ's sake. How could you pass that up? This is the World Series of peacemaking!'

'I don't play baseball.'

'No. OK.' He was talking more quietly now and in a different tone. She recognized it for what it was, a change in tactics. 'What I mean is, you're a mediator. It's your calling. It's what you were born to do. You're good at it and you love doing it. This is the chance to return to the work you love. At the highest possible level.'

She thought of the pictures she had seen on TV that morning, and the feeling she had had, but not admitted, even to herself. Envy. She had envied the men and women sitting at the head of the negotiating table in Jerusalem, the people charged with that weightiest and most thrilling of tasks, brokering peace. She had pictured them the instant she saw the news item. Like fishermen, reeling in a rare and prized specimen, they would be exerting both enormous strength and great gentleness. Pulling with all their might one moment, then backing off, letting out some more line the next. Knowing when the rod could bend, and knowing what would make it break. It was skilled, demanding work. But it was also the most exhilarating activity she had ever known.

Bonham read her face. 'You must miss it. You wouldn't be human if you didn't. I mean counselling couples is valuable, no question. But the stakes are never as high, are they? You're never going to feel the thrill you did at Dayton or Geneva. Not here. Are you?'

Maggie wanted to shake her head in agreement. This man seemed to know her own mind better than she did. But she resisted, turning her head to stare out of the window.

'Not that this is some kind of sport to you, I know that. It never was. Sure, you like the professional challenge. But that came second. To the *goal.* The pursuit of peace. You're one of the few people on the planet who knows how much these efforts matter. What can happen if things go wrong.' Her mistake.

'And few matter more than this one, Maggie. Thousands of Israelis and Palestinians have died in this conflict. It's gone on and on and on. Our whole adult lifetimes. And it will keep going. You'll turn on your TV set in ten years' time and there'll still be Palestinian kids shelled in playgrounds and Israeli teenagers blown to pieces on buses.'

'And you think you can stop it?'

'Me? *I* can't stop it. I can't stop anything. But you can.'

'I don't believe that. Not any more.'

'Come on. You haven't changed that much.'

'Look, I didn't suddenly forget that people are dying there and everywhere else. I know only too well how much death and killing goes on in every fucking corner of this planet. But I happen to have realized there is nothing I can do about it. So it's better I stay out of it.'

'The White House doesn't agree.'

'Well, the White House can just shove it, can't it?'

Bonham sat back, as if assessing his prey. After a pause he said, 'This is because of . . . what happened, isn't it?'

Maggie stared out of the window, willing her eyes to stay dry.

'Look, Maggie. We know what went on there. You fouled up very badly. But it was one black mark on an otherwise exceptional record. The White House view is that you've done your penance. And you don't help anyone by staying in exile like this. You're not saving any lives here. It's time you came back.'

'You're saying I'm forgiven.'

'I'm saying it's time to move on. But, yes, if you like, you're forgiven.'

For the first time Maggie met his gaze. 'But what if I haven't forgiven myself?'

'Ah, that's a different problem, isn't it? Shouldn't be too tricky for you, though. That's a Catholic specialty, isn't it? Cancelling out the sin through repentance? Redemption and all that? So this is your chance.'

'It's not as simple as that.'

'True. You're not going to bring back the lives that were lost because of what happened. Your mistake. But you can prevent more lives being lost. And that's got to count for something. Hasn't it?'

She was about to say that she had once promised Edward that she wouldn't travel again. But she said nothing.

'It's your choice, Maggie. If you believe that nothing else matters but your life here, your relationship here—'

She knew he'd heard the row in the kitchen.

'—you'll ignore me and send me away from here. But if you miss the work you were born to do, if you care about ending a conflict that's spread so much bitterness around the world, if you want to make things right, you'll say yes.'

'Tell me something,' she said after a long pause. 'Why the house visit? Why all this cloak and dagger bullshit, pretending to be a client?'

'We tried phoning you, but you didn't return our calls. I didn't think you'd let me into the building.'

'You called?'

'We've been leaving messages here since yesterday afternoon. We left a couple early this morning.'

'But,' she stammered. She was sure she had checked, sure that there was nothing on the machine.

'Maybe someone deleted the messages before you got to them.' She felt the air seep out of her lungs. *Edward.*

Judd threw an envelope on the table, thick and heavy. 'Tickets and briefing material. The plane for Tel Aviv leaves this afternoon. The choice is yours, Maggie.'

CHAPTER FOUR

JERUSALEM, SATURDAY, 11.10PM

After-dark meetings were part of the tradition of this office. Ben-Gurion had done it in the fifties, debating and deciding till the early hours; Golda, too, always worked late at night, most famously when the Egyptians launched their surprise attack on Yom Kippur in 1973: legend has it the old lady barely slept for days. Somehow this room, with its single high-backed chair, reserved for the Prime Minister, lent itself to such encounters. It was small and intimate, with two couches forming an L-shape on which advisers or aides could sit around and talk for hours. The desk was functional, built for use rather than to impress. Rabin used to sit here alone deep into the night, with his own ink-pen, letters to the parents of soldiers – which, being Israel, meant every mother and father in the land.

Rabin was long gone now, taking the ashtrays that accompanied his chain-smoking habit with him. The current incumbent preferred, when stressed, to nibble on sunflower seeds, a habit which made him the peer of bus drivers and stallholders across the country. He gestured now to the man from Shin Bet, Israeli's internal security service, to begin speaking.

'Prime Minister, the dead man was Shimon Guttman. We all know who we're talking about: the writer and activist, aged seventy-one. The first reports suggesting he was armed have now been discounted. Our investigators found no sign that he carried any weapon. Examination of the body showed he was killed by a bullet to the brain.'

The PM grimaced, then cracked one more seed shell between his front teeth.

'As you know, he was found clasping a handwritten note, addressed to yourself. Intelligence say it will take some days to piece it together, the words were obscured by the blood—'

The Prime Minister waved him quiet. The head of Shin Bet put away the paper he had been consulting. The Deputy Prime Minster stared at his shoes; the Foreign and Defence Ministers stared at the PM, trying to gauge his reaction: none wanted to be the first to speak.

Amir Tal, special adviser to the PM and the youngest man in the room, decided to fill the quiet. 'Of course, this has immediate political implications. First, we will come under fire—'

The Prime Minister raised an eyebrow.

'Sorry. We will be criticized for making a bad mistake, killing an innocent man. That kind of flak could come our way anytime. But, second, if we are about to sign a peace deal, this will make things much harder. The right were already boiling; now they're claiming their first martyr. They insist it is not a coincidence: Guttman was one of our loudest critics. And not just ours. He said the same thing during Oslo and again during Camp David: "Anyone who talks peace with the Arabs is a criminal who should be on trial for treason." Arutz Sheva was on the air an hour ago saying "So now we know the government's plan; they want to silence dissent with gunfire".'

'Could they be right?' It was the Foreign Minister, addressing Tal, avoiding the boss's eye.

'Excuse me?'

'I don't mean that we deliberately killed him. But that it was not a coincidence. Could it be deliberate in the other direction, the opposite of what Arutz Sheva are saying?'

'How do you mean?'

'I mean, was this a set-up? Guttman knew how things worked. You can't just rush towards the Prime Minister, shouting and screaming, and then reach into your jacket. He was a smart guy. He'd have known that.'

'Are you saying—'

'Yeah. I'm wondering if Guttman *wanted* to get shot. If he was deliberately luring us in, daring us to kill a famous opponent of the government.'

'This is crazy.'

'Is it? This is a guy who his whole life has gone in for the grand spectacular gesture, the great protest. And now, finally, it's the big one: we're about to make peace with the Arabs, to give away holy Judea and sacred Samaria. To prevent such a calamity, a fanatic like Guttman would have to come up with the biggest possible gesture. One that might actually mobilize the right.'

'He would sacrifice his own life?'

'He would.' The Prime Minister had uttered his first two words since the meeting began. Until now, he had sat back, listening to the debate. That was his style. First, hear the arguments among the competing members of his court. Then, pepper them with questions. *So how should we respond? What are our options?* The cabinet had braced itself for just such an interrogation. But instead the Prime Minister had just leaned forward, saying nothing, cracking open yet another salty seed shell. Until those words: 'He would.'

After a long pause, as if completing a thought that had been unspooling in his own head, he added, 'I know this man. Inside out.'

The Chief of Staff, dressed in pressed olive green trousers and beige shirt, with a beret under his epaulette – the uniform of the soldier whose battlefield was politics – broke the silence that followed with what felt to him like a related question. He asked what everyone in the room – along with everyone who had heard the eye-witness accounts on TV – had wanted to know from the beginning. 'How come he called you Kobi?'

'Ah,' said the Prime Minister.

'I thought he hated your guts. Yet here he's talking to you like you're old chums.'

'Rav Aluf, you of all people should know the answer to that question.' The PM sat back, though he still preferred to look into middle distance rather than at any of his colleagues. 'Kobi was the man I was a long, long time ago.' The Defence Minister shuffled awkwardly in his seat, shooting a glance at the General. 'It was what my friends called me. In the army. We were a good unit, one of the best. In '67 we took a hill, just us: thirty-odd men. And you know who was the bravest, much braver than me, despite what Amir here tells the newspapers? A young scholar from the Hebrew University by the name of Shimon Guttman.'

CHAPTER FIVE

JERUSALEM, MONDAY, 9.28AM

For the first time since she got here the people checking her bags were Arabs. Everyone she had met since coming off the overnight flight at dawn this morning had been Israeli Jews. Now at the entrance to the US Consulate on Agron Street, she was waiting to be processed by Palestinian Arabs – albeit wearing shirts bearing the crest of the United States. Ordinarily an official of the United States government, as she now was once more, would be waved through. But these were extra-tense times, the driver explained, so it would take a little longer. One of the guards wanted Maggie to hand in her mobile phone, until a more senior man waved him away.

She was ushered into a small security lobby, staffed by a US marine behind thick glass watching a bank of TV monitors. As she gazed at the flickering images, she rewound her scene with Judd Bonham for the dozenth time. He had played her like a master, making every move she would have made. He had appealed to her conscience and flattered her ego, just as she had done to countless delegates, ambassadors and presidential aides. He had both dangled a stick, revealing what he knew, and offered a carrot. And, just as the rulebook dictates, the latter had been designed to reach the reluctant party's weakest spot: in her case, her desire to wipe the slate clean. You always tried to know a participant's greatest vulnerability. It pained her to think hers was so obvious.

Bonham must have known it would be a breeze. First some light intimidation, then a show of apparent kindness and empathy. It was the classic pattern. Police interrogator kicks away the chair, then puts a hand on the shoulder and offers to take the pain away. Good cop, bad cop, even if it was the same person. She had done it herself a dozen times.

Her gaze went to the marine. She couldn't quite believe she was back to all this again. Instinctively, she scrutinized the scene before her. Natural that the serious security would be entrusted only to an American. The choice of local hires was also a statement. Use of Palestinian staff to underline that the consulate in Jerusalem was the US mission to the Palestinians; a wholly different operation from the embassy in Tel Aviv, which represented America to the Israelis.

A door buzzed, opening up for a tall, fair-haired man. 'Welcome to the madhouse! Jim Davis, Consul, good to see you.' He stuck out a hand to shake.

'As you can see, we work in the most beautiful pair of buildings the State Department owns anywhere in the world,' he said as they walked into a garden, a wide, square lawn laid out before a grand, colonial house. The noise of Agron Street was shut out now. The only sound was the hummed melody of an aged gardener, bending over to prune a rosebush.

'And this is our newest acquisition, the Lazarist Pères Monastery.' Davis pointed to his left, to a structure that seemed part church, part fortress. It was modest; no fussy steeples or fancy turrets, but each arched window was decorated with a brick surround, as if reinforced against incoming fire. And all of it was built in the same pale, craggy stone that dominated this city. Every building, every house, every office, every hotel, even the supermarkets – they were all made of it. 'Jerusalem stone' the driver had called it on the way from the airport. 'It is the law, it is the law!' he had said, his stubbled face peering over his shoulder, prompting Maggie to nod eagerly towards the road, encouraging him to do the same.

She had been here before, a couple of times, nearly a decade ago. But she hadn't been close to the action. The White House ran that show: they were happy to let the do-gooders of State do Africa or East Timor and, on a good day, the Balkans. But the Middle East was the glamour assignment, the diplomatic big one, the only foreign story that consistently made the front page. So Maggie had always been kept back.

She looked up, shielding her eyes with the palm of her hand. The light was so bright here, reflecting and bouncing off all that pale, sand-coloured stone. A monastery in Jerusalem. Had probably been here centuries, all the way back to the Crusades. It reminded Maggie of the convent of her schooldays.

'Took that over just a while back,' Davis was explaining. Unusually for a long-time diplomat, his Southern accent was perfectly intact. 'The brothers, or fathers, strictly speaking, have vacated most of the building. A few of them are hanging on, in a little corner that will stay theirs. Otherwise it now belongs to the United States of America.'

He was babbling, a male reaction Maggie was used to. She had seen it in Davis's eyes the moment he had greeted her, the initial instant of surprise, followed by a regrouping and the concentrated effort to act normally. She had thought this would stop as she moved into her late thirties, that she would become less of a magnet for male attention. But, even with the dressing down, it hadn't faded much. She was still tall, at five foot nine, and her figure had held its shape pretty well. Her hair was still thick and warm brown and, when she let it down, it was long enough to trail over her shoulders.

'So here's the deal.' Davis had led them to a cluster of iron chairs, shaded by the cypress trees. 'As you know, the White House is convinced this is the week. Aiming for a permanent agreement signed in the Rose Garden within a matter of days. Just in time for election day.'

'On re-election day as I think the President likes to call it,' she said. 'Is he going to get what he wants?'

'Well, we've had two delegations over at Government House sitting face to face for nearly two weeks now. That's a breakthrough right there.'

'What, that they've done two weeks?'

'No, I meant talks on the ground.'

'Right. Sorry.' Maggie swallowed. This would take some time; she was rusty.

'It's never happened before. Camp David, Wye River, Madrid, Oslo, you name it. But never here. Camp David's been spooked since 2000. And the White House, in its infinite wisdom, decided it would be good for the parties to do the business in their own backyard.'

'And are they? Doing the business?'

'Course not. We could have told them that. These guys are leaking to their media more than they're talking to each other. You can't do a news blackout when you're right in the middle of the freakin' conflict zone.'

'But the White House went ahead anyway?'

'It's their show. But, believe me, they're running to us every time someone sneezes.'

'No change there, then.'

'Excuse me?'

'Forget it. So State's having to do some of the heavy lifting?'

'Some? Try most. But everyone's trying to get their oar in. EU, UN, the British. Arab states, Indonesia, Malaysia. We got a billion

Muslims on the edge of their seats, waiting to see what happens. Imams and mullahs from here to Mohammadsville, Alabama preaching that this is the front line in the war between Islam and the West. Armies being mobilized in the Arab world. If they all decide the Palestinians are being pushed into some kind of sell-out deal, some surrender to the evil West, then it's not going to be just a few angry folks in Gaza or the odd demo in Damascus. The whole region could go *boof*.' He made a little mushroom cloud of his hands. 'And that's World War Three, right there.'

Maggie nodded, allowing Davis to know his little dramatic exposition had struck home.

'Up till now things have gone OK. But it's crunch time now, R & J, and the parties are getting antsy.'

'They haven't talked about refugees and Jerusalem until now?' She wanted Davis to know that she knew the code. Like every field, diplomacy had its jargon; within that, Middle East diplomacy had its own dialect. After a year spent a million miles away, Maggie hoped she'd be able to keep up.

'There's been a ton of groundwork on right of return,' said Davis. 'Though, one tip: don't let anyone catch you saying those words or the Israelis will eat your lunch. It's not a "right", it's a claim. And it's not necessarily "return", because some of the Palestinians came from somewhere else first. And it's not "home" because this is the homeland of the Jewish people, blah, blah. You know all this.'

Maggie nodded, but she had stopped listening. She was remembering the row she had had with Edward. He hadn't even attempted to deny that he had deleted those messages from Judd: he simply said he had done it for Maggie's own good. She had been furious, accusing him of trying to cage her, to tame her into some little Washington wife with a sideline in couples' therapy. He was denying who she really was, or at least who she had been. He said she had swallowed too many counselling manuals and was now simply vomiting them back up. She insisted that he was on some weird mission to prevent her ever getting over what had happened in Africa, as if he somehow liked her in the state he had found her: broken.

After that, there wasn't much to say and they hadn't said it. She had packed her bags quickly and left for the airport. She felt guilty, knowing all that Edward had done for her when she was at her lowest. And she felt tremendous sadness, that her attempt at a normal life had collapsed so spectacularly. But she could not, in all conscience, say she felt she had made a mistake. Why, she wondered now, had she never unpacked those boxes? She knew what she would say if this were about someone else: that unconsciously she was holding back, that she was refraining from ever fully moving in with Edward. Like a child who refuses to take his coat off at school, those two boxes, waiting to be unpacked, were her way of saying she was just passing through.

So she had boarded the plane, looked down at Washington as it receded, imagining Edward receding with it, and then promptly distracted herself by plunging into the three-hundred-page briefing pack Bonham had prepared for her.

'So you can imagine, this assassination thing has everyone extra jumpy. They're all on a hair trigger at the best of times, but now more than ever. Which is why they sent in the cavalry.' He gestured towards her. 'Closing the deal.'

'Right. Though not in the room just yet.'

'How's that?'

'Washington has decided that the mood has "deteriorated" in the few hours I was in the air. Apparently, the moment is not "ripe" for me to come in just yet.'

'Oh, right.'

'For now my immediate role is to keep everyone calm. Out and about, keeping the constituencies on side.'

'Ah, the "constituencies".' Davis made little quote marks with his fingers. 'Well, after what happened last night, the Israeli right are the first guys who are gonna need stroking. They're going ape, saying the dead guy's a martyr.'

'They think it was deliberate?'

'They're saying all kinds of things.' A look of sudden comprehension crossed Davis's face. 'So that's why you're going to the *shiva* house.'

'What?'

'The house of mourning. I just got passed a note saying you're to go, as an unofficial representative. The Israelis asked for it, apparently. Shows respect to the guy, proof that he wasn't being taken out because he opposed the "US-backed" peace process; proof that no one regarded him as an enemy.'

'But not too official, or it looks like we're endorsing his views.'

'Right. They think it might help cool things down.'

'And we've agreed.'

'We have. Funeral was this morning, as soon as they got the body back from the autopsy. They do them quick here; religious thing, like everything else in this place. But the *shiva* goes on all week. You've probably got the details on your BlackBerry.'

'Ah. No BlackBerry, I'm afraid.'

'Oh, Comms will fix you up with one of those, no problem. I'll get—'

'I mean, I don't use a BlackBerry. Never have. Keeps you on too tight a leash. Means you're listening to Washington or London or whoever, when you should be listening to the people in the room. Can't stand the things.'

'Okay.' Davis looked as if Maggie had admitted a heroin addiction.

'I wouldn't carry a cellphone either if I could get away with it. Same reason.'

Davis ignored that. 'Your hotel's just a block away. You can freshen up and the driver will take you there. Widow's name is Rachel.'

CHAPTER SIX

JERUSALEM, MONDAY 7.27PM

The street was jammed, cars parked on both sides, their tyres spilling onto the pavements. It was a well-to-do neighbourhood, Maggie could tell that much: the trees were leafy, the cars BMWs and Mercs. Her driver was struggling to get through, despite the discreet Stars-and-Stripes pennant flying from the bonnet. It had been getting chilly in DC. Here it was still warm in the late evening; there was a sweet, sticky smell coming off the trees.

The path to the building was packed, all the way to the front door. As she squeezed through, she noticed that look again from several of the men in line, their eyes following her as she went past.

'You are from the embassy, no? From America?' It was a man at the door, staff or relative Maggie couldn't tell. But clearly he knew she was coming. 'Please, inside.'

Maggie was pressed into what would ordinarily be a large room. Now it was jammed with people, like rush hour on a subway train. Her height was an advantage: she could see the crowd of heads, the male ones covered in skull caps, and at the front a bearded man she took to be a rabbi.

Yitgadal, v'Yitkadash . . .

The room hushed for this murmured prayer for the dead man. Then the rabbi spoke a few sentences of Hebrew, turning occasionally to a row of three people sitting on strangely low chairs. From their red eyes and moist noses, Maggie guessed they were Guttman's immediate family: widow, son and daughter. Of the three, only the son was not weeping. He stared straight ahead, his dark eyes dry.

Maggie could feel the crowd behind her. She was not quite sure what she was supposed to do. She should wait her turn to meet the family, but the room was heaving. It would take an hour to get to the front. But if she left now, it could be interpreted – and written up – as a snub. Meanwhile, she could hardly turn to strangers and strike up chitchat. This was not a party.

She smiled politely as she inched her way through. Her height and black trouser suit persuaded most of the mourners that she was some kind of VIP and they made way for her. (Wearing the suit felt strange: it had been so long since she had dressed this way.) Still, she could only move slowly.

She was making progress until she was blocked by a large bookcase. In truth the whole room seemed to be filled with books. They were broken up by the odd ceramic pot or plate, including one with a strikingly ornate blue pattern, but mainly it was books. Across each wall, and from floor to ceiling.

Her face was pressed up close enough to read the titles. Most were in Hebrew; but there was a cluster of books on American politics, including several of the neo-conservative tomes which had once dominated the *New York Times* bestseller lists. *Terrorism: How the West Can Win. Inside the New Jihad. The Coming Clash. The Gathering Storm*. She felt she had a good handle on this Mr Guttman. After all, Washington was not short of men who shared his politics. She had encountered more than one of them, at some reception or other, as Edward worked the room while she stood watching, as if from afar, even when she was right next to him. The memory had barely popped into her mind when she felt the accompanying pang. *Edward.*

'Please, please, come.' Her unofficial host had somehow reappeared and now drew Maggie forward. People were forming a line to meet the mourners. She tried to hear what those in front were saying, but she could understand none of it: Hebrew.

At last, it was Maggie's turn to shake hands with the family, nodding respectfully to each one, trying to mould her lips into the shape of pity. First, the daughter, who gave her only a fleeting moment of eye contact. She looked to be in her mid-forties, with short, dark hair interrupted by a few strands of grey; she was attractive, with a face that radiated solid practicality. Maggie guessed she was the person in charge here.

Then the son. Half-standing, half-sitting, he looked at her coldly. He was tall, and more casually dressed than she would have expected in a house of mourning, in dark jeans and a white shirt, both of which looked expensive. His hair, a full, dark head of it, was well cut, too. From the way people hovered around him, it appeared that he was successful or important in some way. Late thirties, Maggie noted; no sign of a wife.

And finally the widow. Maggie's guide bent down, so that the grieving woman could hear him. Self-consciously he spoke in English.

'Mrs Guttman, this lady is from United States. From the White House, from the President.'

Maggie toyed with correcting him and let it go. 'I'm so sorry for your loss,' she said, bending almost double and extending a hand. 'We wish you to know that you and your family are in the prayers of the American people.'

The widow looked up suddenly. Her hair was dyed black, her eyes nearly the same colour. She gripped Maggie by the wrist, so that Maggie was forced to look into those dark eyes which, still wet, focused intently.

'You are from the President of the United States?'

'Well—'

'You know my husband had an important message. For the Prime Minister.'

'That's what I understand and it's such a tragedy—'

'No, no you don't understand. This message, he had been trying to get it to Kobi for days. He called the office; he went to the Knesset. But they would not let him anywhere near. It drove him mad!' Her grip on Maggie's wrist tightened.

'Please don't upset yourself—'

'What is your name?'

'Maggie Costello.'

'His message was urgent, Miss Costello. A matter of life and death. Not just his life or Kobi's life, but the lives of everyone in this country, in this whole region. He had seen something, Miss Costello.'

'Please, Mrs Guttman—' It was the man who had introduced them, but the widow waved him away.

Maggie crouched lower. 'You say he had seen something?'

'Yes. A document, a letter maybe, something, I don't know for sure – but something of the greatest importance. For the last three days of his life, he did not sleep. He just said the same thing over and over. "Kobi must know of this, Kobi must know of this".'

'Kobi? The Prime Minister?'

'Yes, yes. Please understand, what he had to tell Kobi still needs to be told. My husband was not a fool. He knew the risk he took. But he said nothing was more important. He had to tell him what he had seen.'

'And what had he seen?'

'*Ima, dai kvar*!' It was the son, his voice firm, the voice of a man used to giving instructions. *Mother, enough already.*

'He didn't tell me. I only know it was some document, something written. And he said, "This will change everything." That's what he said. "This will change everything".'

'What will change everything?'

The son was now getting up.

'I don't know. He wouldn't tell me. For my safety, he said.'

'Your *safety*?'

'I know my husband. He was a serious man. He would not suddenly go crazy and run and shout at the Prime Minister. If he had something to say, it must have been just as Shimon said – a matter of life and death.'

CHAPTER SEVEN

BEITIN, THE WEST BANK, TUESDAY, 9.32AM

He wouldn't need to be here long. Just ten minutes in the office, collect the papers and leave.

Except 'office' was not quite the right word. The two heavy padlocks guarding the metal door testified to that. 'Workroom' was more like it, even 'storehouse'. Inside, it smelled like a potting shed. The fluorescent strip lights flickered on to reveal shelves filled not with papers, files or computer discs but stiff cardboard boxes. And inside those were fragments of ancient pottery, material Ahmed Nour had excavated from this very village.

He worked this way on every dig. Set up a base as close to the site as possible, allowing the latest findings to be brought back, catalogued and stored right away. He liked to do the job daily if he could: leave even a few burnt pottery shards around for too long and they would soon vanish. Looters, the curse of archaeologists the world over.

Ahmed found his desk: modest, metal, as if it belonged to the foreman on a construction site. Not so far off, he thought to himself. We're both in the business of human homes: they build new ones, I dig up old ones.

The papers he needed for his meeting with the head of the Palestinian Authority's Department of Antiquities and Cultural Heritage were right there, in a neat pile. Sweet Huda, he thought to himself. His young protégée had left everything in order: the permit renewal form, seeking permission to carry on digging in Beitin, and the application for a grant, begging for the cash to do it. Huda took care of all contact with the outside world now. She left him alone with no distractions – no phone calls, no emails, no blaring radio or crackling TV – so that he could bury himself in his work. If he concentrated hard, he could shut out modernity altogether.

That's what he had done this weekend. And he would have carried on doing it all week if it hadn't been for this damned meeting. The head of antiquities was an ignoramus. With no archaeological training, he was little more than a political hack. He wore a beard, which meant that the politics in question were of the new variety: religious.

'My preference, Dr Nour,' he had explained to Ahmed in their first meeting, 'is for the glorification of our Islamic heritage.' No surprise there. The new government was half Hamas. Translation: I'll pay for anything after the seventh century; if you want to dig up anything older, you're on your own.

The irony of it was not lost on Ahmed. Once he had been a hero to the Palestinian political class. He had been a founder member of a group of scholars who, decades ago, had insisted on looking at the ground beneath their feet in a radically new way. Until then, ever since the expeditions of Edward Robinson in the nineteenth century, those taking a shovel to this landscape were looking for one thing only: the Bible. They weren't interested in Palestine or the people who had lived here for thousands of years. They were searching for the Holy Land.

They were outsiders, of course, Americans or Europeans. They would arrive at Jaffa or Jerusalem giddy with scripture, yearning to see the route Abraham trod, to gaze at the Tomb of Christ. They longed to find the vestiges of the ancient Israelites or of the early Christians. Palestinians, ancient and modern, were an irrelevance.

The new generation, Ahmed among them, was trained in biblical archaeology – what other kind was there? – but they soon developed their own ideas. In the 1960s, several of them assisted a team of Lutheran Bible scholars from Illinois as they excavated Tell Ta'anach, a mound not far from Jenin in the West Bank. The Americans dug there for several years, such was their excitement. Ta'anach was mentioned in the Bible as one of the Canaanite cities conquered by Joshua, military leader of the Israelites.

But Ahmed and his colleagues began to see something else. They returned to the site, their focus now not Biblical Ta'anach but the Palestinian village at the foot of the mound: Ti'innik. These new archaeologists wanted to learn all they could about day-to-day life in this ordinary community, which had sat on the same spot for most of the last five millennia. Every heave of the archaeologist's shovel, every push of a spade, was making a political statement: this would be a Palestinian excavation of Palestine.

That put Ahmed Nour firmly into the bosom of the burgeoning Palestinian national movement. In whispers he was told that the Palestine Liberation Organization, then still secret, banned and run from abroad, approved of his work. He was nurturing 'national pride' and handily proving, at a time when most Israeli leaders were still denying even the existence of a Palestinian people, that the communities of these lands had the deepest possible roots.

His reputation only increased when he led students on a dig at an abandoned refugee camp, digging up the trash, the old sardine cans and plastic bags which revealed the way of life of people just a generation gone, those who had fled their homes in 1948. And his work here at Beitin had boosted his reputation yet further.

Previous scholars had thrilled at this place as the Bet-El of the Bible, the spot where Abraham, heading south, stopped and built an altar, the place where Jacob rested his head on a pillow of stone and dreamed of the angels going up and down a ladder. But Ahmed was determined to examine not just the ruins around Beitin, but the village itself. For humble, tiny Beitin had been ruled by Hellenists, by Romans, by Byzantines, by Ottomans. It had been Christian and it had been Muslim: in the late nineteenth century, a mosque had been built on the ruins of a Byzantine church. You could still see the remains of a Hellenistic tower, a Byzantine monastery and a Crusader castle. All three. To Ahmed's mind, that was the glory of Palestine. Even in a forgotten speck like Beitin, you could see the history of the world, one layer on top of another.

That gave him an idea. He reached for one of the newer boxes, one that would contain the freshest finds from the site. He peered inside, his nose crinkling at the musty smell: human skulls from the early Bronze Age, some five thousand years ago, along with storage jars and cooking pots. He smiled, knowing he could do better, that he could go back even further. He unlocked a cupboard, to find the flint tools and animal bones that had first been found at Beitin in the 1950s and which had been traced back some five millennia before Christ. He would tell that oaf at the antiquities department about the traces of blood that had been spotted, a sure sign of ritual sacrifice, establishing that Beitin had once been the site of a Canaanite temple. Maybe it was playing the old biblical game, thought Ahmed with a pang of guilt, but he had to use whatever he'd got.

It still might have no effect. The man from Hamas would

doubtless perk up at the reference to the nineteenth-century mosque and yawn at the rest. Or perhaps there was a chance he would see Beitin for what it really was, a place packed with the history of this land.

On tiptoes, stretching to put the most precious box back on the top shelf of the locked cupboard, he heard a noise. Metallic.

'Hello? Huda?'

No reply. Probably nothing. He must have left the metal door to the workroom ajar and the wind had clicked it shut. No matter. He would seal this box and be on his way.

But then there was another sound. This time a footstep, unmistakable. Ahmed turned around to see two men coming towards him. Both were wearing black hoods which covered their faces entirely. The taller man was holding up a finger, which he theatrically placed over his lips. *Hush*.

'What? What is this?' said Ahmed, his knees buckling.

'Just come with us,' said the tall man, something strange in his accent. 'Now!' And for the first time Ahmed saw the gun, lifted and aimed straight at him.

CHAPTER EIGHT

THE US CONSULATE, JERUSALEM, TUESDAY, 2.14PM

'Our information is that the body, riddled with bullets, was dumped by two hooded men in Ramallah's main square about 10.45 local time. The corpse was propped up and displayed to the crowd for about fifteen minutes, then taken away by the same two hooded men who'd brought it there.'

'Collaborator killing?'

'Exactly.' The CIA station chief turned towards Maggie, offering extra tuition to the newcomer to the class. 'This is standard punishment meted out by Palestinians to any Palestinian deemed guilty of collaborating with Israeli intelligence. Usually they're accused of tipping off Israel as to the whereabouts of wanted terrorists or have warned the Israelis when an attack's coming.'

'What's the Israeli reaction?' The questions were coming out of a speakerphone pulled to the centre of the polished wood table: the voice of the Secretary of State in Washington. He had left it to his deputy to manage this last stage of talks on the ground. He had wanted to keep his distance, in case of failure.

'So far pretty muted. Some boilerplate about Palestinians needing to prove they believe in the rule of law. But that was only a low-level spokesman, when prompted in a media interview. Nothing from any of the principals. I think they want to treat this as an internal—'

'No chance they'd break off talks over this?'

'We don't think so, sir.'

'Unless they're looking for an excuse.'

'Which they're not at this stage.' It was his deputy, raising his voice to be picked up by the phone. 'The talks are painfully difficult right now, but no one's walking away.'

'Still hung up on refugees?'

'And Jerusalem. Yes.'

'Remember, we can't let this go on forever. If we're not careful, it's one delay, then another and before you know it—'

'—it's November.' This from Bruce Miller, officially titled Political Counsellor to the President, unofficially his most trusted *consigliere*, at his side since his first run for Attorney General in Georgia more than twenty-five years earlier. They spent more time together than either man did with his wife. His presence in Jerusalem confirmed what they all knew. That this push for peace was inseparable from American domestic politics.

'Hello, Bruce.' Maggie detected a sudden meekness in the Secretary of State.

'I was just about to agree with you, Mr Secretary,' Miller began, his voice twanging between a down-home southern accent and the Nicorette gum he chewed from morning till night. He had given up cigarettes eleven years ago, aided by a variety of nicotine substitutes. The patch had gone, but not the gum: it was his new addiction.

'I mean, they've only had sixty years to think of an answer to all this. Jesus! We can't maintain this pitch forever.' He was leaning forward now, his wiry frame hunched so that his mouth would be closer to the telephone. His neck seemed to jut out at key moments, the two horns of hair bestriding his bald pate floating upward as he did so. Maggie tried to work out what he reminded her of. Was it a cockerel, its head popping forward and back metronomically? Or a feisty bantamweight in an illegal ring, somewhere in the backstreets of old Dublin, ready to fight dirty if he had to? He was mesmerizing to watch.

'We keep saying—' he gestured at a TV set in the corner, silently showing Fox News, 'this is about to get resolved this week. If nothing happens, we're back to square one. Only trouble is, there's no such place in the Middle East. Doesn't fucking exist! You never can just stand still. Screw it up here, and you go right back. Look what happened after Camp David. Israelis were shooting Arabs in the streets and Arabs were blowing up every café in Jerusalem. Because the folk who sat in these chairs tried to get it right and they screwed up.'

Silence, including from the speakerphone. They knew what this was: a rollicking from the top, doubtless with more to come.

'We do have more on this collaborator killing,' said the CIA man, a tentative attempt to alter the mood.

'Yes?' The Secretary of State.

'As I said earlier, ordinarily such a minor incident wouldn't warrant any discussion at all. At the height of the last *intifada*, these summary executions were happening all the time, at the rate of nearly one a week. But since the parties are supposed to be on a ceasefire, even an internal infraction like this one could turn—'

'This is background. You said you had more information.' Miller, conveying another message from the boss: *cut to the chase, there's no time to waste*.

'Just a couple of oddities. First, the dead man was in his late sixties. That's older than the usual profile, which tends to match that of the militants themselves.'

Miller raised a damning eyebrow. *Militants*.

'Or rather the terrorists themselves. Second, we've had a word with our Israeli counterparts today and they tell us this man was precisely what he seemed to be, an elderly archaeologist. He had done no work for them that they knew of.'

'So the Palestinians got the wrong guy?'

'That's possible, Mr Secretary. And death by mistaken identity is not unheard of in this part of the world. But there are other possibilities.'

'Such as?'

'It could be the work of a rebel faction. Security's so tight in Israel just now that they can't pull off a terrorist outrage here—' He left a subtle emphasis on the word 'terrorist', for Miller's benefit. 'So killing one of their own, especially an innocent, well-respected Palestinian like Nour, is the next best thing. It sows dissension among the Palestinians and could provoke the Israelis into breaking off negotiations. Destabilizes the process.'

'Sounds a long shot to me,' said Miller, still craning forward in concentration. 'Israel could say it shows Palestinians are lawless, can't be trusted with their own state. But Israeli public opinion would never swallow it. Break off the whole peace process just because one Arab's blown away? Never. What else?'

'The other curiosity relates to eye-witness reports from Manara Square in Ramallah. The hooded men hardly spoke but when they did, we're told they had unusual accents.'

'What kind of accent?'

'I don't have that information, sir. I'm sorry.'

'But they could be Israeli?'

'It's a possibility.'

Miller fell back into his chair, took off his glasses and addressed the ceiling. 'Christ! What are we saying? That this might be an undercover Israeli army operation?'

'Well, we know Israel has always run undercover units. Codenamed Cherry and Samson; special forces dressed as Arabs. This could be their latest operation.'

Still rubbing his eyes, Miller asked: 'Why the hell would they do that now?'

'Again, it might be an effort to destabilize the peace talks. It's widely known that elements within the Israeli military are fiercely hostile to the compromises the Prime Minister wants to make—'

'And if this got out, then the Palestinians would be so pissed, they'd walk away. The killing of one of their national heroes.'

'Yes. And even if the Authority were ready to let it go, the Palestinian street wouldn't let them.'

'Hence the accidentally-on-purpose slip of the accent.' The words were barely audible through the chewing.

'Its one of the lines of enquiry we're pursuing.'

'It's like a hall of fucking mirrors here!' Miller threw himself back in his chair. 'We have the Israelis and the Palestinians at each other's throats. And now we've got rogue elements on both sides.'

'The possibility at least. Which is why we're taking a close look at the Guttman killing.'

'What's that got to do with it?'

'We're asking some questions about the security detail that protects the Prime Minister, wondering if it's possible it was infiltrated. We don't want to rule out the scenario that the man who shot Guttman did so deliberately, following some other agenda.'

Maggie leaned forward, about to mention her strange encounter with the Guttman widow, the previous night. *His message was urgent, Miss Costello. A matter of life and death.* Maybe it would sound flaky to bring that up here. On the other hand—

It was too late. Miller was getting up out of his chair.

'OK, people, I think that's enough Oliver Stone for one session. Mr Secretary, we're going to keep pushing the talks at this end as if none of this other stuff was happening. Is that OK with you?'

'Of course.'

'And shall I leave you to brief the President?'

'Sure. Yes.' Everyone in the room, including the Secretary of State seven thousand miles away, knew this was an empty courtesy: Miller and the President spoke a dozen times before breakfast, no matter how many time zones stood between them. If there was any briefing to be done he would be doing it, probably within minutes.

Miller looked up. 'Anything else?' He looked towards Maggie, who shook her head, and then to the consul who did the same. 'OK.'

The room broke up, every official eager to show the man from the White House that they were hurrying to return to their duties. Maggie filed out behind Davis.

They all left too fast either to see Miller pull out his cellphone or to hear the three short, staccato words he whispered into it once he was connected to Washington: 'Everything's on track.'

CHAPTER NINE

JERUSALEM, TUESDAY, 3.17PM

Maggie headed to the room Davis had set up for her, a work space for all State Department visitors. Just a desk, phone and computer. That's all she would need. She closed the door.

First, she checked her email. One from Liz, in response to a message Maggie had left on her phone, telling her of the sudden trip to Jerusalem. Subject: *You go, girl!*

> *So my serious sister, you've finally made it into my crazy world. You know you're now a character in Second Life? You know, the online thing where I waste WAY too much of my time. Seriously. You're in some Middle East peace talks simulation thing. It even looks like you: though they've given you a better arse than you deserve. Here's a link: take a look . . .*

Maggie clicked on it, intrigued. Liz had mentioned Second Life to her a couple of times, insisting it was not just another dumb game but a virtual addition to the real world. Liz loved it, evangelizing about the way you could travel and meet people – not orcs or dragon-slayers but real people – without ever leaving your computer. It sounded horrendous to Maggie, but her curiosity was piqued. What did Liz mean, that Maggie was now a 'character' in it? A 'peace talks simulation thing' she understood: there were several of those online, where graduate students would role-play their way through the latest round of Middle East negotiations. Impressive that they already knew she was in Jerusalem. She guessed there had been a paragraph in one of the Israeli papers.

The computer eggtimer was still showing, before eventually freezing in defeat. A message popped up saying something about a security block on the consulate network. Never mind, thought Maggie. Some other time.

She went back through the inbox. Still nothing from Edward. She wondered if that would be it, if they would ever speak again, other than to arrange the removal of what was left of her stuff. Which, thanks to him, was not much.

She clicked her email shut then, out of habit, brought up the *New York Times* and *Washington Post* websites. The *Times* had a story about the Israel shooting on Saturday night, including a profile of the dead man. Happy for the distraction, she read through it.

Shimon Guttman first came to prominence after the Six Day War in 1967, in which he was said to have performed with military distinction. Seizing the chance to make the most of Israel's new control of the historic West Bank territories of Judea and Samaria, Guttman was among the group of activists who famously found an ingenious way to re-establish a Jewish presence in the heavily Arab city of Hebron. Disguised as tourists, they rented rooms in a Palestinian hotel, ostensibly to host a Passover dinner, or seder. Once installed, they refused to leave. In the stand-off with the Israeli authorities that followed, Guttman was especially vocal, insisting that the Jewish connection to Hebron was stronger than with anywhere else in the land of Israel. 'This is the spot where the Oak of Abraham stands, the ancient tree where Avraham Avinu, Abraham our father, pitched his tent,' he told reporters in 1968. 'Here is the Tomb of the Patriarchs, where Abraham, Isaac and Jacob are all buried. Without Hebron, we are nothing.' Guttman and his fellow activists eventually struck a deal with the Israeli authorities, vacating the hotel and moving instead to a hill northeast of Hebron where they established the Jewish settlement of Kiryat Arba. That hilltop outpost has since flourished into the modern city that exists today, though speculation mounts as to its fate in the new peace accord which could be signed as soon as this week.

That would explain it, thought Maggie. Guttman was worried that the settlement he had founded was about to be surrendered to the Palestinians, along with the scores of other Jewish towns and villages Israel was bound to give up. He had been trying to persuade the Prime Minister to change his mind. And he clearly enjoyed the dramatic gesture. He had climbed a roof in Gaza a few years back and had, she now saw, seized a hotel in Hebron a generation before that. A regular performance artist, she thought.

She Googled him, looking into the handful of English language websites carrying Israeli news. They all told similar stories. Guttman had been first a war hero and then a right-wing extremist with a knack for the big stunt. One site contained a clip of video, apparently from a protest, Guttman at the front of a crowd on some dusty hilltop, all of them waving Israeli flags. Maggie guessed it was some settlement, either about to go up or come down.

He had been an imposing figure, a thick plume of grey hair blowing in the breeze, a healthy belly spilling over the top of his trousers. He filled the frame. 'The Palestinians need to look at the history,' he was saying. 'Because the history says it as clear as can be: the Jews were here first. This land belongs to us. All of it.'

It all seemed pretty straightforward. He was a hawk, determined to make his last stand by appealing to the Prime Minister direct. He got too close and was gunned down. Simple.

And yet there was something about what Rachel Guttman had said, and the way she had said it, that nagged at her. She had insisted that her husband had *seen* something – *a document, a letter* – that would change everything, in the last three days of his life. Maggie looked at her wrist, where the widow had gripped her so tightly. Poor woman. To be so stricken with grief that she had started ranting at her, a total stranger. Maggie had seen other people who had lost loved ones trying, madly, to detect some higher meaning in the violent death of their husband, wife, mother or child. Claiming that the slain person had somehow foreseen their own death; that they were about to do one last great deed; that they were poised to make everything right. Maybe Rachel Guttman was suffering from that same, melancholy delusion. Maggie rubbed her wrist.

There was a knock on the door. Without waiting for an answer, Davis walked in.

'OK, the United States has decided to deploy its secret weapon.'

'Oh yes, what's that?'

'You.'

Davis explained that, as feared, the Palestinian delegation to Government House were now threatening to pull out over the death of the archaeologist. They suspected the hand of Israel. 'We need you to talk them off the ledge. Deputy Secretary wants to see you in five minutes.'

Maggie collected her papers and moved to turn off the computer. She was about to shut down the website of the Israeli newspaper, *Haaretz*, the last one she had searched for information on Guttman, when she changed her mind, quickly checking the front page, just in case there was fresh word on the Nour case.

There was a news story, which she skim-read. It was written up as a straight collaborator killing: no mention of any possible Israeli involvement. But accompanying it was a picture of the dead Palestinian, what seemed to be a snap from a family album. The archaeologist, with his thick salt-and-pepper moustache, was smiling at the camera, holding up a glass. A disembodied arm was draped over his shoulder, as if he were posing with an unseen friend.

Maggie got up to go, following Davis, but something drew her back to the picture on the screen. She had seen something familiar, without being able to identify what it was. She looked at Nour's eyes, but they gave nothing away. What was it she had seen? For a fleeting moment, she thought she had grasped it – only for it slip back below the surface, out of reach. She would see it again, though – and much sooner than she expected.

CHAPTER TEN

RAMALLAH, THE WEST BANK, TUESDAY, 4.46PM

Her first surprise was at the brevity of the journey. She had climbed into the back of one of the consulate's black Land Cruisers only fifteen minutes earlier and yet now her driver, Marine Sergeant Kevin Lee, was telling her that she was crossing the Green Line, out of 'Israel-proper' and into the lands the country took in the Six Day War of 1967.

But it was an invisible border. There were no markings, no guards, no welcome signs. Instead, they were in what looked like another residential Jerusalem neighbourhood – one apartment building after another in that smooth, gleaming stone – when Lee gestured, 'This is Pisgat Ze'ev. Even the people who live here don't realize this is across the Green Line.' He turned to look at Maggie. 'Or they don't want to realize.'

Maggie stared out of the window. No wonder everything about these negotiations was a nightmare. The plan was for Jerusalem to be divided between the two sides – 'shared' was the favoured US euphemism – becoming a capital for both countries. But she could now see that splitting it would be all but impossible: east and west Jerusalem were like trees which had grown so close, they had become entwined. They refused to be untangled.

'Now you get more of a sense of it,' Lee was saying, as the road began to bend. 'Pisgat Ze'ev on one side,' he said, pointing to his right. 'And Beit Hanina on the other.' Gesturing to the left.

She could see the difference. The Arab side of the road was a semi-wasteland: unfinished houses made of grey breeze blocks, sprouting steel rods like severed tendons; potholed, overgrown pathways, bordered by rusting oil barrels. Out of the car's other window, Pisgat Ze'ev was all straight lines and trim verges. It could have been an American suburb, cast in Biblical stone.

'Yep, it's pretty simple,' said Lee. 'The infrastructure here is great. And over there it's shit.'

They drove on in silence, Maggie's eyes boring into the landscape around her. You could read a thousand briefing notes and study a hundred maps, but there was no substitute for seeing the ground with your own eyes. It was true in Belfast and in Bosnia and it was true here.

'Hold up,' Lee said sharply, looking ahead. 'What have we got here?'

Two thin lines of people were standing on either side of the highway.

'Can we stop?' Maggie asked. 'I want to see.'

Lee pulled off the road, the gravel crunching under the vehicle's tyres. 'Ma'am, let me get out first. To see if it's safe to proceed.'

Ma'am. Maggie tried to guess the difference in age between herself and this Marine Sergeant Lee. He could have been no more than twenty-two: she was, theoretically anyway, old enough to be his mother.

'OK, Miss Costello, I think it's clear.'

Maggie got out of the car, to see that the people were forming a line that stretched off the side beyond the road, trailing down the hillside and into the distance. In the other direction, on the other side of the road, the same thing. Some were holding banners, the rest were holding hands. It was a human chain, breaking only for the highway itself.

Now she understood it. They were all wearing orange, the colour of the protest movement that had sprung up to oppose the peace process. She looked at the placards. *With blood and fire, Yariv will go,* said one. *Arrest the traitors,* said another. The first had mocked up a portrait of the Prime Minister wearing a black and white keffiyeh, the traditional Palestinian headdress. The second had Yariv wearing the uniform of a Nazi officer, down to the letters SS on his collar.

The woman holding the keffiyeh banner saw Maggie looking. She called over: 'You want to save Jerusalem? This is the way!' A New York accent.

Maggie came closer.

'We're "Arms Around Jerusalem",' the woman said, handing Maggie a flier. 'We're forming a human chain around the eternal, undivided capital of the Jewish people. We're going to stay here until Yariv and all the other criminals are gone and our city is safe again.'

Maggie nodded.

The woman lowered her voice, as if enlisting a co-conspirator. 'If it were down to me we would have called it "Hands Off Jerusalem". But you don't win every battle. You should stay here a while, see what true Israelis feel about this great betrayal.'

Maggie gestured towards the car, her features crinkled into an apology. As she walked back, she could hear a song drifting up from the hillside. It was out of time, as different people in different places struggled to keep up with each other; but even so it was a haunting, beautiful melody.

As Sergeant Lee ushered her back into the car and they continued on their way, Maggie thought about what she had seen.

Against opposition this committed, Yariv surely had no chance. Even if he were able to make the final push with the Palestinians, he had his own people to overcome. People who were prepared to ring an entire city, day and night, for weeks or even months.

By now they were on a smooth road with hardly any traffic on it except the odd UN 4x4 or a khaki vehicle of the Israel Defence Force, the IDF. Any other vehicles, Lee explained, belonged to settlers.

'Where are the Palestinians?'

'They have to get around some other way. That's why they call this a bypass road: it's to bypass them.'

Lee slowed down to join a checkpoint queue. A sign in English indicated who was allowed to approach: international organizations, medical staff, ambulances, press. Below that, a firm injunction: 'Stop Here! Wait to be called by the soldier!'

The driver reached across for Maggie's passport, wound down the window and passed it to the guard. Maggie dipped her head in the passenger seat, to get a good look at his face. He was dark and skinny, with a few random wisps on his chin. He couldn't have been more than eighteen.

They were waved through, past an empty hulk of a building that Lee identified as the City Inn Hotel. It was pocked all over with bullet holes. 'During the second *intifada* they fought here for weeks. Took the IDF ages to finally clear the Pals out.' He turned to smile at Maggie. 'I hear the room rate's real low now.'

Just a few minutes after they had been driving through Israeli suburbia, they were in a different country. The buildings were still made of the pale stone she had seen in Jerusalem, but here they were dustier, forlorn. The signs were in Arabic and English: Al-Rami Motors, the Al-Aqsa Islamic Bank. She saw a clutch of wicker rattan chairs on a street corner, young men loafing on them, thin cigarettes between their lips. The furniture was for sale. Walking in the road, sidestepping the potholes, were children on their way from school, labouring under oversized rucksacks. She looked away.

On every wall and pasted on the windows of abandoned stores were posters showing the faces of boys and men, the images framed by the green, white, red and black of the Palestinian national flag.

'Martyrs,' said Lee.

'Suicide bombers?'

'Yeah, but not only. Also kids who were shooting at settlers or maybe trying to launch a rocket.'

The car dipped suddenly, caught by a deep pothole. Maggie kept staring out of the window. Here, as in almost every other place she had worked, the two sides had ended up killing each other's children. It seemed everyone doing the killing or being killed was young. She always knew that, but in the last few years she couldn't see anything else. Time after time, in place after place, she had seen it and it just sickened her. An image, the same as always, floated into her head and she had to close her eyes tight to push it away.

They threaded through crammed roads, passing a coffee shop filled with women in black headscarves. Lee dodged a couple of wagons, pulled by young boys, loaded with fruit: pears, apples, strawberries and kiwis. Everyone used the road: people, cars, animals. It was slow and noisy, horns blaring and beeping without interruption.

'Here we are.'

They had parked by a building that looked different from the others: it was substantial, the stone clean, the glass in the windows solid. She saw a sign, thanking the government of Japan and the European Union. A ministry.

Inside, they were ushered into a wide spacious office with a long L-shaped couch. The room was too big for the furniture inside it. Maggie suspected that grandiosity had dictated the size, with practicality and need coming a remote second.

A thickset man came in carrying a plastic tray bearing two glasses of steaming mint tea, for her and her Marine escort. Maggie had seen a half dozen more men like him on her way up, sitting around like drivers at a taxi dispatch office, smoking, sipping coffee and tea. She guessed they were officially 'security'. In reality, they were that group she had seen in countless corners of the world: hangers-on, blessed with a brother-in-law or cousin who had found them a place on the state payroll.

'Mr al-Shafi is ready. Please, please come.' Maggie collected her small, black leather case and followed the guide out of the room and into another, smaller one. Furnished more sparely, it looked as if proper work was done here. On one couch and in several chairs, assorted aides and officials. On the wall, a portrait of Yasser Arafat and a calendar showing a map of the whole of Palestine, including not just the West Bank and Gaza, but Israel itself. An ideological statement that said hardline.

Khalil al-Shafi rose from his seat to shake Maggie's hand. 'Ms Costello, I hear you have broken your retirement to come here and stop us children squabbling.'

The joke, and the inside knowledge it betrayed, did not surprise her. The briefing note from Davis had told her to expect a smart operator. After more than a decade in an Israeli jail, convicted not only on the usual terrorism charges but also on several counts of murder, he had become a symbol of 'the struggle'. He had learned Hebrew from his jailers and then English, and had taken to issuing, via his wife, monthly statements – sometimes calls to arms, sometimes sober analyses, sometimes subtle diplomatic manoeuvres. When the Israelis had released him three months earlier, it had been the most serious sign yet that progress was possible.

Now al-Shafi was recognized as the de facto leader of at least one half of the Palestinian nation, those who did not back Hamas but identified with the secular nationalists of Arafat's Fatah movement. He held no official title – there was still a chairman and a president – but nothing on the Fatah side could move without him.

Maggie tried to read him. The photos, of a stubbled face with broad, crude features, had led her to expect a streetfighter rather than a sophisticate. Yet the man before her had a refinement that surprised her.

'I was told it was worth it. That you and the Israelis were close to a deal.'

'"Were" is the right word.'

'Not now?'

'Not if the Israelis keep killing us in order to play games with us.'

'Killing you?'

'Ahmed Nour could not have been killed by a Palestinian.'

'You sound very certain. From what I hear, Palestinians seem to have killed quite a lot of other Palestinians over the years.'

His eyes flashed a cold stare. Maggie smiled back. She was used to this. In fact, she did it deliberately: show some steel early, that way they'll resist the temptation to dismiss you as some lightweight woman.

'No Palestinian would kill a national hero like Ahmed Nour. His work was a source of pride to all of us and a direct challenge to the hegemony and domination of the Israelis.' Maggie remembered: al-Shafi had taken a doctorate in political science while in jail.

'But who knows what else he was doing?'

'Believe me, he was the last person on this earth who would collaborate with the Israelis.'

'Oh come on. We know he wasn't a big fan of the new government. He couldn't stand Hamas.'

'You're informed well, Ms Costello. But Ahmed Nour understood we have a government of national unity in Palestine now. When Fatah went into coalition with Hamas, Ahmed accepted it.'

'What else could he say publicly? Last time I checked, collaborators weren't wearing T-shirts with "collaborator" written on the chest.'

Al-Shafi leaned forward and looked unblinking at Maggie. 'Listen to me, Miss Costello. I know my people and I know who is a traitor and who is not. Collaborators are young or they are poor or they are desperate. Or they have some shameful secret. Or the Israelis have something they need. None of these fit Ahmed Nour. Besides—'

'He knew nothing.' Suddenly Maggie realized the obvious. 'He was a middle-aged scholar. He didn't have any information to give.'

'Yes, that's right.' Al-Shafi looked puzzled; he was looking for the trap. The American had folded too early. 'Which is why it must have been the Israelis who killed him.'

'Which would explain the strange accent of the killers.'

'Exactly. So you agree with me?'

'What would be their motive?'

'The same as always, for the last one hundred years! The Zionists say they want peace, but they don't. Peace scares them. Whenever they are close, they find a reason to step back. And this time they want *us* to step back, so they kill us and drive our people so mad that Palestinians will not allow their leaders to shake the hand of the Zionist enemy!'

'If the Israelis really wanted to wind up the Palestinians, wouldn't they kill a whole lot more people than just one old man?'

'But the Zionists are too clever for that! If they drop a bomb, then the world will blame them. This way, the world blames us!'

Something in al-Shafi's tone struck Maggie as odd. What was it? A false note, his voice somehow a decibel too loud. She had heard this before: once in Belgrade, a Serb official talking at the same, unnatural volume. *Of course.* Al-Shafi was not speaking to her, she realized. He was *performing.* His real audience was the other men in the room.

'Dr al-Shafi, do you think we could talk in private?'

Al-Shafi looked to the handful of officials and, with a quick gesture, waved them out. After a rustle of papers and clinking of tea glasses, they were alone.

'Thank you. Is there something you want to tell me?'

'I have told you what I think.' The voice was quieter now.

'You've told me you believe that the men who killed Ahmed Nour yesterday were undercover agents of Israel.'

'Yes.'

'But you don't really believe that, do you? Is there something you didn't want to say in front of your colleagues?'

'Is this how you make peace, Miss Costello? By reading the minds of the men who are fighting?' He gave her a rueful smile.

'Don't try flattering me, Dr al-Shafi,' Maggie said, returning the smile. 'You suspect Hamas, don't you?' Taking his silence as affirmation, she pressed on. 'But why? Because he was a critic of theirs?'

'Do you remember what the Taliban did in Afghanistan, just before 9/11? Something that grabbed the world's attention.'

'They blew up those giant Buddhas, carved in the mountain-side.'

'Correct. And why did they do this? Because the statues proved there was something before Islam, a civilization even older than the Prophet. This is something the fanatics cannot stand.'

'You think Hamas would kill Nour just for that, because he found a few pots and pans that predated Islam?'

Al-Shafi sighed and leaned back in his chair. 'Miss Costello, it's not just Hamas. They are under pressure from Islamists all around the world, who are calling them traitors for talking to Israel at all.'

'Al-Qaeda?'

'Among others, yes. They are watching what is happening here very closely. It's possible that Hamas felt they had to show their balls – excuse me – by killing a scholar who uncovered the wrong kind of truth.'

'But why would they disguise that as a collaborator killing? Surely they would make it look like a state execution, if they wanted to boost their standing with al-Qaeda.' Maggie paused. 'Unless they also wanted to make it look like Israel, so that Palestinians would be too angry to go ahead with the peace deal. Is that possible?'

'I have wondered about it. Whether Hamas is getting, how do you say, cold feet?'

Maggie smiled. She was always wary of first impressions, including her own. But something about the knot of angst on this man's forehead, the way his mind seemed to be wrestling with itself, made her trust him.

Al-Shafi rubbed his beard. Maggie tried to read his expression. 'There's something else, isn't there?'

He looked up, his eyes holding hers. She did not break the contact; or the silence.

At last, he got up and began to pace, staring at his feet. 'Ahmed Nour's son came to see me an hour ago. He was very agitated.'

'Understandably.'

'He said he went through his father's things this afternoon, looking for an explanation. He found some correspondence, a few emails. Including one – a strange one – from someone he does not recognize.'

'Has he spoken with colleagues? Maybe it's someone he worked with.'

'Of course. But his assistant does not recognize the name either. And she handled all such matters for him.'

'Maybe he was having an affair.'

'It's a man's name.'

Maggie began to raise her eyebrows, but thought better of it. 'And the son thought this person might somehow be linked to his father's death?'

Al-Shafi nodded.

'That he might even be behind it?'

He gave the slightest movement of his head.

'What kind of person are we talking about?'

Al-Shafi looked towards the door, as if uncertain who might be listening. 'The email was sent by an Arab.'

CHAPTER ELEVEN

JERUSALEM, TUESDAY, 8.19PM

Maggie lay back on her bed at the David's Citadel Hotel. The hotel was cavernous, built in a modern, scrubbed version of Jerusalem stone – and, as far as she could tell, packed with American Christians. She had seen one group form a circle, their eyes closed, in the lobby while their Israeli tour guide looked on, patiently.

Davis had put her here. It was a block away from the consulate; she could see Agron Street from her window. She and Lee had driven back from Ramallah in the twilight, the road even emptier than before, and in silence. Maggie had been thinking, doing her best not to believe that this mission, far from being destined to save her reputation, was doomed to fail.

What Judd Bonham had billed as a simple matter of closing the deal was deteriorating instead into yet another Middle East disaster. No one had kept count of how many times these two peoples had seemed ready to make peace, only to fail and sink back into war. Each time it happened the violence was worse than before. Maggie dreaded to think what hell awaited if, in the next few days, they failed all over again. She had learned to recognize the telltale signs, and high-profile killings on both sides, whatever the circumstances, were a reliable warning of serious trouble ahead.

She reached for the minibar. With a glass honeyed by a whisky miniature, she sat at the desk and stared out of the window. She could see a man emerge from the neon-lit convenience store across the street, carrying a flimsy plastic bag: inside it, a plastic bottle of milk, maybe a jar of honey. A man off home for the night.

It was such a simple sight yet it fascinated Maggie. For some reason such basic, humdrum domesticity had eluded her. She envied that man, heading home with a bottle of milk for the children to drink with their bedtime story. He probably did the same thing every night. Somehow he had managed it without ever trying to break free.

Draining her glass, she considered calling Edward. She wondered if her number would show on his phone and, if it did, whether he would pick up. She imagined what they would say, whether he would apologize for what he had done, or expect her to apologize for having gone to Jerusalem. Maggie sat still, drinking one and a half more whiskies as Edward's words two days ago, slung across the kitchen of their apartment in Washington, did circuits in her head. Was he right, that she always ran away, that she couldn't stick long enough at anything to make it work? Maybe he was. Maybe a normal person would have got over what happened last year and moved on by now.

She dialled his number, using her mobile so he would know it was her and would have a choice to screen her out if he wanted to. As she heard the first ring, she looked at her watch. Half-past one in Washington. He picked up.

'Maggie.' Not a question, not a greeting. A statement.

'Hi, Edward.'

'How's Jerusalem?' A pause. Then, 'You save the world yet?'

'I wanted to talk.'

'Well, now's not a great time, Maggie.' She could hear the clink of silverware and low string music in the background. Lunch at La Colline, she reckoned.

'Just give me two minutes.'

She could hear the muffled sound of Edward excusing himself from the table, pulling back his chair and finding a quiet corner. Truth be told, he wouldn't have been so unhappy to do it: interrupting a meal to take an urgent phone call was standard Washington practice, a way of signalling your indispensable importance.

'Yeah,' he said finally. *Fire away.*

'I just wanted to talk about what's going to happen with us.'

'Well, I was planning on you coming to your senses and coming back home. Then we could take it from there.'

'Coming to my senses?'

'Oh come on, Maggie. You can't be serious about all this, playing the peacemaker.'

Maggie closed her eyes. She wouldn't rise to it. 'I need to know you understand why I was so angry. About those boxes.'

'Look, I don't have time for this—'

'Because if you don't understand, if you can't understand—'

'Then what, Maggie? What?' He was raising his voice now. People at the restaurant would be noticing.

'Then I don't know how—'

'What? How we can carry on? Oh, I think we're past that, don't you? I think you took that decision the moment you got on that plane.'

'Edward—'

'I offered you a life here, Maggie. And you didn't want it.'

'Can we just talk—?'

'There's nothing more to say, Maggie. I've got to go.'

There was a click and eventually a synthetic voice: *The other person has hung up, please try later. The other person has hung up, please try later.*

Maggie expected to cry, but she felt something worse. A heaviness spreading inside her, as if her chest were turning to concrete. She leaned forward, elbows on her knees. It was over. Her attempt at a normal life had failed. And here she was again, in a foreign hotel room, quite alone.

It was all because of what happened last year, she understood that. She had thought her relationship with Edward might slay the ghost, but in the end it had been consumed by it. She raised her head and gazed out at the darkness of Jerusalem, knowing that it was quite within her to stay like that, staring and frozen, all night. The prospect was appealing, and she surrendered to it for the best part of an hour.

But eventually another feeling surfaced, the sense that she had been handed a chance to break free of those dreadful events of a year ago, to balance the ledger somehow. To seize that chance she would have to do what she had done so many times before, push away her feelings and concentrate only on the job. She would have to make this current assignment work. She could not afford to fail.

OK, she thought, as she splashed her face with water, forcing herself to make a fresh start. What is the problem? Internal opposition on both sides, prompted by two killings: Guttman and Nour. First priority is to get to the bottom of both cases and somehow reassure both publics that there's nothing to worry about and that the talks should go ahead.

She checked the *Haaretz* site again and saw the same picture she had seen five hours ago: Ahmed Nour, smiling that enigmatic smile. She whispered almost aloud, 'What happened to you?' And then: 'Is this entire peace deal going to screw up because of you?'

She had done her best with al-Shafi, urging him to keep the faith, to stick with the process. She had assured him that if Hamas were going wobbly, there were things the US could do to bring them back on side. She stressed Washington's absolute conviction that the Israelis were serious, that a Palestinian state could be theirs within a matter of days. She said he bore a historic responsibility and, not meaning to, had glanced up at the portrait of Arafat as she said it.

There was no way of knowing if it had worked. He had ushered her out of his office quietly, summoning his aides and colleagues back in. He was in a corner, she understood that: suspicious of his coalition partners in Hamas, suspicious even of his own inner circle, doubtful of their loyalty. He feared he was being led into a trap, extending his hand to Israel only to be denounced by the Islamists as a traitor. That would secure their domination for decades, if they could cast Fatah as patsies of Israel. He had not spent seventeen years in an Israeli jail for this.

She stared at the picture of Nour as if her eyes might somehow drill down into his and extract the answers she needed. If they could only resolve the Nour killing, tidy it up and put it out of the way, then maybe things could get back on track.

She scrolled down, to see that *Haaretz* had now posted an extended 'appreciation' of the life of Shimon Guttman. She could see from the items around it that the story was still running big. 'Settlers' leaders demand state inquiry into Guttman slaying,' ran one headline. 'Militant rabbi calls for holy curse on Prime Ministerial protection squad,' reported another.

She skimmed this new, longer profile. The same details were there: the early war record; the bluff, bullish persona; the inflammatory rhetoric. But now there were more anecdotes and longer quotations. She was two thirds down and about to give up, when her eye caught something.

In the 1967 campaign and afterwards, Guttman showed his debt to those earlier Israeli heroes Moshe Dayan and Yigal Yadin. He, like them, combined his military prowess with a scholar's passion for the ancient history of this land. He became what polite society refers to as a muscular archaeologist – and what the Palestinians call a looter in a tank. Every hill taken and every hamlet conquered were seen not only as squares on the war planners' chessboard, but as sites for excavation. Guttman would swap his rifle for a shovel and start digging. His admirers – and enemies – said he had amassed a collection of serious importance, a range of pieces dating back several thousand years. All of them had one quality in common: they confirmed the continuous Jewish presence in this land . . .

Maggie cracked open another miniature bottle of Scotch. Maybe this was just a coincidence: Guttman and Nour, both archaeologists, both nationalists, both killed within twenty-four hours of one another. She read on.

. . . he was self-taught but became a respected authority, with ancient inscription an esoteric specialism. Did he cut corners, both ethical and legal to build up his hoard? Probably. But that was the man, the last of the Zionist swashbucklers, an adventurer who belonged in the generation of 1948, if not of 1908 . . .

Two men, not that far apart in age, both digging up the Holy Land to prove it belonged to them, to their tribe. It was a fluke, Maggie told herself. But it was odd all the same. One killing had fired up the Israeli right, the second was whipping up the Palestinian hardliners and both now threatened to shut down the best hope for peace these two nations were likely to see this side of the Second Coming.

Maggie glanced over at the minibar, pondering a refill. She looked back at the screen, heading for the Google window. She typed in a new combination: *Shimon Guttman archaeologist.*

The page filled up. A decade-old profile from the *Jerusalem*

Post; a Canadian Broadcasting transcript of Guttman interviewed in a West Bank settlement, describing the Palestinians as 'interlopers' and a 'bogus nation'. Both made frustratingly fleeting reference to what the *Post* called his 'patriotic passion for excavating the Jewish past'.

Next came *Minerva*, the International Review of Ancient Art and Archaeology. She couldn't see any obvious pieces about Guttman, so she did a text search and even then it was barely visible. Just his name, small and italicized, alongside someone else's at the foot of an article announcing the discovery of an unusual prayer bowl traced to the Biblical city of Nineveh.

She scoured the text, looking for . . . she didn't know what. It made no sense to her, all the talk of 'embellishments' and 'inlays' and cuneiform script. Perhaps this was a dead end. She rubbed her forehead, pressed the shutdown button on the computer and began closing the lid.

But the machine refused to turn off. It asked instead if she wanted to close all the 'tabs', all the pages she was looking at. Her cursor was hovering over 'yes' when she saw Guttman's name again, small and italic. And now, for the first time, she read the name next to it: Ehud Ramon.

Maybe this man would know something. She Googled him, bringing up only three relevant results: one more of them a reference in *Minerva*, all three appearing alongside Shimon Guttman. Of Ehud Ramon on his own, as an independent person in his own right, there was nothing.

She found a database of Israeli archaeologists and typed Ehud Ramon into the search window. Plenty of Ehuds and one Ramon but no Ehud Ramon. Same with the Archaeological Institute of America. Who was this man, tied to Guttman yet who left no trace?

And then she saw it. Her skin shivered, as she fumbled for a pen and paper, scribbling letters as fast as she could, just to be sure. Surely this name, apparently belonging to an Israeli or American scholar couldn't be . . . And yet, here it was, materializing before her very eyes. There was no Ehud Ramon. Or rather there was, but that wasn't his real name. It was an anagram, just like the ones Maggie had unscrambled at uncanny speed as a teenager during those interminable, dreary Sunday afternoons at the convent. Ehud Ramon was a scholar, committed to exhuming the secrets of the soil. But he was the unlikeliest partner for Shimon Guttman, right-wing Zionist zealot and sworn enemy of the Palestinians. For Ehud Ramon was Ahmed Nour.

CHAPTER TWELVE

BAGHDAD, APRIL 2003

Salam had headed to school that morning more out of habit than expectation. He didn't really believe that his classes would go ahead as normal, but he had gone along anyway, just in case. Under Saddam, truancy from school was, like any other act of disobedience, a risk no one who valued their safety would ever take. Saddam might have been on the run, his statue in Paradise Square toppled for the world's TV cameras, but amongst most Baghdadis, the caution bred over the course of twenty-four years endured. Salam was not the only one who had dreamed of the dictator rising like Poseidon from the Tigris, drenched and angry, demanding that his subjects fall to their knees.

So he went to school. Clearly others had suffered the same fear: half of Salam's classmates were milling around outside, kicking a ball, trading gossip. They made no outward show of exhilaration: too many of their teachers were Baathists, apparatchik supporters of the regime, to risk that. Even so, Salam sensed a nervous energy, an electrical charge that seemed to pulse through all of them. It was a new sensation, one none of them would have been able to articulate. Had they known the words, and had they been free of the fear that was bred into them, they would have said that they were, for the first time, excited by the idea of the future.

Ahmed, the class bigmouth, sauntered over, with a quick glance over his shoulder. 'Where were you last night?'

'I was nowhere. At home.' The reflex of fear.

'Guess where I was?'

'I don't know.'

'Guess.'

'At Salima's?'

'No, you dumb ape! Guess again.'

'I don't know. Give me a clue.'

'I was making a fortune for myself, man.'

'You were working?'

'You could call it that. Oh, I was hard at work last night. Made more money than you'll ever see in your whole lifetime.'

'How?' Salam whispered it, even though Ahmed was happily broadcasting at full volume.

Ahmed beamed, showing his teeth. 'At a store packed with the most priceless treasures in the world. They had a special offer on last night: take as much as you want, free of charge!'

'You were at the museum!'

'I was.' The proud smile of the young businessman. Salam noticed the fluff on Ahmed's chin, and realized his friend was trying to style it into a beard.

'What did you get?'

'Ah, now that would be telling, wouldn't it? But, as the Prophet, peace be upon him, says, "The hoarded treasures of gold and silver seem fair to men" – and they certainly seem fair to me.'

'You got gold and silver?'

'And much else that will seem fair to men.'

'How long were you there for?'

'I was there all night. I went back five times. For the last four trips I took a wheelbarrow.'

Salam took in Ahmed's wide smile and made a decision. He would not let on that he too had been at the museum last night, not because he feared the law – there was no law now – or any Baathist punishment, but because he was ashamed. What had he taken from the National Museum but a single useless lump of clay? He wanted to curse God for making him such a coward. For, as always, he had been too meek, holding back from danger and allowing others to barge past him to glory. It was the same on the football field, where Salam never plunged into a tackle, but kept his distance, gingerly avoiding trouble. Well, now that habit had cost him his fortune. Ahmed would make it, he would be a millionaire, he might even escape Iraq and live like a prince in Dubai or, who knows, America.

That evening Salam looked under his bed with none of the fever he had felt when he had checked there that morning. His booty was still in place but now as he pulled it out he saw it as drab and worthless. He imagined Ahmed's stash of rubied goblets and gold-encrusted figurines and damned himself. Why had he not found those treasures? What had sent him poking around in a dark basement when the dazzling glories of Babylon were there for the taking? Fate was to blame. Or destiny. Or both of them, for ensuring that, no matter what, Salam al-Askari would be a loser.

'What's that?'

Salam instinctively doubled over the clay tablet, as if he had been winded. But it was no good: his nine-year-old sister had seen it.

'What's what?'

'That thing. On your lap.'

'Oh this. It's nothing. Just something I got at school today.'

'You said there was no school.'

'There wasn't. But I got this outside—'

Leila was already out of the room, skipping down the corridor to the kitchen: 'Daddy! Daddy! Salam has something he shouldn't have, Salam has something he shouldn't have!'

Salam stared at the ceiling: he was finished. Now he would take a beating and for nothing, for some worthless piece of dust. He held the tablet, stood on the chair by his bed and began fiddling with the window. He would chuck this chunk of clay out of the window and be done with it.

'Salam!'

He turned around to find his father in the doorway, one hand already moving to the buckle of his belt. He moved back to the window, working harder now, his fingers trembling. But it was jammed, it would open no more than an inch wide. No matter how hard he pushed, it was stuck.

Suddenly he felt a hand gripping his wrist, pulling his arm back. He could feel his father's breath. The two of them were wrestling, Salam determined to get that window open so that he could hurl this damned lump to the ground.

The chair beneath him began to wobble; his father was pushing against him too hard. He could feel himself toppling over, falling backwards.

He landed hard on his backside. He let out a cry of pain at the impact on the base of his spine. But that, he realized, was the only sound. There had been no crash, no shattering onto the stone floor. And yet the clay tablet was no longer in his hands. He looked up to see his father calmly pick it up from the bed where it had fallen.

'Dad, it's—'

'Quiet!'

'I got it from the—'

'Shut it!'

What a mistake this had been from beginning to end; how

he wished he had never set foot in that museum. He began to explain: how he had got swept up in the fervour of last night, how he had been carried in there with the mob, how he had stumbled on this tablet, how everyone had taken something, so why shouldn't he?

His father was not listening. He was studying the object, turning it over in his hands. He paid close attention to the clay 'envelope' that held the tablet within.

'What is it, Father?'

The man looked up and fixed his son with a glare. 'Don't speak.' Then he headed out of Salam's bedroom, walking slowly and with extreme care, his eyes on the object in his hands. A moment later the boy could hear the muffled voice of his father on the telephone.

Not daring to venture out of the bedroom, lest he provoke his father's anger anew, Salam perched on the end of his bed, thanking Allah that he had been spared a beating, at least for now. He stayed there like that until, a few minutes later, he heard his father open the apartment door and step out into the night. Salam pictured the ancient tablet that had been his for less than a day and knew, in that instant, that he would never see it again.

CHAPTER THIRTEEN

JERUSALEM, TUESDAY, 8.45PM

Amir Tal knocked on the door with two brisk taps, then, without waiting for an answer, walked into the Prime Minister's office. Yaakov Yariv's chair was swivelled round, its back to the door: Tal could see only the corona of silver around his head. He wondered, as he had before, whether the old man was taking a catnap.

'Rosh Ha'memshalah?'

The chair spun around immediately, revealing that the Prime Minister was wide-eyed and alert. But, Tal noticed, there was no pen in his hand, no half-complete document on the table. No sign, in fact, that he hadn't been asleep. A trick the boss had learned in the army, no doubt.

'Sir, I have some important news. The technicians say they've cracked the note left by Shimon Guttman. They've cleansed it of blood and human material and got it to a point where it can be read. The lab will send over the results in the next few minutes.'

'Who else knows about this?'

'No one else, sir.'

There was another tap on the door: the Deputy Prime Minister. 'I hear we have some news. From the lab?'

The PM shot Tal a weary look. 'Convene a meeting here in fifteen minutes. Better have Ben-Ari here too.'

Yariv pulled out of his desk drawer the text that he had been working on for the last twenty-four hours. Drafted in the White House, it bore the hand-written annotations of the President himself: they had all worked on this so long, Yariv could recognize his oddly-sloping scrawl instantly. The President had summarized the points of agreement and the remaining differences. Yariv had to hand it to him, he had done a brilliant job, cleverly emphasizing the former and distilling the latter so concisely that they took only a few words. Yariv exhaled deeply as he reflected that those short half-sentences – some of them describing disputed strips of land not two yards wide, no bigger than a grass verge – probably looked to most outsiders like mere technical matters, fine-print detail that surely could be resolved by two teams of lawyers. But Yariv knew that each one could, in fact, represent the difference between serenity for his people, at long last, and another generation of bloodshed and weeping.

When he heard Tal and the others return, he shoved the paper back inside the drawer and, in the same moment, pulled out a bag of *garinim*, the sunflower seeds that had become his trademark. None of his cabinet colleagues had seen the American president's draft. Nor would they, until he and his Palestinian counterpart had agreed on it. No point in fighting a cabinet revolt over a hypothetical peace accord: he would save that for the real thing. He nodded at Tal to get things started.

'Gentlemen, the scientists at Mazap, the Criminal Identification Department, have worked 24/7 to see through the blood and tissue fragments and reveal what message it was Shimon Guttman wished to convey to the Prime Minister. They warn that the version they have is provisional, contingent on final tests—'

The Defence Minister, Yossi Ben-Ari, cleared his throat and began fidgeting with the yarmulke on his head. It was of the crocheted variety, a sign that Ben-Ari was not just religious but from one of Israel's specific tribes: a religious Zionist. Not for him the black suit and white shirt uniform of the ultra-orthodox, many of whom had little interest in, if not outright hostility towards, a secular state. Rather, Ben-Ari was a modern, muscular Israeli and a raging nationalist, the leader of a party whose core belief was that Israel should have the largest, most expansive borders possible. Guttman had denounced him as a traitor to their cause just for sitting in Yariv's cabinet, as had the rest of the hardcore settler movement. Ben-Ari believed he was doing vital patriotic work, acting as the brake on Yariv that would prevent him 'selling the Jewish people's birthright for a mess of pottage', as he liked to put it. He would stop Yariv giving away land that was too historically significant to be surrendered – or at least he would keep those losses to their barest minimum. And, if the Prime Minister went too far, Ben-Ari would simply quit the cabinet, thereby unravelling Yariv's fragile coalition, mockingly referred to in the press as 'Israel's national disunity government'. That gave him enormous veto power, but there was a cost: if he ever used it, Yossi Ben-Ari would be cast in Israel and abroad, now and forever, as the man who prevented peace.

Tal saw the fidgeting and understood what it meant. He cut to the chase. 'It turns out this was more than a note. It was a letter. Guttman had written on both sides of the paper, in a tiny crabby script, which is why it took the technicians so long to decipher. I'll read it out:

My dear Kobi,

I have been your enemy for longer than I was your comrade in arms. I have said some harsh things about you, as you have about me. You have good grounds to distrust me. Perhaps that is why every attempt I have made to contact you has been blocked. That is why I have resorted to this desperate move tonight. I could not risk giving this letter to one of your staff, so that they could throw it straight into the trash. Forgive me for that.

I write because I have seen something that cannot be ignored. If you were to see what I have seen, you would understand. You would be changed profoundly – and so would everything you plan to do.

I have toyed with sharing this knowledge with the public, through the media. But I believe you have a right to hear it first. Accordingly, I have tried to keep this knowledge a secret – one so powerful it will change the course of history. It will reshape this part of the world and so the world itself.

Kobi, I am not a hysterical man, despite what you have seen on TV. I have exaggerated sometimes, perhaps, in the cause of politics, but I am not exaggerating now. This secret puts me in fear for my life. The knowledge it contains is timeless and yet, in the light of everything you are doing, impossibly urgent. Do not forsake me, do not cast me out. Hear what I have to say: I will tell you everything, holding nothing back. But I will tell only you. When you have heard it, you will understand. You will tremble as I have done – as if God himself had spoken to you.

My number is below. Please call me tonight, Kobi – for the sake of our covenant.

Shimon

Tal put the paper down quietly, aware that a new atmosphere had entered the room, one he did not want to disturb by moving too briskly. He noticed the Deputy Prime Minister and Defence Minister glance at each other, then away. He found he couldn't bring himself to meet the boss's eye and realized then that he had no idea how the Prime Minister would react. The silence held.

'He'd obviously cracked.' This from the Deputy PM, Avram

Mossek. 'A bad case of Jerusalem Syndrome.' The term referred to an acknowledged medical condition, cited by psychiatrists to describe those whose heads had been turned by the Holy City. You could spot them from the Via Dolorosa to the back streets of the Jewish Quarter, usually men, usually young – with the beard, sandals and wild staring eyes of those convinced they could hear the voices of angels.

Ben-Ari ignored that remark; now was not the time to defend religious fervour. 'Can I see that?' he asked Tal, nodding in the direction of the text.

His eyes scanned it. 'It doesn't sound like Guttman at all. He was not an especially religious man. A nationalist, of course. But not religious. Yet here he implies that God himself has spoken to him. And he quotes the Rosh Hashana liturgy: "Do not forsake me, do not cast me out." I wouldn't put it as robustly as Mossek here but maybe Guttman had indeed lost his mind.'

They all looked to Yariv, waiting for his verdict. A one-word dismissal, even a gesture, and the matter would be forgotten. But he simply sucked on a sunflower seed, staring at the copy of the text Tal had handed him.

As so often, his assistant found the silence awkward and moved to fill it. 'One curiosity: he says he has "tried" to keep this knowledge a secret. That suggests he may not have succeeded. If we decide to take this further, we will have to find out who else Guttman spoke to: friends, family members. Maybe, despite what he says about the media, some right-wing journalists. He certainly knew plenty of those. Second: the stuff about fearing for his life could backfire very badly. On us, I mean. If the right were to get hold of this text, it would fuel their conspiracy theories: a man whom we insist was killed by accident was in fear for his life. Third: this is all clearly about the peace talks. "In the light of everything you are doing," he says. Adding that you, Prime Minister, would "tremble" if you knew what he knew.

Which implies that you would realize you are making a terrible mistake and would not go ahead.'

'Guttman was against the peace process – there's a big surprise,' said Mossek dryly.

Yariv raised his hand and leaned forward. 'These are not the words of a madman. They are urgent and passionate, yes. But they are not incoherent. Nor is this a martyr's letter, despite the premonition of his own death. If it were, he would have spoken clearly and transparently about the treachery of giving up territory and so on. He would have wanted a text to rally his troops. This is too,' he paused, sucking a tooth as he tried to find the right word, 'enigmatic for that. No, I believe this is what it says it is: a letter from a man desperate to tell me something.

'The task now is to ensure that no one breathes a word of the contents of this letter. Amir will say that the lab tests were inconclusive, that no words can be made out clearly. If so much as a syllable of it leaks out, I will sack both of you and replace you with your bitterest party rivals.' Mossek and Ben-Ari drew back, astounded by this sudden show of suspicion, which both interpreted as pent-up anger. 'And Amir here will tell the press you betrayed a crucial state secret to the enemy during the peace negotiations. Whether through malice or incompetence we will let the press decide. Meanwhile, Amir, it is clear that Shimon Guttman harboured a secret for which he was prepared to risk his life. Your job is to find out what it was.'

CHAPTER FOURTEEN

JERUSALEM, TUESDAY, 10.01PM

She was meant to travel nowhere except with her official driver, but there was no time for that. Besides, something told her this was a visit best paid discreetly, and it was hard to be discreet in an armour-plated Land Cruiser. So now she rattled towards Bet Hakerem in a plain white taxi.

She had moved fast. Once she had unpicked the anagram, everything else seemed to fit into place. She had stared hard at the photograph of Nour, to find whatever it was that had nagged away at her when she first saw it. She had looked into his eyes, as she had done before, but then her gaze had shifted to the background.

He was clearly standing indoors, in a home rather than an office, in front of what seemed to be a bookcase. Visible was a complex floral pattern in blue and green. When Maggie clicked on the image to make it larger, she could see that this was not wallpaper, as she had first guessed, but a design on a plate, resting on the shelf just behind Nour's shoulder.

Of course. She had seen that pattern before; indeed, she had been struck by its beauty. She had seen it just twenty-four hours earlier, when she had made a condolence call at the home of Shimon Guttman. In a house full of books, the ceramic plate had stood out. And here was Nour, standing in front of one just like it. Could it be that the two of them had discovered this pottery together, perhaps taking a piece each? Were these two men, whose politics made them sworn enemies, in fact collaborators?

She smiled to herself at the very thought. The CIA chief had declared Nour's death a typical collaborator killing: maybe he was right, he just had the wrong kind of collaboration in mind.

And then her eye had moved away from the ceramic, noticing again the disembodied arm looped over Nour's shoulder. Was it possible that this picture had been taken in front of the very bookcase Maggie had seen on Monday night, right here in Jerusalem? Did that arm embracing the Palestinian belong to none other than the fierce Israeli hawk, Shimon Guttman?

She had reached for her cellphone, about to call Davis with her discovery. Or to go up a level, to the Deputy Secretary of State who had sent her to see Khalil al-Shafi. But she paused. What exactly did she have here? A coincidence that was odd, granted, but hardly clear evidence of anything. On the other hand, the chances that there really was an Ehud Ramon toiling away in some university faculty somewhere, leaving no trace on Google, were close to zero.

The truth was, this connection between the two dead men had gripped her because of the conversation she had had in the mourning house with Rachel Guttman. So far she had said nothing about that to anyone. If challenged, she would have said that she had not taken the old lady's words seriously, that she had regarded them as the ramblings of a traumatized widow. That was at least half-true. But Mrs Guttman's words had nagged away at her. And now this link – if that's what it was – to the dead Palestinian.

It was all too speculative to be worth briefing colleagues about, at least in this form. She didn't want them concluding that her spell in the wilderness had turned her into a conspiracy nut. Yet she couldn't quite leave it either. The solution was to make this one visit, find out what she could, then present her findings to her bosses. The CIA station chief would be the obvious destination: she should tell him what she knew and he could see what it meant. All she needed was to ask the Guttman widow a couple of questions.

That decision had been taken no more than half an hour ago. Now, the taxi pulled up on the corner of the Guttmans' street: soon she would have her answers. 'I'll walk from here,' she told the driver.

The vigil that had been held there since Saturday night – right-wingers and settlers, determined to keep up the pressure on the government – was smaller now. A handful of activists with candles, keeping a respectful distance from the house.

Maggie checked her watch. It was late to visit like this, unannounced, but something told her Rachel Guttman wouldn't be asleep.

She looked for a doorbell, finding a buzzer with a Hebrew scrawl on it which she took to be the family name. She pressed it quickly, to minimize the disturbance. No reply.

But the lights were on and she could hear a record playing. A melancholy, haunting melody. Mahler, Maggie reckoned. Someone was definitely home. She tried the metal knocker on the door, first lightly, then more firmly. At her second attempt, the door came open a little. It had been left ajar, just like the mourning houses Maggie remembered from Dublin, open to all-comers, day and night.

The hallway was empty, but the house felt warm. There was, Maggie felt sure, even the smell of cooking.

'Hello? Mrs Guttman?'

No reply. Perhaps the old lady had dozed off in her chair.

Maggie stepped inside hesitantly, not wanting to barge into this stranger's house. She made for the main room, which last night had been jammed with hundreds of people. It took her a second to get her bearings, but she soon found it. There, in the space between the tall, leather-bound volumes, was the ceramic plate. No mistaking it: the pattern was identical to the one in the newspaper picture of Ahmed Nour.

She tried again. 'Hello?' But there was no response. Maggie was confused. The house was open and gave every sign of being occupied.

She stole another glance at the plate, turned out of the main room and tried to follow the warmth and the smell. It took her down a corridor and eventually to a door onto what Maggie guessed was the kitchen.

She pushed at it but it was tightly shut. She knocked on the door, almost whispering. 'Mrs Guttman? It's Maggie Costello. We met yesterday.'

As she spoke, she turned the handle and opened the door. She peered into the dark. It took a few seconds for her eyes to adjust, to make out the shape of a table and chairs at one end, all empty. She looked towards the sink and the kitchen counter. No one there.

Only then did her gaze fall to the floor, where she saw the outline of what seemed to be a body. Maggie crouched down to get a better look – but there was no doubt about it.

There, cold and lifeless, its hand gnarled around a small, empty bottle of pills, was the corpse of Rachel Guttman.

CHAPTER FIFTEEN

BAGHDAD, APRIL 2003

He only had a rumour to go on. His brother-in-law had mentioned it at the garage yesterday, not that he would dare ask him about it now. If he did, he would only demand why he was asking and before long it would get back to his wife and he would never hear the end of it.

No, he would find this out himself. He knew where the café was, just after the fruit market on Mutannabi Street. Apparently everyone had been coming here.

Abdel-Aziz al-Askari took a seat close to the back, an observation post, so that he could see who came in and who came out. He signalled for mint tea, served here piping hot and in a *stikkam*, a narrow glass as tall as your first finger, and looked around. A few old-timers playing *sheshbesh*; several puffing on the *nargileh* pipe; a group clustered around a TV set watching footage of the statue of Saddam falling, apparently played on a loop. They were men and the talk was louder than usual, but there was none of the loud euphoria he had always imagined this day would bring. Liberation! The fall of the dictator! He had pictured screaming, dancing ecstasy; spontaneous hugs between strangers on the street; he had seen himself kissing beautiful women, everyone falling into each other's arms at the sheer delight of it all.

But it was not like that. People were holding back, just in case. What if the secret police burst in, announcing that the Americans had been defeated and anyone who had so much as smiled at Saddam's alleged defeat would be hanged? After all, few believed the hated *Mahabarat* had simply vanished overnight. What if the pictures on Al-Arabiya were in fact an elaborate hoax, designed by Uday and Qusay to test the Iraqi people, to flush out those who were disloyal to the regime? What, above all, if Saddam had not gone?

So the customers here, like everyone throughout this city, were watching and waiting. Happy to chat, but not quite ready to commit. Even those watching the replayed scenes from Paradise Square confined themselves to blandly neutral remarks.

'It's certainly an historic event,' said one.

'People will be seeing this around the world,' nodded another. Both kept open the option of adding that it was a 'wicked act by Zionist counter-revolutionaries who must be punished at once'.

Abdel-Aziz kept sipping his tea, patting Salam's school satchel intermittently to be sure his son's discovery was still inside. He had been there maybe fifteen minutes when a younger man, perhaps in his mid-thirties, came in, all smiles and confidence.

'Good afternoon, my brothers!' he said, beaming. 'And how is business?' He laughed loudly. There were nods in his direction, even a couple of hands proffered for shaking. 'Mahmoud, welcome,' said one man, by way of greeting.

Mahmoud. Abdel-Aziz cleared his throat. This must be him. I should seize the moment, talk to him right away. Mind you, I mustn't seem too eager.

But it was too late. The newcomer, in a black leather jacket and with some kind of bracelet around his wrist, had already spotted Abdel-Aziz, catching the look in his eye.

'Welcome, my friend. You are looking for someone?'

'I am looking for Mahmoud.'

'Well, maybe I can help.' He turned towards the door of the cafe, pretending to shout. 'Mahmoud! Mahmoud!' Then, turning back to Abdel-Aziz: 'Oh look! I'm right here.' His face disintegrating into an exaggerated, fake laugh.

'I hear you—'

'What did you hear?'

'That people who have—'

'What have they been saying about Mahmoud? Eh?'

'Sorry. Maybe I made a mistake—' Abdel-Aziz got up to leave but he found Mahmoud's hand on his arm, pushing him back into his seat. He was surprisingly strong.

'I can see you're carrying something rather heavy in that bag of yours. Is that something you want to show Mahmoud?'

'My son got it. Yesterday. From the—'

'From the same place as everyone else. Don't worry. I won't tell. That would be bad for you, bad for me, bad for business.' He dissolved again into the fake laugh. Then, just as suddenly, the smile died. 'Bad for your son, too.'

Abdel-Aziz wanted to get away; he did not trust this man one bit. He glanced back at the others in the café. Most were watching the TV, live coverage of a briefing by the US military from Centcom, central command in Doha, Qatar. They were announcing their capture of yet another presidential palace.

'So shall we do some business, yes?'

'Is it safe? To show you, here?'

Mahmoud pulled Abdel-Aziz's chair with a single tug, shifting him round so that their shoulders touched. Now they had their backs to the rest of the drinkers. Between them, they shielded their small, square table from view.

'Show me.'

Abdel-Aziz unbuckled the satchel, peeled back the leather flap and offered it for Mahmoud's inspection.

'Take it out.'

'I'm not sure I—'

'If you want to do business, Mahmoud has to see the merchandise.'

Abdel-Aziz laid the satchel flat on the table and slowly eased the object out. Mahmoud's expression did not change. Instead, he reached over and, without ceremony, unsheathed the tablet from its envelope.

'OK.'

'OK?'

'Yes, you can put it back now.'

'You're not interested?'

'Normally, Mahmoud wouldn't be interested in such a lump. Clay bricks like this are ten a penny.'

'But the writing on it—'

'Who cares about writing? Just a few squiggles. It could be a shopping list. Who cares what some old hag wanted from the fishmongers ten thousand years ago?'

'But—'

'But,' Mahmoud held up a finger, to silence him. 'But it does come in an envelope. And it's only had the odd knock to it. I'll give you twenty dollars for it.'

'Twenty?'

'You wanted more?'

'But this is from the National Museum—'

'Uh, uh, uh.' The finger was up again. 'Remember, Mahmoud doesn't want to know too much. You say this has been in your family for many generations and given the, er, recent events, you believe now is the time to sell.'

'But this must be very rare.'

'I'm afraid not, Mr . . . ?'

'My name is Abdel-Aziz.' *Damn.* Why had he given his real name?

'There are a thousand items like this floating around Baghdad right now. I could step outside and find many like it, with a click of my fingers.' He clicked them, as if to demonstrate. 'If you want to do business with someone else—' He rose to his feet.

Now it was Abdel-Aziz's turn to extend a restraining hand. 'Please. Maybe twenty-five dollars?'

'I am sorry. Twenty is already too much.'

'I have a family. A son, a daughter—'

'I understand. Because you seem a good man, I will do you a favour. I will pay you twenty-two dollars. Mahmoud must be crazy: now he will make no money. Instead he makes you rich!'

They shook hands. Mahmoud stood up and asked the café owner to find him a plastic bag. Once he had it, he slipped the tablet inside and peeled off twenty-two American dollars from a thick, grubby wad and handed them to Abdel-Aziz who left the café immediately, his son's school bag swung over his shoulder, now light and entirely empty.

CHAPTER SIXTEEN

JERUSALEM, TUESDAY, 10.13PM

Maggie had seen plenty of dead bodies before. She had been part of an NGO team that tried to broker a ceasefire in the Congo, where the one commodity that was in cheap and plentiful supply was human corpses: four million killed there in just a few years. You'd find them in forests, behind bushes, at roadsides, as regular as wild flowers.

But never before had she been this close to one so . . . fresh. The fading warmth of the woman's flesh as Maggie touched her back appalled and confused her. She shuddered, instinctively tugging at the woman's arm, trying to pull her into an upright position, so that she wouldn't just be lying here, like a, like a . . . corpse.

That was when she heard the creak of a footstep on the floorboards outside. Maggie wanted to cry out for help. But some reflex squeezed her throat and prevented the words from escaping.

Now the footsteps were heading nearer and Maggie was frozen. The kitchen door swung open. She looked round to see a man's shape filling the doorframe and, in the shadow, the clear outline of a gun.

This much she had learned from roadblocks in Afghanistan: if a gun is pointed at you, you raise your hands in the air and become very still. If you have to speak, you do so very quietly.

With her arms up, Maggie stared at the barrel of the revolver that was now aimed at her. In the gloom she could see next to nothing.

The gunman's arm made a sudden movement: Maggie braced herself for a bullet. But instead of firing, he reached to his left, his hand finding the light switch. In a flash, she saw him – and he saw the lifeless woman on the floor.

'*Eema*?'

He fell to his knees, the gun falling from his hands. He began to do as Maggie had done, tugging at the arm, touching the body. Except now, kneeling beside it, he let his head sink onto the corpse's back, his head shaking in a way Maggie had never seen before. It was as if every part of his being was crying.

'I found her here no more than three minutes ago, I swear.' She hoped this man recognized her as quickly as she had recognized him.

He said nothing, just remained hunched over the body of his dead mother. She tiptoed around him, getting out of his way and closer to the door.

His face stayed hidden, his head still trembling in a dry sob over the body of his mother. But his hand was moving, reaching without sight for the revolver he had dropped. Maggie stood rigid, as his arm lifted in a smooth, almost mechanical arc until, even without looking, the gun was aimed straight at her face.

She ran.

In an instant, she had yanked the door open and darted into the hallway, making for the front door. Surely he wouldn't have been crazy enough to fire, would he?

Which is when she heard the whizzing sound, the one she

had learned to fear in her very core. It strangely came before the bang of the gun being fired, even though, she would recall later, that made no sense at all. But it was the whizz, the whoosh of air sliced by a bullet, that froze her. There, in the hallway, facing the door, she stopped dead.

'Turn around.'

She did as she was told. Her mind raced. One thought, almost euphoric, sped fastest. *Good: Now I will have a chance to explain everything!* But, not far behind, was a gloomier notion. *He's out of his mind with grief! He won't listen to a word I say!*

She tried anyway. Negotiating was a reflex, even, she now discovered, when her own life was on the line. 'I was trying to see if I could save her.'

He lifted the gun so that it was aimed at her face.

'I came here to tell your mother something. About your father. The front door was open. And then I found her, in there.'

The gun stayed locked onto her. The man holding it seemed strangely at odds with the weapon, even though he handled it expertly. He certainly had the build for it: he was tall and she could see the muscles of his arms were taut and flexed. But his eyes were not those of a gunman. They were too curious, as if they were meant to scan the pages of a book rather than assess a target. His nose and mouth were substantial enough, but they suggested conversation, inquiry even. She guessed this was a man more prone to talking than shooting. Or not talking, so much as listening.

'Please,' Maggie began, gambling that she had assessed him correctly. 'I came here to help. If I had come here to do harm, do you think I would be just standing here? Wouldn't I be wearing a mask so that no one could see me? Wouldn't I have a gun? Wouldn't I have killed you the moment I saw you?'

The gun wavered, the hand now shaking ever so slightly.

'I swear to you, someone else did this. Not me.'

Slowly, no faster than the sweep of the second hand on a wristwatch, the arm lowered. The gun steadily arcing downward, away from her. But only once he had stood with his arm at his side for what felt like a full minute did she dare to move.

She inched towards him slowly, her eyes never leaving his. Then she surprised him and herself by extending both her arms, placing them around his shoulders until, still stiff and unmoving, he was wrapped in her embrace. She held him like that for a minute, then another minute and then another, the thump of her heart gradually quietening, while he stood as still as marble.

Eventually she persuaded him to sit down, while she repeated that he had suffered a terrible shock, that he needed to give himself time to absorb what had happened, to think straight. She knew he wasn't listening but she hoped that he would at least, like other angry men before him, be soothed by the sound of her voice. She wanted to make him a cup of sweet tea, or at least fetch a glass of water. But she knew she could suggest no such thing. That would mean going back into the kitchen.

It was he who decided to go in. 'I want to see her again,' he said. He had been gone perhaps five minutes, when Maggie heard an almost animal howl of pain. She ran into the kitchen, where the corpse of Rachel Guttman still lay slumped on the floor. Her son was standing over her, except where he had been pale, his face was now flushed red.

'What is it?'

He held out his hand. In it was a single sheet of paper. She stepped forward to take it.

Ani kol kach mitsta'eret sh'ani osah l'chem et zeh.

אני כל כך מצטערת שאני עושה לכם את זה

Hebrew, typewritten. 'I'm afraid I can't—'

'It says, "I am so sorry to do this to all of you."'

'Right.'

'Not right. Wrong!'

'I don't understand.'

'This is BULLSHIT!'

Maggie jumped back, shocked by the volume of his voice. 'This is meant to make us think my mother killed herself. She would never, ever do such a thing. Never.'

Maggie wished they were back in the other room, sitting down. Who knew what he might do here, with his dead mother at his feet? She still hadn't dared ask his name.

'She gave her whole life to looking after us. And, since Saturday, she was desperate to do something, to take action. You saw it yourself. Remember how she took hold of you. She wanted your help, to finish off whatever it was my father started. Because she believed something important was at stake.'

'A matter of life and death, she said.' As she recalled Rachel Guttman's words, and the way the old lady had gripped her wrist, Maggie felt a twinge of guilt: this woman had tried to enlist her as an ally and she had done nothing.

'Yes. Does someone plead for something to be done and then do,' he gestured down at the body on the ground, unable to look at it, 'this?'

'Maybe she had given up. Lost hope. Perhaps she got frustrated that nobody was listening to what she was saying.'

'So she types a note on a computer. My mother, who does not know how to switch on the TV. And saying sorry to "all" of us. Not calling me and my sister by name, or at least leaving a note to "both" of us. Believe me, I know my mother. She did not do this.'

'So who did?'

'I don't know, but someone very, very wicked—' He stopped himself before he choked. He was standing close now, almost looming over Maggie. His head of thick dark hair was scruffier than when she had seen him here yesterday, as if he had spent the intervening twenty-four hours running his hands through it over and over again. She pictured him, hunched over, bent double with grief, his head cradled in his hands. And that was before this terrible thing had happened to his mother.

He gathered himself. 'Wicked, but also very stupid. Imagine it: a typewritten suicide note.'

'Why would anyone want to kill your mother?'

'For the same reason my mother wanted to talk to you. Remember, she said that my father knew something very important, something that would change everything. Remember?'

'I remember.'

'So someone thought she knew this thing too. And they wanted to kill her before she told anyone else.'

'But she insisted she didn't know what it was. She said your father wouldn't tell her. For her own safety.'

'I know that. But whoever did this was not so sure.'

'I see.' She looked down at the floor, without meaning to. 'Look, do you think perhaps we ought to call the police, get an ambulance maybe?'

'First, you tell me why you came here.'

'It . . . it seems ridiculous now. It's not urgent. Really, you have so much to deal—'

'I don't believe someone working for the American government drives to a private home late at night unless there is a good reason. So you just tell me what business you had with my mother, OK?'

'Perhaps I ought to go, leave you some time to be alone.'

He reached for her arm, yanking her back. The same spot on her wrist where his mother had grabbed her a day earlier. 'You have to tell me what you know. I, I—'

Ordinarily, Maggie would have slapped a man who had dared grab her that way. But she could see this was not an act of aggression, but one of desperation. The composure, the haughtiness even, she had seen at the house yesterday had gone now. For the first time, Maggie saw the eyes of this grieving son glisten.

'If you can trust me enough to tell me your name, I'll tell you what I know.'

'My name is Uri.'

'OK, Uri. My name is Maggie. Maggie Costello. Let's sit down and talk.'

Calmly, Maggie filled a glass with water from the tap and handed it over. Then she led him back out of the kitchen and sat him down, her body reeling from the adrenaline.

'You think what happened tonight has something to do with this information, of your father's.'

Uri Guttman nodded.

'Do you think your father was killed deliberately, because of that information?'

'I don't know. Some people say so. I don't know. But I tell you what: I will find out who did this to my family. I will find them and I will make them pay.'

She wanted to tell him that his mother's death was almost certainly the result of horrible, intense grief. His father had been killed accidentally and now his mother had taken her own life, as simple as that. But she couldn't say that because she wasn't sure she believed it.

Instead, she told him what she had just discovered. That Ahmed Nour, the Palestinian archaeologist slain earlier that day, had secretly worked with his father.

At first, he refused to accept it. He sat back in his chair with the pretence of a smile, cruel and bitter. No way, he said more than once. An anagram? It was absurd. But once Maggie had explained that his father and Nour had both trained as specialists in biblical archaeology, and once she had mentioned the unusual but recurring ceramic pattern, he fell quiet. It was clear that Maggie could have come up with no more shocking fact about Shimon Guttman. A lifelong mistress, a teenage lover, a secret family – she guessed Uri could have accepted any one of those revelations more readily than that his father might have had a working partnership with a Palestinian.

'Look, if I'm right, it means that there may indeed be something going on here. Whatever secret it was your father was carrying, it seems to bring great harm to those who know it.'

'But my mother knew nothing.'

'Like you said, maybe whoever did this didn't know that – or didn't want to risk it.'

'You think the same people who killed this Palestinian killed my mother?'

'I don't know.'

'Because if they did, then I know who will be the next to die.'

'Who?'

'Me.'

CHAPTER SEVENTEEN

APRIL 2003, BAGHDAD

Mahmoud was regretting this decision. He should be above this now, he said to himself; as he was thrown into the air yet again, his bottom landing on the hard plastic seat of the bus as it hit the thousandth bump in the road. He should be the Mr Big who hired runners, yet here he was, working as a humble courier himself. Ten hours down, five more to go on the clapped-out old charabanc they laughingly referred to as the Desert Rocket.

For the last couple of weeks he had been working on a different business model. He would sit in the café on Mutannabi Street, waiting for pieces to come his way – and, let Allah be praised, they kept coming – and then pass them on via one of the countless boys who had emerged, like rats from a sewer, the instant Saddam was toppled. Mahmoud marvelled at the sudden proliferation of these teenage entrepreneurs. No one had planned for it; no one had ever discussed it. There had been no training; not even a rumour that there would be money to be made the day you-know-who was gone. Yet here they all came, slipping out of every backstreet and flea-ridden alley.

The trade was brisk, with mobile phones the preferred means

of communication. Mahmoud would call, say, Tariq, who he knew had a shipment going to Jordan that night, telling him that he had a couple of items that needed transportation. He would hand those to one of the boys, who would run them across town. Then Tariq would pass them onto another runner, who would take the Desert Rocket to Amman. There he would meet al-Naasri or one of his rivals among the big Jordanian dealers. Al-Naasri would work out a price, and the courier would take the cash back to Iraq. Thanks to the phone network, the runners knew better than to slice off a cut. If they did, there were no shortages of ditches along the Tigris for them to fall into.

Mahmoud had been doing that profitably for a while. Business had been constant since the statue came down, but he had been close to the trade for longer than that. It was not spoken of in whispers; it was not spoken of at all, but there had been some – how should he put it? – *movement* of antiquities since the first war, the mother of all battles, back in 1991. Until then, looting had been unheard of, but the American bombardment loosened things up a little: even Saddam couldn't keep an eye on everything when there were Cruise missiles falling from the sky. Not that he did not come down hard on the guilty men. Mahmoud, like every other 'dealer' in Iraq, remembered the fate of the eleven men found guilty of sawing the face off a magnificent Mesopotamian winged bull: the beast itself was too heavy to transport anywhere. Saddam made sure it was known that he signed the death warrant for that crime himself. And, with characteristic flair, it was Saddam who decreed that these thieves should suffer the same fate they had inflicted on the mighty bronze creature. Their executioner duly took an electric saw and sliced the faces off each one of them in turn. And each, waiting for his own death, had had to watch as it came to his fellows. When the eleventh man was killed, he had already witnessed the punishment that awaited him ten times over.

Despite that deterrent, some grand pieces did get out. Mahmoud never saw, but he had heard about, the section of a relief taken from the ancient Palace of Nimrod. Rather poignantly, Mahmoud thought, it depicted slaves in chains. He imagined that image, smuggled out to the West by the suffocated people of Iraq: it was like a distress signal.

The route then as now was Jordan and the conduit, then as now, was the al-Naasri family. The traffic in treasures along that path had never been heavier than it was now; trinkets and pots from every age of man, from the eras of the Assyrians and the Babylonians, the Sumerians and the Persians and the Greeks. Mostly it was fragments that were taken, though the tale was told of Tariq's boys who lugged an entire statue to Amman, stashing it in the boot of the Desert Rocket. Apparently they slipped the driver a dollar or two – and told him their cargo was only a corpse. Such was the topsy-turvy morality of Baghdad in the spring of 2003.

Mahmoud had sent nearly a dozen runners to Amman in the last fortnight, each of them following the route he had taken himself when he was starting out. But something told him he was due a visit in person. He needed to see al-Naasri eyeball-to-eyeball. With business expanding at the rate it was, and the sums at stake, there were bound to be opportunities to bend the rules. Mahmoud wasn't going to be a sucker. He wanted to be sure al-Naasri was playing it straight.

So he had filled a holdall with his latest hoard of three or four items, including a couple of ancient seals, that clay tablet he had got from the nervous man in the café and the *pièce de résistance*, a pair of gold-leaf earrings which, though it was anyone's guess, his valuer had estimated to be four and a half thousand years old. He wasn't about to entrust those to some spotty fourteen-year-old from Saddam City. All the more reason why he was spending fifteen hours in the company of the sputtering bone-trembler that was the Desert Rocket.

He had dozed off in the final hours of the journey, waking up with a start when the bus juddered to a halt. He had kept the bag on his lap throughout, the handles entwined around his wrists lest the thieving scum around him get any ideas. Even before he had opened his eyes, he had patted the bag, to make sure he could still feel the shapes within; he tested its weight. As for the earrings, he knew they were somewhere completely safe.

It was midnight by the time he got off the bus. He hadn't realized how bad it smelled until he was off it, the odour released in waves as the unwashed, exhausted passengers emerged into the night. He breathed in the Amman air, inhaling the excitement of a place that wasn't Baghdad. Last time he had been here it had been even more thrilling: handling bank notes that did not have *his* face on them, seeing statues that depicted men other than *him*. There were no real elections here either, but at least the Jordanians had not shamed themselves by approving their tyrant with a one hundred per cent vote.

One of al-Naasri's boys was waiting for him, bored and listless by the railings. He said nothing, nor did he offer to take Mahmoud's bag – not that Mahmoud would have let him – as he set off for the short walk down King Hussein Street. Before long there were signs for the Roman Amphitheatre, which meant the *souk* was close by. As they headed down the cobbled alleys, the boy increased his speed; Mahmoud had to run to keep up. Some kind of mind game, Mahmoud decided.

Most of the stalls were closed at this time of night, their steel shutters down. The boy was turning through the market, twisting left and right, so fast that Mahmoud knew he would never be able to find his way out alone. He reached inside his suit jacket, under his arm, to check that his dagger was still there, in its leather holster.

Eventually Mahmoud caught a smell: fresh pitta bread. There must be a night bakery near here. Sure enough, the row after row of empty, unmanned stalls was broken by a cluster of lights just around the next corner. Tinny music was playing on a radio; men were sitting outside, drinking coffee from small cups and mint tea from glasses. Mahmoud sighed his relief. This felt like home.

The runner made his way inside, Mahmoud following. He reached the table where a man was sitting alone. The runner nodded curtly and left just as quickly. From beginning to end, he had not said a word.

Mahmoud did not recognize the man at the table. He was too young, younger than Mahmoud himself. 'I'm sorry, perhaps there has been some mistake. I am looking for Mr al-Naasri.'

'Mahmoud?'

'Yes.'

'I am Nawaf al-Naasri. I am my father's son. Come.'

He led Mahmoud out of the coffee shop and down another alleyway. He could stab me here, thought Mahmoud, take my bag and no one would ever know.

Instead Nawaf was tapping lightly on one of the steel shutters. After a second or two, it began to crawl upward, apparently operated by some electric mechanism. Inside, fluorescent lights flickered on to reveal what looked like a souvenir shop: big glass windows and fifty-seven varieties of junk inside.

'Come, come. Some tea?'

Mahmoud nodded as he surveyed the merchandise. Clock faces on highly-polished slices of timber; jars of coloured sand and bottles of water 'Guaranteed from the River Jordan'. It was crap, doubtless aimed at the Christian pilgrim market. One day, Mahmoud thought, we'll have trash like this on sale in Baghdad: 'Guaranteed from the Gardens of Babylon'. And the tat stores in Iraq will do the same job as they do here in Jordan, serve as fronts for the antiquities business.

'Mahmoud! A pleasure.'

He wheeled round to see al-Naasri senior beaming a wild

smile. Mahmoud, who had an eye for clothes, could see that the Jordanian was wearing a well-tailored suit, the fabric hanging properly. He was ashamed of his own black leather jacket, rumpled after the marathon bus journey, its patches worn almost to baldness. It wasn't just the suit: all over, al-Naasri had the gloss that comes with wealth. It had only been a matter of weeks since the treasure had started flowing from Baghdad, but already it seemed to have transformed Jaafar al-Naasri. Maybe serious money worked its magic fast. Whether or not that was true Mahmoud was determined to find out for himself.

'So, my friend, to what do I owe this pleasure?'

'I thought maybe we would meet for a later night cup of coffee, perhaps a piece of cake. Talk about old times.'

Al-Naasri turned to his son, who was fussing in the back of the store. 'I forgot that our friend from Baghdad is something of a joker with us!' Then he turned back to Mahmoud, still smiling. 'Would you forgive me, Mahmoud, if we got straight to business. It's late and I am a busy man.'

'Of course.' Mahmoud tried flashing his own smile: he wanted to learn from this wealthy man, to copy him. He reached into the holdall, bringing out the first of the two seals that a young cousin had brought him within hours of what Mahmoud liked to think of as the museum's grand opening. Others had reached him later, chipped and damaged. But none were as good as this one.

Al-Naasri took it from him, checking its weight in his hands, testing its solidity. He reached into the breast-pocket of his suit and pulled out a pair of half-moon reading glasses.

'It's real, I assure you. Mahmoud wouldn't spend fifteen hours getting his arse pounded on that bus for a fake—'

Al-Naasri halted him with an upward glance of the eyes, peering out from above the lenses. The expression demanded quiet. The Jordanian was concentrating. 'OK,' he said finally. 'What else?'

Mahmoud produced the second seal, larger and more ornate.

He had the sequence of items all worked out, building to what he thought would be an irresistible climax.

Al-Naasri submitted the seal to the same scrutiny then placed it down on the table so he could examine Mahmoud with similar thoroughness. 'You have done well here, my friend. I am impressed. Do I have the feeling the best is yet to come?' He flashed the teeth once more.

'You do, my friend, you do indeed.' Mahmoud pulled the bag up onto his lap, and dug both hands in to bring out the clay tablet that had come to him in the café a few days earlier.

Al-Naasri extended his hands to take it from him. He held the envelope in one, and pulled out the tablet with the other. Suddenly he called over his shoulder to his son: 'My glass, please!'

Nawaf brought out a jeweller's eyeglass, which al-Naasri expertly lodged in his left eye. The older man hunched over the table, studying the object closely. He let out a low murmur, but said nothing.

'So what do you think?' Mahmoud couldn't help himself.

Al-Naasri leaned back, the glass still wedged in place, so that his left eye was magnified grotesquely. 'I think you have earned the right to see the al-Naasri collection.' He let the glass fall out, catching it in his hand.

Without prompting, Nawaf began to unlock a door behind the shop counter which opened, Mahmoud presumed, onto a storeroom. All the big dealers worked like this: trinkets sold out front, the real deal hidden behind. Hurriedly, he stashed his hoard back in the bag and got up.

They walked in single file through a back room that was filled with cardboard boxes and two giant rolls of bubble wrap. This, surely, was where the treasure was to be found. But the al-Naasri men did not linger; they did not even switch on a light. Instead, with the father in front of Mahmoud and the son behind him, they kept walking, until they reached a second door. This one was sturdier and more heavily secured; al-Naasri had to use three keys to unlock it.

To Mahmoud's surprise it opened onto the outside, a cool breeze of night air touching his face. Down a couple of stairs, and the three men were standing in a decent-sized backyard.

'Nawaf, do you have the spade?'

Mahmoud swung round to see the young man holding a solid metal spade. Instinctively Mahmoud's free hand reached for his dagger and whipped it out, thrusting it in Nawaf's direction.

'Oh, my dear brother, don't be so ridiculous!' said Jaafar al-Naasri, catching Mahmoud's hunted expression and laughing broadly. 'Nawaf here is not going to hit you. The spade is so he can show you our collection.'

Mahmoud's head was spinning. Sleep-deprived and confused, his eyes adjusted to see that this barren scrap of land was in fact covered with sandy brown earth, like a vegetable patch. And now, directed by his father and apparently unfazed by Mahmoud pulling a blade on him, Nawaf was standing in the middle of it, digging.

'What's going on?'

'Wait and see.'

Al-Naasri and Mahmoud stood, watching Nawaf as he dug, in a smooth, easy rhythm, into the ground. Mahmoud noticed Nawaf's arms, knotted with muscles.

Slowly, out of the ground, a shape began to emerge. Nawaf dug harder, then threw aside his spade and crouched, scratching at the soil with his bare hands. In the moonlight, Mahmoud could make out a figure, an animal of some kind. Nawaf beckoned them over.

As he got nearer, Mahmoud saw it clearly. Pulled from the ground was a statue, a ram on its hind legs, its front hooves gripping a slim tree trunk, its horns caught in the tree's ornate flowers. As Nawaf dusted off the soil, and in the light of the night sky, Mahmoud could see this extraordinary sculpture was carved from the most delicate copper, silver and gold.

Mahmoud gasped.

Al-Naasri senior smiled. 'You recognize it, yes? Perhaps you have seen it in the newspapers.' Mahmoud nodded, unable to speak. 'It is the Ram in the Thicket, found in the Great Pit of Death at Ur,' al-Naasri went on, enjoying the moment. 'You probably saw it on a school trip to the National Museum when you were a child. I know I did. It was one of the highlights.'

'And now you have it here?'

'Have you not seen it with your own eyes?'

'You are showing me this so that I will know that what I have brought is worthless. Is that right? You want to humiliate Mahmoud by this comparison.'

'Not at all, my friend. You worry too much. I am showing you this so that you might know what glories you are to live among.'

Mahmoud smiled with relief. 'Really? You think the pieces I have brought are worthy of being kept here, in the collection?' He liked sounding complicit with this man, the equal of this genius of the trade.

'Not just the pieces, Mahmoud. I also plan to keep *you* here.' And, with barely a flick of his hand, he beckoned his son to move, precisely as they had planned. Mahmoud reached for his blade, but it was too late: the spade had already thudded against his skull, knocking him to the ground. He oozed a final breath, but Nawaf pounded him with the metal head of the tool twice more, just to be sure.

'Our very own Great Pit of Death,' Jaafar al-Naasri murmured, almost to himself. 'Strip him and bury him,' he ordered his son. 'Right away.'

Jaafar al-Naasri picked up the holdall, checking that the seals and clay tablet were still in place, and headed back inside. He was turning the second of the three locks on the door when he heard his son laughing loudly. He turned round to see Nawaf, standing over the fresh corpse, rocking back and forth in mirth.

Al-Naasri walked back until he stood alongside his son. He could not see the joke at first, until Nawaf pointed at the dead man's chest. There, glinting in the light of the stars, one attached to each of Mahmoud's nipples, were two fine, golden earrings. Mahmoud believed he had hit upon the perfect hiding place: their revelation was to be his grand finale. And so it turned out.

CHAPTER EIGHTEEN

JERUSALEM, WEDNESDAY MORNING, 9.45PM

She met Uri at the Restobar Café. Not that he called it that. 'Meet me at the café that used to be moment,' he had said, in a voice-mail message on her mobile phone. She didn't understand it. Was it some kind of philosophical riddle: a café that used to be moment?

She asked the hotel concierge who seemed wholly familiar with the question, instantly instructing her to 'head out of the hotel, up the hill, second turning—'

'But what does it mean?'

'That used to be the Moment Café. It was bombed a few years ago. A suicide bombing.' He pronounced both *b*'s. 'So they changed the name.'

'But no one remembers the new name, so they all call it "the café that used to be Moment".'

'Right.' He smiled.

Uri was already there, at a corner table, hunched over a full cup of black coffee. He hadn't so much as sipped it. Unshaven, he looked as if he hadn't slept for days.

Maggie took the seat opposite and waited for Uri to make eye contact. Eventually she gave up waiting.

'So when's the funeral?'

'I don't know. It should have been today. But the police are holding on to my mother's body. Autopsy. It might not be till Friday.'

'I see.'

'Even though they say there is nothing to investigate.'

'What do you mean?'

'I mean—' He looked up, meeting her gaze for the first time. His eyes, so black, were now ringed with red. Even like this, Maggie felt ashamed to notice, he was extraordinarily handsome: she had to force herself to look away.

'I mean they are insisting that it is suicide.'

'You've told them what you think?'

'I said to them, over and over, that it is beyond doubt that my mother did not kill herself. But they insist that those pills belonged to her. And that there was no sign of a break-in.'

'Right.'

'But that means nothing. The front door has been open all week. Since my father . . .' His voice trailed off and he stared back into his coffee.

'But you're certain that she didn't do that to herself.' She couldn't utter the word kill, still less murder. Not to his face.

'No doubt at all. Not my mother.' He looked up again. 'My father maybe. This is the kind of macho stunt he might pull. The big heroic gesture, to get everyone's attention—'

'Uri—'

'It's his fault, you know.'

'You don't mean that.'

'No, I do. Always we had to suffer for his crazy beliefs. When we were kids, he was always arrested or he was on the TV or he was screaming at somebody. Do you know what that's like for a kid?'

Maggie thought of her own parents. The closest they got to

taking a political stand was when her father resigned from the committee of the Dun Laoghaire Bowls Club in a row with the treasurer. It was over payment for the biscuits at teatime.

'But he had principles. That's something to admire, isn't it?'

He looked up again, his eyes sparking with anger. 'Not if they are the wrong principles, no. That is not something to respect.'

'Wrong?'

'All this worship of land: every inch must be ours, ours, ours. It's a kind of sickness. Idol worship or something. And look where it led. He is dead and he has taken my mother with him.'

'Did your father know you felt this way?'

'We argued all the time. He always said that's why I stayed away, in New York. Not because it might actually have been good for my career, because there I had the chance to make movies properly—'

'You make movies?'

'Yeah, documentaries mainly.'

'Go on.'

'My father didn't believe I had gone to New York to make films. He said I ran away because I couldn't face losing the argument.'

'The argument over—'

'—over everything. Voting for left-wing parties, working in the arts. "You live like some decadent dropout from Tel Aviv!" That's what he would say to me. Tel Aviv. The number one insult.'

Maggie paused, looking away, then back at the man opposite her. 'Look, Uri. I know you're in pain. And I know there is so much to talk about. But we have to find out what the hell's going on here.'

'Why do you care?'

'Because the government I work for doesn't want the whole bloody Middle East peace process going down the pan over these killings, that's why.'

'You know my father would be happy if what you call the "peace process" fell to pieces. He called it the "war process".'

'Yes. But he wouldn't be happy to see his wife dead and maybe his son, too, would he, no matter how much you disagreed?'

'You think my life is in danger? And you care about that?'

'Not really. But you should.'

'Look, the danger to me doesn't matter. I don't care about it. What I care about is finding the people who did this.'

She exhaled. 'Good. Well you can start by telling me what you know.'

For the second time in two days she was back on the West Bank, though now her guide was a man who called it Judea and Samaria, even if the phrase seemed to come wrapped in fairly large quotation marks. Uri Guttman pointed out of the window, just as Sergeant Lee had done, though he was not indicating this or that site of Palestinian suffering, but the landmarks of the Old Testament.

'Down that road is Hebron, where Abraham, Isaac and Jacob, the three patriarchs, are all buried. And the matriarchs too: Sarah, who was married to Abraham; Rebecca, wife of Isaac, and Leah, second wife of Jacob.'

'I know my Bible, Uri.'

'You are a Christian, no? A Catholic?' He separated each syllable: *Cath-o-lic.*

'I was born and raised that way, that's right.'

'What, and you are not a Catholic now? I thought it was like being a Jew. Once you are, you are.'

'Something like that,' Maggie said quietly, wiping the moisture from her window.

'There are many Christian sites around here too. This is the Holy Land, remember.'

'"Never to be surrendered".'

'Are you quoting my father?'

'Not only him.'

The guided tour was interrupted only once, when Uri turned on the radio news. The latest word was desperately bleak. Hizbullah had launched a rocket bombardment from Lebanon, breaking their own long-held ceasefire. Israeli civilians in the north were cowering in bomb shelters and Yaakov Yariv was under pressure to hit back, pressure from his own supporters. If he was about to make peace, they said, he had to prove he was no soft touch. Maggie had discussed this with Davis on the phone that morning: Hizbullah did nothing without the backing of Iran. If they were attacking now, it was because Tehran expected a regional war. And soon.

They had driven around and then above Ramallah and were now pulling into Psagot, a Jewish settlement perched on a hill that loomed over the Palestinian city. Maggie was struck by the simplicity of it all. It was almost medieval. Fortresses on hilltops, as if packed with archers ready to rain arrows down on the enemy below. It made her think of France or England, or Ireland, for that matter. The castles were either gone or in ruins now but only a few centuries ago the European countryside would have looked much like this, too: a battleground, with every mountaintop and hillside a strategic prize to be seized or feared.

The road was winding and steep, but eventually they came to a boom gate. Uri slowed down, giving enough time for the guard on duty to emerge from his sentry box, decide that this car was Israeli and therefore legitimate and wave him on. The guard was middle-aged and paunchy, wearing ill-fitting jeans and a plain T-shirt under a green soldier's anorak. Slung over his shoulder was an M16 rifle, its butt bound with black gaffer tape. Maggie couldn't decide if the casualness of the scene made it more or less sinister.

Once out of the car, she tried to get her bearings. At first glance these Jewish settlements really did look like American suburbs transplanted into the middle of dusty Arabia, the houses complete with their trademark red roofs and grass lawns. At the end of one street a group of teenage girls were playing basketball, though they were all wearing denim skirts long enough to cover their ankles.

She looked further, keen to take in Ramallah from this vantage point, but her view was blocked. Only then did she notice the thick concrete wall that bordered one side of Psagot, shutting out entirely any sight of the city below.

Uri caught her gaze. 'It's ugly, no?'

'You're not kidding.'

'They had to build it a few years back to stop the sniper fire from Ramallah. Every day there would be bullets landing here.'

'And did it work?'

'Ask the girls who can play basketball in the street now.'

On closer inspection, Maggie could see that if this was an American suburb, it was one of the more down-at-heel variety. The housing units were basic and the central administrative building, into which Uri was leading her now, was a drab affair. The place was surprisingly empty. As Uri waited for a secretary to appear at the front desk, he explained that everyone was either at demonstrations in Jerusalem or in the human chain.

Eventually, a woman appeared and instantly gave Uri a long look of deep sympathy, her eyes damp. It was becoming clear that, whatever views he held personally, Uri Guttman was the grieving son of settler aristocracy: word about his mother's death had spread, following an announcement on the radio that morning. With no appointment, she gestured for him to come into the office of the man who Uri had explained was not just the head of Psagot but of the entire settlements council of the West Bank.

The second Uri was through the door, Akiva Shapira was on his feet, striding over to welcome the younger man. Big and bearded, he immediately placed his hand on Uri's head and uttered what Maggie took to be some kind of prayer of condolence. *'HaMakom y'nachem oscha b'soch sh'ar aveilei Tzion v'Yerushalayim.'* His eyes were closed as he said the words.

'Akiva, this is my friend Maggie Costello. She is from Ireland, but she is here with the American team for the peace talks. She is helping me.'

Maggie offered a hand, but Shapira had already turned around, heading back to his desk. Whether he was avoiding a handshake on political grounds, because she was a servant of an American administration despised for imposing surrender on Israel, or on religious grounds, because she was a woman, she couldn't tell.

'You're both welcome,' he said breathing heavily, as he squeezed himself back into his seat. The first surprise: a New York accent. 'By rights I should be the one doing the visiting. You have suffered the most profound loss, Uri, and you know you have the wishes of all the people of Eretz Yisroel, the whole land of Israel.'

Maggie understood the translation was for her benefit, as was perhaps the phrase itself. That 'whole' was not lost on her.

'I need to talk to you about my father.'

'Of course.'

'As you know he was very agitated in the last days of his life, frantic.'

'He was desperate to see Yariv. To tell him what madness he was committing, but this so-called Prime Minister of ours wouldn't see him.'

'Is that what he wanted to say? That the peace talks were "madness"?'

'What else? He thought this was sane, giving up the very heart of our land? Are you serious?'

Maggie knew that this, too, was for her sake. Shapira was barely looking at Uri.

'He knew that this was an act of a people who have lost their collective minds. A re-run of the great Jewish mistake. From Pharaoh to Hitler himself, the clever Jew has always reckoned he can make the wolf go away. And what is this Jewish secret weapon? I'll tell you, Uri. It is surrender! That's right! That is the great genius of the Jews, the nation of Marx and Freud and Einstein. Surrender! And now Yariv is trying the same trick. We give the enemy what he wants, without a fight, and we'll call it peace. It is surrender, no more and no less. Am I wrong, Miss Costello?'

She wished she hadn't come. Uri on his own would have been spared this performance. But he wasn't fazed. She saw him lean forward, like an interviewer.

'Akiva. What I want to know is what specifically my father had on his mind in the last days of his life.'

'And for this you came all this way? This you couldn't work out by yourself? What he had on his *mind*? Isn't that just so obvious a child in kindergarten could give you the answer?' He turned away from Uri, again. 'Tell me, Miss Costello – Uri says you're Irish. I have no idea whether you're a Protestant or a Catholic, but tell me this: when the IRA were planting bombs every five minutes, did the Protestants say, "OK, here, take Belfast. Split it down the middle and we'll have whichever bits you don't want. Oh, and while we're at it, all the millions of Catholic Irish who left on boats for the last one hundred and fifty years – all of them can come back and live here, in our little bit of Protestant Northern Ireland." Tell me honestly, did you ever hear a Protestant in Northern Ireland say such a thing? Did you?'

'Akiva, I'm here to talk about my father—'

'Because that is what our beloved Prime Minister and our so-called government, may God rain justice down upon them, are doing here. The same thing! Let every Palestinian whose great-uncle once pissed in a pot in Jaffa come here and claim a mansion in Tel Aviv. And sure, let's split Jerusalem in two. Do you know how many times Jerusalem is mentioned in the Koran? Tell me, do you?'

Uri was staring at the ceiling, struggling to hide his frustration. Maggie spoke instead. 'Really, we're not here—'

'Zero.' He made the shape with his thumb and forefinger. 'A big fat zero. We pray for a return to Jerusalem three times a day for two thousand years; we build our synagogues facing east so that we can face Jerusalem, no matter if we're in New Jersey or Dublin; we ask Ha'shem, the Almighty, to make our tongues cleave to the roofs of our mouths and for our right hand to lose its cunning if we should forget thee O Jerusalem – and yet *we* have to give it up! We have to surrender a city to these Arabs who don't even mention it – not a mention – in their so-called holy book!' His face flushed, he now leaned forward, jabbing a finger at Maggie.

'So yes, I know what Shimon Guttman had on his mind. The suicide of the Jewish people! Do you hear me? The self-destruction of the Jewish people. That is what he wanted to prevent.'

Uri raised a palm in request, like a pupil asking a teacher for permission to speak. Maggie could see he was suppressing his own views. Whether that was because he was too drained to summon the energy for a fight, or because he had made the smart decision that there was nothing to be gained from a political row, she couldn't tell. But she was grateful for Uri's instinct. They needed Shapira to be helpful, otherwise their trip would be wasted.

'He told my mother he had seen something specific,' Uri began, the picture of politeness and filial duty. 'Something that would change everything. Do you know what that was?'

Shapira turned towards Uri and softened his voice. 'Your father and I talked all the time these last weeks. He and I—'

'I'm talking about the last three or four days. That's when he saw whatever it was—'

'He could be quite a private man, Uri. If he didn't want to share with you what he had seen, maybe there was a reason for that.'

'What kind of reason?'

'How do the Psalms put it? "As a father has compassion on his children, so the Lord has compassion on those who fear him."'

'I don't understand.'

'Compassion for his children, protecting his children. It's the same thing.'

'You think he was protecting me?'

'He was a devoted father, Uri.'

'But what about my mother? He tried to protect her too. And look what happened to her.'

'Are you sure he didn't pass on whatever information he had to her, Uri? Can you be certain of that?'

Uri reluctantly shook his head, as if he had been caught out.

Maggie realized that it was possible that Mrs Guttman had found out something last night, just hours before her death. Maybe she had tried to make a call. Perhaps that way she had alerted her killers. Or maybe, despite Uri's protestations, she had seen something which had so appalled her, filled her with such despair, that she had taken her own life.

'You see, my dear Uri, the Master of the Universe has a plan for the Jewish people. He doesn't allow us to see it, of course. He gives us a glimpse, here and there, in the texts, in the sources. It's only a glimpse. But he performs miracles, Uri. Your own faith probably teaches you that, too, Miss Costello. Miracles. And the history of the Jewish people is a story of miracles.

'We suffer the greatest tragedy in human history. The Holocaust. And how long do we have to wait before redemption? Three years! That's all! The Nazis fall in 1945 and in forty-eight we have a state of our own. After two thousand years of exile and wandering, we return to our ancient land. The land which God promised to Abraham nearly four thousand years ago. What do you call that, Miss Costello, if not a bona fide, copper-bottomed, fourteen-days-at-home-or-your-money-back miracle? Our darkest hour, followed by the moment of greatest light!

'Same in sixty-seven. The Arabs surround us, all of them sharpening their knives to slit our throats, to push the Jews into the sea. And what happens? Israel destroys their air forces in a matter of hours and their armies in days! Six days. "And God saw every thing that he had made and, behold, it was very good." And on the seventh day he rested.

'Well, would you bet against the Almighty redeeming us once more? Yes, things are dark now, no denying it. Your government in Washington, Miss Costello, plans on robbing the Jewish people of its birthright, telling us to give up land we were promised by God. And collaborating with you is a man who we once trusted, a traitor who is ready to betray his people so that he can parade before the anti-Semites in Europe as the good Jew, the nice Jew, the dove with a Nobel Prize clasped in his beak, while the bad Jews are left to be murdered in their beds by the Arabs.

'It all seems to be over, it's our darkest hour all over again, when look! A hero of the Jewish people, Shimon Guttman, intervenes to stay the hand of the traitor and lo, Guttman the hero is slain. And now the people of Israel begin to understand. They now see the threat that faces them: a government that is willing to shoot its own citizens. Even, and for this please forgive me, Uri, to kill the wife of the hero!

'This is the way the Almighty works. He gives us signs, clues if you will. Because he wants us to see what's going on. He took your mother so that we would be under no illusions. It's a message to us, Uri. Your parents and the tragedy that has befallen them is a message. It's telling us to say no to this huge American trick. To say no to mass Jewish suicide.'

All of this came at such a speed, and at such loud, full-throated volume, there was no choice but to wait for it to stop. This

Shapira was a practised speaker, that much was clear, who had mastered the technique of the seamless segue from one sentence to the next, brooking no interruption. Maggie had been in the meeting when the US team famously sat listening to the Syrian President talk for an unbroken six hours, deploying the exact same trick. The only suitable response was stamina and patience. You just had to wait till your foe, or partner, it made no difference, had talked himself out. That moment seemed to have arrived.

'Mr Shapira,' Maggie began, leaping in ahead of Uri. 'That's all really helpful. Would I be summarizing your views accurately if I were to say that you suspect the hand of the Israeli authorities themselves in the deaths of Uri's parents?'

'Yes, because what the United States of America needs to realize—'

Big mistake, thought Maggie. Should not have formulated it as a question, inviting a bloody answer.

'Thank you, that's clear. They did this to silence the Guttmans, because they feared whatever information it was they had discovered.' The inflection was downward now, indicating a statement. 'Yet what you have described are the views Shimon Guttman held for many years. He most certainly would have wanted to convey them to the Prime Minister. But they were hardly new. How do you explain the frantic urgency? How do you explain why the Israeli authorities would act this way to suppress an opinion that was already well known?'

'Opinion? Who said anything about opinion? Not me. I've been using the word information. *Information,* Miss Costello. Different thing. Shimon had obviously uncovered some information that would force Yariv to realize the lunacy of his ways. I think he wanted to get it out there any way he could.'

'What kind of information?'

'Now you're asking too much of me, Miss Costello.'

'Does that mean you won't tell us or you don't know?' It was Uri, operating as if he and Maggie were a tag team. Akiva ignored him, his eye remaining fixed on Maggie.

'Why don't you take some advice from someone who's been around this neighbourhood a little longer than forty-eight hours? What I know, you don't want to know. And, Uri, you don't want to know either. Believe me, big things are at stake here. The fate of God's chosen people in God's Promised Land. A covenant between us and the Almighty. That's too big for a few jumped-up, sleazeball politicians to try to tear up, no matter how important they think they are, whether here or in Washington. You can tell that to your employers, Miss Costello. No one comes between us and the Almighty. No one.'

'Or else?'

'Or else? You're asking "or else"? This is not a question to ask. But look around you. Uri, take my advice. Leave this alone. You have parents to mourn for. You have a funeral to arrange.'

There was a knock on the door. The secretary poked her head around, and mouthed something to Shapira. 'Sure, I'll call him back.'

He turned back to Uri. 'Do yourself a favour, Uri. Mourn your mother. *Sit shiva*. And leave this thing alone. No good can come of poking around. Your father's task has been fulfilled. Not the way he intended, maybe. But fulfilled. The people of Israel have been roused.'

Uri was doing his best, Maggie could see, to disguise his eye-rolling contempt for what he was hearing. Occasionally he slumped into his seat, like an insolent schoolboy, only to remember himself and sit up straight. Now he leaned forward to speak. 'Do you know anything about Ahmed Nour?'

Maggie leapt in. 'Mr Shapira, you've been very generous with your time. Can I thank you—'

'What, you're trying to blame me for the death of that Arab?

Is that what they're saying on the leftist radio already? I'm surprised at you, Uri, for sucking up that bullshit.'

Maggie was on her feet now. 'It's been a very troubling time, you can imagine. People are saying all kinds of things.' She knew she was babbling, but her eyes were doing the work, desperately trying to say to Akiva Shapira: *He's just lost both his parents. He's gone a little nuts. Ignore him.*

Shapira was now standing up, not to bid farewell to Maggie but to embrace Uri.

'You can be very proud of your parents, Uri. But now let them rest in peace. Leave this alone.'

CHAPTER NINETEEN

AMMAN, JORDAN, TEN MONTHS EARLIER

Jaafar al-Naasri was not a man to rush. 'Those that hurry are those that get caught,' he used to say. He had tried explaining that to his son, but he was too dumb to listen. Al-Naasri wondered if he had been cursed to be surrounded by such stupidity, even in his own house. He had made sure to marry a clever woman. They had done everything right, sending their children to one of the best schools in Amman. Yet his daughter was a slut who modelled herself on the whores on MTV; and his boys were no better. One a lumpen oaf, whose only value lay in his fists. The other brighter, but a layabout. Up at noon, with aspirations to be a playboy.

It pained Jaafar al-Naasri. Yes, he was a wealthy man now, thanks in part to the generosity of Saddam Hussein and the United States military. Between them, they had opened the door to the great treasure house of mankind, the repository of the very origins of human history. Was it an exaggeration? Jaafar was prone to the occasional lapse into hype, he could not deny it: what salesman was not? But the Baghdad Museum needed no selling. It had served as the keeper of man's earliest memories.

Mesopotamia had been the first civilization and those beginnings were all there, under glass, tagged, indexed and preserved in the National Museum of Antiquities. The first examples of writing, anywhere in the world, were to be found in Baghdad, in the thousands of tablets written in cuneiform, the language of four millennia past. Art, sculpture, jewellery and statuary from the days when these were all new forms, relics of the age of the Bible and before, they were to be found in Baghdad.

For decades they had stayed in alarmed cases and behind steel doors, protected by the greatest security system in the world: the tyranny of Saddam Hussein. But thanks to those GIs in their tanks and the bomber pilots in the skies above, Saddam had fled and the doors to the museum had been flung wide open. The American soldiers who had surrounded the Ministry of Oil, placing its files and papers, its precious secrets of black gold, under round-the-clock armed guard, thankfully did nothing to protect the Museum. A single tank came, days too late. Otherwise, it was left naked and exposed, as open and available as a Baghdad whore. And Jaafar and his boys had been able to feast on her again and again, without disturbance.

Make no mistake, he had done well, filling the al-Naasri collection in his backyard with enough delights to start a museum of his own. His fool of a son had been digging morning, noon and night for months, stashing away the booty his wide network of runners brought daily from Iraq. Sometimes, if Jaafar suspected they were two-timing him, supplying a rival dealer, here in Amman or further afield, in Beirut or Damascus, then Nawaf would have to use his spade for another purpose. He had only had to do that half a dozen times, maybe less. Jaafar was not counting. But he could not say he was happy. By now, after a blessing like the US invasion, he should have been at the very top of his game, like that bastard Kaslik, who had built an empire across the region thanks to the 2003 war. But Kaslik had sons he could rely on. Jaafar al-Naasri could rely only on himself.

Which is why he was stuck here, now, in his workshop doing a job he should have been able to delegate. He could not entrust such a task to staff: the risk of betrayal, either stealing the goods or tipping somebody off, was too great. But he had once imagined a team of junior al-Naasris, as skilled as he was, beavering away, only too eager to take on the most sensitive work.

And this was certainly sensitive. The downside of Saddam's fall was that after it, the rules suddenly tightened. Governments around the world who had turned a blind eye to the trade in stolen Iraqi treasures before 2003 were no longer so forgiving. Maybe they felt it was OK to steal from a dictator, but not quite right to steal the inheritance of 'the Iraqi people'. Personally, Jaafar blamed the television news. If it hadn't been for the pictures of the Baghdad looting, things could have gone on as before. But after they had seen it, the denuding of the grand museum by wheelbarrow and sack, the high-ups in London and New York had got anxious. They couldn't be accomplices to this great cultural crime. So the word went out to customs officials and auction houses and museum curators from Paris to Los Angeles: nothing from Iraq.

Which meant Jaafar had to be creative. More than ever, he would have to conceal the products he was sending out. The item on the bench in front of him was a source of particular pride. It was a flat plastic box, divided into two dozen compartments, full of brightly coloured beads, under a clear lid – a jewellery-making set, aimed at the younger end of the teenage girl market. His wife's sister had bought it for Naima's twelfth birthday after a trip to New York. His daughter had played with it for a while, then tired of it. Jaafar had come across it a couple of months ago, quite by accident, and had realized its potential immediately.

Now, trying to ape the garish tastes of an adolescent girl, he reached for a pink bead, threading it onto the string, which already carried a fake ruby, a purple sequin and the metal top from a bottle of Coca-Cola. He smiled. It looked like a tacky charm bracelet, a medley of novelty items that a teenager might wear, break and never remember again.

Unless they looked too closely at one of the items on the string. It was not the only golden piece – there was also a brassy miniature poodle – but it was the finest. A simple gold leaf, delicate and finely engraved. But you would have to look, and Jaafar had been around precious things long enough to know that context was everything. Had it been in a museum, resting on a cushion, far away from the beads and the bottle-tops, then maybe you might have guessed that this was an earring buried four and a half thousand years ago with a princess of Sumeria. On Jaafar's worktable, cheek-by-jowl with trash, it looked like nothing.

Next came the seals, small stone cylinders embossed with a unique cuneiform pattern. Five millennia ago these would have been rolled onto clay tablets to denote a signature. Ingenious for their time, but no more ingenious than the home Jaafar had found for them. He reached down to the big brown carton that had arrived a week ago from Neuchatel, Switzerland. Inside was a bulk load of toy wooden chalets, complete with painted windows and surrounded by matchstick picket fences. Lift the roof and you would discover that this mantelpiece ornament had another function. A slow, tinny melody would begin, picked out by the shiny metal mechanism within.

It had taken him months to source this exact music box. He had looked on dozens of websites and spoken to more technicians than he could count until he was satisfied that this one had the right specifications. Now, as he prized out the mechanism with his screwdriver, he saw his patience had been rewarded. The central rotating drum, punctuated with tiny spears which caught a hammer to produce the melody, was hollow, just as he had been assured. His hand, gloved in latex, reached for the first of the cylinder-seals which he had lined up on a shelf at eye level. Slowly, carefully, he eased the seal inside the metal drum. It fitted perfectly. He exhaled his relief, looking again at the hoard of seals he had amassed, lined up before him like soldiers awaiting inspection. They were all sorts of shapes and sizes, but now he felt confident, glancing down at the carton from the Swiss company, who had sent him the full range of music boxes, from very small to 'our grand model, sir'. This might just work.

But he could do it so much quicker if he had some decent help. He glanced over at the tea chest by the big roll of bubble wrap. That alone represented about three months of hard, solitary labour. Inside it were the several hundred clay tablets he had accumulated since April 2003. He had a plan for those, too. Not fiddly, but time-consuming.

He checked the calendar, with its soft-focused portraits of the king and his gorgeous American-styled wife on each page. All being well, he would have this lot boxed up, labelled as handicrafts and on its way to London by the spring. There was no need to rush. In the business of antiquities time was never your enemy, only your friend. The longer you waited, the richer you became. And the world had waited four and a half thousand years for these beauties.

CHAPTER TWENTY

JERUSALEM, WEDNESDAY, 1.23PM

The drive back from Psagot had been tense. Maggie had administered a bollocking to Uri before the engine had even started. 'Mentioning Ahmed Nour, what on earth was that for?'

'I thought he might have something to tell us.'

'Yeah, like "piss off before I kill both of you, too".'

'You think Akiva Shapira killed my parents? Are you out of your mind?'

Maggie backed off. She had to remind herself that Uri was still in the immediate shock of a double bereavement. But she was fed up with treading on eggshells. Calm self-possession and control might be the order of the day in the divorce mediation room, but not here.

'Tell me. Why is that so crazy?'

'You saw the guy. He's a fanatic. Just like my dad. They loved each other, these guys.'

'OK, so not him. Then, who?'

'Who what?'

'Who killed your parents? Go on. Who do you suspect?'

Uri took his eye off the road and looked at Maggie, as if in disbelief. 'You know, I'm not used to working like this.'

'Like what?'

'With another person. When I make a movie, I do everything myself. Interviewing, shooting, cutting. I'm not used to having some Irish girl next to me, chipping in.'

'I'm not "some Irish girl", thank you very much. That kind of sexist crap may play in Israel, but not with me. OK?'

Uri shot a glance back at Maggie. 'OK, OK.'

'As it happens, I'm not used to it either. When I'm in the room, I'm on my own. Just me and the two sides.'

'How come?'

'I find it just works better that way. No aides, advisers—'

'No, I mean how come you do this? How come you're so good at it?' She guessed he was trying to make amends for 'some Irish girl'.

'At mediation, you mean?'

'Yes.'

She was about to tell the truth, to explain that it had been a while since she had engaged in an international negotiation, that the last dispute she had brokered had been over weekend access to Nat, Joey and Ruby George of Chevy Chase, Maryland. But she said none of that.

'I got it from home, I suppose.'

'Don't tell me. Your mum and dad used to fight all the time and you became the peacemaker?'

'No, don't be soft.' Though she had to admit she was impressed: as it happened, the broken home appeared in the personal histories of dozens of mediators. 'The opposite. My parents were rock solid. Best marriage on the street. Not that that was saying much. Everyone else was rowing and fighting, husbands getting in drunk, mothers having it off with the milkman, all sorts. They used to come to my mother for advice.'

'And you watched her?'

'I never planned to. But couples would appear in our front

room, asking my mother to arbitrate between them. "Let's see what Mrs Costello has to say." It became a catchphrase round our way. I watched what she did and I suppose I picked it up.'

'She must be very proud of you.'

'They both are.'

Uri said nothing, allowing the hum of the car to fill the void. Maggie scolded herself: it was crass to have referred to her two parents in the present tense so breezily, rubbing their aliveness in his face. But she had got carried away. It was rare for her to be asked about herself like that and she had enjoyed the chance to answer. It had probably seemed obvious to Uri, who earned his living getting people to talk about themselves, but she couldn't remember the last time anyone else had asked, 'How come you're a mediator?' It struck her that Edward had never once asked that question.

While they sped towards Jerusalem, past roads she knew were choked with Palestinians moving at a fraction of their speed, if they were moving at all, she tried to focus on the meeting with Shapira. He seemed pretty clear: Guttman had told Shapira what he had found – *You don't want to know what I know* – and, Shapira believed, the Israeli government had killed him for it. But Shapira was a big, puffed-up blowhard. Why hadn't he told Uri what his father had discovered? Maybe because she was in the room. Though that made no sense: if there was some devastating new ammunition against the peace process, he'd have seized his chance to hurl it at the Americans. Was it possible Shapira knew nothing, but simply wanted to make the Guttmans look like martyrs to the cause?

She was too lost in thought, and Uri the same, to look closely in the rear-view mirror and notice what was behind them: a white Subaru that kept three cars back. And never let them out of its sight.

They were back in the home of Shimon and Rachel Guttman. The instant Uri let them in, she shuddered. The house was not cold, but a chill hung in the air all the same. This was a place of death, twice over. She admired Uri for being able to set foot inside it.

The doormat was piled high with notes and cards: well-wishers from abroad, no doubt. Everyone else would be at Uri's sister's house now, where the *shiva* for his father would continue and where the *shiva* for his mother would begin once she had been buried. Maggie worried that Uri was absenting himself from a process he needed. She knew from wakes back at home that all this fuss wasn't for the dead, but for the living, to give them something to do, to distract them from their grief. When you have to talk to two dozen relatives in an hour, you haven't got time to be depressed. Yet here Uri was with her, denying himself that sedative for the pain.

'In here.' He switched on the light in a room that was, thankfully, at the opposite end of the house from the kitchen where she had discovered Rachel Guttman's dead body the previous night. It was small, cramped and lined, floor to ceiling, with books. There were also piles and piles of paper on every available surface. In the middle of a simple desk, just a plain table really, was a computer, a telephone and a fax machine with a jumble of electronic gadgetry, including a video camera, pushed to one side. Maggie checked the camera straight away: no tape inside.

'Where on earth do we start?'

Uri looked at her. 'Well, why don't you quickly learn Hebrew? Then it will only take us a few months.'

Maggie smiled. It was the closest thing to laughter they had shared since they had met.

'Maybe if you look at the computer. A lot of that was in English. I'll start on these piles.'

Maggie settled herself into the seat and pressed the power button. 'Hey, Uri. Can you give me the cellphone again?'

He pulled out the transparent plastic bag he had collected from the hospital on their way back from Psagot. Inside it were 'the personal effects of the deceased', the things his father had with him when he was killed. He passed her the phone. She switched it on, then selected the message inbox. *Empty*. Then the 'sent' box. *Empty*.

'And you're definitely sure your father used to send text messages?'

'I told you already. He sent some to me. When I was on border duty in Lebanon, we used to text all the time.'

'So this phone has definitely been wiped.'

'I think so.'

'Which means his email account is likely to have gone too. Whoever did that to your mother probably came in here too. But let's look.'

The familiar desktop appeared on the screen. Maggie went straight for the email account. A box appeared, demanding a password. *Damn*.

'Uri?'

He was clutching a bundle of papers to his chest, adding to it each time he examined a sheet from the pile on the desk in front of him. She could see progress was going to be painfully slow.

'Try Vladimir.'

'Vladimir?'

'As in Jabotinsky. The founder of Revisionist Zionism. The first serious hardliner. My dad's hero.'

She keyed in the letters slowly. Without fanfare, the screen began to fill up with email. Uri smiled. 'He always used that. Used to write love letters to my mother under that name.'

Maggie scrolled down, looking at the unopened messages. They had kept coming, even now, since his death. Bulletins from the *Jerusalem Post*; a soldiers' relief fund; circulars from Arutz Sheva, the settlers' radio station.

She went back earlier, to those that had arrived before his death. Still the same round robins and circulars. Hold on: some personal ones. A request to speak at a demo next Wednesday. That was today. An inquiry from German TV; a request to be on a BBC radio panel. She looked further, hoping for a message from Ahmed Nour or anything which might explain the fevered words of Rachel Guttman in this very house just two days earlier. She checked the sent box, but there was not much there that stood out, and certainly no communication with Nour. *How stupid could she be?* With confidence, she searched for the codename she had unscrambled, Ehud Ramon, certain it would be here. Not in the inbox, not in sent messages. Nothing.

Maybe Maggie's assumption was right. Whoever had killed Rachel Guttman had stopped in here first, methodically deleting any emails of significance. She looked in the recycle bin, just on the off-chance. Nothing in there since Saturday, the day of Guttman's death. Which meant that either someone had hacked into this computer and was skilled enough to cover their traces – or the dead man simply avoided using email for any communication that mattered.

'Are you certain your father used email? I mean properly.'

'Are you kidding? All the time. Like I said, for a man his age, he is very modern. He even plays computer games, my father. Besides, he is a campaigner. They live on the internet, these people.'

That gave her an idea. She clicked the email away and looked instead for the browser. She opened it up and went straight to the favourites. A couple of Hebrew newspapers; the BBC; the *New York Times*; eBay; the British Museum; Fox News. *Damn*. Her hunch had been wrong. She shut down the browser and stared at the desktop which, at this moment, looked to her like an electronic brick wall.

She stared hard at the icons on it. A few Word documents, which she opened. She saw Yariv1.doc and her heart leapt. But it was only an open letter, in English, addressed to the Prime Minister and headed 'For the Attention of the *Philadelphia Inquirer*'. Whatever it was Guttman had wanted to say to Yariv, he had not left it lying around here.

Then, at the bottom of the screen, an icon she had on her own machine but had never used. She clicked on it and saw it was another internet browser, just not a very famous one. She looked for the favourites, here called *Bookmarks*, and there was only one.

gmail.com

It was what she had been hoping for. An email account, separate to his main one, effectively hidden away. Here, she had no doubt, was where Guttman's serious correspondence would be kept.

A box appeared, this time asking for both a name and a password. She typed in Shimon Guttman, with Vladimir as the password and waited. No luck. She tried Shimon on its own. Nothing. She tried lower case, upper case and then no spaces. None if it worked.

'Uri, what would he use besides Vladimir?'

So she tried Jabotinsky, Jabo, VladimirJ and what seemed like three dozen other permutations. No luck. And then it hit her. Without pausing, she pulled out her cellphone and punched at the numbers. 'The office of Khalil al-Shafi please.'

Uri reared back, dropping a clump of papers onto the floor as he did so. 'What the hell do you think—'

'Let me speak to Khalil al-Shafi please. This is Maggie Costello from the State Department.' It was her Sunday best accent.

'Mr al-Shafi. Do you remember you told me that Ahmed Nour had received some mysterious emails prior to his death, requesting a meeting? That's right. From an Arab name his family did not recognize. I need you to tell me that name. It will go no further than me, I assure you.'

She checked the spelling back twice, making sure every letter was right, knowing there was no room for error. She thanked the Palestinian negotiator and hung up.

'Do you speak any Arabic, Uri?'

'A little.'

'OK. What does *nas tayib* mean?'

'That's very simple. It means a good man.'

'Or, if we were to translate it into German, a *Gutt man, nein*?

CHAPTER TWENTY-ONE

LONDON, SIX MONTHS EARLIER

Henry Blyth-Pullen tapped the steering wheel along to the *Archers* theme tune. *Tum-tee-tum-tee-tum-tum-tum, tum-tee-tum-tum-tum-tum*. He was, he decided, a man of simple tastes. He might have spent his working life surrounded by sumptuous antiques and precious artefacts, but his needs were modest. Just this – an afternoon drive through the spring sunshine, with no more onerous obligation than listening to a radio soap – was enough to cheer his spirits.

He always liked driving. Even this, a forty-five-minute run from the showroom in Bond Street to Heathrow Airport, was a pleasure. No phone calls, no one bothering him. Just time to daydream.

He did the drive often. Not to the main terminals, teeming with passengers and all kinds of *hoi polloi* on their way to their tacky vacations in heaven knows where. His destination was the turning almost everyone else ignored. The cargo area.

He pulled into the car park, finding a space easily. He didn't get out straightaway, but stayed to listen to the end of the episode: Jenny breaking down in tears for a change. He got out, straightened his jacket – a contemporary tweed, he liked to call it – shot an admiring glance at his vintage Jaguar, polished to a shine, and headed for the reception.

'Hello again, sir,' said the guard the instant Henry walked into the Ascentis building. 'We can't keep you away, can we?'

'Oh come on, Tony. Third time this month, that's all.'

'Business must be good.'

'In truth,' he said, mimicking a courtly bow, 'I cannot complain.'

At the window, he filled in the air waybill. On the line marked 'goods' he wrote simply 'handicrafts'. For 'country of origin', he wrote 'Jordan' which was not only true but suitably unremarkable. Imports from Jordan were entirely legal. Asked for his 125 number he wrote down the string of digits Jaafar had given him over the phone. He signed his name as an approved handling agent and slipped the form back under the glass.

'All right, Mr Blyth-Pullen, I'll be back in a tick,' said Tony.

Henry took his usual seat in the waiting area and began leafing through a copy of yesterday's *Evening Standard*. If he looked relaxed, it was because he felt relaxed. For one thing, he was dealing with the staff of BA, not Her Majesty's Revenue & Customs department. Sure, Customs would look at the forms but he couldn't think of the last time they had asked to open anything up, let alone a crate that had been vouched for by a recognized, and highly respectable, agent like him. The truth was, they were not really bothered with the art trade. Trafficking, whether in drugs or people, that was their game. The lead had come from the top. The politicians, pushed by the tabloids, wanted to keep out crack, smack and Albanians – not the odd mosaic fragment. As Henry had explained to his over-anxious wife more than once, the uniformed men at Heathrow were playing at *The Sweeney*, not *Antiques* bloody *Roadshow*.

Sure enough, Tony soon emerged with a set of papers and his usual smile: Customs must have nodded the forms through. Henry Blyth-Pullen wrote out a cheque for the thirty pounds release fee and went back to his car, waiting, with Radio 4 now deep into an afternoon play, to be called into the secure area. Eventually he was beckoned forward, driving through the huge, high gates until he reached Door 8, as instructed by Tony. Another short wait and soon he was putting a single brown box into the boot of the Jag. One more signature, to confirm receipt, and the shipment was officially signed, sealed, delivered – and one hundred per cent legitimate.

When it came time to open the crate in the back room of his Bond Street showroom, he felt the same pulse of pleasure he experienced whenever a truly special consignment arrived. It was almost sexual, a stirring in the loins, that he had first known as a teenager, smoking an illicit joint at his boarding school. He levered open the top, taking care to avoid the splinters these tea-chests could skewer into your fingers. But his mind itched with that most delicious of questions, known to any child tearing away at ribbons and paper on Christmas morning: *what's inside?*

Al-Naasri had told him over the phone to expect tourist souvenirs. Henry had been intrigued, assuming this was code for items brought to Jordan from somewhere else. But as he peeled off the first layers of styrofoam and bubble wrap, he felt uneasy. He saw a set of six music boxes, each in the form of a Swiss chalet in luridly cheap colours. He lifted the lid of the first one and, to his great disappointment, it played a tune. *Edelweiss.*

Below them were horrible, shoddy glass frames an inch thick containing patterns of coloured powder, complete with a transparently fake sticker, announcing each one as 'Genuin Sand from Jordan River'. Al-Naasri had never let him down before but this, Henry Blyth-Pullen had to admit, had him foxed. Finally, encased in triple layers of bubble wrap and tissue paper, were a dozen nasty charm bracelets, the kind, Henry decided instantly, oiks might buy from a coin-operated machine on Blackpool pier. Of all the shipments he had received in his eighteen years in the business, this was easily the most disappointing. Handicrafts, my eye. This was tourist tat, plain and simple.

When they had spoken, Henry had thought 'souvenirs' was simply a euphemism, necessary when talking on the telephone. But that bloody Arab wasn't kidding. Still, he had worked with Jaafar al-Naasri for a long time now. He had never been let down before. Falling into a chair, he now reached for the phone. He would get this sorted. He dialled and waited for the long drone of an international ring.

'Jaafar! Thanks for this latest arrival. It's – how shall I put it – *surprising*.'

'Do you like the song?'

'On the music boxes? Yes, er, yes. Most . . . tuneful.'

'Ah, that is because of the workmanship, Henry. Look inside the cylinder drum; you can see a technique there that is very old. Ancient even.'

'I understand.' Listening to Jaafar, with the phone cradled in his ear, Henry moved back to the crate, where he picked out the first music box. He wrenched the wooden roof off its hinges to get a closer look at the mechanism. He would need a screw-driver.

'And these are a local product?' Henry asked, stalling.

Too impatient to find his tool box, Henry grabbed a kitchen knife and levered out the innards of the first music box. It was stubborn – too bloody meticulous, the Swiss, that was their trouble – but eventually it pushed out. And there, inside, sure enough, was a perfect example of a cylinder seal.

'Oh, I now see what you mean about these music boxes, Jaafar. The mechanisms are exquisite! They could only have come from the very birthplace of the, er, music box. The place where it all began!'

'And what about the sand displays?'

'Well, their immediate appeal is a little less obvious.'

'You know of course, that every grain of sand was once a much larger stone. One that has been changed, its appearance altered by time. Look hard in any grain of sand and you can see the rocks and stones of the past.'

Henry picked up the first display and smashed it against the side of his oak desk, sending sand all over the carpet. He peered out through the doorway, hoping no one out front – staff or, worse, a customer – had heard the sound of breaking glass.

There, filling the palm of his hand, was a clay tablet. Etched on it was line after line of cuneiform writing. It was covered in sticky sand now, like party glitter, but it brushed off easily.

'Oh, and my dear Jaafar, these sands from the River Jordan are perfect. And I see you have sent me at least—'

'Twenty, Henry. Exactly twenty.'

'Yes, twenty it is. Quite so.'

'And, my friend, the bracelets are especially charming, don't you think? Do they not perhaps remind you of the leaves on the trees in springtime?'

Henry had to marvel at the ingenuity of it. It was brilliantly done. Jaafar had surpassed himself. He had seen the opportunity of 2003, bided his time and then come up with a flawless disguise. Henry felt honoured to be part of it.

The next day he made an appointment to see his friend, Ernest Freundel, at the British Museum. They had jointly run the Art Club at Harrow, where Freundel, even then, was the more accomplished scholar. When Henry came up with the wheeze of combing the art books for female nudes, then charging boys 10p a time to look at them, it was clear which of the two was headed for business and which for the academy.

Ordinarily, Ernest Freundel was happy to indulge his old pal, even if he couldn't help but resent the ever-widening gap between their incomes. He would decipher whatever piece had landed in Henry's lap, then give him a rough value for it. Once or twice he had even urged the trustees of the Museum to purchase one of Henry's items for the permanent collection. But this time was different. Henry had barely pulled the first clay tablet from his bag when Ernest all but recoiled, refusing even to touch it.

'Where has this come from, Henry?'

'From Jordan, Ernest.'

'Don't insult me. *Via* Jordan, possibly. But I think we both know where this comes from.'

'Isn't that what makes it worth so much?'

'Theoretically.'

'How do you mean?'

'I mean that nobody with half a brain cell is going to buy this stuff. It's radioactive. There are half a dozen conventions banning the trade in looted antiquities from Iraq.'

'Ssssh!' Then in a whisper, 'Aren't you going to examine it? Aren't you even curious?'

'Of course I am. But this is one of the greatest cultural crimes in human history, Henry. I won't be an accomplice to it. I should really call the police this second and have you arrested.'

'You won't tell anyone, will you?'

'No. But I should. Go. And take that bag of swag with you.'

Henry refused to be disheartened. Freundel was just a goodie-goodie, always had been. But he was right. The I-word had become a taboo in the antiquities trade. Governments had got heavy on stolen Iraqi goods and most collectors and buyers were fighting shy. Wait for the dust to settle, they said. Wait till London and Washington have got something else to worry about, something even more embarrassing than the rape of Baghdad, and then we can talk. For now, we'd rather not.

The only solution was to give Jaafar's hoard a patina of legitimacy. If he could make it look legit, then he could begin the more pleasurable task of selling it. But no one would risk buying any of these treasures if they lacked 'provenance'. It would be too risky: any day they could be seized and repatriated to Iraq, with meagre compensation. The world's collectors had seen what happened to the Munchs and Klimts that had been looted by the Nazis. Their new owners had to give them up, even decades later. No multi-millionaire wanted to repeat that mistake.

Henry Blyth-Pullen waited a day or two then called up an old academic acquaintance, Paul Cree, one with even less money and far fewer scruples than Ernest. Henry suggested they operate in the usual way. Cree would see the items, take photographs of them, then submit an article for one of the journals, perhaps *Minerva* or the *Burlington Magazine*, which specialized in publicizing new finds. Once they had been written about in a respectable outlet, they would be on a fast track to legitimacy; the aura around them would change. They would no longer be looted, but rather *discovered*. Their history would be entered and logged in neat black and white type. Future buyers could check the *Burlington Magazine* and see that Henry was not flogging any old rubbish but rather works that had featured in a prestigious journal: *I happen to have a copy right here, would sir perhaps like to take a look?* In return Cree would be compensated for his time and expertise. In other words, he would either get a wad of twenties from Henry's Bond Street till or, less likely, a slice of the profits from the eventual sale.

But even the shabby Cree would not do business.

'I'm sorry Henry, dear boy—'

The 'dear boy' was a particular irritant to Henry, who knew it was hardly natural lingo for a comprehensive boy from Bedfordshire, which is all Neather was.

'—I'm sorry, but the mags have all clammed up. Tighter than a nun's whatchamacallit these days. They won't feature just anything. Not any more.'

'But, Paul, this is not just anything.'

'I know old boy, I know. But the *journeaux* worry when things might have, how shall we put it, a dubious provenance.'

'Dubious?'

'If they've fallen off the back of a Baghdad lorry. After Iraq, everyone's lost their bloody marbles.'

'What am I supposed to do?'

'I'm sorry, Henry. But you'll just have to find another way.'

Henry chose not to relay any of this to al-Naasri, but the messages the Jordanian was leaving on his voicemail were getting less and less friendly.

'I need to speak to you, Henry. Remember, those souvenirs belong to me and cost me a lot of money. I hope you are not letting me down. For your sake.'

Henry was beginning to sweat. He had stashed the items in the heaviest, double-doored safe in the shop, but he was still anxious. He knew these were items of serious value: Jaafar would not have taken such painstaking care to disguise them if they were not.

He called Lucinda at Sotheby's, a move that always smacked of desperation.

'Hello, darling,' she drawled, audibly exhaling cigarette smoke. 'What do you want this time?'

'Lucinda! What makes you think I want anything?'

'Because you never, ever ring me unless you want something.'

'That's not true,' Henry said, even though it was. Apart from one highly regrettable snog tumbling out of the Christie's Christmas party, their relationship had only ever been about what Henry could get out of her. Maybe including the highly regrettable snog. If he thought about it, about the girl who, in their college days, had been quite a beauty but who had descended rapidly into blowsy, he would have felt sad for Lucinda. But Henry didn't think about it.

'On the contrary, I have something of an opportunity.'

He went to see her that same afternoon, Lucinda being easily enticed by the promise of a gin and tonic afterwards.

'So what are these delights you have to show me, Henry?'

He produced a small jewellery box, holding it in the palm of his right hand.

'Oh, Henry, you're not going to propose, are you? Here?'

Henry rolled his eyes indulgently, then popped open the box, revealing a pair of fine gold earrings, each one consisting of a single leaf. Extracting them from the charm bracelets and putting them back together had taken a delicate touch, but it had not been too difficult. Luckily the earrings had been photographed more than once, and he had found a clear colour picture in a reference book. 'Photo reproduced by kind permission of the National Museum of Antiquities, Baghdad,' the caption had said.

'Good God, Henry. Those are . . . those are . . .'

'Four thousand five hundred years old.'

'Magnificent was what I was going to say. Four thousand five hundred years old? Incredible.'

'You know what I want you to do, don't you?'

'I can guess. But why don't you tell me?'

'I want you to sell them. So that I can buy them off you.'

'And that way they're kosher. "Purchased under auction at Sotheby's".'

'Lucinda, that's what I love about you. So quick.'

'Except you don't love me, Henry. Anyway, it's impossible.'

'Why?'

'Well, let's say we were actually allowed to sell pieces from . . . *there*. If we were, these would go for an absolute bloody fortune. They're priceless. Far out of your reach. We'd have to lie about what they were. And that would defeat the object rather, wouldn't it?'

'You could say they've been bought from a private collector in Jordan. That is in fact how I got them.'

'Except we all know what private collector means, don't we? Come on, Henry. Everyone's on the lookout for stuff from you-know-where. It's the kiss of death. We can't touch it.'

Henry stared into the puddle of gin at the bottom of his glass. 'Well, what the hell am I going to do? I have to sell this stuff somehow.'

'In the old days, I could have introduced you to some very rich people who would have been happy to take them from you on the QT. But it's different now. This whole ghastly Nazi business has everyone terrified. Unless you can give them ten certificates in triplicate, signed and countersigned, no one will buy a bloody thing.'

'What would you do?'

'I'd sit tight, darling. Eventually this stuff will be in major demand. It's too good to go to waste. But now is not the time.'

When Henry spoke to Jaafar al-Naasri that evening it was only after he had fortified himself with two more stiff drinks. He prepared a script for what he would say, which he delivered with much less fluency than he had planned, the fault of the alcohol and his nerves. But he spat out his basic message. Jaafar would have to be patient and he would have to trust him. Henry would hold back on the prestige, high-value items, which he could continue to keep in the showroom safe or, if Jaafar wished, they could be transferred to a safety deposit box at Henry's private bank, an institution known for its discretion. They would wait till the market was more propitious. 'You'll get the same story all over the world, Jaafar,' Henry told him when the Jordanian threatened to take his custom to a New York dealer. 'The Americans are even more uptight on all this than we are.'

Besides, it was not all gloom and doom. Henry had held back some good news, to lighten the call. For the less glamorous items, he had a plan, a way to realize some value sooner rather than later. No, it would not be wise to go into details over the phone. But Henry knew exactly where those clay tablets would be going. And he would take them there himself.

CHAPTER TWENTY-TWO

JERUSALEM, WEDNESDAY, 3.14PM

'I hate the media in this country, I really do.' Uri was standing at the window, pulling back the curtain just enough to see the street outside.

'Hmm.'

'They're like vultures. Look at them, Channel 2 outside in their satellite TV truck. It's not enough they all had to come here to show the world the death of my parents. They have to stay.'

'Not only in this country, Uri.' Maggie was not looking in his direction, but keeping her eye fixed on the computer. She was about to try out her hunch on the gmail account she had discovered on Shimon Guttman's computer. She logged in as Saeb Nastayib, the name of the man who had sent those mysterious last emails to Ahmed Nour. And, as it happens, an approximate translation of the name Shimon Guttman. For the password, she tried Vladimir as before. 'Login failed.' *Damn.*

She pushed the swivel chair away from the desk, got to her feet and stretched. The worst thing about this line of work, she remembered, was the lack of exercise. As she stretched her arms backwards, her hands meeting in a knot behind her back, she caught Uri's gaze and realized that, without intending to, she was pushing her breasts forward: his eyes had widened. She hastily repositioned her arms, but she could tell that the image lingered.

'We need to crack this password thing, Uri. The prompt seems to demand ten characters: Vladimir is only eight.'

'He always did Vladimir, on everything.'

'So we need two more letters.' She opened up a new window, Googled Jabotinsky and discovered his alternative, Hebrew name: Ze'ev.

'OK,' she said, typing in VladimirZJ. Nothing. VladimirJ1. Also nothing. VZJabotins. VZJabotin1. She went through at least a dozen permutations.

'What about a number? What if he did Vladimir12 or Vladimir99? Is there any two digit number that might be significant?'

'Try 48. The year the state was established.'

'Oh, that's good.' She spoke as she typed: 'Vladimir48.'

Login failed.

Uri came over to the desk, standing by her side. He bent down, to get a closer look at the screen. She could see the stubble on his cheek.

'I really thought that would work,' he said. 'Maybe I am wrong about Vladimir—'

'Or maybe we just got the year wrong. For a right-wing—' She caught herself just in time. 'For a passionate nationalist like your father, there's one year that is just as important as 1948. Maybe even more so.'

She typed in Vladimir67 and suddenly the screen altered. An egg-timer graphic appeared, and a new page began loading: the email inbox of Saeb Nastayib.

At the top of the page, still in bold and therefore unread, was a name which gave Maggie a start: Ahmed Nour. She looked at the time the email was sent: 11.25pm on Tuesday evening, a good twelve hours after he was reported dead. She clicked the message open.

Who are you? And why were you contacting my father?

'It seems Mr Nour Junior knew as little about his father as you did about yours.'

'It could be a woman. Could be his daughter.'

'Uri, do you mind if we look at the messages your father sent?'

'Aren't you going to reply?'

'I want to think about it. Let's see what these two had been saying to each other first.'

She brought up the sent messages, all of which were to Ahmed Nour. This was obviously the back channel the two men had used, an Arabic name so that if anyone was monitoring Nour's email, they would have no grounds for suspicion.

The last one was sent at 6.08pm on Saturday, just a few hours before the peace rally at which Guttman was shot dead.

Ahmed, we have the most urgent matter to discuss. I have tried your telephone but without success. Are you able to meet me in Geneva?
Saeb

Maggie instantly scrolled down to the next message, sent at 3.58pm that same day.

My dear Ahmed, I hope you got my earlier message. Do let me know if your plans permit a trip to Geneva, hopefully in the very near future. We have much to talk about.
My best wishes,
Saeb

There was another at 10.14am, and two the previous evening. All of them mentioning a planned trip to Geneva. As far as Maggie could see, Ahmed Nour had not replied to any of them.

Had they fallen out? Was Ahmed blanking his Israeli colleague? And what was all this about an upcoming trip to Geneva?

Uri had left the piles of papers and pulled up a second chair. He was looking at the screen, but it was clear from his facial expression that he was as baffled as she was. Predicting her question, he turned to her, shaking his head. 'I didn't even know my father had been to Geneva.'

'It seems there was quite a bit about him you didn't know. Did he keep any kind of diary? You know, a desk planner.'

Uri began rummaging, at one point on hands and knees, eyeing the book shelves side on, while she went back to the computer. She called up the browser's history, seeing the cache of web pages Guttman had consulted in the last days of his life, looking for a travel agent, Swissair, a guide to hotels in Geneva, anything which might yield a clue as to what Guttman and Nour were planning. This connection between the two men, unlikely and unknown to those closest to them both, was intriguing. And she felt sure it was connected to what was happening right now, the first turns of a cycle of violence that would, if left unchecked, destroy the peace process.

'Uri, pass me the cellphone again.'

She grabbed it, realizing that she had made a stupid oversight. She had looked at the text messages, all of which had doubtless been wiped, but had not checked the call register, the record of outgoing calls. She stabbed at the keys until she pulled up the dialled numbers. There, at the top, was a call made on Saturday afternoon. It showed up on the display not as a number, but a name.

'Uri, who's Baruch Kishon?'

'At last, something that is not a mystery. He is a very famous journalist in Israel. He writes a column in *Maariv*. The settlers love him; he has been denouncing Yariv every week for a year. He and my father were great friends.'

'Well, I think we ought to pay Mr Kishon a visit. Right now.'

CHAPTER TWENTY-THREE

JERUSALEM, WEDNESDAY, 3.10PM

Amir Tal was working hard to conceal his amazement, even his excitement. He had dealt with intelligence often; since taking this job in the Prime Minister's bureau, it was hard to avoid it. Reports, assessments, analyses, they all crossed his desk.

But he had never seen how it was done, how the raw information that formed that paper mountain was gathered. His army service had kept him inside the belly of an armoured personnel carrier. It was prestigious enough – he served in the Golani Brigade – but nothing like this. Now, in this office, he was seeing how it worked, up close. And, best of all, he was the man in charge.

'Can I listen?' he said, gesturing at the woman who sat at the centre of the multiple computer screens, with what looked like a DJ's mixing desk before her. She took off her headphones and gave them to Tal, who wore them the way she had, one ear on, one ear off.

'The man's voice you hear is Uri Guttman, son of the deceased. The woman's voice is the American, Maggie Costello.'

'Irish,' Tal murmured, mainly to himself. The voices were remarkably clear. Costello was asking Guttman for his father's cellphone. Tal could even hear papers rustling. Say what you like about the Shin Bet, they were an impressive bunch: they had mounted this entire surveillance operation within a few hours of his demanding it.

'And you can do all this from that TV satellite truck parked outside?'

'With directional microphones aimed at the windows – through the glass – you can do a lot. Better if you have something on the inside too.'

'Which you don't. So how come the sound's so good?'

The woman was plugging in a second pair of headphones into the side of the computer, so that she could listen in at the same time. She gave Tal a crooked smile.

'You *do* have something in there! How?' He quickly altered his features: mustn't look too eager.

'Well, there have been a lot of flowers arriving in that house, and food parcels, too. Let's just say one of the bouquets does more than look nice.'

Amir took off the headphones, and put his hand on the shoulder of the woman. *Keep up the good work.*

There was no point listening any further. Another operative was listening closely, taking a shorthand note. Anything of substance, he would report it immediately.

'Amir, you might want to see this.' It was the man who had remained glued to a computer screen since they had got here, at least as far as Tal could tell. He had wondered what this man was up to, but hadn't dared ask.

Now what he saw disappointed him. It was a standard webmail page, an inbox no different from the one he used for his personal correspondence at home. Nothing hi-tech or espionage about that.

And then he saw it. The cursor moving around the screen without any apparent human intervention; the operator's hands remained still.

'What is this?'

'You're looking at Shimon Guttman's computer, the one his son and that woman are working on right now.'

'Are these surveillance pictures?'

The man smiled in a way Tal didn't like, as if he was entertaining a question from a slow child.

'No, there's no hidden camera. Just a simple SilentNight program.' He waited a beat or two – standard techie practice, to let the ignorance of the explainee sink in – then went on: 'It's a neat little program that installs itself on someone else's machine and gains the kind of system-level privileges we need.' He could see that the penny had not yet dropped. 'It gives us total access to their computer. We could operate it remotely, from here, if we wanted to.'

'What, I could start typing at this keyboard, and it would show up on their screen?'

'Yep. But don't do it!' He placed his hand protectively over the keyboard and cursor, like a swot shielding his exam paper to prevent the other kids taking a peek. 'If they see their cursor moving around, they'll know we're onto them. Either that, or they'll think it's Guttman's ghost trying to freak them out.'

'So we just watch.'

'Exactly. Anything they type, I see it. Right now, for example, they're trying to hack into his gmail account.'

The woman with the headphones called out. 'OK, we have a phone call. Costello's just dialled Khalil al-Shafi in Ramallah.' Tal headed over, waiting to be passed a set of headphones of his own. But the woman was concentrating too hard, listening to each word, to help the boss. By the time she had connected him, the phone call was over. Instead he heard Maggie Costello speaking to Uri Guttman.

'*OK. What does* nas tayib *mean*?'

A moment later and it was the computer operator who was

getting excited, forcing Amir Tal to rush back to his side. He felt slightly ridiculous, like a kid at a video arcade, watching as his older brothers played games, hopping from one machine to another to keep up with the action.

The computer guy was wide-eyed. 'Hey, this is *interesting.*'

'What are they doing?'

'Watch that window right there. They're logging on as that name we just heard. Saeb Nastayib. Now they're trying different passwords.' A series of asterisks appeared in the password box on the screen. The operator clicked open a small window and suddenly real characters appeared, one by one. 'Having a go at VladimirJ. Nope.'

'How can you see that? Even their screen doesn't show up the password.'

'That's why this SilentNight programme is such a beauty. It records every keystroke. So even if the screen doesn't show what buttons they pressed, we can still see them. Oops, Vladimir48. Wrong again.'

'OK, let me know when you have something useful.'

Amir Tal didn't have long to wait. Within ten minutes the surveillance team parked in the Channel 2 truck outside the Guttman residence reported that Costello and Guttman Junior had left the house, apparently heading for the home of journalist Baruch Kishon. Meanwhile, computer analysis suggested a correspondence between the late Shimon Guttman and the late Ahmed Nour, the former using an Arab codename, combined with the intensely Zionist password of Vladimir67. They were arranging to meet in Geneva.

'OK, gather round, people,' Tal began, enjoying taking command. 'I want whatever intel we can get on Nour: who was he, why did he die and what the hell was he talking about with Shimon Guttman? What were they planning? Was this some kind of alliance of the extremes, two guys both opposed to the peace process agreeing to work together to derail the talks? Talk to Mossad in Geneva. Find out whether they'd met before. Travel plans for the last year. If that yields nothing, go back further. Everything you can get, I want it.

'Also Khalil al-Shafi. What's he been saying to Costello? Why did she call him? And what's his precise connection to Ahmed Nour? We need answers on this right away. Is he onside for these peace talks or not? If he is sabotaging from the inside, I want to know about it.

'I hope the most crucial thing goes without saying. We keep following Costello and Guttman. And, whatever happens, we get to Baruch Kishon before they do. Go!'

CHAPTER TWENTY-FOUR

THE AFULA-BET SHEAN ROAD,
NORTHERN ISRAEL, WEDNESDAY, 8.15PM

Their orders were very clear. Get in, search and possibly destroy, get out. Above all, don't get caught. The Director of Operations had spelled it out: this was not to be a suicide mission.

There were four of them in the car. They had not met before and only went by the names they had been given: Ziad, Daoud, Marwan and Salim. Ziad would be in charge.

He checked his watch and worried again that this operation had begun with a fatal flaw. It was too early. Much better to strike in the dead of night. But the boss had said it was urgent; no time to waste.

'OK. Turn off here.' It was a slip road, narrowing rapidly into a dirt track. Suitable for a tractor, but tricky for a rented Subaru. 'Drive off, into the crops. OK. Kill the engine.'

It was a cotton field, planted high enough to conceal a car, just as they had been briefed. The reconnaissance boys had done a good job.

The four men began to change into black clothing. Ziad handed each of them balaclavas to put over their faces and made sure they had removed any other form of identification. Each of them had a small torch in his pocket, a lighter, a knife and a Micro Uzi submachine gun. Ziad and Marwan had cyclists' water pouches strapped to their backs. Both of these contained petrol.

They all knew the plan: they would walk twenty minutes through the fields belonging to the kibbutz until they were within sight of their target. Once they were certain no one was around, they would move fast and get out.

Ziad could see the lights of the perimeter. Soon the crops would give way to the asphalt of the visitors' car park and service roads. They would be lit too. This would be the area of greatest danger.

Sure enough, he soon saw the sign in English and Hebrew, welcoming guests to 'Kibbutz Hephziba, Home of the Legendary Bet Alpha Synagogue'. Silently, he gave the order to duck down. One at a time, the four men ran in a low crouch towards the area Ziad's map had described as the site entrance. The door was locked, as anticipated. He gave the nod to Marwan, who produced a wire and jimmied the door open. They slipped in, Ziad looking back to make sure no one had seen the movement of the door in the lamplight of the car park.

Inside there was complete darkness. The men waited till they were deep within before switching on their torches: too risky to let light leak out through the glass walls of this visitors' centre. Ziad was first to use his, shining it down on the centrepiece of this location, the treasure that had brought sightseers here since the 1930s.

It was a Roman-style mosaic, perfectly intact, stretching some ten metres long and five metres wide. Even in this light, Ziad could see the clarity of the colours formed by the countless tiny squares: yellows, greens, ochres, browns, a deep wine red, a coarser shade like reddish brick as well as sharp blacks, whites and multiple variants of grey. As he had been told, the floor was divided into three distinct panels. Furthest away, what seemed to be a sketch of a synagogue, including a pair of traditional Jewish candelabra, the menorah. At the bottom, a primitive, almost childlike, depiction of Abraham's sacrifice of his son Isaac.

But the eye was drawn immediately to the larger, middle panel. It showed a circle, divided into twelve segments, one for each sign of the zodiac. Ziad let his torch pick out each image, stopping to take in the clearest: a scorpion, next to it a pair of twins, a ram, an archer. He had not meant to linger, but he couldn't help it. This ancient artwork, over fifteen hundred years old, was so vivid that it was impossible to look away.

'OK, you know what to do.' Marwan began checking the top panel, Daoud the lower, while Salim examined the central zodiac. Even the slightest sign of recent activity – fresh digging or tampering of any kind – and they were to summon the others. If something had been buried here in the last few days, they were to find it.

Ziad, meanwhile, had specific instructions. He was to locate the museum office – and take it apart, searching it meticulously. Every drawer, every filing cabinet. If there was a safe, he should get it open and leave not a speck of dust unexamined. The Director had been clear: 'He needed to hide this item in a hurry. He will not have been able to conceal it well. If it's there, you'll find it.'

Ziad worked through the desk drawers first. The usual crap: rubber bands, business cards, sticky tape, envelopes. There was an old metal box, like the kind that used to hold pipe tobacco, which seemed to have potential: it felt the right weight. But inside was simply a bundle of Friends of the Museum membership cards, tied together so that in the tin they sounded like a single thick object.

He was starting on the filing cabinet when he heard a noise, the crunch of a foot on the gravel outside. A beat later, and the room filled with a sweep of torchlight, as if a beam had been passed across the whole exterior of the building.

'Mee zeh?' Who's there?

Without needing an order from Ziad, the team instantly killed their own flashlights and froze. Do that and, most times, a night-watchman will tell himself that what he had seen was a trick of the light, a reflection from his own torch, and walk away. Given the choice of going to the bother of opening a locked building or doing nothing, lethargy usually won out. The unheralded friend of intruders and thieves the world over: the sheer indolence of security staff.

But this man was different. He advanced, the beam thrown by his torch getting larger as he approached the glass door. Ziad, stock still in the office, his hand gripping the drawer he had just pulled out of the filing cabinet, heard the jangle of keys. In a second, this guard would discover that the lock had been forced.

There was no time to lose. Ziad drew his weapon from the holster and stepped out into the main lobby, where he had a clear line of sight to the door. He saw the guard look up and notice not Ziad or the others, but their shadows, now giant against the walls, rendered colossal by the guard's very own torch. Without hesitation, Ziad aimed his Micro Uzi and sent a 9mm-calibre bullet straight through the glass and into the man's skull.

The sound of the door shattering, and the guard's brain exploding, were the cue for an immediate change of tactic. His aim was no longer to find the object but to disguise the nature of this mission. Ziad returned to the office and, abandoning his meticulous examination, now turned the place upside down. He yanked out each desk drawer, emptying its contents onto the floor, finding nothing. Next, he shoved the filing cabinets to the ground, before sweeping the desk with a single movement of his arm, so that every item was sent flying. Then, he used his gun to break each window in turn.

He turned around to find Marwan and Daoud, carrying the corpse of the guard like a stretcher. Silently they counted one, two, three then swung his body onto the ground, amid all the debris of the office. There was a crunch as the flesh landed on the shattered glass; then, in a single, smooth action, Marwan removed the cyclist's water pouch from his back, took off the cap and began dousing the room with petrol.

Outside Salam was switching his torch back on, lighting up a wall covered in panels explaining the Bet Alpha exhibit. He produced a can of spray paint and, slowly and calmly, daubed the wall in red graffiti. In Arabic he wrote: 'No peace for Israel till there is justice for Palestine. No sleep for Bet Alpha till there is sleep for Jenin'.

His work done, he turned to the other three who were now standing outside the door of the museum office. A silent, interrogatory look to each of them – *Ready? Ready?* – then Ziad took his cigarette lighter, sparked it up and threw it to the ground, where it made instant contact with the petrol-soaked body of the security guard.

The flames erupted immediately, leaping so high that Ziad and the team could see them for most of their twenty-minute, wordless return hike through the fields of the kibbutz. The first fire engine arrived at about the same time the quartet found the car they had left in the cotton fields. As they drove back to Afula, they counted at least two more fire trucks and several police cars, heading in the opposite direction. Ziad reached for his cellphone to send a text message to the Director: 'The hiding place is no more.'

CHAPTER TWENTY-FIVE

BEN-GURION AIRPORT, FIVE WEEKS EARLIER

Henry Blyth-Pullen hated flying at the best of times. Even before the war on bloody terror, and the fear that some maniac with a pair of scissors was going to ram the plane into Big Ben, he had been terrified of the damn things. Take-off was the worst. While everyone else was flicking through the *Daily Telegraph* or *Hello!* magazine, he would be gripping the buckle of his seat belt until his knuckles turned white. The grinding engines, the straining to lift off the ground, all of it sounded dangerous to Henry. And not just dangerous. *Unnatural.* As if this huge hunk of metal was meant to float in the air, defying gravity if not the will of the Almighty. No wonder there were so many accidents: it was God's way of telling us to know our place, to keep our feet on the ground. Remember Icarus . . .

Henry gave himself this lecture every time he strapped himself into one of the bloody contraptions. It had acquired the status of a ritual. Though he would never admit to superstition, Henry had come to believe his little mental apology to the Creator – expressing regret for mankind's hubris in taking to the skies – had protected him. If he ever failed to think it, if he took flying for granted, why, then the plane was sure to tumble through the clouds like a stone.

This time, though, Henry's anxiety had had days to build, long before he got anywhere near the runway. Inside his luggage was a consignment of clay tablets which he had decided to offload three thousand miles away from London. They would not make his fortune – the items that could do that were safely stashed away in a safe, waiting for a change in the political climate – but they would at least make his monthly bank balance look a little bonnier. Besides, he needed to tell Jaafar al-Naasri he had at least sold something. The fact that he was taking the goods back to Jaafar's very own patch, or near as dammit, was a detail he would not share. Not with anyone, as it happened. It smacked so much of selling sand to the Sahara, that he was embarrassed by it.

How to get them there, that was the issue. You couldn't just pitch up with a bag-load of bloody precious antiquities. Jaafar had gone to great lengths to get them out; Henry couldn't just waltz them back in.

As it happens, it was lovable old Lucinda who hit on the answer. Not consciously of course, she wasn't *that* bright. No, she just stumbled on it. She was burbling on about some ex-pat friends of hers who'd set up home in Barbados or somewhere, how they didn't miss the English weather – no fear! – they didn't miss the telly, but the one thing they did miss was the chocolate. Or choccy, as Lucinda, flush with her third G&T, put it. 'Apparently the choccy there doesn't taste of anything,' she had said, halfway towards slurring. 'Not even real chocolate. Made with vegetable extract or something.' Henry was barely listening. 'Anyway, now every time a friend comes over from Blighty, they're under strict orders to bring a *caseload* of Fruit & Nut, Dairy Milk and as much Green & Black as they can afford. Sophie says they've both put on at least a stone . . .'

That was it, Henry had realized before Lucinda had even finished speaking. On his way home that night he had stopped at a garage, and picked up more chocolate than he had bought in his life, one of almost every bar on the market. The next day he had sat in the back office at the showroom, experimenting with a clay tablet in one hand and an Aero or Twix in the other, trying to find a perfect match for length, width, thickness and, crucially, weight. Finally, he struck gold with a mid-size bar of Whole Nut.

Methodically, he removed the paper sleeve, taking care not to tear it. Then he unfolded the inner foil, as if handling the most precious gold leaf. He removed the chocolate bar, putting the clay tablet in its place. Then, to both the head and foot of the bar, he glued two rows of Whole Nut, each row three squares wide. Then he refolded the foil and sheathed the whole hybrid chocolate-and-clay bar back in its paper wrapper. He got through close to a hundred bars that way, ripping the foil, tearing the paper, until finally he had twenty perfect specimens ready to transport to his fictitious, but chocolate-hungry ex-pat relatives.

He had laid them neatly in his small carry-on suitcase. He had wondered about packing them into a strongbox for safekeeping, but he knew that would look suspicious: Cadbury's was good, but it wasn't that good. So he just had to chance it, leaving them in his bag as casually as if they really were nothing more than a high-fat treat for a nephew or niece missing home.

The security check at Heathrow was his first worry. Talk of liquid explosives on planes had not only given nervous fliers like Henry more to panic about, it also led airport staff to be much more vigilant about previously ignored food items. But, Henry told himself, if he was stopped he would keep calm and stick to his story.

He placed the bag on the conveyer belt and walked through the metal detector, as nonchalantly as he could manage.

'Excuse me, sir,' one of the airport staff had said, stretching his arms out wide, inviting Henry to do the same. Some forgotten change in Henry's trouser pocket had set off the beeper. They waved him forward.

He reached for the bag, just off the belt, exhaling his relief.

A hand stopped his. 'One moment please, sir. Can you open the bag for me?'

'Yes, of course.' Henry smiled and unzipped the case.

'A computer?'

'Yes.'

'The sign says, computers must go in separately, sir. Please will you do it again?'

Henry could feel his hands go clammy. What were the chances that the twenty chocolate bars could evade discovery *twice*?

And yet, as the bag went through a second time, he saw the man charged with examining the x-ray monitor turn away to share a joke with his colleague. He stayed away from the screen for three or four seconds, just as the clay tablets, now bereft of the computer which had shielded them the first time around, lay exposed and in full view. Henry went on his way.

While Henry's fellow passengers watched the in-flight film, Henry replayed that scene in his head over and over, thanking God, Jesus and anyone else who came to mind for his luck. But as the plane began its descent for Tel Aviv, relief at the first stage of his journey gave way to anxiety about the next.

He had no luggage to collect, so he headed straight for immigration control.

'And why you are in Israel?' the girl, who could have been no more than eighteen, asked him.

'I'm visiting my nephew who' s studying here.'

'And where is he studying?'

'At the Hebrew University. In Jerusalem.' Henry had a couple of Jewish friends whom he'd called up last week: as casually as he could, he had asked after their sons, both of whom were currently on gap years, and promptly taken down and memorized all the details.

Only one more stop: Customs. As a white middle-aged man, the sorry truth was that he had always passed through customs at Heathrow like a breeze, watching the poor souls, almost always black or Asian, who were asked to empty out their suitcases, take out their clothes and squeeze every last tube of toothpaste. Racism was a hideous thing to behold, of course, but for a traveller like Henry Blyth-Pullen, it could be rather convenient.

Except this time he was stopped, the first time it had ever happened. A bored, unshaven officer waved him over to one side and then nodded wordlessly at Henry's suitcase, which he'd been wheeling behind him. Henry pulled it up onto the metal counter between them and unzipped it.

The guard rifled through the Y-fronts, socks, toilet bag, before coming to the stash of chocolate. He looked up at Henry, raising a sceptical eyebrow.

'And what is this?'

'It's chocolate.'

'Why you bring so much?'

'It's for my nephew. He misses home.'

'Can I open it?'

'Sure. Why don't I help?'

Henry was certain his hands were trembling, but he kept them busy enough so that the officer wouldn't notice. He picked a bar at random, pushed up the chocolate an inch, just as he had practised on his kitchen table, and tore off the foil to reveal a solid three squares of English milk chocolate.

'OK.'

Without thinking, Henry broke off the chocolate and offered it to the customs official, an expression that said 'peace offering?' on his face. The man refused and then nodded his head towards the exit. Henry's examination was over. Which was lucky, because if the guard had looked closely he would have seen the next row of the bar he had tested was strangely lacking in nuts, whether whole or half, and was instead unappetizingly solid.

Clutching the handle of his suitcase more tightly than ever, Henry left the airport and joined the queue for a taxi. When it came to his turn, he said loudly, pumped up with relief, 'Jerusalem please. To the Old City market.'

CHAPTER TWENTY-SIX

Tel Aviv, Israel, Wednesday, 8.45pm

For a small country, Maggie couldn't help thinking, Israel couldn't half be confusing. They had been driving less than an hour and yet she felt as if she had travelled through time. If Jerusalem was a town carved in the pale stone of Biblical times, each rock, each narrow cobbled path, coated in the stale must of ancient history, Tel Aviv was noisily, brashly, chokingly modern. On the horizon were gleaming skyscrapers, their highest storeys lit like checkerboards, and by the roadside line after line of concrete apartment blocks, their roofs covered with solar panels and bulbous cylinders which, Uri explained, were hot water tanks. As they pulled off the highway and into the city streets, Maggie was transfixed by the frenzy of billboards and shoppers, burger bars and pavement cafés, traffic jams and office blocks, girls in crop-tops and boys whose hair peaked in a series of peroxide spikes. Just a short drive from Jerusalem, where holiness hung like a cloud, Tel Aviv seemed a temple to throbbing, urgent profanity.

'OK, his building is number six. Let's park here.' They were on Mapu Street, which, judging by the class of cars parked at the kerb, seemed to be one of Tel Aviv's more upscale neighbourhoods. The building itself was nothing special, rendered in the same white concrete. They walked through a kind of underpass, past the lines of metal mailboxes, and found the entrance and its intercom. Uri pressed number seventy-two.

There was no reply. Impatient, Maggie reached past Uri and pressed the button again, for much longer. Still nothing.

'Try the phone again.'

'It's been on voicemail all afternoon.'

'And you're sure this is the right apartment?'

'I'm sure.'

Maggie began pacing. 'How come there's nobody in? They can't all be out.'

'There is no "they". It's just him.'

Maggie stopped, puzzled.

'He's divorced. Lives alone.'

'Bollocks. What the hell can we do now?'

'We could break in.'

Maggie suddenly became aware of the cold. What on earth was she doing here, shivering on a Tel Aviv street corner when she should have been picking out sofa-beds in Georgetown? She should be home, with Edward, cosy on their couch, ordering takeout, watching TV or whatever it was normal people did once they stopped being twenty-five-year-old maniacs who worked all hours, hopping from one nuthouse country to the next. Edward had managed it, making the transition from backpacking idealist to Washington suit, so why couldn't she? God knows, she had tried. Maybe she should just call Judd Bonham and tell him she was pulling out. They weren't using her properly anyway. She was a mediator, for Christ's sake, she should be in the room. Not playing at being a bloody amateur detective. She reached into her pocket and felt her cellphone.

But she knew what Bonham would say. That there was no point in her being in the room until the two sides were ready. And the way things were going, that moment was getting more remote by the day. Pretty soon, there'd be no room to be in. Her job was to get the two sides back on track, and that meant closing down this Guttman/Nour problem, whatever it was. They couldn't afford for her to fail. She knew, better than anyone, what happened if a peace effort came close only to fall apart. For an instant she saw it again, the flash of memory she worked so hard to keep out. She had to succeed. Otherwise, that would be her career, even her life story. It would be reduced to one single, lethal mistake.

Quietly, she turned back to Uri and said, 'No, we can't break in. Imagine if we got caught: I'm an official of the United States government.'

'I could do it.'

'Yeah, but you're with me, aren't you? Still trouble. Is there any other way?'

Uri shook his head and punched his fist against the door of the building, sustaining what looked like serious pain without so much as a wince.

'All right,' said Maggie, turning away. 'Let's think. What happened when you called the newspaper?'

'It was just the night news desk – said they didn't know the movements of their columnists. Gave me his cellphone number.'

'Which we already had.'

The silence lasted for more than a minute, Maggie straining to think of a next move. Then, suddenly, Uri leapt to his feet and all but sprinted back to the car.

'Uri? Uri, what is it?'

'Just get in the car.'

As they drove, Uri explained that in the army he had dated a girl whose brother had gone to India with Baruch Kishon's son. When he saw Maggie's face, a scrunch of incredulity, he smiled and said only, 'Israel's a small country.'

A few calls later and he had a cellphone number for Eyal

Kishon. Uri had to shout into the phone: Eyal was in a club. Uri tried explaining the situation, but it was no good. They would have to go there.

While they drove, Uri put on the radio news, giving a brief translation at the end of each story. Violence on the West Bank, some Palestinian children dead; Israeli tanks re-entering Gaza; more Hizbullah rockets in the north. Talks with the Palestinians now in the deep freeze. Maggie shook her head: this whole thing was unravelling. Then: 'A poll in America has the president five points behind. He did badly in the TV debate, apparently.' Last item: 'They're getting reports of a fire at a kibbutz in the north. Might be arson.'

They parked on Yad Harutzim Street and walked straight into the Blondie club. The noise was immediate, a pounding rhythm that Maggie could feel in her guts. There was a steady bombardment of light, including one sharp, white beam that swept across the dance floor like a searchlight.

The place was hardly full, but already there seemed to be lithe, sweaty bodies in every corner. Maggie was struck by the range of faces. In front of her were two girls, blonde with porcelain skin, while just behind was a tall black man with an Afro and thin, sharp features. Dancing alongside were a man and woman, each with dark, corkscrew curls. Maggie thought back to the briefing pack Bonham had given her, the page about the multiple tribes of Israel: Russians, Ethiopians, the *Mizrachim*, those from Arab countries. They were all here.

Maggie caught a glimpse of herself on a mirrored wall and was sufficiently shocked by what she saw to stop and stare. All her working life, she had been the youngest in the room. At negotiations between middle-aged men, she was the novelty: not only a woman, but a young and, let's be honest, attractive woman. They didn't know what to make of her. How many times had she been asked when her boss, the mediator, would be along?

Or asked to be a love and bring three coffees over to the French delegation. Or told how nice it was to have some decoration in these dull, grey talks.

She had got used to it and, of course, used it to her advantage. It wrongfooted the negotiators, made them more candid than they intended to be. They said things to her they would not have said to a 'real' mediator, as if talks with her were a kind of dress rehearsal. Only once the deal was done would they fully understand that she was indeed the real thing. But her greatest asset was the competition. Without realizing it, these suits would compete for her attention. She first spotted it when she ran a back-channel session for the Sri Lankan civil war, held in a log cabin in Sweden. At mealtimes, she noticed, the participants would jostle to be seated near her. They wanted her to laugh at their jokes, to nod at their insights. They couldn't help themselves: it was how they were conditioned to behave around an attractive woman. But for her it was inestimably useful. Every little move she pushed them to make, inch by tortured inch, was one they knew would keep them in her affections. If they held out over this word in a treaty, or that line on a map, she would be disappointed in them. And they didn't want that.

But she didn't look like that here. Now, surrounded by these gorgeous creatures, none older than twenty-five, with their glowing skin and skimpy tops, she realized she must be the oldest person in the place. She saw the black trousers, Ann Taylor jacket and Agnes B shirt of her own outfit: fine for work, positively elegant when meeting diplomats and ministers. But here it was dull. And those crow's feet around her eyes, or the creases when she smiled . . .

'He's over there.'

Uri gestured towards a man sitting back watching the dancing, his hand around the neck of a beer bottle, nodding to the music. He looked part-stoned, part-drunk – and fully out of it.

Uri sat beside him and, after a brief, seated embrace, spoke into his ear. While they spoke, Maggie scoped the club. By the entrance she could see a man, newly arrived, who looked as out of place as she was. He wore rimless glasses, which declared him 'adult' amongst these partying children.

She could see from Eyal's expression that Uri had reached the point in the story where he had lost both his parents. Eyal was shaking his head and pulling on Uri's shoulder, as if initiating another hug. But Uri was already bringing out the cellphone to show Eyal that the last call Shimon Guttman had made had been to Baruch Kishon.

Eyal shrugged apologetically; he didn't know anything. Uri kept up the questions, now turning back to Maggie with snatches of translation. When had he last spoken with his father? On Sunday morning. His father was off on 'assignment'. Nothing unusual there. The old man was always going away; that's why he and Eyal's mother had broken up. Had he said anything about where he was going? Nothing Eyal could remember. Mind you, he had been off his face the night before. Eyal smiled.

'Eyal, did your father mention a trip to Geneva?'

Careful, thought Maggie.

'As in, like, Switzerland? No. He usually tells me when he's going abroad. Likes me to check on his apartment. Pretty anal that way.'

'So you don't think he's abroad?'

'Nope.'

'But you haven't spoken to him since Sunday? And you're not worried?'

'I wasn't worried. Till you guys started freaking me out.'

They drove back fast, with Eyal, no longer blissed out, in the back. Uri kept up the questioning, extracting only one more detail: that when Eyal and his father spoke on Sunday morning, Baruch

Kishon had seemed in a good mood. He said he had a 'hot' story to work on. Or maybe it was cool. Eyal couldn't remember.

The eleven o'clock news came on, Uri passing on only that the kibbutz arson story was now the lead item: they had found among the wreckage some charred human remains. An IDF spokesman said there was firm evidence that this was a terror attack, mounted by Palestinians from Jenin. Speculation was already mounting over the political fallout. This raid was bound to be seen as a threat to the already fragile peace talks in Jerusalem, and a further blow to the standing of Prime Minister Yariv.

Maggie pulled out her phone and saw that she had missed a call. The noise of the club had drowned it out, no doubt, dulling her senses even to the silent vibration of an incoming call. She listened to the voicemail: Davis, letting her know about Bet Alpha. *'An attack on a kibbutz now, Maggie. The Deputy Secretary asked me to give you this message. "Whatever else Maggie Costello is up to, remind her that her job is to stop relations between these two sides deteriorating any further. Make sure she's got that." OK, you got it, verbatim. Sorry to be the bearer of bad news.'*

The worst thing was, she couldn't argue. The Deputy Secretary was right: she had to keep the lid on this violence. And she knew how it would look, her taking off on some speculative quest involving anagrams and pottery patterns. Yet she was sure that the two key deaths, Guttman's and Nour's, were linked. Finding out how was surely the best way, maybe even the only way, to stop this current round of killing. The alternative was to hold an endless round of meetings where people would make the right noises – but the violence would just keep on going. She had been round that track before and was determined not to go round again.

They were at Kishon's apartment twenty minutes later. Eyal seemed nervous about opening up the place. After what he had heard about Uri's parents, he was clearly fearful of what he might find. He walked in first, switching on lights, calling out his father's name.

'Eyal, look around.' It was Uri, scoping the apartment as if it was a movie location. 'Look carefully. Tell us if you notice anything different, anything out of place. Anything at all.'

Maggie herself could see nothing: the place was preternaturally tidy. Anal was right. Mindful of her success at the Guttman house, she asked Eyal where his father worked. He directed her to a desk in the corner of the living room, while he went to check the bedroom.

'Hey, Eyal, there's no computer here.'

He reappeared in the doorway. 'Oh, yeah. I forgot. He always works on a laptop. That's the only machine he uses. Sorry.'

Damn. In this place, as neat as a mausoleum, it had been her best hope. There were no stray pieces of paper, no piles of books to work through. This was a dead end.

She took one last look at the desk. *Think, Maggie, think*. Just a phone, a fax, a blank message pad, a picture of what she assumed was Eyal and his sister as kids, and a pen in a stand. Nothing.

She stepped away, then turned back. She pulled the pad towards her, picked it up and held it up to the light.

'Uri! Come here!'

There, as if engraved into the page, were the inkless markings of what she hoped was Hebrew handwriting. She imagined it: Baruch Kishon taking the call from Shimon Guttman, scribbling a note on his message pad, peeling it off, rushing out the door – leaving the impression of the note on the page below.

Uri saw it, too. He held the piece of paper above his head, trying to divine its meaning through the ceiling light. He squinted and he grimaced until eventually he gave a small smile. 'It's a name,' he said. 'An Arabic name. The man we want is called Afif Aweida.'

CHAPTER TWENTY-SEVEN

JERUSALEM, THE PREVIOUS THURSDAY

This was the sound Shimon Guttman wanted to hear, the throb of carnival. The whistles, blown repeatedly; the steady pounding of dustbin lids; the clamour that could only be generated by a group of people strong in number and, above all, strong in conviction.

He had been at a hundred demonstrations in his time, but this one made him prouder than all the rest. The crowd, gathered here at Zion Square, was enormous, a mass of people packed together, some carrying placards, the rest either waving their fists in the air or clapping in unison. They looked striking, each one of them clad in orange. T-shirts, hats, even shorts and face-paint, all in the brightest, most luminous orange. But what made Shimon tremble with pride, a glow rising from deep within, was that this massed rally against Yariv and his treachery consisted entirely of the young.

When he had issued the call, he had no idea if it would be heeded. The conventional wisdom these days held that Israel's young had grown apathetic. They were the internet generation, more concerned with Google than the Golan, happier bumming around India or trekking in Nepal than pioneering in Judea or tilling the soil in Samaria. His own son, Uri, who had given up a career in army intelligence to pursue some limp-wristed job in films, was proof of the malaise.

Yet here was compelling evidence that such pessimism about the state of Israel's youth was misplaced. Look at them, Guttman thought, massed on the streets, determined to save their nation from the surrender and appeasement plotted by their own prime minister. Those of his contemporaries who always moaned about kids today, complaining that they wouldn't have the gumption to fight the way our lot did back in sixty-seven – they should be here now. This sight would soon shut them up.

For this was shaping up to be a fight, good and proper. Facing the army of orange, separated by a thin line of police and the odd news photographer and TV cameraman, was another crowd, nearly as packed, almost as vociferous. They had no single colour, but just as many placards as their opponents. He saw one, carefully placed near the news crews, that read simply, and in English: *Yes to Peace*.

Shimon Guttman had been at the head of the orange column – one of only a half dozen oldies granted such elevated status – but as the trouble started, they were ushered out of the way. Partly for the seniors' own safety, partly he suspected to allow the young men of action to get stuck in. From his vantage point on the sidelines he could see that this would soon descend into a medieval pitched battle, two armies charging at each other. All that was missing were the horses.

Soon a young man was emerging, an orange Venus from the water, out of the crowd, elevated by some hidden hand until he was able to stand unsteadily on somebody's shoulders to deliver his speech. As the youngster barked into a megaphone, Guttman concluded that he was an inexperienced speaker, unaware that, when amplified, it wasn't necessary to shout.

Shimon was smiling, reflecting back on his younger self, when a pleasing thought dawned on him. The movement he had helped build was, after all, in safe hands. Whatever perfidy Yariv had in mind, there was a new generation ready to arise and resist. 'I am not needed here,' Guttman thought. He quietly withdrew, happy to let the young people get on without him. It also meant he would now gain a precious hour in a day jammed with this rally, a television debate this evening and a strategy meeting with Shapira and the settlers' council in between. He checked his watch. The sensible course would be to slope off to a café, have a smoke and recharge his batteries. But Guttman decided he would grant himself a rare treat. He would go somewhere else entirely.

A quick visit wouldn't delay him too badly. As he walked through the Jaffa Gate, ignoring the kids hawking cans of soda and postcards of the Old City, turning into the Arab market, he realized that this was his greatest weakness. Other men could be diverted from their duty by wine or women, but Shimon Guttman had only one comparable passion. Drift the scent of the ancient past before his nostrils and he would forget everything else. He would be a bloodhound, following the trail until he had found his prey.

He walked briskly down the cobbled alleys of the *shouk*, as the Israelis referred to it, a soft 'sh' where the Arabs would sound an 's'. Not that Israelis ever came here. Since the first *intifada* in the late 1980s, few Jewish Israelis dared set foot inside the Old City, except of course for the Jewish Quarter and the *Kotel*, the Western Wall. It had become a no-go area; a spate of fatal stabbings had seen to that.

But Guttman was not frightened. He believed as a matter of principle that Jews should have full access to all of their capital city, that they should not be intimidated into retreat from any part of it. That was one reason why he had left Kiryat Arba when he did. His comrades in the settler movement were populating the outer edges of Samaria and stretching to the beach shores of Gaza, but they were neglecting the beating heart of the Land of Israel, the heart of Zion: Jerusalem. The Israeli right were taking the eternal city for granted, not realizing that, as they stretched out their hand to liberate land elsewhere, the great pearl of Jerusalem was slipping from their grasp. If they were not careful, they would find they had lost East Jerusalem the way the British acquired an empire: in a fit of absent-mindedness.

So Shimon Guttman made it his business to travel around the mainly Arab eastern part of the city as freely as he would amble around the predominantly Jewish west. True, he didn't come here anything like as often as, ideologically speaking, he should. True, too, that he looked over his shoulder every five or six steps and that his heart raced the instant he left behind the smooth stone and scrubbed, lit streets of the Jewish Quarter for the dust and noise of the Arab neighbourhoods. Still, he tried to walk as relaxedly as he could given those constraints, like a man who was simply strolling in his home city. As if he owned the place. Which, as a matter of principle, he believed he did.

There were a few shops he stopped into whenever he was in the market, which, he now realized, he had not visited for well over a year. (The campaign against Yariv had been all-consuming; everything else had slipped.) He checked in at the first, whose entrance was obscured by rail after rail of leather bags, satchels and purses. They had a pot that was intriguing, but hard to date. The second and third shops were apologetic; they had sold the best stuff and were waiting for more. They didn't need to spell out where these new shipments would be coming from: Iraq had transformed the entire trade. A fourth had some coins which Shimon made a note of: he would tell his friend Yehuda, an obsessive numismatist, to stop being such a wimp and take a trip down here.

He was heading out when he caught a glimpse of the shop he had almost forgotten. Like the rest here, it had no front window, just a pile of merchandise outside which extended inside. To enter was to stand in the narrow floor space that was not filled with stuff, a canyon of goods on either side. At eye level and above, there was silverware, candlesticks mainly, including several of the nine-branched variety, the traditional menorah used by Jews during the festival of Chanukah. It always struck Guttman as the ultimate in commercial pragmatism, this willingness of the Arab traders to sell Jewish kitsch.

He surveyed the shelves almost hoping there would be nothing worth seeing, so that he could hurry away and get back on schedule.

'Hello, Professor. How nice to see you again.' It was the owner, Afif Aweida, emerging from behind the jeweller's counter at the far end, a glass case housing a collection of rings and bracelets on velvet beds. He offered his hand.

'What a remarkable memory you have, Afif. Good to see you.'

'To what do I owe this pleasure?'

'I was just passing through. Window shopping.'

Afif gestured for Guttman to follow him through the shop, up a couple of stairs into a back office. The Israeli looked around, noting the large, bulky computer, the old calculator, complete with paper printout, the layer of dust on the shelves. Times had been hard for Aweida, as they had for everyone in this area. The inhabitants of East Jerusalem, like the Palestinians in general, were the victims of what Shimon often thought of as a bad case of divine oversight, fating them to live in a land promised to the Jews.

Afif saw Shimon check his watch. 'You cannot wait till my son brings us some tea? You are in a hurry?'

'I'm sorry, Afif. Busy day.'

'OK. Well, let me see.' He was on his feet, surveying his stock. 'Nothing too dramatic, but there is this.' He held out a cardboard box with perhaps a dozen mosaic fragments inside. Shimon rapidly arranged them, like a child's jigsaw, to discover the shape of a bird. 'Nice,' he said, 'but not really my area.'

'Actually, there is something you can help *me* with. A new shipment arrived this week. I am told there is more where this came from, but for now, this is what I have.' He leaned down, resting one arm on a shabby leather chair which was disgorging some of its stuffing, to pick up a tray from the floor.

On it, arranged in four rows of five across, were the twenty clay tablets Henry Blyth-Pullen had brought to him just a few days earlier. Despite Aweida's downbeat pitch, it was not dull – merely handling such clear remnants of the ancient past always excited Shimon Guttman – but it was hardly scintillating either. He checked his watch: 1.45 p.m. He would get through these, then be off to Psagot for that three o'clock meeting.

'OK,' he said to Aweida. 'The usual terms, yes?'

'Of course: you'll translate all of them and keep one. Agreed?'

'Agreed.'

Aweida brought a notepad to his lap and waited. His familiar pose, the secretary taking dictation. Guttman brought the first tablet out of the tray, felt the pleasing weight of it in his palm, not much bigger than an old tape cassette. He moved it closer to his eyes, lifting his glasses to get a sharper view of the text.

He gazed at the cuneiform markings which, even in as banal a context as this, never failed to thrill him. The very idea of a written record that stretched back more than five millennia into the past was, to him, intensely moving. The notion that the Sumerians had been writing down their thoughts, their experiences, even trivial jottings, thirty centuries before Christ and that they could be read right here, on tablets no grander or more imposing than these small bars of clay, was exhilarating. He imagined himself as one of those enormous radio telescopes, arranged in rows in the New Mexico desert, their yawning wide dishes primed to receive a signal emitted by a remote star millennia ago. Someone had written these words thousands of years ago, yet here he was, reading them right now, as if the ancient past and the immediate present were facing each other in conversation.

The first time he had been taught how to interpret the marks which gave cuneiform its name – the word literally translated as 'wedge-shaped' – he had felt the emotional charge of it. To the naked eye, they were just squiggles that looked like little golf tees, some vertical, in pairs or threes, some on their side, also in twos and threes, arranged in various patterns, filling line after line. But ever since Professor Mankowitz had shown him how those cryptic impressions could be decoded as 'In my first campaign, I . . .' or 'Gilgamesh opened his mouth and said . . .' he had been seduced.

He dictated to Aweida. 'Three sheep, three fattened sheep, one goat . . .' he said after a glance. He could not read and understand these as quickly as he could English, but certainly as fast as he could read and translate, say, German. He knew it was a rare expertise, but that delighted him all the more. In Israel, there was no one to match his knowledge, with the exception of Ahmed Nour (not that Ahmed would ever declare himself to be living in Israel). Otherwise, now that Mankowitz had gone, it was just Guttman. Who else? That fellow in New York; Freundel at the British Museum in London; but only a handful of others. The journals always said there were only one hundred people in the world at any one time who could read cuneiform, but he suspected that was, if anything, an overestimate.

He picked up the next one. Instantly, merely from the layout of the tablet, he could see what this was. 'A household inventory, I'm afraid, Afif.' The next one showed the same line repeated ten times. 'A schoolboy's exercise,' he told the Palestinian, who smiled and noted it.

He continued like that, setting the translated tablets onto

Aweida's desk, until there were only six left in the tray. He picked up the next one, and read to himself the opening words as if they were the first line of a joke.

'*Ab-ra-ha-am mar te-ra-ah a-na-ku* . . .' He put the tablet down and smirked at Aweida, as if he might be in on the gag, then brought the tablet back to his eye again. The words had not vanished. Nor had he misread them. The cuneiform, of the Old Babylonian period, still read *Abraham mar Terach anaku*. I Abraham, son of Terach.

Shimon felt the blood draining from his face. A kind of queasy panic washed over him, starting in his head, then cascading through his chest and into his guts. His eye sped forward, as far as they could before the letters became cloudy and indistinct.

I Abraham, son of Terach, in front of the judges have attested thus. The land where I took my son, there to make a sacrifice of him to the Mighty Name, the Mountain of Moriah, this land has become a source of dissension between my two sons; let their names here be recorded as Isaac and Ishmael. So have I thus declared in front of the judges that the Mount shall be bequeathed as follows . . .

What reflex restrained Guttman at that moment, preventing him from saying out loud what he had just read to himself? He would ask himself that question many times in the days that followed. Was it an innate shrewdness that made him realize that if he spoke now he would almost certainly lose this great prize? Was it no more than the savvy of the *shouk*, the habit of a veteran haggler who knows that to show enthusiasm for any item immediately doubles its price, moving it potentially out of reach?

Was it a political calculation, a comprehension in a fleeting second that what he was holding in his now-trembling hand was an object that could change human history no less dramatically than if he were grasping the detonator of a nuclear bomb? Or was there a simpler explanation, one less noble than all the others: had Guttman bitten his tongue because every instinct in his body would hesitate before sharing a secret with an Arab?

'OK,' he said finally, hoping, by economy of speech, to hide the shakiness in his voice. 'What's next?'

'But, Professor, you haven't told me what that one said.'

'Didn't I? Sorry, my mind wandered. Another household inventory, I'm afraid. Woman's.'

He proceeded to the next one, a tally of livestock in a farm in Tikrit. And somehow he ploughed through the rest, though he felt as if he were performing the entire task under water. The hardest moment, he knew, was yet to come.

He was no poker player. He had no idea if he would be able to conceal his emotions. He assumed he would not. His life was spent speaking from the heart, deliberately displaying all the conviction he could muster. He was not a politician, practised in the art of dissembling, but a campaigner, whose stock in trade had to be sincerity. And this man, Aweida, was a market trader: he had seen every trick; he knew how to read any customer instantly, upping the price for those who feigned indifference, dropping it for those whose lack of interest was genuine. He would see through Guttman instantly.

Then it came to him.

'So the usual terms?' he said, his throat parched. 'I can pick one?'

'As we agreed,' said Aweida.

'Good. I'll have that one.' He pointed at the ninth tablet he had examined.

'The letter from a mother to her son?'

'Yes.'

'Oh, but Professor, you know that was the only one of any special interest. All the rest are so, how shall I say, day-to-day.'

'Which is why I want that one. Come on, your buyers won't care one way or the other.'

'Ordinarily that might be true. But I have a collector coming in from New York in the next few days. A young man, coming here with his own art expert. He is obviously in a position to spend some money. This story – a mother and a son – will perhaps appeal to him.'

'So tell him that that's the story of that one.' Guttman pointed at the tablet engraved with the schoolboy punishment.

'Professor. These buyers get such items independently verified. I cannot lie. It would destroy me.'

'I see that, Afif. But I am a scholar. This is what interests me historically. The rest are very ordinary.' He was aware of the sweat on his upper lip. He wasn't sure how long he could keep this up.

'Please, Professor. I do not want to beg you. But you know what these years have done to us. We are earning a fraction of what we once could make. This month I suffered the indignity of accepting money from a cousin in Beirut. With this sale—'

'OK, Afif. I understand. I don't want to push you too hard. It's fine.' He reached for the tablet that began *I Abraham, son of Terach*. 'I'll take this one.'

'The inventory?'

'Yes. Why not? It's not so dull.'

Guttman rose to his feet, slipping the tablet in his jacket pocket as casually as he could manage. He shook hands with Afif, only realizing as they made contact that his own palm was clammy with sweat.

'Are you all right, Professor? Would you like a glass of water?'

Guttman insisted he was fine, that he just needed to get to his next appointment. He said goodbye and headed briskly out. As he ascended the tiered steps of the market, heading back towards the Jaffa Gate, he kept his hand firmly inside his pocket, gripping the tablet. Eventually, once out of the *shouk* and beyond the walls of the Old City, he stopped and paused for breath, gasping like a sprinter who had just run the race of his life. He felt as if he might faint.

Even at that moment, his hand stayed wrapped around the chunk of clay that had made his head spin and heart throb, first with excitement, then fear and finally, now, awe. For at that moment Shimon Guttman knew he held in his hand the greatest archaeological discovery ever made. In his grasp was the last testament of the great patriarch, the man revered as the father of the three great faiths, Judaism, Christianity and Islam. In his hand was the will of Abraham.

CHAPTER TWENTY-EIGHT

JERUSALEM, THURSDAY, 12.46AM

Their first stop had been the central police station in Tel Aviv, dropping off a distraught Eyal Kishon so that he could file a missing person's report on his father. He was convinced that whatever curse had killed Shimon and Rachel Guttman had now passed, like a contagion, to his family.

All the while, even as he drove, Uri was working his mobile, starting with directory inquiries, trying to get any information he could on Afif Aweida. The phone company said there were at least two dozen, though that narrowed down to nine in the Jerusalem area. Uri had to use all his charm to get the operator to read them all out. There was a dentist, a lawyer, six residential listings and one Afif Aweida registered as an antiques dealer on Suq el-Bazaar road, in the Old City. Uri smiled and turned to Maggie. 'That's the *shouk*. And that's our man.'

'How can you be sure?'

'Because my father already had a dentist and he already had a lawyer. And he hardly had hundreds of Arab friends. Antiquities: that's about the only thing that could have made him talk to an Arab.'

As they approached Jerusalem, well past midnight, Uri was wondering whether he shouldn't head for the market there and then, try to track down this Aweida immediately. Eventually he conceded that it was pointless, that all the stores would be closed. Unless they knew the address of his home, not just his shop, it would be impossible to find him.

He drew up among the taxis outside the Citadel hotel, ostentatiously pulling up the handbrake to signal the journey was over.

'OK, Miss Costello. This is the end of the line. All change here.'

Maggie thanked him, then unlatched her door. Before getting out, she turned back to him with a single word: 'Nightcap?'

He was not a drinker, she could see that. He nursed his whisky and water as if it were a rare and precious liquid that had to be observed, rather than consumed. Her own style – a quick knock-back and then ordering a refill – looked positively uncouth by comparison.

'So what about this film-making then?' she said, removing her shoes under the corner table they had taken and enjoying the relief that coursed through her feet and upward.

'What about it?'

'How come you're good at it?'

He smiled, recognizing the return of his own inquiry. 'You don't know if I'm good at it.'

'Oh, I think I can tell. You hold yourself like a successful man.'

'Well, it's kind of you to say so. Did you see *The Truth about Boys*?'

'The one that followed those four teenagers? I saw that last year: it was brilliant.'

'Thank you.'

'That was you?'

'That was me.'

'Jesus. I couldn't believe what those lads said on camera. I thought there were hidden cameras or something, they were so honest. How on earth did you get them to do that?'

'No hidden cameras. There is a big secret though. Which you mustn't let on. It's commercially sensitive.'

'I'm good with secrets.'

'The one thing you have to do, and this is really the key to the whole thing. You have to . . . No, I can't.' He screwed his eyes into a look of mock suspicion. 'How do I know if I can trust you?'

'You know you can trust me.'

'The secret is listening. You have to listen.'

'And where did you learn that?'

'From my father.'

'Really? I didn't imagine him as the listening type.'

'He wasn't. He was the talking type. Which meant we had to listen. We got really good at it.'

He smiled and took another sip of the amber liquid. Maggie liked the glow it made around his mouth and eyes. He had, she told herself, one of those faces that you wanted to look at.

'Anyway, you only answered half my question before. I get how you're a mediator, but not really why.'

'You asked me "how come".'

'Right. And that's part how and part why. So tell me the why.'

Maggie looked at this man, leaning back in his chair, also relaxing now for the first time since they'd met. She was aware that this was some kind of respite for him, a break from mourning, a chance for lightness after the weight he had been carrying around for four days. She was aware that it was a fleeting mood, that it could not possibly last. Yet she couldn't help herself: she was enjoying this moment between them. She wouldn't just swat aside his question with a joke or a change of subject, as she had learned to do with the countless men who had come on to her in late-night bars in foreign capitals. She would be honest.

'The why sounds so corny no one ever talks about it.'

'I like corny.'

Maggie looked at him hard, as if she was handing him a fragile object. 'The very first time I'd been abroad was when I volunteered in Sudan. While I was there, a civil war was raging. One day we were driving back and we saw a village that had been razed to the ground. There were bodies on the roadside, limbs, the whole thing. But the worst of it were these children, alive, but wandering around aimlessly, stumbling really. Like zombies. They had seen the most awful things, their parents killed, their mothers raped. And they were just dumbstruck. After that, I thought if I could do anything, anything at all, to stop a war lasting even one day longer, then it would be worth it.'

Uri said nothing, just kept his eyes locked onto hers.

'Which is why I couldn't bear to be kept away from it all this time.'

He furrowed his eyebrows.

'I haven't told you, have I? This is my first assignment for over a year. I've been brought back out of retirement.' Maggie drained her glass. 'Forced retirement.'

'What happened?'

'I was in Africa, again. Mediating in the Congo: the war no one ever talked about. No one gave a fuck, even though millions died there. Anyway, it had taken eighteen months, but we finally had all the parties on board for a deal. We were days away from a signing, maybe weeks. But very close. And I made—' She looked up at him, to see if he was still with her, and he was, his concentration absolute. 'I made a mistake. A terrible, terrible mistake.' Her voice was cracking now. 'And because of that mistake, because of *me,* the talks broke down. The deal was off.

'I had to leave the Congo a few days later and when I did, when I took the main road out to the airport, I saw them again. Those faces, those kids, teenagers, young girls, that same stunned look in their eyes. And I realized that they were like that because of me, because I had fucked up so badly.' A tear trickled down her cheek. 'And those faces will haunt me for the rest of my life, no matter what I do.'

Only then did Uri put down his glass and lean forward out of his chair to touch Maggie's hand. He held it tightly, until he eventually stood up and brought Maggie up with him, so that her head was resting on his chest. Without saying a word, he stroked her hair, over and over, which only made the tears come faster.

They moved upstairs, to her room, in silence. Once the door was closed, they stood together for a while until, without any act of volition either of them could remember, their lips touched. They kissed slowly, shyly, their tongues making the lightest possible contact with each other.

Her hands were the first to move, placing themselves on his chest, feeling its muscled hardness. He moved gently, his right palm only grazing the side of her breast, a touch which made her shudder with pleasure.

When his left hand found the space between the top of her skirt and her shirt, his fingers tingling across her naked skin, she pulled away.

'What? What is it?'

Maggie stumbled backwards, until she was sitting on the bed. She leaned across and found the light switch, dazzling them both and breaking the spell between them.

'I'm sorry, I'm sorry,' she said, shaking her head and avoiding Uri's eye. 'I just can't do it.'

'Because of the man at home.'

It should have been because of Edward, she realized with a guilty start; but it wasn't. 'No. No, it's not that.'

Uri turned his face away from her. The look in his eyes changed, as if a protective cover was being drawn over them.

'Uri, please. I want to tell you.'

He let his eyes meet hers, then lowered himself into the chair at the desk.

'You see, I didn't tell you everything about my mistake. Back in Africa. It wasn't a—' She struggled to find the right word. 'It wasn't a . . . professional error. I didn't screw up the negotiations.' She gave a bitter smile, realizing the linguistic trap she had just walked into. 'I screwed one of the negotiators. That was my mistake. A leader of one of the rebel groups.' She looked up at Uri, expecting the disapproval to be etched into his face. But he just listened. 'Of course, everyone found out. And when they did, they said I could no longer be impartial. And that therefore the United States was no longer impartial. The talks were suspended.'

Uri sighed. 'And that's why they sent you into exile, away from your job. To punish you.'

'No, not really. That was me who did that. Punishing myself.' She offered him a wan attempt at a smile, but she could barely see his reaction: her eyes were too blurred with tears. It was such a relief to be telling him. 'You know, people keep telling me I should move on. Edward would say it again and again. Move on. But I just can't. Do you understand that, Uri? I can't move on. Not until I've made things right. And I won't do that if I make the same mistake again.'

'But, Maggie.' He smiled. 'I'm just some guy you met. I've got nothing to do with the peace talks.'

'No, but you're an Israeli. And you know how crazy this place is: that counts as taking sides.'

'You're assuming people would find out.'

'Oh, they'd find out.' She was trying not to look at him for too long, her eyes darting back and forth to the floor instead. She feared that if she saw him as she had seen him just a few moments ago, her resolve would crumble.

She got up off the bed and opened the hotel room door, wide enough so that both of them could see the corridor outside. Uri rose to his feet. Her eyes still wet, Maggie said quietly, 'I'm sorry, Uri. I really am.'

CHAPTER TWENTY-NINE

JERUSALEM, THURSDAY, 7.15AM

Maggie bolted upright, her heart thumping. She was confused, taking a second or two to look around the room and realize where she was. It was the phone that had done it, shocking her out of deep sleep. No matter that she had arranged a wake-up call from the hotel operator for this hour. Any sudden sound, whether an alarm clock or a telephone, always came as a shock.

'Yerrrr.'

'Maggie? This is the Deputy Secretary.'

Jesus. Maggie pushed the phone away from her mouth and cleared her throat. 'Yes. Hello.'

'I need to see you in fifteen minutes. Meet me downstairs.'

Over coffee, Robert Sanchez set out just how bad things were. Both sides seemed to be trying to keep the lid on the violence, though there had been armed clashes in Jenin and Qalqilya and Israel had reoccupied whole swathes of the Gaza Strip. Palestinians meanwhile claimed a dozen children had been killed in the last two days of fighting, while word was coming through of a minibus full of Israeli school pupils that had been blown up that morning by a suicide bomber just outside Netanya.

Worse, the whole region seemed to be preparing for war. Not only was Hizbullah hurling rockets from Lebanon onto Israel's northern towns and villages, but now Syria was mobilizing its troops around the Golan Heights. Egypt and Jordan had both recalled their ambassadors from Tel Aviv. Sanchez held a clutch of printouts from the American press: both the *New York Times* and *Washington Post* were drawing comparisons with 1967 and 1973, wars that engulfed the entire Middle East. 'This time it will be worse,' said Sanchez. 'Half of these countries have got nukes now. They'll soon suck in the whole damn world.'

The prognosis could not have been gloomier. Yet Maggie found it comforting to be sitting with Robert Sanchez again. He was one of the very few people in the current State Department she knew at all, and certainly the only familiar face in the US team in Jerusalem. His reappointment as number two had surprised Washington; he was a holdover from the previous administration. Press consensus said he was there to hold the hand of the new Secretary, an immediate vote of no confidence from the President in his own choice for the top job. But Maggie couldn't have cared less about all that. She had worked with Sanchez twice before and come to respect and, even rarer in this business, trust him. He had led the second string US team on the Balkans to which Maggie was attached when she was a novice and she had watched his patient, deliberate method of working. No grandstanding, no media leaking, dogged preparation. He had slipped quite naturally into the role of mentor then and later, when they met again during the north-south talks in Sudan.

He was a doubly unusual fixture on the Washington diplomatic landscape. For one thing he was a real diplomat, not just some high-dollar donor to the party in power, rewarded with a juicy ambassadorship. As a career officer rather than a political appointee, he had gone as far as he could go: he could never be Secretary of State. That he had become the deputy was rare in itself.

More relevant, at least to Maggie, was that Sanchez was one of the few Hispanic-Americans to be found at the upper reaches of the US government. They made an unlikely pair, the big, bear-like guy from New Mexico and the slender girl from Dublin, but among the buttoned-up white males of the State Department, they were both outsiders. That much they had in common.

'It's only lucky we're not in Camp David or somewhere,' Sanchez was saying. 'If we were, the parties would have gone home by now. As it is, Government House is virtually empty.'

Maggie forced herself to wake up, glugging back the coffee. 'Don't tell me: the two sides have pulled back their negotiators for "consultations"?'

'Exactly.'

'And this started with the killings?'

'Yep. First it was Guttman, then Nour. To say nothing of the Jenin raid on the kibbutz last night—'

'Sorry, Jenin raid?'

'Yep. Turns out it was some kind of Palestinian cell from Jenin. They crossed over and got through to Bet Alpha.'

'The Israelis know that for sure?'

'Yeah, the terrorists sprayed some slogan on the wall. *No sleep for Bet Alpha till there is sleep for Jenin.*'

'And the Israelis are saying that's grounds to break off talks.'

'Well, they haven't gone that far yet.'

'Just "consultations".'

'Right. But what's got them freaked is that they thought they had stopped attacks from Jenin. Ever since they built the wall—'

'I think you mean the "security barrier", Robert.' Maggie was smiling.

'Whatever you want to call it, it's been keeping out attacks from the West Bank. Yariv's got the right wing killing him, saying that he's been so busy sucking up to the Palestinians that he's left the country exposed, so now he's negotiating under fire.'

'And does Yariv know how they got through?'

'That's the thing, Maggie. Even our intel guys are stumped by it. The Israelis say they've checked the length of the wall – excuse me, the barrier – and they can't find a breach.'

'So what could it be?'

Sanchez lowered his voice. 'The Israelis are worried it represents some kind of escalation. That maybe the Palestinians are stepping up the degree of sophistication. As a warning.'

'Have the Israelis responded?'

'Only a statement. Unless you count the killing last night.'

'What killing?'

'Didn't you get the CIA note?'

Doubtless sent at 6am, thought Maggie. When the rest of the State team in Jerusalem were already up, showered and briefed she was sleeping off a light night in the bar with—

'There was a stabbing in East Jerusalem last night. In the street market. Some trader.'

Maggie paled. 'A trader? What kind of trader?'

'I don't know. But listen, Maggie. I know you've been trying to talk to the settlers, to al-Shafi, find out what's going on. But we've got to raise our game here. Seems the bad guys on both sides are trying to derail this thing. OK. Shhh.'

Maggie turned around to see exactly why Sanchez had clammed up. Bruce Miller was strolling past the breakfast buffet towards their table. *Damn.* She wanted to finish hearing what Sanchez knew. Now he would be on his best behaviour in front of the President's man. The Deputy Secretary of State rose slightly for Miller, as if to render in physical form their precise positions along the Washington hierarchy.

'Hello, Bruce. I was just bringing Maggie Costello here up to speed.'

Maggie offered a hand, which Miller took, keeping hold of it a moment too long. He did a tiny dip of his head – the Southern gentleman – as he said, 'Pleasure's all mine.'

Maggie couldn't help but notice that this little performance allowed Miller to give her a good once-over, his eyes examining her body from her ankles to her chest.

'So,' he said finally, apparently satisfied with the results of his inspection. 'Whatcha got so far?'

Maggie proceeded to tell him how she believed there was a link between the Guttman and Nour killings and that she was using the relationships she had built up on both sides to discover what that link might be. (She noticed something flicker across Miller's face at the mention of the word 'relationships'.) She couldn't bring herself to describe the Nour anagram, but said only that she was now certain that, whatever this connection was, it would explain the current threat to the peace process.

'What kind of connection, Ms Costello?'

'Archaeology.'

'Excuse me?'

'Both Guttman and Nour were archaeologists. I believe they had even worked together. Guttman had seen something that he told his wife would change everything. Two days later he's dead – and so's she.'

'Police said that was suicide. She couldn't handle the grief.'

'I know that's what the police say, Mr Miller. But her son is convinced otherwise. And I believe him.'

'You working pretty closely with him, Ms Costello?'

Maggie could feel her neck reddening. *This is what happened last time*, she thought, cursing herself. She, who could keep everything hidden during negotiations, holding the secrets of each side without ever betraying so much as a hint to the other, would always crack when the subject at issue was not demilitarization of a buffer zone or access to seaports, but *herself*. Then she would go to pieces, giving it all away. She had done that back then, too. It had cost her so dear, you would have assumed she'd have learned to control it. But no. Here she was, repressing a blush.

'Uri Guttman has proved an invaluable resource.'

'Archaeology, you say?' Bruce Miller was tucking the napkin into his shirt collar. 'Does that make last night a coincidence or what?'

'Last night?'

'The attack on Bet Alpha.'

'You mean, the kibbutz?'

'Yeah, it's a kibbutz.' *Kiboootz*. 'Also the site of one of the great archaeological treasures of Israel. Take a look.'

He passed over the English language edition of *Haaretz*. 'Page three.'

She turned to see the top half of the page dominated by a photograph of a night sky turned orange as a building burnt to the ground. The caption identified it as the Bet Alpha Museum and Visitors' Centre, which 'last night appeared to have been the target of a Palestinian raid'.

Inset was a smaller photo depicting a stunning mosaic, divided into three panels, the middle section devoted to what seemed to be a wheel. The caption explained that this was the mosaic floor of the oldest synagogue in Israel, estimated to date from the Byzantine period of the fifth or sixth century. 'Preserved intact for 1500 years, experts now worry for its survival.'

While she was reading, Miller had turned to Sanchez to discuss their next moves. No point in the Secretary coming now, they agreed, with the two sides not even talking. Smarter to hold him back for the final phase—

'It's too much of a coincidence,' Maggie said, aware that she was interrupting two much more senior officials.

'Bet Alpha?'

'Yes. So far everyone hurt on both sides since this sudden deterioration has been connected with all this,' she gestured at the photograph in the paper. 'With archaeology, with ruins. With the past.'

Miller gazed at her, a smile on his lips, as if Maggie was somehow amusing him. 'You think we gotta ghost problem? Spirits of the ancient come to haunt the present?' He made a spooky, Hallowe'en gesture with his hands.

Maggie chose to ignore the condescension. 'I don't yet know what it is, but I bet you it explains why these talks are in meltdown.'

'Face it, Ms Costello. Everything in this goddamn country—' He suddenly remembered himself and lowered his voice. 'Everything in this place is tied up to all this,' he picked up the newspaper, scrunching up the page showing the Bet Alpha mosaic. 'It's all rocks and stones and temples. That's the whole freakin' point. It don't explain nothing. We have a serious *political* problem here, which is gonna take some serious political solving. And I need you to start living up to your goddamned five star reputation and do some solving right now. Do I make myself clear, Ms Costello?'

Maggie was about to insist that she was not wasting her time, that the connection was real, when they were interrupted by a buzzing sound on the table. Miller's BlackBerry, vibrating to announce a new message.

'Israeli police have just confirmed the name of the man killed in the market last night.'

'I bet he was a trader of antiques, wasn't he, Mr Miller? Antiquities? Archaeological relics? Am I right, Mr Miller?'

He looked back at the handheld device, using his thumb to scroll down through the message.

'As a matter of fact you're wrong, Ms Costello. The dead man was, it seems, a seller of fruit and vegetables. Nothing ancient about that. He was a greengrocer. Name of Afif Aweida.'

CHAPTER THIRTY

JERUSALEM, THE PREVIOUS THURSDAY

Shimon Guttman's hand trembled as he put his key in the lock. The journey back home had been dizzy, his mind oscillating between excitement and alarm. Not once in all his years in Jerusalem had he ever feared mugging, but today he had looked over both shoulders, eyeing everyone who came near him with suspicion. He imagined the tragedy of it: some lout approaching him in the street, demanding he empty his pockets. He couldn't let that happen. Not today. Not with this in his hand.

'I'm home,' he called as he walked inside. He prayed there would be no reply, that he would be alone.

'Shimon? Is that you?' His wife.

'Yes, I won't be long. I'll be in my study.'

'Did you eat yet?'

Shimon ignored her and headed straight for his desk, closing the door behind him. With his arm, he swept a pile of junk – video-camera, digital sound recorder and piles of paper – to one side, to clear a space. Slowly he took out the clay tablet Afif Aweida had given him an hour earlier. For the last half of his journey he had wrapped it in a handkerchief, to keep the sweat of his own clammy hands at bay.

As he unwrapped it now, reading again those first few words, he felt his body convulse with anticipation. In the market he had been able to make out only the opening words: the rest were obscured, their meanings out of reach. To decode the full text, he would have to study it closely, using some of his most arcane reference books. He would labour over it all night.

The thought thrilled him. He hadn't felt this way since . . . since, when? Since his work on the Bet Alpha site, discovering the houses that adjoined the synagogue, which proved the existence of an entire Jewish village from the Byzantine period? Since his work, as a student of Yigal Yadin at Masada? No. The exhilaration he felt now was on an entirely different scale. The closest comparison, he was ashamed to realize, was with the moment when, as a shy sixteen-year-old, he had lost his virginity to Orna, the nineteen-year-old beauty on his kibbutz. The ecstasy rising in him now was explosive, just as it had been then.

I Abraham, son of Terach . . .

He was desperate to find out what it said, but there was a feeling in his gut like a lead weight. What if he were wrong? What if this was an extraordinary case of mistaken identity?

Shimon tried to calm himself. He got out of his chair, shook his head, like a dog shaking off drops of rain, and sat down again. The first task was to confirm that this really was the word of Abraham; the meaning would come next. He breathed deeply and started again.

The text was in Old Babylonian language. That, thought Guttman, fitted: it was the dialect that would have been spoken eighteen centuries before Christ, when Abraham was commonly believed to have lived. He looked back at the text. The author gave his father's name as Terach and identified his sons as Isaac and Ishmael.

It was conceivable that there had been other Abrahams who were sons of other Terachs, even possible that they lived at that time and in that place. These other Abrahams might even have had two sons. But two sons with those exact names, Isaac and Ishmael? It was too much of a coincidence. *It had to be him.*

The door opened. Instinctively, Shimon placed his hand over the tablet to hide it.

'Hello, *chamoudi*. I wasn't expecting you back. Aren't you meant to be with Shapira?'

Shit. The meeting.

'Yes. I was. I mean, I am. I'll phone him.'

'What is it, Shimon? You're sweating.'

'It was hot out. I was running.'

'Why were you running?'

He raised his voice. 'Why all these questions? Leave me alone, woman! Can't you see I'm working?'

'What's that on your desk?'

'Rachel!'

She turned around, slamming the door behind her.

He tried to calm himself, looking back to the text, his eye tracing the line in which the author named his hometown as Ur, the Mesopotamian city where Abraham was born. He saw the seal on the reverse side of the tablet, in the space between the text and the date at the bottom, and repeated in another corner and again on the edges. It had not been made by a cylinder, the seal used by kings and men of wealth, the carved stone tube that could be rolled into the soft clay, thereby leaving a unique marking, a signature. Nor was it a series of crescent shapes, etched into the clay by the use of the author's right thumbnail. No, it was a pattern found much more rarely than that, one that Guttman instantly recognized – and found unaccountably moving.

It was a roughly circular pattern, formed by a criss-cross of lines. Shimon had seen it only twice before, and one of those was in a photograph. It was formed by pressing into the clay the knot found at the fringes of a male garment, of the kind worn by Mesopotamian men at exactly Abraham's time. Such fringed garments had faded from history, with one exception: the Jewish prayer shawl. Shimon would only have to step outside his house to find an ultra-orthodox Jew waiting at a bus stop, or buying a paper, wearing the exact same garment now, nearly four thousand years later. And here was its mark, pressed deep by Abraham, son of Terach.

Regardless of what it said, the importance of this object, no more than four inches high, less than three inches wide and barely half an inch thick, could not be overestimated. It would be the first significant archaeological evidence of the Bible ever discovered. Sure, there was the Black Obelisk of Shalmaneser III, on display among the pharaohs and mummies of the British Museum. One of the five scenes shown in the obelisk's sculptured relief depicted the Israelite king Jehu, paying tribute to the Assyrian monarch. Jehu appeared in the Bible and this obelisk, found by Henry Layard in the nineteenth century, corroborated it.

But Jehu was a minor character in the great Bible story. Of the lead players, from the patriarchs to Moses to Joshua, the archaeological record had yielded nothing. Until now. Here it was: physical confirmation of the great forefather himself.

Surely it was too good to be true. What if it was a fake? Guttman thought back to the scandal that had spooked scholars and historians the world over. He and his friends had followed it with a mixture of *Schadenfreude* and fascination. In 1983 the British historian Hugh Trevor-Roper had declared the Hitler diaries genuine and had paid for it with his reputation. His mistake was simple. He had *wanted* to believe they were real. Now, sitting in his Jerusalem home, Shimon Guttman knew how Trevor-Roper must have felt: he wanted so desperately for this tablet to be what it seemed.

He looked at its reddish-brown clay, precisely the shade any expert would expect from Iraq in that period. It was craggy and weathered, the way pieces of this vintage always looked. Guttman brought the tablet closer to his eyes: the angle of each line of the cuneiform script, each syllabic character, was entirely as it should be. And the wording. Every phrase, every formulation, was idiomatically and historically fitting: *in front of the judges have attested thus* . . . There were only about half a dozen people in the world who could fake an item as well as this – and he, Guttman, was one of them.

But a fake made no sense. Trevor-Roper had got the Hitler diaries wrong because he had overlooked a crucial fact. Someone had brought them *to* him, wanting his validation. A vast fortune rested on his verdict. There was always a risk of a con.

This was not like that. No one had come to Guttman, trying to pass off this tablet as the last will of Abraham. On the contrary, *he* had found it. If it hadn't been for his impulse visit to Aweida it would still be in that marketplace now, sitting in a tray, ready to be sold off to some know-nothing collector. A smile spread across Shimon Guttman's face. Logic was on his side.

To believe this was a fake, you would have to believe a series of wildly unlikely propositions. That someone had gone to painstaking and expensive trouble to inscribe a clay tablet that could pass as a four-millennia-old Mesopotamian relic. That this trickster had then, without mentioning it, dumped his handiwork in the hands of an East Jerusalem market trader, in the hope that fate would bring one of the world's few cuneiform experts into the trader's shop. That this expert would see this item in particular, picking it out from everything else in the shop, that he would translate it and comprehend its profound significance. The faker would be gambling that all those circumstances would materialize, and for what? What would this con artist have earned from his trick? Certainly not money, since Guttman had paid nothing to a trader who had no idea what he was giving away. No, if this was a fake, the trickster would surely have brought it to Guttman demanding millions of dollars.

The cold, rational truth was that it made more sense to believe this tablet was genuine than to believe it was phoney. The logical leap entailed by the latter was greater than the former. It had to be real.

His mind was racing. How on earth had it got here? It had come to Jerusalem from Iraq, part of the huge outflow of antiquities since the fall of Saddam: that much was obvious. Whether it had come via Beirut, Amman, Damascus, it hardly mattered. How it had been found in Iraq, whether it had been in the ground until recently or plundered from a collection, perhaps even a museum, was unknowable. Maybe the authorities under Saddam had found it and hidden it from view; perhaps they had never realized its significance.

What fascinated Shimon Guttman was its earlier journey. The tablet was written in Hebron, the place where Abraham was buried, the place so holy in Judaism that Guttman and his fellow radicals had been determined to restore a Jewish presence there as soon as they could after 1967. Did this mean that Abraham had lived his last days in Hebron, then? His two sons had been involved in his burial, but did this discovery mean there was some kind of final deathbed scene, involving the father and his two heirs? Had there been a dispute the aged patriarch had to resolve?

Guttman wondered how the tablet would then have got back to the land of Abraham's birth, Mesopotamia. Perhaps one of the sons had taken it there. There was no mention in the Bible of Isaac returning to Ur, but perhaps Ishmael had gone back, to see for himself the town where it had all begun.

This, he realized, could be his life's work. Translating this tablet, decoding its history, displaying it in the great museums of the world. It would make his name forever – it would be known as the Guttman tablet – he would be on television, hailed at the British Museum, toasted at the Smithsonian. Scholars would tell and retell the story of how he had stumbled across the founding document of human civilization in a street market on a hot afternoon in Jerusalem.

This small, silent object had taught him something he had not expected to discover about himself. He realized that he was, despite his recent decades of activism, an archaeologist first and foremost. The mere discovery of this tablet, whatever its ultimate meaning, thrilled him as a scholar. It was the connection with Abraham, the sense that he had, like those telescopes in New Mexico, made contact with a faraway world, that delighted him more than he could say.

But the other voice in his head, that of the political campaigner, would not be stilled. It had been nagging away throughout, desperate to know the exact meaning and significance of this document, and now its impatience boiled over. Guttman duly reached for the three or four key volumes required in the deciphering of cuneiform and got to work.

I Abraham, son of Terach, in front of the judges have attested thus. The land where I took my son, there to make a sacrifice of him to the Mighty Name, the Mountain of Moriah, this land has become a source of dissension between my two sons; let their names here be recorded as Isaac and Ishmael. So have I thus declared in front of the judges that the Mount shall be bequeathed as follows . . .

Guttman couldn't help it. He was overwhelmed all over again. Here was Abraham referring to one of the defining episodes in world culture, the *akeda*, when the great patriarch led his son up Mount Moriah, there to sacrifice him to the god in whom he had become the first believer. For centuries, Jews had struggled to understand what kind of father could slay his own child and what kind of God would ask him to do it. And, make no mistake, Abraham had been ready to do it, raising his blade, only staying his hand when an angel descended to announce that God did not demand this act of child sacrifice after all. It was a moment that would bind Abraham and Isaac and their children to God for ever more, sealing them into the covenant between God and the Jews.

Now here was textual proof of that event. But that was not what made Shimon Guttman giddy. He read the words again, syllable by syllable, in case he had made a mistake.

> *The Mountain of Moriah . . . has become a source of dissension between my two sons, let their names here be recorded as Isaac and Ishmael.*

Mount Moriah. The Temple Mount, Judaism's holiest site. Tradition held that this spot, where the angel had saved Isaac, was the centre of the world, the Foundation Stone on which the universe had been created. The Jews of ancient times had built their temple here and, when it was destroyed by the Babylonians, they had built it again. All that was left now was the Western Wall, but this place remained the spiritual centre of the Jewish faith.

Yet Mount Moriah was holy to Muslims, too, those who traced their ancestry back to Ishmael. For them it was Haram al-Sharif, the Noble Sanctuary, the place where Mohammed had ascended to heaven on his winged horse. After Mecca and Medina, it was the Haram that was holiest.

> *. . . this land has become a source of dissension between my two sons; let their names here be recorded as Isaac and Ishmael. So have I thus declared in front of the judges that the Mount shall be bequeathed as follows . . .*

Here the characters were faded, as if the carving had gone less deep. Guttman opened a desk drawer and pulled out a magnifying glass. Some of the formations were novel: they required checking against other texts, looking for repetitions that might suggest a specific local usage. More than two hours later and it was done.

When it was, Shimon Guttman gripped the desk in front of him. He needed to feel the solidity of the wood, its mundanity. For the enormity of these words was now apparent. Forget the fame and glory of an unprecedented historic discovery. What he had in front of him would change everything. People had fought for millennia over control of this holy site, all sides believing themselves to be the children of Abraham. At different times, Jews, Muslims and Christians had claimed it, each believing they were its true heirs. And now he, Shimon Guttman, held the document that would settle this question forever. All who regarded themselves as the descendents of Isaac and Ishmael, Jews and Muslims, would have to be bound by this, the word of the great father himself. It would change everything.

He fumbled for his phone before realizing that he didn't know by heart the number he meant to call. He quickly logged onto the computer, searching for the website. He called up the contacts page and immediately dialled the number.

'My name is Professor Shimon Guttman,' he said, his voice parched. 'I need to speak to the Prime Minister.'

CHAPTER THIRTY-ONE

RAMALLAH, THE WEST BANK, THURSDAY, 8.30AM

Khalil al-Shafi knew that, in reality, this was only half a meeting. He had the head of the presidential guard, along with the heads of three other security forces here. But the leaders of the military wing of Hamas were not here, nor of the Gaza police force. If this was a unity government, he had joked with his wife that morning, then he would hate to see a disunity government.

In jail he had planned and strategized for this moment over many years. He had anticipated every Israeli move and prepared a series of possible countermoves. To each of those, he had predicted a range of Israeli reactions, calculating in advance the appropriate Palestinian response to each. If you opened up his head, he thought, you would see a flow chart more complex than the circuit board for the space shuttle.

But he had not factored in sufficiently the durability of Palestinian divisions. He had assumed that by the time serious talks came around there would be a single Palestinian leadership. Indeed, he had taken for granted that his own release would only have come about if the Palestinians had formed a united front. They had cobbled together a coalition, but that was not the same thing.

He had made another error during those long stretches inside Ketziot jail, confined to a cell measuring six feet by four and a half feet for twenty three hours a day. He had always anticipated that the final straight of negotiations would be punctuated by outbreaks of violence on both sides. There would always be hardliners who would move to sabotage progress and atrocity would be their obvious tool. It had happened in every peace process the world over. Al-Shafi knew: he had studied them in footnote detail.

What he had not prepared for was this, attacks which no one claimed and no one could explain. He turned to Faisal Amiry, head of the security operation that was the closest the Palestinians came to an intelligence agency.

'How is it possible that this attack was staged from Jenin? It's far, no?'

'It is far, sir. But if a team were able to get over the wall—'

'We would know about it. Wouldn't we?'

'There may be others who knew.' It was Toubi, a veteran of the old PLO struggles going back decades. He hated Hamas with a passion.

'The trouble is, it doesn't seem like them,' Amiry replied. 'It's not their style. A raid, in then out.'

'With no martyrs,' said Toubi. 'I agree it's strange. If they wanted to blow up the talks they'd have blown up themselves. On a bus. In the centre of Jerusalem.'

'Rogue elements?' asked al-Shafi.

'That would be something, wouldn't it, if our friends in Hamas were losing their legendary discipline?' It was Toubi, with too much of a smile on his face for Khalil's taste.

'I don't think so,' said Amiry. 'So far they have stayed remarkably united. The political bureau in Damascus has decided that these talks should work. That we should get an agreement, then call the Israelis' bluff and demand they honour it. That's the strategic decision they've taken.'

'And without Damascus, there's nothing any of the rogue elements can do?'

'Correct, Mr al-Shafi. They just don't have the equipment, the training, the money. Nothing.'

'Jihad?'

'We wondered about Islamic Jihad. But we have a very good source inside there. He says they are as surprised by this as we are.'

'What about the target?'

'That is the strangest thing of all. If you were aiming for loss of life, you'd have turned right out of the kibbutz fields, aiming for the residential buildings. But they were at the museum. Where they only took one life.'

Toubi was nodding. 'Or not gone there at all. Once they got over the wall, they could have struck Magen Shaul. Why hike all the way to Bet Alpha?'

'I know why.' It was al-Shafi, who had got out from behind his desk and was now attending to a chessboard he kept in the corner of his office. A leftover from prison, the chess. He would play entire games in his head, taking both sides, sometimes lasting days. During the spells of solitary confinement, it kept him sane. Now he always had a game on the go.

'Bet Alpha is the site of an ancient synagogue. Fifteen hundred years old. The Zionists love it because it "proves" they've been here as long as we have. If it's gone, that's one bit less proof.'

'You're not serious.'

'Why not? What else do you think the Jerusalem team at Government House is talking about all day?' He had still not looked up, his eyes remaining fixed on the white bishop he held between his fingers, hovering over the black rook. 'It's all about this.' He captured the castle, replaced it with his bishop and moved back to his desk.

'I don't follow.'

'It's all about the *past*. All about who was here first, who has the prior claim. Do you know what drove the Israelis completely apeshit during Camp David in 2000?'

Toubi shifted in his seat. He resented being lectured to by this younger man.

'Of all the things, there was one statement by President Arafat that drove the Israelis insane. He denied that there had ever been a temple for the Jews in Jerusalem. "How can this be the Temple Mount?" he said. "Why do you call it the Temple Mount? There was no Temple here. It was in Nablus!"'

'What's that got to do with Bet Alpha?'

'It's the same thing. An attempt, while we're thrashing out who gets what, to weaken the other side's claim. To tilt the scales in our favour. "Look, there's now one less ancient Jewish site here. Maybe it never existed!"'

'This is nuts.'

'It *is* nuts. But I think some Palestinian took it into his head to do us a favour. To lend us a helping hand.'

'I don't believe it.'

'Do you have a better explanation?'

There was silence, broken eventually by Amiry. 'And there's the trader. This man Aweida, stabbed to death in Jerusalem.'

'What can you tell me?'

'Not very much. Apparently there was some Hebrew message pinned to the body. A page of the Torah. And Army Radio in Israel is reporting a claim of responsibility from a group nobody's ever heard of. The Defenders of United Jerusalem.'

'Settlers?'

'Maybe.'

Al-Shafi rubbed his chin, scratching at his stubble. 'In which case, Yariv is sweating right now.'

Toubi chipped in. 'They always thought the *Machteret* would resurface eventually.' *Machteret,* the Jewish underground. Like al-Shafi, he had learned his Hebrew in an Israeli jail.

'If it has, they'll be killing us. But it's him they want to hurt.'

'What would you like us to do, Mr al-Shafi?' It was Amiry, who had risen through a movement of ideologues by remaining determinedly practical.

'I want you to find out whatever you can about the incident in Bet Alpha. Comb the Israeli papers: read the military correspondents. Anything the army finds out, they always leak. And see what people here know about Afif Aweida. He has cousins in Bethlehem, I'm told. Talk to them. Was this man picked out at random, or is there a reason why a few Israeli fanatics would kill a greengrocer?'

'Anything else?'

'Yes. I want to know what that American woman, Costello, is up to. She called me with more questions about Ahmed Nour. There are at least three mysterious murders here, my friends. Unless we understand what's going on, there will be more. And a lot of Palestinians will be dead – along with the best chance of independence any of us will ever see. I think you know what to do.'

CHAPTER THIRTY-TWO

EAST JERUSALEM, THURSDAY, 9.40AM

For the second time in a week she was entering a house of mourning. This was a new development for her, though she knew of others for whom it was a standard ploy in the mediator's repertoire. At a critical week in the Northern Ireland peace talks, for example, two young men, good friends – one Protestant, the other Catholic – were shot dead in a pub. The killings were designed to halt the peace process, but they did the opposite, reminding everyone why they were sick to the back teeth of war. The negotiating teams visited the bereaved families and came out with their resolve doubled. Maggie remembered it well: she had followed it all on a crackling shortwave radio, deep in southern Sudan. And when London and Dublin announced the Good Friday Agreement she had sat in her tent with tears rolling down her cheeks.

These killings in Jerusalem lacked the moral clarity of the Belfast deaths. Truth be told, they had no bloody clarity at all. Shimon Guttman might have been shot simply because he appeared to be threatening the life of the prime minister; Ahmed Nour could have been a collaborator, executed for his crime;

Rachel Guttman might have killed herself; the kibbutz up north might have been firebombed by angry Palestinian teenagers. Only the murder of Afif Aweida, claimed by some fringe Israeli group, seemed to be a clear attempt to sabotage the peace talks. But no one could be sure.

So Maggie's visit to the Aweida mourning house didn't quite carry the emotional weight of the equivalent journey in Belfast all those years ago. She wasn't there to mourn two lads, a Jew and an Arab, who had been shot dead while drinking together. In truth, she wasn't there to mourn at all. She had come to find out what the hell was going on.

The house was full, as she had expected. It was noisy, with a piercing wail that rose and fell like a wave. She soon saw the source of it, a group of women huddled around an older woman, swathed in shapeless, embroidered black. Her face seemed to have been worn away by tears.

A path formed for Maggie as she made her way through the mourners. There were women constantly brushing their cheeks with the palms of their hands, as if trying to banish a dust that would never clear. Some were crouched low, pounding the floor. It was a scene of abject grief.

Eventually Maggie reached the front of the room where she found a woman whom she guessed was around her own age, dressed in simple, Western clothes. She was not crying but seemed simply stunned into silence.

'Mrs Aweida?'

The woman said nothing, staring past Maggie, into the middle distance. Her eyes seemed hollow.

'Mrs Aweida, I am with the international team in Jerusalem trying to bring peace.' Something told Maggie 'American' was not the right word to use here. 'I came to pay my respects to your husband and to offer my condolences on your terrible loss.'

The woman still stared blankly, seemingly oblivious to Maggie's words and the noise all around. Maggie stayed there, crouching down, looking at the widow as long as she could before eventually placing a hand on hers, squeezing it and moving away. She would not intrude.

A man materialized to steer Maggie away. 'Thank you,' he said. 'Please, you to know we thank America. For you to come here. Thank you.'

Maggie nodded and smiled her weary half-smile. But he hadn't finished speaking.

'He was a simple man. All he did was sell tomato and carrot and apple. He no kill anyone.'

'Oh, I know. It's a terrible crime that happened to your—'

'My cousin. I am Sari Aweida.'

'Tell me. Do you also work in the market?'

'Yes, yes. All of us, we work in market. For many year. Many year.'

'What do you do?'

'I sell meat. I am butcher. And my brother he sell scarf, for the head. *Keffiyeh*. You know what is *keffiyeh?*'

'Yes, I do. Tell me, are you all called Aweida?'

'Ah, yes. Yes, we are all Aweida. Aweida family.'

'Tell me. Is there anyone in your family who sells old things. You know old stones, pots. Antiquities?'

He looked puzzled.

'Jewellery perhaps?'

'Ah! Jewels! I understand. Yes, yes. My cousin, he sell jewel.'

'And antiques?'

'Yes, yes. Antique. He sell in the market.'

'Can I see him?'

'Of course. He live near to here.'

'Thank you, Sari.' Maggie smiled. 'And what is his name?'

'His name also Afif. He is Afif Aweida.'

CHAPTER THIRTY-THREE

JERUSALEM, THURSDAY, 10.05AM

As they threaded through the back streets, narrow and made of the same pale stone as the rest of Jerusalem, Maggie realized that no one in the family had suspected that the Afif Aweida they were about to bury had been the victim of a case of mistaken identity. If it was a random killing, how could the killers have got the wrong man?

Because it was not a random killing. Of that Maggie was now certain. She pulled out her mobile to dial Uri's number. A text message had arrived while she was in the Aweida house. From Edward. He must have sent it in the middle of the night.

We need to talk about what to do with your stuff. E.

Sari Aweida must have seen the expression on her face, the brow knotted. 'No to worry, Maggie. We nearly there.'

She cleared Edward's message, without replying, and hit the green button for the last number she had dialled. She would speak as if last night had not happened.

'Uri? Listen. Afif Aweida is alive. I mean there's another Afif

Aweida. A trader in antiquities. It has to be the right one. They must have got the wrong one.'

'Slow down, Maggie. You're not making any sense.'

'OK. I'm on my way to meet Afif Aweida. I'm sure he was the man your father mentioned on the phone to Baruch Kishon. He deals in antiquities. It's too much of a coincidence. I'll call you later.'

Like most people talking on a mobile while walking, Maggie had spoken with her head down, staring at her feet. She now looked up to find no sign of Sari. He had obviously walked on so fast, he hadn't noticed that she wasn't keeping up. She stopped and looked around at the warren of streets, with turnings and alleyways every few yards, and realized he could have gone anywhere.

She walked a few yards forward, peering to her left down a turning so narrow it was dark, even in this morning sunlight. Its width was spanned by a washing line, and in the distance she could see two kids, boys she guessed, kicking a can. If she went down here, perhaps she could ask their mother—

Suddenly she felt a violent jerking backwards, as if her neck was about to be snapped. A gloved hand was over her eyes and another was covering her mouth, muffling her cry. She heard the sound as if it belonged to someone else.

Now she could feel herself being dragged backwards, even as her eyes and mouth stayed covered. She tried to pull her arms free, but they were held fast. She was dragged into an alleyway and shoved hard against the wall, the bricks pounding against the ridges of her spine. The hand covering her mouth moved down now, clamping her throat. She heard herself emit a dry rasp.

Now the hand came away from her eyes but, for a second, she still saw only darkness. Then a voice, which she realized was right in front of her, coming from a face entirely covered in a black ski mask. It was barely an inch away, the mouth close enough to touch her lips.

'Stay away, understand?'

'I don't—'

The hand around her throat tightened, until she was gasping for air. She was being strangled.

'Stay away.'

'Stay away from what?' she tried to croak.

The hand came off her throat, so that it could join with the other in taking hold of her shoulders. He held her like that for a second, then moved her whole body forward about six inches, so that she was tight against him. Then, still holding both shoulders, he rammed her hard in the other direction, straight into the wall.

The pain shuddered all the way through her, reaching the top of her skull. She wondered if he had shattered her spine. She wanted to double over, but still he held her upright, as if she was a doll that would slump into a heap if he let go.

Suddenly she heard a new voice, whispered directly into her left ear. For an instant she was confused. The black mask was still in front of her, its mouth only inches from hers. How was he speaking into her ear at the same time? Now she understood. There was a second man, invisible in the shadows, who had been pinning her to the wall from the side. 'You know what we're talking about, Maggie Costello.'

The voice was strange, indeterminate. It sounded foreign, but from where Maggie couldn't say. Was it Middle Eastern? Or European? And how many of these men were there? Was there a third attacker she hadn't seen? The surprise of the assault, combined with the darkness, had disoriented her entirely. Her senses seemed to have short-circuited, the wires crossed. She wasn't sure where the pain was coming from.

Now she felt a hand on her leg, squeezing a thigh. 'Do you hear me, Maggie?'

Her heart was thumping, her body still writhing in futile

protest. She was trying to work out what kind of voice she was hearing – was it Arab, was it Israeli? – when she felt a sensation that made her quake.

The breath on her ear had turned moist, as she registered the unmistakable sensation of a tongue probing inside it. She let out the first sounds of a scream, but the gloved hand was back, sealing her mouth. And now the other hand, the one that had been gripping her thigh, relaxed – only to move upward, clamping itself between Maggie's legs.

Her eyes began to water. She was trying to kick, but the first man was pressed too close: she could hardly move her legs. And still this hand was squeezing her, grabbing her crotch the way it would grip at a man's balls if trying to inflict the maximum punishment.

'You like that, Maggie Costello?' The voice, its accent still so elusive, was hot and breathy in her ear. It could have been Arab, it could have been Israeli. Or neither. 'No? Don't like it?' She felt the tongue and face move six inches away from her. 'Then fuck off.' The first man let go of her shoulders, then pushed her to the ground. 'Otherwise we'll be back for more.'

CHAPTER THIRTY-FOUR

JERUSALEM, THURSDAY, 11.05AM

Tradition held that this hour was reserved for the forum, the informal kitchen cabinet of advisers that had surrounded Yariv since he first considered an entry into politics three decades ago. Every Thursday morning, the working week nearly over, was the hour to digest and analyse events, spot mistakes, devise solutions and plot the next moves ahead. They had been doing it when Yariv was Defence Minister, then Foreign Minister; when he was in the wilderness of opposition. Even, truth be told, when he was still in uniform serving as Chief of Staff. That was a politician's job, whatever they might pretend, and don't believe anyone who tells you otherwise.

There had only been one change in the personnel. The two old buddies from army days still came, one now in advertising, the other in the import business. And so was his wife, Ruth, whose counsel Yariv weighed seriously. The only change was of necessity. His son, Aluf, had been a regular until he was killed in Lebanon three years ago. Amir Tal had taken his place, a fact seized on by the Israeli press who constantly described the young adviser as the PM's adopted son, even, in a phrase that punned in Hebrew, Aluf Bet – Aluf the Second.

Ideally, the meetings happened at home, with Ruth bringing coffee and strudel. But not today. Things were too serious, he told Amir, to leave the office early. The forum would be just the two of them.

The talks at Government House were now effectively on hold, only a skeleton presence maintained on both sides. Neither Israel nor the Palestinians wanted to be accused by the Americans of pulling the plug, so they hadn't dared walk out completely. But no serious work was being done. It meant the centrepiece of the Yariv – the peace effort – was collapsing before their eyes. He was taking heat from the right – the settlers with their damned human chain around Jerusalem – and he was ready to take it, but not if there was nothing to show for it. He remembered the man who had sat in this office just a few years ago, who had seen his premiership crumble in a matter of months once the Camp David attempt unravelled.

What was worse, he now confided in Amir Tal, as he spat the sunflower seeds into his hand, was that he felt confused.

'Look, a *pigua*', a suicide bombing, 'from Hamas or Jihad I fully expected. They did it to Rabin and they did it to Peres. They even did it to Bibi, for God's sake. Anyone gets close to a deal, they're on an Egged bus with dynamite strapped to their belly. I expected that.' He raised his hand, signalling that he had not yet finished.

'Even the *Machteret* I was expecting to hear from.' They had both assumed that a resurgence of the Jewish underground was on the cards. Back in the 1980s, a handful of settlers and religious fanatics had sent bombs in the post or planted them under cars, maiming a series of Palestinian politicians. Several of their victims were still active, appearing on television in wheelchairs or with terrible facial disfigurement.

'Maybe,' Yariv continued, 'they'd firebomb an Arab playground or two. Even do the Mosque.'

He didn't need to say which mosque. They both knew the wilder elements of the *Machteret* dreamed of blowing up the Dome of the Rock, Islam's most cherished site in the Holy Land, thereby clearing the ground for the rebuilding of the Jewish Temple on the same spot.

'But these attacks? They make no sense. Why would the Palestinians attack some visitors' centre in the north? Why do it at night when no one's around? If you want to screw up the talks, do it in the day! Kill lots of people!'

'Unless it was a warning.'

'But that *would* be a warning. Whenever they wanted to send a message before, that's how they did it.'

'Al-Shafi has denied all responsibility for it,' said Tal.

'Of course. But Hamas?'

'They have too. But—'

'But we don't know whether to believe them. And this stabbing in Jerusalem. I don't believe the claim of responsibility. Defenders of United Jerusalem or whatever bullshit name they gave themselves. Why haven't we heard of them before? There's always some crackpot group ready to claim credit for actions they didn't take. Could be just some street crime.'

'Not necessarily.'

'What do you mean?' The Prime Minister was now cracking and spitting at a frantic speed.

'You know we've been pursuing the Guttman investigation. We've had the son, Uri, under surveillance. He's working closely with Maggie Costello of the State Department—'

'The mediator? What the hell's she got to do with it?'

'It seems she was passed some kind of message by Rachel Guttman. And, in the absence of any action at Government House, the Americans are letting her pursue it. She's obviously persuaded them that if she doesn't close down this Guttman business, there'll be no peace to negotiate.'

'So?'

'So, as you know, Costello and Uri Guttman have established a connection between the Professor and the dead Palestinian, Nour. Well, we think there might be a further connection with the killing in Jerusalem last night.'

'Go on.'

'We didn't have much time to establish surveillance on the apartment they visited last night in Tel Aviv – the home of Baruch Kishon – but we did get a muffled voice recording. It had to be enhanced, but our engineers say that, just before they left, Guttman and Costello had found something, a piece of paper, with a name on it.

'What name?'

'Afif Aweida.'

'I see.'

'So,' Tal went on, 'it seems Guttman spoke to Kishon, mentioned Aweida's name. And suddenly Aweida ends up dead.'

Yariv paused. There was silence, but for the sucking sound as a particularly fat seed lodged between his teeth. 'Well, who else was listening—?'

'That's why I'm glad we're meeting here alone today, Prime Minister.'

'You don't think—'

'Military intelligence are the only people besides you and me who have access to our surveillance.'

'That's crazy. What, you think Yossi Ben-Ari, the Defence Minister of the State of Israel, could be running his own rogue operation? Killing this Arab in the market?'

'If his people were listening in last night, he would have had the name.'

'Why would he do it?'

'I don't know why he would have picked out this specific man. We'd have to know what this whole Guttman business was all about to understand that. But the bigger picture—'

'—is that he's trying to sabotage the peace talks. Bring me down; take over himself. *Jesus*.'

'I know it's not—'

'Possible partners?'

'Maybe Mossek. Perhaps the Chief of Staff.'

'It's a military coup!'

'We can't be sure.'

'Why, who else could have done this?'

'If we accept that this was not a random crime, that this was indeed the man Kishon knew of, well, then the suspects could be anybody who knew of his identity. Of his connection to the Guttman business.'

'But that could only be the American woman and Guttman's son.'

'We can't rule it out.'

'It doesn't make any sense. This is not one of your crazy videogames, Amir. This is the real world.'

'We have to follow every lead.'

The Prime Minister leaned back in his chair, balling up the paper bag that had once been full of sunflower seeds but which was now empty. He sighed deeply.

'What you are suggesting here—'

'I'm not suggesting anything.'

'—is that there are rogue elements within the military establishment of the state of Israel, killing and doing God knows what else to topple the elected government of this country. And to deny us the best chance of peace in a generation.'

'You know the army's attitude to what we're doing. They never liked the pull-out from Gaza; you think they're going to like this? Tearing down settlements in the West Bank? Handing over half of Jerusalem?'

Yariv smiled, the wistful smile of an old man who thought he had seen it all. 'I promoted Ben-Ari, you know. Made him a general. "But Brutus is an honourable man . . ."'

'What do you want me to do, Prime Minister?'

'I think you have to set up an intelligence team answerable solely to this office. Check them for political allegiance. Make sure they have no doubts about the peace talks. Use leftists and druggie dropouts if you have to. Just make sure they're loyal. Cut defence and the IDF out of the loop. And then, once you have the team in place, set them on Mossek and Ben-Ari. Bug their phone calls and their meetings. I want to see their emails, their text messages, the colour of the paper they use to wipe their arses in the morning.'

'It's done.'

'Just to prove you're wrong, that's the only reason I'm doing this. And one other thing.'

'Yep.'

'Keep on Costello and Guttman Junior. Don't let them out of our sight. If they're about to find the explanation for all this madness, then good. They can lead us to it.'

CHAPTER THIRTY-FIVE

JERUSALEM, THURSDAY, 11.11AM

She had no idea how long she had remained stuck on the ground. It might have been a minute, five or ten. She had stayed there, inert, since they had dumped her and fled. She had not watched where the men had gone. She had not phoned for help. She had been too frozen for that, temporarily too stunned by what had happened. Unhelpfully, her body insisted on repeating the sensation of the tongue in her ear and the hand on her crotch. Her skin, her flesh, remembered these invasions with perfect accuracy.

Maggie had just begun the effort to pull herself together, to persuade herself that it could have been much worse, that they could have killed her, when a hand reached out.

It belonged to a woman, staring down, her face a picture of concern and puzzlement. After a long while, the creases in her face briefly relaxed. 'You are the American lady. From the Aweida house.' Only to tense up all over again. 'What are you doing here?'

It forced Maggie to get up and dust herself down, to deploy the protective shell she had had to grow these last few years. She said nothing, gasping only at the pain that shot up her spine, fizzing like a firework, as she stood: a silvery flash that made her eyes water.

The woman was leading her down the alley, towards the washing line. At the end of it, there were two small steps down into a tiny yard, no more than a couple of metres square. Then a room, with a kitchen in the corner, a TV set and a child at a table, drawing. Perhaps he was one of the boys she had seen playing football earlier. Maybe he had seen something. Or perhaps the boys had not been playing here at all but at the other end of the alley. She had lost her bearings entirely.

She was now perched at the end of a couch, while her rescuer fired up a small gas-ring stove to make mint tea, when all Maggie yearned for was a cup of her mother's old Typhoo, the way her dad used to have it, with three sugars. She looked at her hands, which were shaking, and realized how far from home she had come. It had been nearly twenty years, and still here she was, in the middle of nowhere, surrounded by men who were ready to commit horrible violence.

'You are welcome in my house.' It was a male voice and it made her jump. She looked up to see a man in a faded blue suit, with a long thin face and a head of closely cropped hair, black turning to silver.

The woman turned around and they began speaking in Arabic. She was explaining what had happened, gesturing towards Maggie at intervals.

'Now you are safe,' he said, flashing a smile that unsettled her. He turned his back and Maggie exhaled; she didn't want him here. But he wasn't leaving: he had simply gone to collect an ashtray.

'So you are American?'

'I'm Irish,' Maggie said, her voice quiet and distant.

'Yes? We like the Irish very much. But you work for the Americans, am I right?' He was smiling throughout, a forced smile that made Maggie want to look away. When the woman brought tea, Maggie was glad of the distraction, glad of the business with the cup and spoon that would keep her from talking to this man.

'And why were you here?'

'Nabil!' In Arabic, Maggie guessed, the wife was telling her husband to leave the girl alone. While they spoke, she dug into her pocket to pull out her phone. There was a text message, from Uri: *Where are you?*

She was beginning a reply, when her host leaned across to her, all but reaching to take the phone.

'You don't need to call anyone. We'll take care of you. What is it you need? Anything you need, please, just to ask.'

Maggie suddenly had the strong urge to get away, to be out of this rabbit warren of streets and into the daylight. She wanted to remove and destroy these clothes and stand under a shower for as long as it would take to wash away the—

'Please. Tell me. If you work for the American government, why are you here on your own? Where is your protection?' The smile was as wide as before, the teeth bared. 'Is there really no one here to protect you?'

Maggie felt her hands, which until then had been as cold and inert as the rest of her, turn clammy. Instinctively, she looked for the doorway where she had come in. It was closed.

The woman brought over more tea, then headed into the next room, shouting the names of her children. Maggie was now alone with this man. She wanted to call Davis at the consulate, or Uri, or Liz in London, anyone, but she feared this man's reaction. Would he snatch the phone off her? Would he grab at her? Who was he?

As casually as she could, Maggie stood up, stretched and, as if she were trying politely to extricate herself from tea with a wearisome great aunt, announced that she really had to be going.

'But where are you going to?'

Maggie was stumped. She didn't know where she was nor how she would get out. 'My hotel is in West Jerusalem.'

'Why you not stay in East Jerusalem? It is beautiful here. You have the American Colony Hotel. All the Europeans stay there. Why never the Americans? You want only to see the Israelis.'

Maggie was too tired for this, a conflict so bitter even your choice of hotel could touch off a diplomatic incident. 'No, no,' she began. 'It's not that at all.' She was heading for the door back out into the alleyway as she spoke. She touched the handle. It turned, but didn't open. Locked.

Now she could feel the man at her shoulder, leaning over her to reach the door handle. His closeness made her shudder, reminding her of the alley and the hot breath. She wanted to shove him away.

Before she had a chance, he had opened the door onto the tiny, square yard. She stepped out, the man right behind her.

'Please I ask again. Why were you here?'

'I was at the house for Afif Aweida.'

'Yes. And where were you going?'

'I wanted to see his cousin. The other Afif Aweida.'

'Please. I take you.'

'No, no. There's no need. I just want to get back to my hotel.'

But he wasn't listening. He took her by the elbow and began marching her back into the maze of streets and alleys of Jerusalem's Old City. *Am I deranged,* Maggie wondered as, for the second time in – what was it, an hour? two? – she followed a stranger through a strange city. This time, though, she had none of the distracted carelessness of before. Her heart was racing; she glanced down each alleyway, checked over her shoulder and, above all, eyed the man leading her. Was this some kind of trap? Had Sari Aweida led her to her assailants? Was this man about to do the same?

She thought about making a run for it. But where? She would

instantly be lost in these streets. They were getting fuller now, as they approached the *souk*, the market. She saw a couple of women, perhaps a few years younger than her, who looked like tourists. She could run up to them. But then what?

Now Nabil was guiding her through paths that twisted and turned, passing stalls teeming with goat-skin bongo drums, thick, woven carpets and tacky, wood-carved souvenirs. There were silver-haired couples shuffling along; even a full Japanese tour party. Apparently the briefing material Maggie had read on the plane was right: trade in this market, which had dried up in the *intifada* years, had lifted as tourists slowly came back to the Old City. Credit for that went to the talks in Government House: even the mere prospect of peace was enough to bring visitors back, whether Christians eager to walk the Via Dolorosa, Muslims keen to pray at the Dome of the Rock or Jews yearning to push a note written to God into the crevices of the Western Wall.

They swerved left into a meat market. Maggie wanted to retch at the sight of rack after rack of carcasses, their ribs exposed, the flesh scarlet and bloody. She saw a line of sheep's heads on a butcher's block, averting her eyes only to find puddles of animal blood on the ground.

'Ah, we are here soon. Just one more minute.'

Suddenly, they were back in the realm of bags and purses and kitsch souvenirs. Maggie felt relieved, that the meat was behind her and that people were still around. They had stopped at a jeweller's.

'Here. Please. This is Afif Aweida shop.'

Gingerly, she stepped inside, followed by Nabil who high-fived a young man sitting behind the counter. In Arabic she heard Nabil utter the word 'American' and gesture in her direction.

A moment later, from a back room, a middle-aged man in a V-neck sweater and dark-rimmed spectacles appeared behind a glass counter packed with silver and gold jewellery. Maggie felt she recognized him. She had seen so many men like him in Africa, well-dressed, middle-aged, trying to maintain, or affect, Western standards as if in defiance of the poverty and chaos all around them.

'A pleasure to welcome you here. Thank you, Nabil.'

Maggie turned around to see Nabil heading out, a sheepish wave over his shoulder. She called out her thanks, but half-heartedly. A few seconds ago she had been suspicious of him, even feared him as a possible attacker. After what had happened to her, it was only natural. And yet he had turned out to be no different from his wife, a stranger who simply wanted to help. She felt confused, and suddenly aware all over again of where she had been touched. With that came the memory of the second man's voice, still hot and breathy: *Otherwise we'll be back for more.* Who was he? She pushed the question below the surface and extended her hand with a smile.

'Mr Aweida. I thought you were going to be dead.'

'You mean because of what happened to my cousin. A terrible crime. Terrible.'

'Do you think you were the real target?'

'I'm sorry, I don't understand.'

'Do you think the men who killed your cousin got the wrong Afif Aweida?'

'How can there be the "wrong" Afif Aweida? My cousin was stabbed at random. It could have been anybody.'

'I'm not so sure. Do you know of any reason why your life might be in danger, Mr Aweida?'

To her surprise, the shop owner seemed genuinely puzzled by the question. He was in mourning for his cousin, but Palestinians were used to grieving for their dead. He was sad for him, and they had always had a bond, sharing the same name. But that did not mean he had to be scared, did it? Maggie realized she would have to start at the very beginning.

'Can we talk somewhere private, Mr Aweida? Perhaps in your back room there?' Maggie nodded towards the door he had walked through when she had arrived.

'No. No need, we can speak freely here.' He clapped his hands, urging the young man at the front to leave.

Maggie got up, walking towards the back door. She wanted to test him out. Sure enough, Afif Aweida leapt to his feet, blocking her path.

'Mr Aweida. I work for the American government, in the peace talks. I am not interested in your business dealings. Or in whatever it is you keep behind that door. But you do need to help me. Because your cousin was not killed at random. And many more people will die unless we can find out what's going on.'

Aweida paled. 'Go on.'

'Did you know Shimon Guttman?'

Again, Aweida seemed agitated. 'I know the name, yes. He was a famous man in Israel. He was killed on Saturday.'

Maggie scanned his face. She saw the same nervousness she had seen a moment earlier, when she had mentioned the back office. A realization began to form.

'Afif,' she began, leaning forward. 'I am not a policewoman. I don't care what you buy and sell here. But I am interested in making sure this peace process is not stopped. If it is, many more Palestinians, like your cousin, and many more Israelis, like Professor Guttman, will die. So I need to ask you again. And I swear it will go no further than this room. Did you know Shimon Guttman?'

Quietly, and looking over Maggie's shoulder to check no one was near, he said, 'Yes.'

'Do you have any idea why he might have mentioned your name to someone last week?'

At this, Aweida's brow furrowed again. 'No, I don't know why he would mention me to anyone.'

'When did you last see him?'

'Last week.'

'Will you tell me what happened?'

Reluctantly Afif Aweida sat down and explained about the brief, unannounced visit Guttman had made to the shop, his first for ages. At Maggie's prompting, and only a half-sentence at a time, he explained their 'arrangement', whereby Guttman translated a set of ancient clay tablets, keeping one for himself.

'And you say that none seemed especially significant?'

'No. They were all standard: household inventories, schoolwork.'

'Nothing else at all?'

Again, the sheepish expression. 'There was one item. A letter from a mother to her son.'

'And did Professor Guttman take it?'

'No.'

'But he wanted it?'

'He tried to persuade me to give it to him, but then he eventually gave up. He let me keep it, and he took something else.'

Maggie leaned back. Something about this scene Aweida had just described seemed familiar. 'Tell me again. Did he fight you hard for that tablet from the mother straight away? Or only after he had read all of them?'

'Miss Costello, this was a week ago.'

'Try to remember.'

'He read all of them. Then he decided that that one was the best.'

No, he didn't. Of course that's why it seemed familiar. She had done the same thing herself. In a Balkan negotiation, she had insisted that access to the coast road was the deal-breaker. Decommissioning of weapons could come later. But an absolute must was access to the coast road: she couldn't possibly go back to the other side without it. As she predicted, they promptly offered to decommission weapons, but on the coast road, they would not budge. Grim-faced, she had said she would see what she could do. Then she had gone into the room where the other side were waiting and told them that they had got exactly what they had wanted most: the decommissioning of arms.

Guttman had done the same trick, fighting for the apple so that he could get what he really wanted: the orange.

'And this tablet he took, do you have any idea what it said on it?'

'He said it was an inventory, a woman's.'

'And you believed him?'

'Madam, I cannot read this ancient language. I only know what the Professor told me.'

'And, one last thing. How did he seem when he left here? What mood was he in?'

'Ah, this I remember. He seemed rather unwell. As if he needed a glass of water. I offered, but he didn't take it. He had to rush off.'

I bet he did. 'And that was the last you heard of him?'

'Yes. Until what we heard on the news.'

'Thank you, Mr Aweida. I really appreciate it.'

As Maggie got up and headed for the exit she had a glimpse of what Shimon Guttman must have felt: the sense of having made an important discovery, and the urgent need to share it with someone.

Once outside, feeling safer now among the tourist throng, she reached for her cellphone, dialling Uri's number.

'Uri, I think I know what's going on.'

'Good. You can tell me on the way.'

'On the way to where?'

'You didn't get my text? My father's lawyer just called me. He says he has something for me. A message.'

'Who from?'

'From my father.'

CHAPTER THIRTY-SIX

LAKE GENEVA, SWITZERLAND, THE PREVIOUS MONDAY

Officially, Baruch Kishon was meant to hate Europe. As a conservative ideologue, writing blistering commentaries for the Israeli press for nearly four decades, he had made a good living lambasting the lily-livered appeasers of the Old World, contrasting them unfavourably with the strong champions of liberty to be found in the New. While the Americans knew right from wrong, the Europeans – the French were the worst, but the British were almost as bad – sank to their knees the moment any dictator with a moustache started strutting on the podium. They had crumbled before Hitler and bowed and scraped to Saddam. And they were ready to sell out Israel the way they had been ready – eager – to betray the Jews in the 1930s. It was congenital with them. He had written as much, more than once. The European Union didn't need a motto, concluded one of his favourite columns, just a single word: surrender.

Yet he had a dirty little secret, one common to many of the Israelis who shared his unbending brand of politics. While he may have hated everything Europe stood for, the place itself he *loved*. He couldn't get enough of it: the sidewalk cafés in Paris, where the *café au lait* and croissants came just so; the splendour of the Uffizi or St Peter's Square; the theatres in London's West End, the shopping on Bond Street. After the chaos, rudeness, dust and grime of Israel, it was such a *relief* to come to a place that was colder, but also cooler and calmer. Where bus queues did not turn into riots and where, yes, the trains really did run on time.

Nowhere did Baruch Kishon feel this more keenly than in Switzerland, where you could eat your lunch off the railway platform and set your watch by the trains. Which is why he had felt only delight when Guttman had mentioned Geneva in that long, rambling monologue he delivered on the phone last Saturday. A call which, Kishon now believed, might well have been the Professor's last.

He and Guttman spoke regularly. To say they were journalist and source would be too thin a description of their relationship. Their roles had blurred more than that. They were co-conspirators, kindred spirits of the nationalist camp, their foremost concern always how they might best serve the cause. If Kishon got a good story out of it, and Guttman yet more publicity, well, then that was a happy bonus. Above all, their goal was the Jewish people's sovereignty over their historic home, the Land of Israel.

He hadn't been surprised when Guttman called him on Saturday afternoon. Yariv was holding his big peace rally that evening; only natural that the right would need to plan its response.

But that's not what Guttman wanted to talk about. Instead he started babbling, as excited as a teenage girl, about something that he had found, something that would change everything. The words came tumbling out: the street market in Jerusalem, cuneiform writing, clay tablets, a man called Afif Aweida, and, you'd never believe it, the last words of Abraham. Well, not the last words. But his will.

'You mean Abraham decided who should inherit Mount Moriah, Isaac or Ishmael, us or the Muslims?!' Kishon had spluttered down the phone. 'And you have the proof? Where is it now?'

Guttman had sounded all but hysterical at that point, saying that they had to plan how all this would come out, that it should be them, the right-wing, who revealed it to the world. That it would be the national camp's finest hour!

Kishon had wondered if his old friend was delirious.

'But first we have to tell Kobi,' Guttman had said.

'Kobi?'

'The Prime Minister.'

'Have you been using some of your drop-out son's hashish?'

No, no, Guttman had insisted, he was perfectly in control. When Kishon asked where the tablet was now, Guttman had started breathing heavily, saying that he had arranged to meet a man in Geneva. That it would be safe there. When Kishon tried to press him for more details, Guttman had rambled some more, then said he had to get to the rally. He promised he would call later. They would meet up, Guttman said. He would give all the details and together they would plan a strategy.

Several hours later Kishon had been eating in one of their favourite restaurants, a French place off Ibn Gvirol, waiting for Guttman to show up, when the newsdesk phoned. Guttman was dead, shot at the rally.

He had dropped everything, gone into the office to write a column excoriating Yaakov Yariv for creating a culture in which a political assassination like this had become inevitable. That done, Kishon knocked out a warm, personal tribute to his friend, the late Shimon Guttman.

But the next day, once it began to leak that Guttman had been unarmed, that he had been striding to the front of the rally to hand the Prime Minister a note, Kishon began to wonder. The fevered phone call his old friend had made could have been the random ramblings of a man who had flipped, in the throes of a breakdown evinced by his kamikaze attempt to buttonhole the PM. Or he might have been making perfect, albeit agitated, sense, his march to the front of the rally evidence only of the seriousness of his intent. Kishon weighed up all he knew of Guttman, the years they had worked together, the professor's combination of steady tactical cunning and deep scholarly knowledge, the fact that he had been speaking coherently when they had talked just a few days previously – he weighed all that up and concluded that Guttman deserved to be trusted, posthumously as much as in life. Shimon had clearly made an enormously significant discovery and he owed it to his old friend to find it and show it to the world. It would be a last act of friendship. Besides, if what Guttman had said on the phone was right, it promised to be nothing less than every journalist's dream: the scoop of the century.

Kishon tried to assemble the few elements he could remember from the phone call. He looked at the note he had scribbled while they had spoken. To his great irritation, he had written down only two words, those that were unfamiliar to him, the name of some Arab trader in East Jerusalem: Afif Aweida. The other details, he had assumed he would get later when he met up with Guttman. He hadn't so much as jotted them down. Now he had to reconstruct them from memory: stolen antiquities, a clay tablet, Geneva, Mount Moriah. The will of Abraham.

He considered contacting Aweida, but decided against it. If he, Kishon, knew Guttman and his methods, this trader probably had no idea what he had just sold. If he had, the professor certainly wouldn't have been able to afford it. No, a better lead would be Geneva, one of the centres of the global antiquities trade. There was a time when almost everything went through there. The Swiss took the old *nemo dat* doctrine – *nemo dat quod non habet*, 'you can't give what you don't own' – rather literally, believing that if you were selling something, then you had to be its rightful owner. It meant that an object bought in Switzerland was automatically deemed legitimate, no questions asked. It didn't matter how it had got to Switzerland. Once it left there, its provenance was deemed sound. No wonder the Swiss capital had become the laundromat for the world market in the looted treasures of the ancient world. Kishon booked a ticket online and was there by Sunday night.

Most journalists, thought Kishon smugly, would have headed straight for one of the freeports, the heavily-fortified warehouses that acted as salerooms for these ancient goodies. But Kishon knew better. Guttman would not have been interested in selling this tablet. His interest was in its political impact; he had said as much on the phone.

Which could only mean that the professor had planned to come here not to have the item valued, but *verified*. Guttman could not have made a declaration to the world – 'Here is proof that Abraham bequeathed Jerusalem to the Jews!' – unless he was rock-solid certain it was genuine. Too much was at stake to get it wrong. So Kishon had Googled 'cuneiform, Geneva, expert' and, to his delight, come up with a name. Professor Olivier Schultheis.

He would be there in another ten minutes or so. He hadn't bothered calling in advance: no point giving a source a chance to say no. Better to turn up in person, get your foot in the door.

And the delight of these motorways was the smooth ease of the journey. Not like the congestion and fist-waving lunacy of the Jerusalem-Tel Aviv highway. But what was this? A car behind, right on his tail, flashing him repeatedly.

Kishon moved out of his way, shifting into the slower lane on the right. But the driver behind, in a black BMW, changed lanes with him, staying right on his tail. Kishon indicated again, changing once more, this time aiming for the outside, and slowest, lane.

But the BMW was sticking to him, hanging on his tail. Kishon honked the horn, urging the driver to back off. But it had the opposite effect. He felt the BMW make contact with his rear bumper.

Kishon hooted again. *Back off.* Now the BMW rammed into the back of Kishon's car. He checked the mirror and looked ahead. There was no alternative. If he was to escape this psychopath, he would have to come off the autobahn and take the next turning.

It was a small, mountain road and Kishon had to negotiate the turn and the sudden deceleration. But he managed it. To his relief, he was now on his own on a single-lane, winding country road. He would stay on the little road for a while, then rejoin the highway.

But then he saw it, its black shape filling up his rear-view mirror, its headlights flashing. The BMW was back. Kishon tried to keep calm. Perhaps this car was not a stalker, but some kind of state vehicle, trying to flag him down. Had he done something wrong? Was one of his lights broken? He would pull over.

But there was no hard shoulder, just the crumbling grey rocks at the side of the road before a sheer Alpine drop. He slowed down all the same but the BMW did not seem to get the message.

Kishon honked the horn, a long, sustained blast. The BMW now revved up and rammed into the back of his car, sending Kishon's neck whiplashing forward. He briefly lost his grip on the steering wheel, so that he could hear his tyres crunching over the loose gravel at the road's margin. As he pulled back onto the road, he was rammed again. Then, in a sudden movement, the BMW pulled out to Kishon's side.

He looked to his left, but the windows were solidly tinted. And now he was being rammed from the side, sending his car juddering towards the edge of the road. He could see from his window the clean, vertical drop. Just ahead, the road bent into a hairpin. Kishon knew he would need room to negotiate the turn, but the BMW would neither drop back nor speed forward. He tried to come to a stop, but each time he did, the BMW banged him from the side.

His only hope was to accelerate and break free. As the turn came he tried it, slamming his foot on the gas just as the road bent. But as he was swerving round, much too fast, the BMW shouldered him harder than ever before. It was enough to send Kishon's right wheels over the edge. Desperately he tried steering himself back onto the road, but he could feel the difference: his car was gripping nothing, the wheels turning freely in midair.

He felt the lightness of it, as his car plunged almost gracefully off the mountainside for five, six, maybe seven seconds before hitting the first outcrop of rocks. The impact shattered his spine, and almost severed his head from his neck. When the Swiss highway patrol eventually found the wreck of his car two hours later, they had to search the rest of the night, under floodlights, until they were satisfied they had found every last trace of the flesh and bones of Baruch Kishon.

CHAPTER THIRTY-SEVEN

Jerusalem, Thursday, 1.49pm

Maggie did her best to conceal what had happened. She strode past the security guards on the hotel door, two young men who asked every guest whether they were carrying a weapon, checking those they suspected, with all the straight-backed purpose she could muster. She had come to know that of all the competing elements of body language, the gait was often the most eloquent. The second-rate negotiators always set great store by the usual macho indicators: iron handshake, unwavering eye contact. But they forgot the first battle had already been won the moment the two sides entered the room. You had to stride in like victors, confident in your case, controlling the space. If you shuffled in, reluctant to be there, you would spend the rest of the time on the defensive, reacting.

All this knowledge Maggie tried to impart to her aching bones and muscles as she came through the automatic door of the hotel to see Uri, pacing, head down, in the lobby. She wanted him to have no idea what had happened to her in the market. Growing up, she had never understood the girls at her school who had not breathed a word about Father Riordan, despite everything he had done to them. But she understood now.

Fortunately, Uri didn't ask how she was, only what she had found out. She told him about the real Afif Aweida, the trader in looted antiquities who had lived while his fruit-selling cousin had been murdered. As she explained, Uri was smiling a bitter, rueful smile.

'What is it?'

'It's just that this happened before. Not to me. But some colleagues of mine.'

'What happened?'

'A very bad case of mistaken identity. It happened during the second Lebanon war, just a few years ago. Israeli special forces snatched the man they thought was the leader of Hizbullah. It was a big coup for Israeli intelligence. Only problem, he was just a Beirut shopkeeper. Same name. Wrong man.'

'You think it was Israeli intelligence who killed Afif Aweida?'

'I'm not saying that. Just that dumb mistakes like that happen. Anyone could have made it.'

They were walking along Shlomzion Ha'Malka Street towards his car. She had wanted to go upstairs to her room, to freshen up, but Uri had been adamant: there was no time. As she got into the passenger seat, she explained what she believed had happened: that Shimon Guttman had visited Aweida's shop, translated several clay tablets and come across one of profound political significance. Some text that would have a huge impact on the peace process. He had called Baruch Kishon, his long-time political partner, to discuss how they could best publicize his find. And then he had set about getting this information to the Prime Minister.

'For my dad to get so excited, it must have been something that showed the Jews have been here forever. Some fragment in Hebrew going back a million years.'

'Like the Bet Alpha synagogue?'

'Maybe.'

Maggie bit her lip and looked outside, at the passing streets. Men in black coats and the trademark wide-brimmed hats, some of them edged in fur, even in this Middle Eastern heat. Women in long, shapeless dresses darting in and out of shops, plastic bags swinging. Uri caught Maggie's gaze.

'The religious. Taking over this place. Anyway, we'll know what it was my father saw soon, I reckon. His lawyer was out of the country until today. He got back this morning and saw this letter waiting for him.'

'Did he say how long it had been there?'

'Apparently my dad dropped it off last Saturday. By hand.'

Uri and Maggie looked at each other.

'I know,' said Uri. 'I thought the same thing. Like he knew something was going to happen to him.'

They drove on in silence, Maggie replaying the events of that morning, and of the previous night. If only there was a way to try to make sense of it all. Maybe she should tell Uri what had happened in the market: maybe together they could work out who her attackers were. But she had already revealed so much about herself last night. She was about to say something when Uri reached for the car radio, turning on the noon headlines. Once again he translated each story as it came.

'They're saying that there are fears across the world for the Middle East peace process after both sides admitted they had effectively broken off negotiations. Satellite pictures show Syrian army units mobilizing on the border. The Egyptian military have cancelled all leave. And apparently the President of Iran has said that if Israel refuses this last chance to be accepted in the region, then the region will have to remove Israel once and for all. Cast this cancer out, he said. Washington has said any first use of nuclear weapons against Israel will be punished, er, how do you say that? "In kind"?'

Jesus. Miller and the others were not kidding. The world really was watching; failure in Jerusalem would trigger some geopolitical catastrophe. Then she heard in the stream of Hebrew babble two familiar and unexpected words. 'Uri?' she said. 'What's happened?'

He held up his hand to silence her. Then he paled, the colour visibly leaving his face. Finally he spoke, his voice barely audible.

'They said tributes are coming in for veteran journalist Baruch Kishon, killed in a car accident in Switzerland. Just outside Geneva.'

'Uri. Pull the car over. Now.'

But Uri was stuck in traffic; he couldn't move across. Maggie's mind was racing. Somebody was one step ahead of every move they were making. She and Uri had deciphered the name of Afif Aweida at Kishon's apartment; within hours a man called Afif Aweida was lying in a pool of his own blood in the Jerusalem market. They had been the only people to get into Kishon's home and to have discovered that Kishon had received Guttman's last phone call. And now he too had been hunted down.

It could only mean one thing: they were being followed and their every conversation bugged. That was it. There could be no other explanation.

Uri was hooting at the cars in front, desperately trying to pull over.

Unless.

Where did Uri say he had done his army service? In intelligence. He was the only person who knew all she knew. She had not mentioned Kishon's name to anyone, yet here he was dead, almost certainly murdered.

She had trusted Uri immediately and completely. Maybe she had made a mistake. After all, she had misjudged people before.

She was feeling queasy, her palms clammy with sweat as she looked at him. She thought of the man who had grabbed her that morning, his hand squeezing her *there*. She had not been able to see his face or place his voice. The accent was so strange; maybe, she now wondered, it was the sound of someone disguising his voice. Was it possible that Uri had followed her there? Could that man in the mask have been . . . ? She waited for the traffic to bring the car to a halt and, when it did, she swiftly reached for the handle to open the door.

But Uri got there first, using the button on his side to lock all the doors. She was trapped here; he had her cornered.

He turned to her and in a voice steady and calm said, 'You're not going anywhere.'

CHAPTER THIRTY-EIGHT

JERUSALEM, THURSDAY, 2.25PM

'Uri, I want to get out.'

'Maggie, you're not going anywhere.'

'Let me out. NOW!' Maggie only very rarely raised her voice, and she knew the sound of it was shocking. Uri finally pulled over.

'Listen, Maggie. You can't walk out on me now. Just because this is getting frightening.'

'It's you I'm frightened of, Uri.'

'Me? Are you crazy?'

'Whenever we've found a name, that person has ended up dead. First Aweida, now Kishon. And I know *I* didn't kill them.'

'So you think it was me?'

'Well, you're the only one who knew what I knew.'

Uri was shaking his head in disbelief, staring down at his lap, the car engine still running. 'This is insane, Maggie. How could I have run a guy off a road in Switzerland, when I was here?'

'You could have told someone.'

'I didn't know he was in Switzerland!' He tried to collect himself. 'Look, I just want to find out what happened to my parents.

Someone killed my mother, Maggie. I'm sure of it. And I want to know who it was. That's all.'

She felt the anxiety recede, as if the blood in her veins was subsiding. 'But you could be passing on what you know to Israeli intelligence.'

'Why would I do that? It was Israeli security who shot my father, remember. They may even be the people behind all this. So why would I help them?'

It was true. It didn't make much sense: a secret agent who loses both his parents, just to maintain his cover. She had allowed herself to panic.

'OK. I believe you. Now unlock the doors.'

He clicked them open and waited for her to get out. When he saw that she wasn't moving, he spoke. 'I only locked them because I need you, Maggie. I can't do this alone.' He held the silence a moment longer. 'I don't want you to go.' She held his gaze until she saw in his eyes what she had seen there last night. The same warmth, the same spark. She wanted to dive into that look, to stay inside it. Instead she turned away, nodding, as if to signal that it was time for him to drive on.

He had driven about a hundred yards when, in a sudden movement, he reached for the volume knob on the radio and cranked it up loud. Then he re-tuned until he had found some pounding rap music. The car seemed to be shaking.

Maggie, her head hurting from the noise, reached for the same knob and turned it down, only for Uri to reach back and turn it even louder, his hand lingering there to block any attempt she might make to reverse his decision. 'What the hell are you doing?' she shouted.

Uri looked back at her, his eyes wide as if he had made an important realization. *Bugs,* he mouthed silently. *The car could be bugged.*

Of course. Security had always been a key factor in past mediation efforts and she had, in her time, taken some extreme precautions, once briefing a Foreign Minister in a hotel bathroom while the water was running. But that was when she was dealing with negotiations. This, she had assumed, was different. Her panic over Uri and now this. She suddenly felt very stupid: her year out, nursemaiding warring couples, had left her rustier than she realized.

He was right, they needed to assume they were being bugged. When they reached a traffic light, Uri leaned across to her, so that he could whisper into her ear without his voice being picked up. 'The computers, too.' She could feel the words as much as she could hear them, Uri's breath caressing her ear. She could smell his neck. 'They will have seen whatever we saw. From now on, talk just like normal.'

He turned the music back down. 'You don't like it? Rap's very big in Israel right now.'

Maggie was too thrown to play-act. If their session on Shimon Guttman's home computer had been monitored, then whoever was doing the monitoring would know all they knew – including the truth about Ahmed Nour. And now, this morning, something had got them rattled; rattled enough to want to scare her away. By seeing Aweida, she was getting too close for their comfort.

Uri pulled over. Once they were out of the car, she began speaking immediately, only for Uri to shake his head and put his finger across his lips. *Hush*.

'Yeah, there's a really thriving music scene here now,' he said, still in fake chat mode. 'Mainly in Tel Aviv of course.' He made a beckoning gesture with his hand, urging her to follow his lead.

Maggie stared at him. He was stubbled from several days without a shave, his hair loose and unkempt, the curls tumbling around his face; and now she couldn't think of a single thing to say, about music, or anything else. Instead, she gave him a look of near-complete bafflement.

He leaned in to her ear. 'Our clothes too,' he whispered.

Reflexively, she patted her pockets, feeling for a tiny microphone. He smiled, as if to say, 'There's no point, you'll never find it.'

They were walking towards what looked like an apartment building, not the law office she was expecting. Were they calling on the Guttman family lawyer at home?

Uri pressed the buzzer by the main entrance. 'Hi, Orli?'

Maggie heard a woman's voice crackle through the intercom. '*Mi zeh?*'

'Uri. *Ani lo levad*.' I'm not alone.

The door buzzed open and after two flights they came to an apartment door that was already open. Framed in the doorway, looking bewildered, was a woman Maggie decided was at least five years younger than her – and unnervingly beautiful. With long dark hair that fell in easy curls, wide brown eyes and a slim figure that even loose, faded jeans could not conceal, Maggie found herself hoping this was Uri's sister – but fearing it was his girlfriend.

Instantly, the pair embraced, a long, closed-eyes hug that made Maggie want to disappear. Were they family? Was this woman consoling Uri on his double loss? A moment later, they were inside, Maggie still standing apart, unintroduced.

Without needing direction, or asking permission, Uri made for the stereo, putting on a CD and turning up the volume. Over Radiohead, he began explaining to Orli what had happened and what he suspected. Then, to Maggie's surprise, he pointed towards what she assumed was the bedroom, urging her to follow him. Now the three of them were in there. Still whispering over the music, Uri introduced the two women to each other, each offering an embarrassed nod and polite half-smile. Then he turned to Maggie and explained in an even lower voice that, first, Orli was an ex-girlfriend and, second, Maggie needed to get undressed.

Then in a louder, more deliberately normal voice, he continued: 'Orli trained as a designer in London. I thought maybe you'd like to take a look at some of her latest clothes.' He made a listening gesture, cupping his ear with his hand, then started pointing. The bug could be anywhere: shirt, shoes, trousers, anywhere.

Next, Uri opened up a cupboard and began to pull out men's clothes. Were those his, still stored here, despite his insistence that the gorgeous Orli was an ex? Or did they belong to Orli's new boyfriend?

She couldn't stare for long because Orli was now standing Maggie before her own closet, assessing her up and down with the brutality women reserve only for each other. As it happened, while Maggie might not have Orli's skinny arms, they weren't too far apart: she would be able to fit most of the clothes on the rail.

Orli picked out a long, shapeless skirt – no mistake that, Maggie suspected. 'What about those?' Maggie said, indicating a pair of neat, grey trousers. She noticed a T-shirt and fitted cardigan that would complete the outfit just fine. Reluctantly, Orli handed them over. Pushing her luck, Maggie also nominated a pair of chic leather boots at the bottom of the cupboard. If she was going to wear another woman's clothes, she thought, she might as well enjoy it.

Orli left the clothes in a pile on the corner of the bed, turned on her heel and strode off. Maggie could hardly blame her. If Edward had marched in one day with another woman, demanding that this stranger get undressed in Maggie's apartment and then raid her wardrobe, she would hardly be delighted. *Edward*. They hadn't spoken for two days.

Within a few minutes, they were saying goodbye, Orli drawing out her embrace with Uri a second or two longer than was strictly necessary. He and Maggie headed down the stairs wearing not only new clothes but, at his insistence, having ditched everything else that might contain a device: shoes, bag, pens, the lot.

'You'd be amazed where they can put a microphone or even

a camera these days,' he said, as they walked towards the car. 'Can of hairspray, baseball cap, sunglasses, heel of a shoe, lapel, anything.'

She looked at him.

'We've done it all, for TV documentaries. Hidden camera investigations.'

'Sure, Uri.' She suspected this knowledge was acquired wearing the uniform of the IDF rather than in the edit suites of Tel Aviv TV-land.

Once in the car, he put the music back on and they drove in silence. It was Maggie who broke it.

'So what's the deal with Orli, then?' She hoped it sounded matter-of-fact, as if she was barely bothered.

'I told you. An ex-girlfriend.'

'How ex?'

'Ex. We stopped seeing each other more than a year ago.'

'I thought you were in New York a year ago.'

'I was. She was with me. What is this, an interrogation?'

'No. But five minutes ago we were in the apartment of a woman I'd never met and suddenly you're dressing me up in her clothes. I think I have a right to know who she is.'

'So this is about your rights now, is it?' Uri was taking his eye off the road to smile at her.

She knew how she sounded. She decided to shut up, to look out of the window and say nothing more. That lasted at least fifteen seconds.

'Why did she dump you?'

'How do you know she dumped me? I might have dumped her.'

'Did you?'

'No.'

'So what happened?'

'She said she was sick of hanging around in New York waiting for me to commit. So she came back here.'

'And is it over? Between you?'

'For Christ's sake, Maggie, what is this? Until this week I hadn't spoken to her for nearly a year. She called me about my parents; said if there was anything I needed, I should call. We needed something; I called. Jesus!'

Maggie was about to apologize, to be gracious, to forgive Uri for having a beautiful ex-girlfriend, all of which were possible now that he had said what he had said, but the chance was taken from her. Her phone rang, displaying the number of the US consulate. She gestured at Uri to pull over, so that she could get out and speak, away from the car and the assorted microphones it might be concealing. The phone could be tapped, of course; a bug could even be hidden inside it. But what could she do? She couldn't throw away her phone, she had to be contactable. And she couldn't ignore a call from the consulate. Now standing on a street corner, she answered it.

'Hi Maggie, it's Jim Davis. I'm here with Deputy Secretary Sanchez and Bruce Miller.' There was a click, as she was put on speakerphone.

'Maggie, it's Robert Sanchez here. Things have got a little worse in the course of the day—'

'A little worse? A *little* worse?' It was Miller, his Southern twang cutting right through Sanchez's soft baritone. She imagined him pacing, while Davis and Sanchez sat. 'Try a *lot* worse, Costello. This whole country's burning up faster than a Klansman's cross. Now we got the Israeli Arabs rioting: Galilee, Nazareth, Garden of fucking Gethsemane for all I know. And Hizbullah are still knocking seven bells of shit out of the north. Israelis are getting mighty restless.'

'I understand.'

'I hope you do, Miss Costello. 'Cause I gotta tell ya, the President and a whole lotta other folks have put way too much into this peace process to see it turn into a pile of buffalo shit now.'

This, Maggie knew, was the kind of talk that made Bruce Miller such a force of nature in Washington, overwhelming anyone unlucky enough to stand in his way. Before he got his man elected to the White House, he was a staple on the talk shows, out-mouthing even the Bill O'Reillys and Chris Matthews with this trademark blend of farm-boy argot and cut-to-the-chase political insight. He was smart and funny at the same time; the TV producers couldn't get enough of him.

'We got three big motives in play here. First up, my job is to get the President re-elected in November. Peace treaty in Jerusalem makes that a sure thing. Not many of those in politics, so if you get one, you grab it. Second, Mid-East peace wins the President a place in history. He succeeds where all the others failed. I like that, too. I like that a lot.'

Maggie was smiling despite herself. In her field, euphemism and circumlocution were the standard speech patterns; undiplomatic candour like Miller's made a refreshing change.

'But here's the point, Miss Costello. Usually doing the right thing and winning votes don't go together. When LBJ gave black folks the vote, that was the right thing to do, but it screwed the Democratic Party in the South to this very day. It was right, but it fucked us in the ass. Now this is different, even a cynical old toad like me can see that. We got ourselves a chance to do the right thing *and* win a ton of votes doing it. And believe me, stopping the Jews and Arabs fighting after they've been killing each other so long, that's the right thing to do. We owe it to them not to fuck it up.' He paused, just to make sure his homily had sunk in. 'So what you got?'

Maggie flannelled a while, claiming some progress on both sides, before falling back on her earlier insistence that their best shot at halting the violence would be discovering the specific cause she believed lay behind several, if not all, of the incidents. She was getting closer to uncovering that cause, but it would take time.

'Time's what we don't have, Maggie.'

'I know, Mr Miller,' Maggie said, hearing the almost plaintive note of desperation in his voice. She felt a surge of guilt, that she had been entrusted with this vital task and she was fumbling it. Miller was not all hardball politics; behind that good ol' boy exterior was a man who clearly yearned to make peace. And she, instead of helping, had so far achieved nothing. She hung up, promising another progress report later that night, and got back in the car, her earlier worry over Orli now seeming shamefully trivial.

For a long time she sat in silence, contemplating a much greater terror: a second, lethal failure. Uri drove on, asking no questions.

By the time they stopped outside the lawyer's offices, the light was mellowing into afternoon. It was an old building, made of the same craggy stone that Maggie had now come to see as unremarkable, the natural material for all buildings. They walked up a single flight of stairs to a door marked 'David Rosen, Advocate'.

Uri knocked gently, then pushed at the door. There was no one at the reception desk, though he didn't seem too perturbed by that. 'Probably knocked off early,' he said, no longer in a whisper. Having shed everything he was wearing, he was confident he had now shaken off whatever bug had been pinned on him. Or her.

He called out, in Hebrew, but there was no reply. The offices seemed empty. Together they looked in at the first room: no one there. The next room was the same.

'What time was he expecting us here?' Maggie said, still whispering.

'I said I would come straight over.'

'Uri! That was ages ago. We wasted all that time at Orli's.'

Uri poked his head around each door he could find, looking for the biggest office, the one that would belong to the senior partner. All of them were empty. As he opened the last door which, as he hoped, revealed the grandest office, his expression changed, the colour draining from his face.

Maggie walked in behind Uri, and stared. This office was not empty. David Rosen was still at his desk. But he was slumped across it, his body as still as a corpse.

CHAPTER THIRTY-NINE

TEKOA, THE WEST BANK, THURSDAY, 3.13PM

Not for the first time since he got to this country nearly twenty-five years ago, Akiva Shapira cursed his American upbringing. He watched the young men on manoeuvres in the vineyard, charging, three at a time, their knives thrust forward, ready to plunge into the easy flesh of three straw-filled mannequins, and he regretted that he would never be like them. It was too late now, of course. At fifty-two, and weighing over two hundred pounds, Akiva Shapira would never be able to join this heroic army of Jewish resistance, not in any active way. What pained him was not that his moment had passed, but his knowledge that it had never really arrived.

As an American, he had grown up in flabby, comfortable, suburban New York. Riverdale, to be precise. While these young Israeli men had been taught the language of tanks, artillery and infantry as their mother tongue, reared as warriors from their infancy, he had been raised to join an army of lawyers, accountants and doctors. He had come to Israel in his mid-twenties, in time to do three months' basic training, but by then it was too late. He would never share in the martial knowledge that formed so much of this society's inner culture. He would never say so publicly, but for all his nationalistic militancy and political influence in Israel, Akiva Shapira could never escape the feeling that he remained an outsider.

The men at his side had no such feelings, that he could tell. They all had long military records, the basic three years in their youth and a couple of wars each after that. They could watch this display and, later, discuss the mechanics of combat with unerring confidence. When they moved on to the shooting range, watching as a team of twenty-year-old marksmen darted out of bushes and popped up out of the undergrowth to fire at the row of watermelons lined up as targets, these men, all of them Shapira's age or older, could whisper useful notes to the instructor. Shapira remained quiet, awed by the explosive *blam* that sent the fruits into a shower of pulp and gore time after time, without fail.

He was relieved when the exhibition was over, when the young recruits were dismissed. Now the older men would talk strategy, Shapira taking his place at the table as an equal with the others.

There were only four of them gathered here, in a meeting whose existence, they agreed, would be denied by each of them. Shapira and the man at his right were the only two who held formal positions within the settler movement. The man in the chair had gained fame, and notoriety, another way, as the quartermaster of the *Machteret*, the Jewish underground which made several terrorist attacks on Arab politicians and others more than two decades earlier. He had served time in jail and had, officially, retreated from public life. Most Israeli journalists believed that he now lived abroad. Yet here he was, deep inside the West Bank, in the heart of Samaria, as Shapira and his comrades would describe it.

And yet, should an Israeli camera crew have stumbled upon this gathering – which they would not, since a heavily guarded perimeter enclosed the entire area – it would not have been the former *Machteret* man whose presence would have shocked most, but that of the figure seated at the outdoor picnic table directly opposite Shapira. This man was the personal aide to none other than Yossi Ben-Ari, the Minister of Defence of the State of Israel.

'We're here, as you know, to talk about Operation Bar Kochba,' the quartermaster began.

Shapira liked the name. After all, he had suggested it, to name this twenty-first century Jewish revolt after the man who had led the second-century equivalent. (That Bar Kochba revolt against the Romans had ended in disaster and exile for the Jews of Palestine, a fact Shapira chose to gloss over.)

'Our preferred option remains mass disobedience within the ranks of the IDF. Yariv can have no peace deal if the army refuses to implement its terms. If he gives the order to dismantle a settlement like this one, like Tekoa, then our people will refuse to obey.'

'But there was Gaza,' said Ben-Ari's man.

'Precisely. There was Gaza. We expected mass refusal then and it didn't happen. So we need a Plan B. Which is what you saw just now. Highly-trained young men who will throw off their IDF uniforms and take up arms to protect their homeland.'

Shapira couldn't help but look over at the aide to the Defence Minister. The fact that he was here at all was symbolic enough. But that he was listening, without protest, to a plan by Israelis to take up arms against the army of Israel – the very army his boss headed! – was extraordinary. That they had this man, and therefore, by implication, Ben-Ari himself on side, was proof of their strength, and confirmation of Yariv's great weakness.

'I repeat, we deploy these forces only once an agreement is signed and once the government starts enforcing its terms.'

'But in the meantime . . .' It was Shapira, his urgent desire to get on with it, to act, getting the better of him.

'In the meantime,' continued the quartermaster, shooting a glare in Shapira's direction, 'there are steps we can take to prevent any such deal. These efforts are already underway. You will have seen our claim of responsibility for the latest action in the Old City market.'

The others nodded.

'These pre-emptive steps then, aimed at destabilizing the government before it can commit national surrender, will be the focus of our energies. We have in the last few days established a small unit dedicated to precisely these activities. For now, gentlemen, our fate is in the hands of these men. Tonight when we *daven* the evening service, I suggest we each offer a silent prayer for the good fortune and success of The Defenders of United Jerusalem.'

CHAPTER FORTY

JERUSALEM, THURSDAY, 3.38PM

The sensation was almost physical, as if her spirits were plunging, like a lift in a shaft. There was no denying it: they brought with them the breath of death. Anyone who got close to her or Uri, anyone who had been close to Uri's father, ended up dead. Shimon's wife, poisoned with pills; Aweida, stabbed in a street market; Kishon, driven off a mountain in Switzerland. And now this man, David Rosen, a lawyer who had been entrusted with Guttman's last words, slumped over his desk before he had time to impart them.

Uri approached gingerly, thinking, Maggie assumed, the same thoughts. He got closer, until he could lean over the desk within touching distance of the body. His hand hovered, unsure where to test first. Lightly, it came to rest on the neck, Uri pairing index and middle fingers to find a pulse. A second after he had pressed his fingers in, he leapt back, as if recoiling from an electric charge. At the same instant the body stirred, until both Uri and David Rosen were bolt upright, each as shocked as the other.

'Jesus Christ, Uri, what the hell are you doing here?' Silver-haired with large, unfashionable glasses, Rosen was thin, with spidery arms and legs. His arms, exposed by his short-sleeved shirt, were blotchy with liver spots. As he collected himself, Maggie could see faint red lines etched down one side of his face, the creases of a man who had fallen asleep on a hard surface. In this case, his desk.

'You asked me to come here!'

'What are you talking about?' Maggie could see Rosen was looking for his glasses, even though he was wearing them. Also, bafflingly, he was speaking in English, with what seemed to be a trace of an English accent. 'Oh yes, so I did. But wasn't that yesterday?'

'It was today. You just fell asleep.'

'Ah yes. Arrived in from London this morning. Overnight flight. I'm exhausted. I must have fallen asleep.'

Uri turned to Maggie, rolling his eyes upward. *And our fate is in the hands of this guy?*

'Yes, Mr Rosen. You called me. Said there had been a letter from my father.'

'Yes, that's right.' He began patting his desk, touching the multiple wobbling piles of paper. 'He delivered it by hand it seems, last week.' Suddenly he stopped and pulled himself up to his full height. 'Uri, I'm so sorry. I don't know what I was thinking. Please, come here.' Uri approached and lowered himself, like an adolescent boy receiving a kiss from a tiny grandmother. Rosen hugged him, muttering what seemed like a prayer. Then, in English: 'I wish you and your sister long life. A long life, Uri.'

Maggie gave Uri a stare.

'Oh, yes. Mr Rosen, this is Maggie Costello. From the American Embassy. She's helping me a bit.' Maggie knew what Uri was trying on here.

'What do you mean, the American Embassy?'

It hadn't worked.

'She's a diplomat. Here for the talks.'

'I see. But why exactly is Miss Costello helping you?'

He may be old and half-asleep, thought Maggie, but he's not stupid.

Uri did his best to explain, giving away as few specifics as he could manage. His mother had trusted this woman, he said, and, now, so did he. She was helping solve a problem that seemed to be expanding exponentially. Uri's eyes said something even simpler: I trust her, so you should trust her.

'OK,' said Rosen finally. 'Here it is.' And, with no more ceremony than that, he handed over a white envelope.

Uri opened it slowly, as if handling an exhibit in a court case. He looked inside, a puzzled expression spreading across his face, and then pulled out a clear plastic sleeve containing a single disc. There was no note.

'A DVD,' said Uri. 'Can we use your machine?'

Rosen began fiddling with his computer until Uri moved round to his side of the desk, placed his hands on the old man's shoulders and gently, but unmistakably, shifted him out of the way. No time for courtesies, not now.

He inserted the disc, then dragged across another chair and waited the agonizingly long wait for the programme to boot up and to offer the various prompts which, at this moment, seemed interminable and more annoying than Maggie had ever realized.

Finally a screen within the screen appeared, black at first, then after a second or two, filling up with a line of white characters. Hebrew.

'Message to Uri,' said Uri, translating.

Then, fading up from the black, a moving image appeared: Shimon Guttman sitting at the desk where Maggie herself had sat just last night. He seemed to be facing his computer. He must have filmed this himself, alone, Maggie guessed, remembering the video camera and other paraphernalia piled up in his study.

She looked hard at the face, so different from the man she

had seen in that archive footage online. Gone was the arrogant bluster of the hilltop speech. Instead, Guttman seemed haggard and harried, like a man who had been chased all night and had hardly slept. He was leaning forward, his face drawn and gaunt.

Uri yakiri.

'My dear Uri,' Uri begain translating in a low murmur, 'I hope you never need to see this, that I will come back to Rosen's office in the next week or so and remove this envelope which I asked him to deliver to you only in the event of my disappearance or, God forbid, my death. With any luck, I'll be able to solve this problem by myself and not need to drag you into it.

'But if by any chance I do not, then I could not let this knowledge die with me. You see, Uri, I have seen something so precious, so ancient and so important I genuinely believe it will change anyone who sees it. I know that you and I disagree on almost everything, and I know you think your father exaggerates, but I think you will see that this is different.'

Suddenly Uri leant forward and stopped the computer playback. He turned to Maggie, mouthing, with a how-could-we-be-so-stupid expression, *Bugs!*

He was right. Rosen had phoned Uri; if Uri's phone was tapped, then Israeli intelligence, or whoever else it was, would have had time to come here and bug this office. Could have done it while Sleeping Beauty was dozing on his desk.

Uri now prowled through the office searching intently, stopping once he saw a TV set. He switched it on, found a channel airing American game shows – plenty of whooping and cheering – turned up the volume and came back to the computer. Then he went back to the TV, swivelling it around so that its screen was facing a back wall. 'Hidden cameras,' Uri mouthed to Maggie. 'Most common place to hide them, the TV.' Rosen looked more baffled than ever.

Now when Uri translated, he did so in a whisper, direct into

Maggie's ear. Involuntarily she closed her eyes. She told herself it was so that she could concentrate on his words.

'In the last couple of days I have come across what is the greatest archaeological discovery of my career. Of anyone's career for that matter. It would be enough to make whoever owns it famous and of course very, very rich.' Uri exhaled loudly.

'Those would be reasons alone for me to fear for my life now that it has come into my possession. But there is something more. As always with your father, this something more is a matter of politics. That doesn't surprise you, eh, Uri?'

Uri shook his head. 'No, Father, it does not surprise me.'

'To get to the point, I have seen the last will and testament of *Avraham Avinu*. You heard right. The final will of Abraham, the great patriarch. I know it sounds insane and, believe me, I have wondered about my own sanity. But here it is.'

At that instant, Maggie's eyes opened wide. Uri stopped talking and they both simply stared at the computer screen, David Rosen as dumbfounded as both of them. Shimon Guttman, now with sweat beading on his forehead, had produced from below, out of vision, an object which he held up to the camera. Brown and around the same size as an old audio cassette, it was hard to make out. But Uri's face shone with recognition. He knew exactly what it was. He must have grown up amongst these things.

'I am not going to show you the text up close,' Uri said, translating once more. 'Just in case this recording should fall into the wrong hands. I don't want anyone else seeing what it says. I know that will sound paranoid, Uri. But I fear that some people would go to extreme lengths if they knew this tablet existed.'

'He's right there,' murmured Maggie.

'You will be asking yourself the obvious question. How do I know this is not a fake? I won't bore you with the technical details – the quality and origin of the clay, the style of the cuneiform script, the seal and the language, all of which are entirely in keeping with the Abrahamic period – but, I swear to you, any expert in the field would be almost certain that this is genuine. I say almost. What makes me one hundred per cent certain is that no one tried to sell me this, no one tried to convince me what it was. I found it, quite by chance, in a shop in the Jerusalem market. My guess is that it was stolen, from Iraq. It might have come out of the ground, it might have come from a museum, even the National Museum. Whether the thief knew what he was taking, we will never know. Whether the museum in Baghdad knew is also an interesting question. But Iraq makes sense. After all, where was *Avraham Avinu*, Abraham our father, born but in the great city of Ur in the land of Mesopotamia?' The on-screen Guttman smiled. 'And the city of Ur still stands today. In Iraq.

'You can take my word for it. This text is real. In it, Abraham has come to the end of his life. He is an old man, an ancient man, who has reached Hebron. It seems his two sons, Isaac and Ishmael, are close by. That makes sense, too: we know from the Torah that Isaac and Ishmael buried Abraham, so maybe they were there when their father died. There seems to have been some kind of dispute over Abraham's will. We know from our texts, where it is repeated again and again, that Abraham bequeathed the Land of Israel to Isaac and his descendants, the Jewish people. I know you and your leftist friends can't bear to hear this kind of thing, Uri, but just take two minutes and pick up the book of *Bereshit*, Genesis, chapter fifty, verse twenty-four, where Joseph tells his brothers, "I am about to die. But God will surely come to your aid and take you up out of this land to the land he promised on oath to Abraham, Isaac and Jacob". Or look at *Shmot*, Exodus, chapter thirty-three, verse one: "And the Lord said to Moses, 'Leave this place, you and the people you brought up out of Egypt, and go up to the land I promised on oath to Abraham, Isaac and Jacob, saying, "I will give it to your descendants".'" Or this to Joshua:

"Be strong and courageous, for you will bring the Israelites into the land I promised them on oath, and I myself will be with you". That, by the way is *Dvarim*, Deuteronomy, chapter thrity-one, verse twenty-three. You get the idea: that the Land of Israel was left to the people of Israel, there is no doubt.

'But Jerusalem, it seems, was a more complicated matter between Abraham's brothers, just as it is today. This text—' on screen, Guttman held up the tablet once more, '—doesn't spell it out, but it's quite clear that Isaac and Ishmael had been arguing and that Abraham had to settle the dispute before he died. He must have called for a scribe to come to Hebron – such people existed, even thirty-seven centuries ago – and take down this testament. So that there would be no confusion.

'In the text the old man speaks only of Mount Moriah; there was not yet the Jerusalem we know today. He does not refer to what happened there, but we all know, just as everyone around that deathbed would have known. Imagine the tension in that family! Mount Moriah was the place where Abraham was ready to kill his son. It is the ownership of this spot that Abraham decides in this text.

'My dear Uri, you know the significance of this. The government of Israel now includes three different religious parties. If this text shows that Abraham gave the Temple Mount to the Jews, clearly and unambiguously, they will not be able to stomach a peace accord which compromises on that sovereignty. And what about the other side, our enemy, the Palestinians? Their government includes Hamas, devout Muslims who revere Abraham. If this text says the Haram al-Sharif belongs to the heirs of Ishmael alone, then how can they defy that will? More to the point, and I have thought about this long and hard, what of the first possibility, that this document gives that sacred land entirely to us, the Jews? What then? How would the Muslim fundamentalists cope with that?

'That's why I am sure that if either side were to know even about the existence of this tablet, they would take the most extreme measures to prevent it seeing daylight. That's why I need to handle this carefully. I need to get this information to those who will treat it properly. Later today I will try to speak to the Prime Minister. But if something happens to me, this grave responsibility will become yours, Uri.'

Maggie placed a hand on his shoulder.

'You'll notice that I am not saying here what the text reveals. I cannot risk that, in case, as I say, this recording falls into the wrong hands. But if I am not here, it will be your job to find it. I have put it somewhere safe, somewhere only you and my brother could know about.

'I know that you and I have had bitter differences, especially in recent years. But now I need you to put them aside and remember the good times, like that trip we took together for your Bar Mitzvah. What did we do on that trip, Uri? I hope you remember that.

'I can tell you only that this search begins in Geneva, but not the city everyone knows. A better, newer place, where you can be anyone you want to be. Go there and remember the times together I just spoke about.

'*Lech lecha,* my son. Go from here. And if I am gone from this life, then you shall see me in the other life; that is life too. Good luck, Uri.'

The screen went black. David Rosen was crumpled in his chair, stunned by what he had just seen. Maggie was speechless. Uri, however, was furious.

He started pounding at the computer keyboard, trying frantically to find something else on the DVD, some further element they had missed. 'It can't finish there! It can't!' He was skipping back through the speech they had just watched. He played the last line again. '. . . Good luck, Uri.' Once more, the screen faded to black. Uri put his head in his hands. 'This is so typical of that bastard,' he said quietly.

'What's typical?' said Rosen.

'This. Another fucking dramatic gesture. He has a secret that got his wife killed, that could get his son killed, and does he reveal it? No. He plays fucking games.'

'But Uri,' said Maggie, trying to calm things down, 'wasn't he trying to tell you where it is? He said we have to start in Geneva.'

'Oh, don't listen to any of that crap. Not one word of it makes sense.'

'What do you mean?'

'I mean it's bullshit, from beginning to end.'

'How can you be sure?'

He looked up, his eyes blazing. 'Well, let's start with the very first thing he said. You know, "I've put it somewhere safe, somewhere only you and my brother could know." It's nonsense.'

'Nonsense? How?'

'It's very simple, Maggie.' He paused to look her in the eye. 'My father didn't have a brother.'

Both Maggie and Uri were too fazed by that, too shocked by what they had seen on the DVD and too rapt in conversation to listen closely as they left the offices of David Rosen, Advocate. If they had, they might have heard the veteran lawyer pick up the telephone, asking to speak urgently to a man both he and the late Shimon Guttman regarded as a comrade, an ideological kindred spirit. 'Yes, immediately,' he said into the receiver. 'I need to speak right away to Akiva Shapira.'

CHAPTER FORTY-ONE

RAFAH REFUGEE CAMP, GAZA, TWO DAYS EARLIER

They were running out of places to meet. The golden rule of an armed underground – never in the same place twice – required an infinite supply of safe houses and Salim Nazzal was fearful theirs was running out. The peace talks in Jerusalem had not been good for business; the Palestinian street was suddenly less sympathetic to those who would put bombs on Israeli buses and in Israeli shopping malls. Give the talks a chance, that had become the favoured position of the man in the café. No one's saying we can't go back to armed struggle if – when – the talks fail. But, for a few weeks, let's see what the negotiators can bring us.

In that climate, there was a limited number of Gazans ready to open their doors to a breakaway from Hamas which, everyone knew, was out to sabotage the talks. The risks were insanely high. If anyone found out who was under your roof, your home could be flattened by an Israeli shell. Or you could be shot dead by the Fatah men who, while officially in coalition with Hamas, had not forgotten the street battles they had fought with the organization not that long ago. Or you could be murdered by your former brothers in Hamas itself, disciplined for daring to rebel against a party line that was said to have the blessing of Allah himself.

So Salim bowed graciously to his host, a man, like himself, in his thirties with the neat, short beard of an Islamist. The house was like all the others here: a basic box made of breeze blocks, its floors covered with thin, threadbare rugs and equipped with a TV set, a cooker and a few mattresses on which an entire family would have to sleep. It wasn't the tent city that international visitors would often expect from the words 'refugee camp'. It was more like a shanty town, an urban slum. There were no streets as such, just networks of alleyways that would crisscross into a neighbourhood. This one was called Brazil, after the UN peacekeeping troops from that country who once had barracks here.

Tonight's meeting was even more clandestine than usual. Salim had crucial, and highly confidential, information to impart. A technician at Jawwal, the Palestinian mobile phone company, had been closing down the account of the late Ahmed Nour when he noticed a last, unplayed message in the dead man's voicemail box. The box was locked with a PIN code, but that was easy to over-ride. Curious about the Nour killing, he listened to it: a rambling, excitable message in English from a man who seemed to be some kind of Israeli scholar. The technician, a long-standing Hamas supporter with deep misgivings about the movement's peace strategy, had then made contact with Salim, saying he wanted to pass this knowledge to Palestinian patriots and faithful Muslims.

'*Masa al-khair*,' he began.

'*Masa a-nur*,' the half dozen men present responded.

'We are blessed to have heard news which will have a great bearing on our struggle. A Zionist activist and archaeologist claims to have bought, from an Arab in Jerusalem, a tablet expressing the last will and testament of Ibrahim.' He paused for effect. 'Ibrahim Khalil'ullah.' *Abraham, Allah's Friend*. The men's expressions broke out into a series of sceptical smiles, and there was more than one mocking snort.

'My reaction too, my brothers. But the indications are – and I beg of you that not a word of this travels beyond this room – that the document could well be genuine. Doubtless, this man will claim this text supports Zionist claims to Jerusalem.

'We all know what the Hamas leadership will argue. They will say the tablet was looted from Iraq—'

There was the sound of a gunshot outside. After midnight in Rafah that was not so unusual. But all six men, including Salim, instinctively checked their mobile phones, to see if there were any messages warning of an imminent attack. None. After holding silent for thirty seconds, Salim continued. 'We know what the leadership will say. Either that this is Zionist theft of Arab heritage, looted almost certainly from Iraq. Or that it is a fake and a forgery that only the Zionist media cannot see through, and so on and so on. We know what they will say because we would say the same.'

The men in the room nodded. Salim was younger than most of them but he was respected. In the second *intifada* he had played an active role in the Izz-ad-Din al-Qassam brigades, Hamas's military wing. He was a bomb-maker, one of the few who had avoided the crosshairs of the Israeli military's targeted assassination policy. That gave him a double credibility: he had killed Israelis and he had not got caught.

'But none of that will matter. The Israeli right will not give up an inch of the Haram al-Sharif if they can point to some text that says Ibrahim gave it to them. The peace talks will be over.'

'What if the document says the Haram belongs to us?'

'I have considered that. I think it's safe to assume that if a Zionist scholar had found such a text in the ground he would have put it straight back there.'

The questioner smiled, nodded and sat back.

'So the decision we have is like this: some Palestinians will, I am sure, work very hard to prevent this document coming to light. They will think the obvious: that if Ibrahim's will is known, it will weaken the Palestinian claim on Jerusalem. Such people will kill and be killed to prevent this ancient text ever being revealed. They have probably already started.

'But there is another view. That if this tablet emerges, and if it gives the Zionists all they want, then they will definitely not agree to the arrangements they have been discussing at Government House. Why would they share Jerusalem when Ibrahim has said it belongs to them, all of it?'

'They will call off talks immediately,' chipped in one of Salim's most reliable lieutenants.

'They will. And this sham of a peace process will be over. No more talk of recognizing the Zionist entity. No more nonsense about a truce with the enemy. We can return to the legitimate struggle, one the Prophet, peace be upon him, has determined we shall win.'

'So,' began another. 'You're saying it is in our interest for this will, this testament, to become public?'

'If we want this betrayal of our people to end, I believe so, yes. But we do not need to decide this yet.'

'What do you mean?'

'I mean that we can decide what to do with this document once we have it. But only once we have it. We must devote all our energies to finding it and capturing it. This is our holy duty. Whatever has to be done to get it, must be done. Do I have your agreement?'

The men looked at each other and then, as if in chorus, they replied. 'God is great.'

CHAPTER FORTY-TWO

JERUSALEM, THURSDAY, 6.23PM

They drove back to the hotel in silence. Uri had turned up the rap music again, so that they could drown out whatever bug was listening, but Maggie couldn't stand it. She would prefer to say nothing than have her head pounded with noise.

Her head was pounding anyway. She had scribbled down a few notes during the Guttman video-message and she looked at them now.

. . . somewhere safe, somewhere only you and my brother could know.

What sense did that make if Uri's father had no brother? There was so much to ask. She yearned just to sit still, in a place where they could speak freely, without shouting over noise or looking over each shoulder. If they were being bugged, they were almost certainly being followed.

Once back at the hotel she led Uri straight to the bar. She ordered a Scotch for each of them and all but forced him to down his before ordering another round. Doubles. She found the early evening gloom of the bar soothing.

'What about this brother then, Uri?'

'There is no brother.'

'You sure? Could your grandfather have had an earlier marriage? A secret family he kept hidden?'

Uri looked over his glass, his eyes reflecting the pale amber of the drink. He managed the faintest smile. 'After everything else, after Ahmed Nour and the last will of Abraham, it wouldn't surprise me if my father had a secret brother. Nothing would surprise me now.'

'So it's possible?'

Uri looked tired. 'I suppose it's possible. If you can keep one secret, maybe you can keep many.'

Without thinking, Maggie placed her hand on his. It felt warm. She let it linger, even after she felt self-conscious, just for a second or two. 'OK, let's put the brother thing to one side. We'll come back to it.' At the other end of the bar Maggie noticed an orthodox Jewish man munching peanuts and reading the *Jerusalem Post,* as if waiting for someone. She couldn't remember if he had been there when they arrived. 'Come,' she said, suddenly and loudly. 'I need to sit on a proper chair.' She eased herself off the stool, beckoning Uri to follow. Once she had found a spot a good distance away from the bar, and directly behind the peanut-muncher, she placed her drink on the table and sat where she would have a clear line of sight. Now if the man wanted to watch them, or read their lips, he would have to turn around and reveal himself. She looked around again, over both shoulders. No one else but them.

She called over a waiter and ordered some food. They waited and then, on impulse really, with no planning, she began to tell Uri what had happened that morning. She kept it brief and factual, working hard to show no self-pity. She spared some of the anatomical details, but still she saw Uri's face turn from horror to anger.

'The bastards—' he began, rising to his feet.

'Uri! Sit down.' She grabbed at his arm and tugged him back into his seat. 'Listen, I'm angry too. But the only way we're going to find these people is if we keep calm. Lash out now and they win.' He paused, looking at her. 'The people who killed your mother will win.'

Slowly he came back to his seat, just as the waiter brought over two plates of sandwiches. Maggie was glad of the diversion.

'Look,' she began, once she was sure Uri would not bolt again. 'You know what I can't work out? Why they follow us, but don't strike. Why they don't just take us out. They're killing everyone else.'

Uri chewed for a while, as if trying to swallow his rage. Eventually he spoke, making a clear effort to sound lighter than he felt. 'Speaking as an ex-intelligence officer of the Israel Defence Forces, I'd say when you follow like this, but don't strike, it can mean one of two things.'

'OK.'

'Either the target is too risky to take out. That would be you. If these are Palestinians who are following us, the last thing they need is to kill an American official. Especially a beautiful, female one.'

Maggie looked downward, unsure how to react. Middle-aged diplomats often flattered her and she would reply with some eyelash-fluttering false modesty. But she couldn't deploy that kind of manoeuvre now, one on one with Uri. Not least because this compliment, unlike the others, meant something to her.

'Imagine how the American public would react if your face was shown for twenty-four hours on cable news, how they would feel about the evil Arabs who had killed you.'

'All right, I get the picture.' Maggie was still enough of a convent girl to feel superstitious about tempting fate. 'The same would be true of the Israelis.'

'Even worse for them in a way,' said Uri, slowly loosening up, helped along by the Scotch. 'Spying on the Americans is bad enough and we've done that a couple of times. But killing them? Not a good idea. Are you still an Irish citizen too?'

'Yep. Never gave it up.'

'Big fight with the Europeans too, then. If they killed you.'

'What's the other possibility? You said there were two.'

'Oh, the other time you stalk but don't strike is when you want the subject alive. To lead you somewhere.'

Maggie took a swig of the drink, letting an ice cube slip between her lips. She let it roll around her mouth, enjoying its chill on her tongue. So they wanted her to pursue this Guttman trail, whoever 'they' were. They would keep away for as long as she was useful. 'But the people who attacked me today told me to back off, to stay away.'

'I know,' said Uri. 'So maybe they're in the first category. They're only not killing you because killing you would bring too much trouble.'

'Or maybe there's more than one group following us. Following me. All for different reasons.'

'Maybe. Like I've said a million times, this country, this whole area, is seriously fucked up.'

Maggie put her drink down. Back to business. She pulled out the Post-it note she had scribbled on in Rosen's office. 'Your father said something about the "good times". Some trip you took together for your Bar Mitzvah. He said he hoped you would remember that.'

'I do remember it.'

'What happened?'

'He took me with him on a working trip to Crete. He wanted to check out the excavations at Knossos. Imagine it: I was thirteen years old, and I was looking at dusty old relics.'

'And?'

'That was it.'

'Come on, there has to be something specific. Was there a museum? Was there a particular piece that had special meaning to your father?'

'It was a long time ago, Maggie. And I was a kid. I wasn't interested in that stuff. I don't remember any of it.'

'Did anything happen?'

'I remember waiting around a lot. And I liked the plane ride. I remember that.'

'Think Uri, think. There must be some reason your dad mentioned this in the message. Did something important happen there?'

'Well, it felt important to me at the time. It was a big treat to be alone, just me and him. It hadn't happened before.' He looked up at Maggie, showing her that rueful smile once more. 'And it didn't happen again.'

'Did you talk about something?'

'I remember him talking about the Minoans, saying they had once been this great civilization. And look at them now, he said. They don't exist any more. That could happen to us, he said; to the Jews. It nearly *has* happened, lots of times. Nearly wiped out. That's why we need Israel, he said. "Uri, after all we've been through, we need a place of our own." That's what he said.'

Anything specific, Maggie was thinking impatiently, straining to stick to her own rule: she knew that sometimes you just had to let people talk, let the words unspool until the crucial sentence tumbled out.

'He told me about his parents, how his mother had been killed by Hitler, how his father had survived. That was an amazing story. He hid, my grandfather, with a family of non-Jews, on a farm in Hungary. They kept him and a cousin in the pig sty. Right at the end of the war, he escaped by crawling through two miles of sewers.

'My father said that the lesson of *his* father's life was that the Jews would have to have somewhere where they would never need anyone else's permission to survive. Where they could fight and defend themselves if they had to. No more cowering in a pig sty.'

The Nazi period . . . Maggie was seized by a sudden thought. She remembered the rows about the Swiss banks who had kept their hands on long-dormant accounts held by Jews who had been murdered by the Nazis. Could there be a connection? 'Uri. You know the message mentioned Geneva? Might your family have left—'

'My family had no money. Nothing. Poor before the Nazis and poor after.'

'OK, so not money. But what about a safe deposit box in Geneva? Maybe your father hid the tablet in a Swiss bank.'

'I just don't see it; that wasn't his world. A vault in Geneva? That would cost serious money. Besides, when would he have had the time to put it there? He said on the DVD he had only just found the tablet.'

Maggie nodded; Uri was right. Geneva must mean something else.

'And what about all this stuff at the end? "And if I am gone from this life, then you shall see me in the other life; that is life too." I was under the impression your father was not a religious man.'

'It's a surprise that he talked this way. But maybe this is what happens when you hold the words of Abraham in your hand. And if you fear death. Maybe you start talking like a rabbi.'

'I'm sorry about all this, Uri.'

'It's not your fault. But it's horrible to realize you hardly knew your own father. All these secrets. What kind of relationship can you have with someone who keeps so much from you?'

'Look,' she said. 'They're closing up here. We better go.'

But instead of heading for the lifts, Maggie strode over to the front desk at reception. Uri watched as she launched into a long story about allergies and dust and how she simply couldn't sleep another hour in her room. The night manager put up some resistance but soon surrendered. He took her old key, replacing it with one for room 302 and despatched a porter to move her things. As she turned around, she gave Uri a wink: 'No bugs in room 302.'

He insisted on walking her to her room. Once they got to the door, she asked where he was going to sleep. He looked as if he hadn't thought about it till that moment.

'Well, my apartment is being watched. And so is my parents' house.'

'Seems like the only reason they're not killing you is because you're with me,' said Maggie, smiling up at him.

'Well, I'd better stay with you then.'

CHAPTER FORTY-THREE

JERUSALEM, THURSDAY, 10.25PM

She knew she should have said no, that she should have insisted he take the lift back down, that he sleep in the car if necessary. But she told herself it would be OK, that he would sleep on the sofa or the floor and that would be that.

She even tried opening a cupboard, looking for the extra blankets and pillows from which she would conjure a makeshift bed. But when she turned around Uri was standing behind her, unmoving, as if refusing to play along with this charade.

'Uri, listen, I explained—'

'I know what you said,' he replied, placing a finger on her lips. Before she could say another word, he had met her mouth with his. His kiss was gentle at first, as it had been the previous night, but that did not last. Soon it was urgent and the current of electricity came from her.

She kissed him hungrily, her lips and tongue desperate for the taste of his mouth. The ferocity of her desire shocked her, but there was nothing she could do to stem it. It had been pent up so long, suppressed for hour after hour, that now that the dam had burst, there was no holding it back.

Her hands were moving through his hair, tugging at it, wanting to bring his face, his smell, closer. It was a sort of devouring, and they both felt the urgency of it. His hands were moving fast, first caressing the side of her face, then her neck, until now they were tearing at her top.

A moment later they had fallen onto the bed, their skin tingling from that first electric contact. Each caress, each taste, brought a new flash of intense sensation, until their bodies were joined. His back became slick with sweat and, as she gripped it, she was sure she could feel not only his desire but also his longing, his need, even his grief. And as she howled her release, she knew he could hear her own need, her yearning to be free after so long. They held each other tight like that for hours, even after the first wave had receded, their ardour barely fading.

Maybe she was too wired, but when she woke up sometime after two am she could not get back to sleep. Uri was slumbering beside her, his chest rising and falling with each long breath. She guessed this was the first deep sleep he had had since his father died. She liked looking at him. For a long time she lay there on her side, just watching him, and felt a kind of peace spreading through her.

Nearly an hour passed that way until eventually Maggie grew restless. She got out of bed, grabbing the large T-shirt she had taken from Edward's closet when she packed up on Sunday afternoon. *State be warned, Commerce kicks butt* read the legend: a souvenir of the interdepartmental softball game last summer, participation in which Edward regarded as crucial to his Washington career.

She crept over to the desk, just a few feet from the bed. She flipped open the lid of her laptop, her face turning blue from the screen glow in this darkened room. Uri didn't stir.

She waited for a connection and opened up her email. Top of the list was a message from Liz.

Mags

My Second Life account tells me you never used that link I sent you. So knew you wouldn't! But you should. Not only is it proof of your 2L stardom, but there's also some pretty cool stuff on there. Here – again! – is my screen-name and password and a few basic instructions: just go on as me . . . btw, we must talk about Dad's 70th. I reckon a big do, you know, fly him and Mum to Vegas, strippers, the works. What do you reckon? Just kidding xx L

Her sister had signed off with a smiley face which, at this moment, made Maggie smile.

The next one was from Robert Sanchez. *Subject: Update*. Inside, with no message, was a digest of the latest cables from the US team in Jerusalem to Washington. Even in a skim read she could discern their message: the situation was grim.

Talks are down to a skeleton presence at Government House, with lowest-level representation on both sides. The progress of less than a week ago, before the Guttman killing, seems distant now . . . two sides trading recriminations . . . hostile noises from the Arab states, sabre rattling from Iran and Syria . . . pro-Israel lobby in the US, led by Christian evangelicals, getting restless, liaising with settler groups here to organize a telethon to run on Christian Broadcasting Network on Sunday night . . . outbreak of violence in the Temple Mount area today as Israeli forces fired tear gas on worshippers at the Al-Aqsa Mosque, two Palestinians dead, one teenager . . . ambush of settler car outside Ofra, two passengers killed, one aged twelve . . .

Maggie ran her fingers through her hair as she regretted again having given up smoking. Jesus, she could die for a cigarette now. She braced herself for message number three.

Edward: no subject

M,

Not that you would care but am off to Geneva this evening. Government business, can't get into it in an email.

We have some practical matters to resolve when we both return. Please advise on your plans.

E

Maggie let herself fall back into her chair. *Please advise*. Had this man really once been her lover? She looked over at Uri, the outline of his sleeping body visible under a single white sheet, and she smiled.

Maggie clicked back to Liz's message. Such a sweetie. She hit Reply.

You're a great sister. I don't deserve you. Will check out that link. Re: Vegas. Can we arrange strippers to come as crown green bowlers?

She was about to hunt out Second Life when she had a sudden sinking feeling. Their phone calls were bugged, they were being followed and, it seemed, her work on Shimon Guttman's computer had been watched. Someone, somewhere, was probably reading this right now. She snapped the lid shut, plunging the room into darkness once more.

She knew she wouldn't sleep, she was buzzing too much. So she pulled on some clothes, creaked open the door and crept outside. She tiptoed down the corridor, heading for the rooms that all hotels maintained even though, in the era of the BlackBerry and wi-fi, hardly anybody used them any more: the Business Center.

Her keycard let her in, to a room that was dark, empty and cold. There was just a single, forlorn terminal. But it worked, asking for her room number and nothing else. That was OK: hotel staff could see what she was doing, it was just the electronic eavesdroppers, hackers and Peeping Toms she wanted to avoid.

She called up Liz's email again, scribbled down the name – Lola Hepburn! – and password she had given her, and clicked on the link. The screen instantly went black, then displayed a message.

Welcome to Second Life, Lola.

She entered her details, then watched as a computer-generated landscape began to fill the screen, as if to herald the start of a video game. In the foreground, with her back to Maggie, was a CGI-version of a lithe young woman wearing tight jeans and a Union Jack bratop. This, Maggie realized, was Lola Hepburn, Liz's embodiment in Second Life, her 'avatar'. Maggie looked at the set of buttons that appeared at the foot of the screen: *Map, Fly, Chat* and a few others whose meaning eluded her. There was an instruction to use the keyboard's arrows to move backwards and forwards, left and right. She tried it and watched, amazed, as the buxom siren on screen moved ahead, jerkily, with arms swinging, in a simulation of human walking.

She seemed to be in some kind of virtual garden, with brown autumnal trees swaying in a gentle wind. It was as if Maggie were operating a camera, lurking a few yards behind and several feet above the avatar, one that followed its – her – every move. Now, as she went through the trees, the leaves loomed larger, in sharp, clear focus, as if the lens of her camera were right up close. It was bizarre and strangely mesmerizing.

She turned left, yet the buxom girl on screen didn't seem to move. Rather the whole frame swivelled, the picture rotating around her as if she had turned left. Now she could see houses, the grey slate of the roof tiles suddenly appearing in pin-sharp detail. And there was a sound, a repeated phrase of music, like a fairground jingle. Sure enough, Maggie could see in the distance a spinning carousel. As she walked towards it, the music got louder. She seemed to be approaching via a meadow: with each step that she took, flowers would sprout from the ground in brilliant shades of violet, yellow and scarlet.

Maggie looked down at the scribbled instructions taken from Liz's email. To get to the room where she would find the virtual Maggie Costello, the venue for the peace simulation game, she had to hit the *Map* button, then find the *My Landmarks* pulldown menu and look for Harvard University, Middle East Studies. It was there, close to the top. Once selected, she hit *Teleport* and smiled as the computer gave off a suitably sci-fi whoosh sound, suggesting a Star Trek-style leap across the universe. The screen darkened, lit up with a message that said 'Second Life, Arriving . . .' and then, an instant later, she saw the girl in the skinny jeans and croptop standing somewhere else entirely, still in the foreground, as if in the lens of a camera hovering overhead.

Now she was surrounded on all sides by buildings, arranged as if on a university campus. Some were rendered in traditional brick, others constructed in more modish steel and glass. As the avatar walked ahead, the arms swinging metronomically, Maggie noticed the surface of the ground, cobbled just as a campus path should be.

In front of her was a ramp, with words printed on it which became legible only as you approached. *Welcome to the Faculty for Middle East Studies*. She moved upward, marvelling at the change in perspective as she did so. There were pictures in the lobby, which swivelled as she hit the arrow keys. There was a reception desk and, at shoulder level, a series of signposts. Maggie took the one marked Peace Simulation.

Suddenly she was inside a room laid out in classic negotiation style: a long, wide wooden table with space for more than twenty people around it. It seemed to be full, avatars sitting in each place, with namecards in front of each one. There was one for the American President, another for the Secretary General of the UN and several more for the leaders of assorted interested parties: the perennial 'moderate' Arab states, Egypt and Jordan, the European Union, Russia and others. Away from the table, ringing the room, were chairs laid out for officials, from the US Secretary of State on down. She moved her cursor over the American team, revealing Bruce Miller and Robert Sanchez, until she came across a female avatar, with long brown hair and a trim figure, wearing a dully vacant expression. A black information bubble appeared: *Maggie Costello, US mediator*.

'At least I'm in the room,' Maggie muttered to herself. She guessed these were dumb avatars, inert mannequins installed inside Second Life as props to add to the authenticity of the scene. You had to give it to the geek community: they certainly cared about detail.

It was then Maggie noticed that two of the figures around the table were not still, but wobbling. They were facing each other, identified by their on-screen bubbles as Yaakov Yariv and Khalil al-Shafi. They had the faces of the two men too, or a very close computer simulation of them. Only the bodies and clothes didn't fit. They were computer-game generic, presumably allocated automatically by Second Life software. Either that or Israel's aged Prime Minister still maintained an ostentatiously muscled chest, while the Fatah leader secretly liked to dress like an urban clubber, complete with tight-fitting T-shirt. Now that she was this near, her avatar standing halfway between the door and the head of the table, she could eavesdrop on their conversation. She checked her watch. Early evening on the East Coast: these were probably a couple of postgrads putting in some extra hours of role play.

A speech bubble appeared by the Yaakov Yariv avatar. A single line of yellow text. *Hello? Can we help you? Are you taking part in the peace simulation?*

Maggie was flummoxed. What on earth should she say? Should she pretend to be someone else? There was only one thing for it. She would have to stay in character. Valley girl, she decided. She hit the *Chat* key and typed. As the words appeared on the screen, she noticed her avatar change posture: its arms were now raised up, the hands flapping. Maggie realized her on-screen alter ego was miming typing.

hope i'm not crashing in here guys, but i'm doing my major in int rels and if i could listen in, it could really help.

Yariv came back a second or two later, the hands of his avatar now waggling in front of him, as if hitting the keys of an unseen keyboard.

Where do you study?

Maggie hesitated, looking again at Liz's avatar.

burbank community college.

There was a pause.

OK.

Maggie waited, enjoying this strange little game. She wondered what kind of antics Liz got up to here. Did she have the boyfriend in Second Life that she lacked in the first one?

The al-Shafi character began. *Have you seen the Silwan map, the latest one?*

There was a delay of a second or two. Then a bubble popped up by the Yariv avatar. *We saw it. It involves a bypass route for the water main.*

Khalil al-Shafi: *Yes.*

Yaakov Yariv: *Who would pay for that?*

Khalil al-Shafi: *We propose three years from the EU-UN fund, eventually to be self-sustaining.*

Yaakov Yariv: *With access to the Jordanian aquifer?*

Khalil al-Shafi: *We imagine so. But we would need your in-principle agreement before we would put that to the Jordanians.*

Maggie nodded her head in professional admiration. You had to hand it to these kids: they were certainly taking their studies seriously, not trading platitudes but getting into the real detail of the negotiations. Water was one of those issues whose importance eluded most outsiders to the Middle East conflict: too busy thinking about oil.

Good for them, she thought. She went back to her keyboard, back to the busty Valley girl.

you guys are really smart! thanks a bunch but i think i'd better study some more before i'm ready for this stuff, wish me luck!

Having said her goodbyes, Maggie mis-hit the arrow keys, haphazardly staggering forward and back. Then, embarrassed, as if she really were in a room with two Harvard post-grads and was fumbling her exit, she hit the *Fly* button. Sure enough, the glamorous avatar rose from the ground and, with a little help from the forward arrow, took flight.

Immediately, she collided with a neighbouring building, smacking her virtual head on it, watching her virtual self flinch for no more than a second. But a few moments later she was soaring above the Harvard campus. The graphics were extraordinarily detailed, like architects' three-dimensional projections, showing the white stucco cladding on the Dunster House clock-tower, even the newsstands and bicycle racks of Harvard Yard.

She carried on flying, her arms outstretched, her body horizontal, like a heavy-chested Superman. Occasionally she would swoop down to take a closer look. She saw hodge-podge buildings, as if constructed one extension at a time, surrounded by their own bumpy landscapes: private homes, she soon realized, with gardens. She flew over a stretch of water, spotting a palm-fringed island. Once she got lower, a notice popped up on her screen: a promotional ad for a concert to be performed there by some eighties rocker tomorrow night. Maggie shook her head in bemused awe.

She carried on flying for a few minutes longer, imagining her sister losing herself in this world of sharp lines and vivid colours. Maggie spotted a cluster of avatars and descended, her curiosity roused the way it would be if she saw a real crowd on a real street. As she landed, her knees bent.

The neon signs gave it away: Second Life's red-light district. Mannequins were wearing shiny PVC corsets, which, as your cursor hovered near, revealed a price tag. Whips, rubber masks, they had it all. Instantly she felt unclothed, her pneumatic breasts an embarrassment. But she was Lola Hepburn now. She could do what she liked.

She approached a male avatar, an absurdly muscled creature who, Maggie guessed, had been designed with the gay market in mind. A graphic popped up immediately, shaped like a pie-chart, each slice given over to a different option: *Chat, Flirt, Touch Me* were the ones Maggie noticed first. She hesitated, looking at the screen showing these two ludicrous cyber-creations – one of them, for now, being her – and wondered what people would make of this scene. In the dead of night, in a room filled with sleeping fax machines and abandoned desks, a US diplomat in a Jerusalem hotel, scoping what looked like internet porn during the darkest hour of the peace process. What, she wondered, would it be like to touch without touching? What could this machine do to simulate that feeling? She remembered the man asleep in her bed upstairs.

Now another man, a bearded avatar with seventies Afro and tight trousers, had entered the room, close enough to address them both with a line of text.

Shaftxxx Brando: Hi guys? What's going down?

Maggie instantly hit the *Fly* button, fleeing this room and the whole sex district. She was now zooming over seas, city skylines, holiday resorts, once descending to find she was in a perfectly reproduced Philadelphia city centre, the streets laid out in a neat three-dimensional grid.

She went back to the *Map* key, taking a few seconds to work out what she had to do. Homesickness decided her first destination. She typed in 'Dublin' and then hit *Teleport*.

A whoosh later and she was standing in a landscape which, even reproduced like this, she found instantly familiar. The water on the Liffey was too static, but the Temple Bar area was there, complete with the clubs and pubs she remembered so well from her teenage years, when she and the other convent girls drank vodka like Russian sailors. But it looked desolate tonight, just her and a few wastrels mooching down Dame Street.

She sniffed at the thought of it. Pathetic really, a grown woman staring at a screen in the middle of the night to remind her of home. She was meant to have given all this up, this wandering the globe, and to have put down roots with Edward in Washington. Yet here she was, in the blue light of a hotel business centre at gone three in the morning, pining for her home town thanks to a glorified computer game. She sat back in her chair, wondering why her plan to settle down had failed. Wrong city? Wrong time? Or wrong man?

She shut the computer down, crept out of the glass-walled business centre and headed for the lifts. She thought of the Dublin she had just seen. Not like any Dublin she remembered. Cleaner, tidier and infinitely lonelier.

Maggie stepped inside the lift and it was only when the doors slid shut that it hit her. *Of course*. That's what Shimon Guttman had meant. The wily old bastard! How could she not have seen it till now?

'Come on, come on,' she said, desperate to get back and wake Uri. She looked up at the numbers, counting the floors. *Seven, eight, nine*. Here.

Hesitantly, she peered out of the lift doors, just in case her shadow, the man or men who had been following her since God knows when, had decided to station himself right outside her hotel room. No one there.

She padded along the corridor, ensuring her heels barely landed on the carpet. She wanted to make no sound. Slowly she slid her keycard into the lock, until it flashed green. She pushed the door open, began crying out Uri's name when she felt a hard, quick blow to the back of the neck. She fell to the floor, making barely a sound.

CHAPTER FORTY-FOUR

JERUSALEM, FRIDAY, AN HOUR EARLIER

First he heard the double click, the signal that they were speaking on a secure line. As always, the boss got straight to the point.

'My worry is that things are spiralling out of control.'

'I understand.'

'We obviously need that tablet.'

'Yes.'

'I mean we need it *now*. Things are getting crazy. The cure is beginning to look worse than the disease.'

'I know how it looks.' He could hear a deep sigh on the other end of the phone.

'How long do you think we should give this whole thing?'

That was the drawback of a job like this, working for the big decision-maker. Such men always expected action immediately, as if merely uttering that something should happen was enough to make it happen. All political leaders became like this eventually, coming to regard their own words as divine speech acts. *I said, Let there be light. Why isn't there light?*

'Well, now we've started, I don't see how we can stop. You've seen the latest. Hizbullah firing rockets at towns and villages in the middle of the night, maximizing risk of casualties. We can't let ourselves be dictated to by them.'

'What about Costello? Has she got anything?'

'We're following her very closely. I think she's making progress. And what she knows, we know.'

Another sigh. 'We need to have this tablet in our possession. We have to know what's in it before they do. So we can act first. Shape events.'

'You know it's always possible that no one will get it. Neither us, nor them.'

'How do you mean?'

'I mean Costello could lead us to it. Or she could fail. The tablet could disappear with Shimon Guttman. It would be as if the whole issue never arose.'

The voice on the end of the secure line did not need to hear more. He could put the pieces together.

'That's not bad.'

'Almost a win-win.'

'If she gets it, we get it. If she doesn't get it . . . If she, for some unforeseen reason, cannot advance this mission, then no one gets it. Problem solved.'

'Could be.'

'OK. Let's talk in the morning.'

He heard the familiar second click, then terminated the call and scrolled through his contacts to find the number of the surveillance team, the unit tracking Guttman and Costello. He was connected within a single ring.

'Do you have the subjects within view? Good. We need to talk about a change in plan.'

CHAPTER FORTY-FIVE

JERUSALEM, FRIDAY, 3.11AM

At first she wasn't sure if she had opened her eyes. The room was in complete darkness. She raised her neck, a reflex, to check the clock, but immediately felt a spasm of pain. Only then did she remember what had happened. She had come out of the lift, ready to tell Uri what she had discovered; she had opened the door and then, in a second, she had been struck.

Where was she now? Flat, the palms of her hands detected the cotton softness of bedclothes. She squinted, just making out the outline of curtains ahead. She was, then, still in her room. What the hell had happened?

Suddenly there was a voice, alarmingly close to her ear.

'I'm so, so sorry. I'm sorry, Maggie.'

Uri.

She tried to haul herself up, but the pain shot through her again.

'I woke up and saw the bed was empty. I thought maybe something had happened to you. I waited by the door and then—'

'And then you hit me.'

'I didn't know it was you. I'm so sorry, Maggie. How can I make it better?'

Maggie decided to push through the pain barrier and sit up. Uri instantly propped her up on some pillows, passing her a glass of water. She took sips, then felt a gentle pressure on her hair – a hand, stroking the side of her head. As her eyes adjusted to the dark, she could see that Uri was kneeling by the bed, and now his warm hand cupped the side of her face.

'Everything I touch gets hurt. Everything I care about ends up hurt . . .'

Maggie could feel the water sliding down her throat; it seemed somehow to unleash the pain in her neck, letting its sore redness radiate outward. 'Fuck, though, where did you learn to hit like that?'

'You know the answer to that.'

'You don't mess around, you Israelis, do you?' she said, rubbing at the pain.

'Here.' At his side was a towel, the edge of which was soaked. He balled it up and placed it at the back of Maggie's neck. First, though, he had to lift up her hair, so that her nape was unguarded, naked. She felt her body register the confusion, an ache and a surge of renewed desire, at the same time. The towel was cold, soothing the redness.

'Uri!' she said suddenly, grabbing the towel from him so that she could face him while she spoke. 'Pass me my jacket, on the chair.'

Unsure whether he had been forgiven, Uri hesitated.

'Uri! Now!'

He got up and brought back Maggie's coat. She patted through the packets, ignoring the pain, till she found it: the Post-it from Rosen's office.

'Turn on the light. OK. Listen. Your father said, "I can tell you only that this search begins in Geneva, but not the city everyone knows. A better, newer place, where you can be anyone you want to be. Go there." Remember?'

'Yes.'

'I think I know where that is.'

'It's Geneva.'

'Yes, but not the city everyone knows.' Maggie scanned ahead, looking at her last, scribbled line. 'Then he said, "And if I am gone from this life, then you shall see me in the other life; that is life too". Now, tell me, Uri, as precisely as you can, what were his exact words. In Hebrew.'

'I don't understand a word you're saying.'

'You will. Just tell me what he said!'

Uri began speaking in Hebrew. 'OK, he said, *"Im eineini ba-chaim ha'ele, tireh oti ba-chaim ha-hem."*'

Maggie looked down at the Post-it. 'And that means, "If I am gone from this life, you shall see me in the other life", right?'

'Yes.'

'OK. Go on.' Maggie could feel the adrenaline coursing through her system, dulling the pain.

'Then he said something odd. *B'chaim shteim*. Which means, I guess "in life too".'

'As in "that is also life".'

'No, no, you heard me wrong. Not "too" but "two". *Shteim* is the number two.'

The excitement was growing now. 'So what he was actually saying was "you shall see me in the other life; that is, life number two".'

'Right.'

'And that's the literal translation, Uri?' Maggie knew she was sounding like some kind of lunatic, but this was not unprecedented behaviour on her part. She had done this at a negotiation once, in the very last hour before a signing, when a dispute broke out between the two sides over the English translation of the accord, which would serve as the binding text under international law. She had to go through the relevant clause word by word, with two interpreters, to make sure one side didn't try to steal a march on the other. No dinner conversation among mediators was complete without someone telling the Menachem Begin at Camp David story, how the Israeli prime minister had succeeded in making the Hebrew version of his agreement with Egypt much less demanding on his country than the English text Jimmy Carter took home to Washington. So pressing Uri like this was not a first. Though she had never done it in bed, with a towel on her neck, before.

'Well, the phrase is weird, but he said "*chaim shteim*". Life two.'

'Or to put it another way,' Maggie said, her eyes brightening, 'Second Life.'

CHAPTER FORTY-SIX

JERUSALEM, FRIDAY, 3.20AM

Maggie flung her arms around Uri's neck and planted a long kiss on his mouth. She felt the sudden softening, and moistening, as his lips began to part.

'I knew it!' she said, her eyes closed as she bathed in the sense of satisfaction. 'It had to be!'

For the first time, she felt this was a problem that could actually be solved. Shimon Guttman was sharp, she knew that: his political stunts had been famous for their attention-grabbing creativity, and she had seen his canniness herself, with the neat little sleight concealing his collaboration with Ahmed Nour by creating an Israeli alter ego, 'Ehud Ramon'. And Uri had told her that, despite his age, his father was utterly at ease with new technology. Didn't Uri even say the old man liked playing computer games?

What he had done was utterly in character. Under pressure, aware that he was holding in his palms, no doubt growing clammier by the minute, a geopolitical timebomb, he had decided to hide the Abraham tablet where no one would think to look. Nowhere in the real world at all. But in the virtual realm, "A better, newer place, where you can be anyone you want to be". He had hidden his treasure, or at least the secret of its location, in Second Life.

And then her stomach gave way. *Oh no.* To have come this far and to have screwed up now. How could they, how could *she*, have been so stupid?

'What is it?' asked Uri, still baffled.

Maggie said nothing, simply placing her finger over her lips. *What idiots.* Ever since the death of Afif Aweida, they had realized that someone was listening to their private conversations. From that point on, they had only spoken against a background of loud music or noise; or had whispered in public places, even exchanged scribbled notes. Yet when she had come round after Uri had whacked her on the neck, neither of them had thought to take precautions. Perhaps she had been too dazed by the blow; maybe he was too sleepy, or too guilty. But they had both forgotten. It wasn't enough that they had changed rooms; their pursuers had had several hours to catch up. Which meant her crucial discovery would now be known by whoever was listening.

Maggie reached for the hotel message pad by the phone, scribbling fast: *Get dressed.* There was no time to waste. She had to get onto Second Life before they did. If she moved now, she might have a head start: it would surely take the Israelis or whoever it was time to work out what she already knew. She was tempted to use her laptop in this room and be done with it. But it was too risky: if they had already hacked into that, they would discover whatever she was about to find the instant she found it.

Uri dressed in the dark. If they were being watched from outside, no point in telegraphing that they were about to leave. She caught the outline of Uri's frame only in silhouette now and felt a stirring of desire.

She checked they were ready then led the way downstairs, back to the business centre. She powered up the machine, reassured by its anonymity: there was nothing that could lead those stalking her to this computer. She immediately logged into Second Life, using the name and password Liz had given her. Uri stood over her shoulder, his face lit up by the reflected, lurid colours on the screen. When Liz's avatar materialized, his eyes widened.

'Wow. Hey, Lola.'

'It's not mine!' Maggie grimaced. 'It's my sister's.'

'Your sister Lola looks like a fun girl.' For that, she slapped him on the arm.

Feeling like a veteran now, Maggie called up the *Teleport* prompt and keyed in the six letters she hoped would unlock this puzzle once and for all. She imagined it, the phone call to Sanchez, telling him she could explain the recent spate of violence; she imagined his response. *You better tell them yourself, Maggie. Get them round the table and get these peace talks back on track. I know you can do it . . .*

Her avatar had now landed in the scrubbed streets of virtual Geneva. She began walking down Rue des Etuves, turning into Rue Vallin. There was hardly anyone about, save for a couple of rabbit-headed avatars on a street corner. Maggie headed down Rue du Temple to avoid them.

'I can't believe this,' murmured Uri. 'You're saying my dad came to this . . . place?'

'Geneva, but not the city everyone knows. That's what he said. Kishon went to the wrong Geneva. What your father had was hidden here somewhere.'

'But you're just wandering down streets. What are we looking for exactly?'

'Right now, I don't know. It could be a map, maybe directions. Something that will tell us where he left the tablet. We'll have to work it out.'

She reached into her pocket, looking again at the Post-it note. *I have put it somewhere safe, somewhere only you and my brother could know.* If only she understood what the hell that meant. She read on. *I need you to remember the good times, like that trip we took together for your Bar Mitzvah. What did we do on that trip, Uri? I hope you remember that. I can tell you only that this search begins in Geneva . . .*

'What did you do on the trip, Uri? Think.'

'I told you. We went to Crete. We talked a bit. I got bored. I'm sorry, Maggie. I just can't think of anything.'

'All right. We'll just have to see if Geneva has some Greek museum or something.'

'Minoan.'

'What?'

'Crete is Minoan.'

Maggie gave Uri a glare. 'Thank you, Professor.' She tried to see if there was a directory of buildings, even a detailed map, of this virtual Geneva. Nothing. She decided to fly, to see if any large structures caught her eye. Perhaps there would be a large museum with a Minoan department. Maybe Shimon Guttman had left this vital clue to the tablet's location in there.

'The funny thing is,' Uri was saying, more to himself than to Maggie, 'the only really strong memory I have of that trip is the flight; it was the first time I had ever been on a plane. That's what really stuck in my mind. I told my father that, probably hurt his feelings. But it was true. We sat together, by the window seat, and I found it amazing, looking down at this beautiful blue water, while he pointed out the different islands below. That was the highlight, really. From then on—'

Maggie suddenly turned to look at him. She could hear Shimon Guttman's voice: *What did we do on that trip, Uri? I hope you remember that.*

'He wants us to do the same thing here,' she said, hitting the arrow keys with new vigour. 'He wants us to fly over Lake Geneva, looking for islands.'

The avatar was hovering above the virtual city, as Maggie directed it first west, then east. She had no idea of the geography of Geneva. She had been there once, for some UN thing, but it had been the usual international diplomacy experience: airport, car, meeting room, car, airport. So she relied on the crudest method possible: looking for a big patch of blue.

Once she had found the shoreline, she slowed down so that her avatar could fly low and close, with time to see what was below.

'There's one!' said Uri, pointing in the bottom left of the screen. Clumsily, Maggie turned herself around and came as close as she could, hovering over what looked like a cartoon depiction of a desert island. It was round with a single flag planted in the yellow sand: it announced times for a weekly poetry discussion group. Maggie hit the *Up* arrow.

There were several islands in the lake, some used as venues for virtual events – Maggie saw signs advertising a concert and a press conference for a software company – some no more than simple plots of land for private owners. None seemed to have any connection to Shimon Guttman. Maggie was growing anxious; this was their only lead.

'Come on,' said Uri. 'Keep flying. If it's here, we'll find it.'

Maggie kept it up, looping and dipping over the blue of Second Life's version of Lake Geneva. For nearly a minute she did that, silently, so that it was as if the pair of them were in a glider, floating through the cloudless, midday skies above a real city, instead of here in this dark, soulless room in the dead of a Jerusalem night.

She was concentrating hard. It wasn't easy to stay at the right altitude: too high and the islands were just dots, too low and they had no sense of perspective. If Uri was right, they needed to recreate the childhood experience he had had in that plane, spotting the islands below.

'Hey, what's that?' said Uri, pointing at a small patch of land below. Maggie had to double back, steering Lola round. When she saw it, she hovered, then steadily lowered herself.

'I don't believe it,' Uri said, shaking his head. 'Even here.'

'What is it, Uri? What?'

'Look at that. Can you see the shape of that island? Look at the shape.' He was pointing at the yellow pixels on the screen.

Maggie could see that it was unusual. Not the rough-edged, vaguely circular blob favoured by the owners of most of Second Life's private islands, but a series of wobbling lines, with a large square protruding from the right. It was a deliberate design of some kind. But it meant nothing to Maggie.

'Uri, what is it?'

'See that on the left? That's Israel. And that big bulge? That's Jordan. This is the map of *Eretz Yisrael*, the complete Land of Israel, according to the right-wing fanatics who worship Jabotinsky. People like my father. They have this shape on their T-shirts. The women wear it as a pendant. *Shtei gadot*, they call it. It means two banks. They even have a song: "The River Jordan has two banks, both of them ours".'

'You're sure?'

'I knew this shape before I knew my alphabet, Maggie. I grew up with it. Believe me, my father did this.'

Maggie clicked to stop flying, landing splashily on the water lapping against the island's shore. She walked forward, but was pushed back. A red line, like a laser beam girdling the island, materialized each time the avatar got too near, effectively bouncing her away. When you looked closely, you could see it was made up of words: NO ENTRY NO ENTRY NO ENTRY. It was an electronic border fence. A small message appeared on screen: 'Cannot enter parcel – not member of the group.'

'Damn. It's locked somehow.' Her avatar was static. Maggie looked at the bottom of the screen, trying to find a box for keying in a password.

'Hey, Maggie. Who's this?'

She looked up and felt a chill run through her. Two avatars were hovering close by. They had the same, eerie bunny heads she had seen just before, but now both were clad in black. She remembered the men in the alley, the black ski-masks, the hot breath.

Maggie looked up at Uri. 'They're following us. They're trying to get whatever information your father stored here before we do. What should I do?'

'Can you talk to them?'

Maggie stared hard at the screen. They were still lingering at her side. She hit *Chat* and typed into the window, trying hard to stay in character. *hey guys, what's up?*

She waited for a reply. Three seconds, four, five. She waited till the Second Life clock in the corner of the screen turned a minute. Nothing.

'They're waiting for us to make a move. They know only what they pick up from us.' With that, Maggie had one more attempt at breaking through the laser cordon that appeared around the island every time she got close. *Cannot enter parcel – not member of the group*.

The rabbit-heads remained close by, unmoving. They were shut outside the cordon too, but something about their stillness unsettled Maggie. She imagined their operators, whoever they were, hammering their way through complex algorithms, running serious de-encryption programmes, working out how they could smash through Guttman's little barrier. If these people were clever enough to have followed Maggie, or Lola Hepburn, to this spot within Second Life, they would hardly let one piffling cordon stand in their way.

Maggie hit *Chat. you again! are you rabbit boys hitting on me?*

'Maggie, what are you doing?'

'Letting them know we know.'

She carried on typing, now using the Second Life search function. The search word: *Guttman*. Maybe there was an obvious way into the island, something they were both overlooking.

'I'm going to get something,' Uri said, heading for the door. 'I'll be back in a second.'

The Guttman search was still chugging through, taking much longer than before. No entries were coming up. 'Come on, come on,' Maggie murmured. Then, as if hearing her command, there was a whooshing sound and everything went blank.

Suddenly the screen was loading with a landscape Maggie did not recognize. She had been teleported somewhere else within Second Life, even though she had clicked no button. Had she fumbled the keyboard without realizing it?

But then she saw them. Not two rabbit-heads but four now, surrounding her. She pressed the forward arrow and moved a few paces, then froze. Then, jerkily, she regained movement again, turning rapidly into a side alley. The four rabbit-men were behind her, gaining ground. She froze again.

Maggie could feel her own, real-life, breath coming short and fast. Whoever was behind the rabbit-heads was paralysing her avatar. Now she wouldn't be able to return to the island in Lake Geneva. Whatever message Shimon Guttman had locked there would be out of reach.

Maggie heard the sound of the lift ping open. She turned around to see the room empty behind her. Where was Uri? She could hear footsteps coming closer and now, through the glass, she could see a man approaching. In the dark it was impossible to make out his face.

The door opened and Maggie saw the figure in full: it was Uri, clutching a neat pile of brown clothes. Without explanation he began unbuckling his trousers and removing his shirt, before stashing them under one of the desks, out of view. That done, he started putting on the items he'd brought in, an outfit that seemed to be made entirely of a noisy polyester material in a sickly shade of beige. The trousers were too short, which required some strenuous downward tugging to make contact with his shoes, but soon the transformation was complete. He was wearing the uniform of a hotel bellboy.

'How on earth—'

'Anyone who's ever worked night shifts in a hotel, as I have, knows one thing: they all have a laundry room somewhere. You just have to find it and break in.'

'But why?'

'Don't you see? These people have been bugging us and following us, so that we would lead them to the tablet. And now they have what they want. They know the answer is on that island and they'll get it. They don't need us any more, Maggie. We're in the way.'

Her heart hammering, she turned back to the screen, where Lola was now surrounded by six rabbit-headed men. She hit the *Fly* button, to escape. It didn't work. She began stabbing, dumbly, at all the buttons, but nothing would happen. The avatars in black were closing in.

And now something else was happening. The face on Lola Hepburn, the fresh-faced Valley girl with the ponytail, was starting to change. The eyes began to droop, as if they were about to dissolve into tears. Now the nose began to descend too, the face of this electronic creature no longer perky but increasingly hideous.

Maggie could only watch as the deterioration spread down Lola's body, the breasts melting into a swirl of red, white and blue like a sundae on a summer's day. Now the torso slid down into the legs, until the entire body was a pool of sludge on this side street, the rabbit-headed avatars still circling, like gulls about to feast on dead flesh. Maggie's only chance to find out what Shimon Guttman knew had gone.

'Maggie.' It was Uri, at the door, about to leave. 'In three minutes' time, go down the fire escape. The entrance is there.' He pointed. 'Don't take the elevator. Walk down the stairs as far as you can. Don't stop at the lobby, but one level lower. You'll come out in the kitchens. As quickly as you can, turn left out of the elevator, and head for the refrigeration area.'

'How the hell—'

'Just follow the cold. At the back will be a loading bay. Get out there and I'll be in a car.'

'How are you going to get—'

'Just do it.'

And then he vanished, for all the world a member of the night team of the David's Citadel Hotel.

Maggie collected the few things she had. Uri was right: their every move was being watched and their pursuers were serious. She had seen that for herself this morning and seen it again now, as they had locked on to and destroyed the avatar lent to her by Liz. Maggie shut down the program and moved towards the fire escape.

As she stepped into the blackness of the staircase, she realized that she had not a clue where she was going or what she was going to do next. Their best hope had been taken from them, reduced to a few computer pixels that had simply melted away.

CHAPTER FORTY-SEVEN

Psagot, the West Bank, Friday, 4.07am

His wife heard it before he did. He had always been a heavy sleeper, but now that he was carrying perhaps twenty or thirty pounds in excess weight, his descent into slumber was positively leaden. His wife was shaking him vigorously when he finally awoke.

'Akiva, come on. Akiva!'

Akiva Shapira groaned before squinting at the clock on the nightstand. One of his proudest possessions, that clock. A mechanical, digital relic of the early 1970s, lodged inside its workings was a bullet, fired by a Palestinian sniper directly into his office. Typical of the Palestinians: it missed him – and couldn't even take out the clock. A joke he had cracked to more than one visiting US delegation.

It was gone four in the morning, yet his wife was not mistaken. The same light tapping on the door was repeated. Who on earth could be calling here so late?

He grabbed a robe, tying the cord across his girth as he shuffled to the front door of the modest red-roofed house that had been his home since this settlement was founded, decades ago now. He only had to open it a crack to see the face of Ra'anan, the aide to the Defence Minister who had been at the meeting the previous afternoon.

'What the hell—'

'I am sorry to call so late. Can I come in?'

Shapira widened the door to let in this man who seemed like some kind of alien, fully dressed in this house of sleep. 'Can I get you something to drink. Water, maybe?'

'No. I can't stay very long. We have very little time.'

Shapira turned back from the sink, where he had been filling a glass, to face his guest. 'OK. What is it?'

Ra'anan's eyes darted towards the bedroom. 'Can we speak freely here?'

'Of course! This is my home.'

Ra'anan nodded towards the bedroom again. 'Your wife?' he whispered.

Shapira moved towards the door which separated the kitchen from the hallway and bedrooms and closed it. 'You happy now?'

'Akiva, in the last hour I have spoken to the other members of our group, seeking permission for a specific action which has just become possible. If we all agree, we have to act at once.'

'I'm listening.'

'The subject we discussed. She is now in our sights. We can strike.'

'Risks?'

'Arrest and capture, minimal. We have the best possible personnel, as you saw today.'

Shapira remembered the demonstration in the field, the watermelons exploded with pinpoint accuracy by snipers he barely glimpsed. Ra'anan was right. The risks for such skilled professionals were no obstacle.

'OK,' said Shapira, finally. 'Do it.'

CHAPTER FORTY-EIGHT

JERUSALEM, FRIDAY, 4.21AM

She got out of the hotel more easily than she expected. Uri's instructions were accurate and the kitchen was empty. She found the large refrigeration area, led not by the chill but the electric hum. There, at the back, as promised, was a wide door, which was bolted and required a mammoth shove to push open.

She felt the blast of cold night air immediately. Her jacket was still in the room upstairs. She stood there, on a raised concrete platform, looking down into the square gulch built for reversing delivery trucks. As she stamped up and down, hugging her sides to keep warm, she took a blast of the smell. It was rank. She realized she was standing by three enormous steel cylinders, each of them spilling over with sackfuls of hotel trash.

Two minutes later, she saw the beam of headlights coming into the area, then swerving around and reversing towards the loading bay. A sleek silver Mercedes was nudging backwards, in her direction. She waited as it filled up the loading bay, the fumes of its exhaust rising and wreathing the whole platform. Its rear lights meant she could now see a set of steps off to the side. She thought about heading down them, then hesitated. What if it wasn't Uri?

She stayed in the shadows, waiting until eventually she heard the slow glide of an electric window, followed by a whispered 'psst'. Uri. She leapt down the stairs and bundled herself into the passenger seat.

'Nice wheels. How did you pull this off?'

'By strolling over to the concierge desk, finding the valet parking box and taking the first key I saw.'

'Hence the uniform.'

'Hence the uniform.'

Maggie nodded, detecting something new in this man whom she had never met a week ago and with whom she now seemed fated to spend every waking hour – and even some sleeping ones. For the first time she saw something like pride: he was pleased with himself.

'So now you've got the limousine, where do you want to go, Miss Costello?'

'Anywhere with a computer. We didn't get through to the island. They melted me before I could break through. They're going to get there before we do.'

'Who's they?'

'The rabbit-heads, whoever they were.'

'You don't think they'll be bounced back from the island just like you were?'

'Uri, these are people who can listen to our conversations, hack into our computers, kill Kishon and Aweida the second we mention their names. Somehow I don't think they're going to struggle with a bit of encryption your father put on that island.'

After all, thought Maggie, the men behind the rabbit-heads clearly had the power to turn her avatar into pixellated goo. Uri had been right: they didn't need her any more. She had led them to the island; they could do the rest.

'Look, that's probably true,' said Uri finally. 'But even if they hack into it, they might not understand what they see. Remember, the message on the DVD from my father? That required knowledge that only I have.' He paused. 'Christ, though, why did he have to make everything so fucking complicated?'

'Actually, I kind of admire it. There are a lot of serious people who want the discovery he made and none of them have got their hands on it.'

'Not yet.'

'All right. But it's pretty impressive if you ask me.'

Uri drove on in silence, the wipers on the car sleekly sweeping across the windscreen at intervals. They barely made a sound.

'So where are you taking me, Mr Chauffeur?'

'One of the few places in Jerusalem that stays open all night. And certainly the only one with a computer.'

He parked the car at the bottom of a pedestrianized area, full of closed cafes and shuttered kiosks. 'This is Ben-Yehuda Street,' Uri said. 'Normally it's teeming. But Jerusalem's not like Tel Aviv. It likes to get its beauty sleep.'

He led them off the main thoroughfare, past a human bundle of rags sleeping in a doorway, down a side alley, still made of the same, ragged stone as the rest of the city. Here, too, there were signs of earlier life: restaurants and cafés, closed for the night. She heard the throbbing of a bar. 'Mike's Place,' he said, hearing it too. 'The one they didn't bomb.'

He kept winding through these narrow, catacomb streets, where each arch or vaulted entrance led to a shop or office; modern life carved out of ancient stone.

'Here we are. Someone To Run With.'

'That's its name?'

'Yeah. It's become a Jerusalem institution. All the runaways and dropouts come here. Named it after a novel.'

'Someone to run with, eh? Like you and me.'

Uri smiled and ushered Maggie inside. She looked around and immediately had a flashback to when she had just turned sixteen. Not that she had ever come to a place like this, but her sixteen-year-old self would have loved it. There were no chairs, only enormous cushions arranged on stone benches and window seats. The air was heavy with the steam of fruit teas and the smoke of tobacco and assorted varieties of weed. In one corner she could see a boy, earnestly hunched over a guitar, a curtain of lank, dark hair hiding his face. Opposite him, with a guitar of her own, was a girl whose head was entirely shaved, wearing a shapeless white T-shirt and knee-length shorts who, despite these heroic efforts, could not conceal her beauty. Maggie surveyed the room, seeing the torn jeans and the braided hair, and felt not the consciousness of her own age, as she had in the nightclub in Tel Aviv, but a twinge of real envy. These kids still had everything ahead of them.

She was glad she had changed clothes at Orli's. If these kids had seen her in her usual get-up, they would have had her down as drugs squad, or some kind of authority figure, right away. Instead they barely glanced up at her or Uri: too stoned to notice probably.

Uri nodded towards the corner of the room where there was a sole, unused computer. Maggie guessed that it was terminally uncool to use it, especially at this time of night. While Uri stood at the counter, asking the girl with a stud in her nose for coffee, Maggie switched on the machine and called up Second Life.

At the name prompt she typed Lola Hepburn, only for an instant error message to appear: I*nvalid username and/or password, please try again*. The avatar created by Liz had been eradicated from the system. She would have to enter as someone else. But who? She didn't know anyone who had an avatar on Second Life. Maybe she should just wake up Liz in London.

And then she heard it again, the voice of Shimon Guttman, as clear she had heard it twelve hours ago in Rosen's office.

You shall see me in the other life, not this one but the next one.

Of course. She was meant to enter Second Life not as Lola Hepburn, the big-breasted party girl created by her sister, but as Shimon Guttman himself. That was surely how the coding worked: the island in Geneva would open up to no one but him.

She hit the search button, aiming to trawl through the directory of names. As she typed his first name and then his last name, she hoped that, just this once, the old man had made it easy.

Invalid username and/or password, please try again.

She tried different variations. ShimonG, SGuttman, and half a dozen other permutations. There were a handful of Shimons, but the rest of their names made no sense. And, when she tried the passwords that had worked on Guttman's home computer, she was blocked every time.

Uri arrived with an oversized cup of steaming coffee. Merely inhaling its aroma made Maggie realize how tired she was. She had been living on adrenaline for days now, and her body was feeling it. Her neck ached where Uri had hit her and her right arm had become tender, around the spot where the masked men in the market had grabbed her.

Uri watched what she was doing. 'Why don't you try the name my father used to email that Arab guy?'

Maggie gave Uri a downturned smile, as if to say, not a bad idea. She searched for Saeb Nastayib and beamed when the computer came back with just one result: a single avatar of that name. She repeated the password as before, Vladimir67, and, before her eyes, a lean male figure, materialized on the screen, naked at first, like a mannequin or a statue made in cool, grey stone, then gradually clothed.

She hit *Map*, typed *Geneva*, hit *Teleport* and, after the few seconds it took the machine to load, she was back, hovering over the bright blue water and green banks of the lake. She searched for Guttman's uniquely-contoured island.

Her first inspection made her anxious: no sign of it. That would make a grim kind of sense. If her pursuers had had no use for Liz's avatar once she had led them to the island, then surely the island itself was just as dispensable, once it had yielded its secrets. What better way to ensure no one else discovered the last resting place of the Abraham tablet than to destroy the only clue to its location?

So she had to fly low, hovering over the blue water, her bearings skewed by the undulating, computer-generated landscape which, on this slower connection, was only forming partially on the screen. But finally a green stain appeared on the blueness of the lake which, as the Guttman avatar drew near, revealed itself as the replica Greater Israel Uri's father had created in the heart of virtual Switzerland.

Maggie approached, bracing herself for the no entry tape and error message. But this time there was no such obstacle: the electronic cordon didn't even appear. Clearly, it was designed to pop up only at the approach of outsiders. The Guttman avatar was allowed to stroll onto the island as easily as Maggie had visited the red-light district all those hours ago. There wasn't even a password.

'We're in,' she said, relieved that the old man had not planted another tripwire in their path.

'Now what?' said Uri, leaning forward, cradling his cup of coffee, enjoying its warmth on his hands.

'Now we look.'

They didn't have far to go. The island had only one structure, a simple glass-and-steel box. Inside it was nothing but a chair and a desk with a virtual computer. Maggie pushed the Guttman avatar forward and had him sit on the chair. The instant he did a text bubble appeared.

Go west, young man, and make your way to the model city, close to the Mishkan. You'll find what I left for you there, in the path of ancient warrens.

'So, Uri. What do we have here?' She looked to her side, expecting to see Uri peering at the words with her. But he was gone, vanished as rapidly as one of the anatomically impossible creatures that still flickered on the screen.

CHAPTER FORTY-NINE

KHAN YUNIS, GAZA, FRIDAY, 2.40AM

He was not asleep. He was not even lying down. He was, as so often these days, sitting bolt upright, turning over one scenario after another in his head. Moves, counter-moves, his mind never stopped churning, least of all at night. He would have so many plans, he would grow impatient for the morning prayer. He would want dawn to come so that he could emerge again into the daylight and get back to work.

He was awake, so he heard the footsteps himself. Instinctively, he removed the safety catch on his pistol and waited in the dark. He saw a curve of candleglow before he heard a voice.

'*Psst.* Salim, it's Marwan.'

'Come in, brother.'

Warily, the younger man tiptoed into the room where Salim Nazzal was bedded down for the night. He looked around, counted three teenage boys, all fast asleep on a single mattress, and lowered his voice still further. He had no idea whose house he was in, which family had opened its doors to their leader for tonight.

'Salim. They say they have something. A sighting, in Jerusalem.'

'Of this tablet?'

'Of the Zionist's son. And the American woman.'

Nazzal replaced the safety catch on his gun. He wanted time to think.

'The unit on the ground want to know whether they should strike.'

'They weren't meant for *this!*'

'But your orders: that recovering the tablet was the highest priority.'

One of the boys on the bed stirred. Salim waited until he was sure he had gone back to sleep.

'Tell them,' he said eventually, 'that they are free to act—'

'OK—' He strode away at once.

'Marwan! Come back here. Tell them they are free to act, *but* only if by acting they either secure the tablet or discover, for certain, its location. No point killing these two, Guttman and the American, if we don't get the tablet. Do you understand?'

'I understand, Salim.'

'I mean it, Marwan.' And he cocked his weapon once more, just to leave no doubt.

CHAPTER FIFTY

JERUSALEM, FRIDAY, 5.23AM

She wheeled around, searching among the blissed-out faces and strumming guitars for Uri, but he had vanished. She stood up, walking towards the entrance. Then she saw him, his forehead lined with anxiety. He was in the doorway, staring hard into the street.

'Uri, what is it?'

'I don't know, but I heard something. Could be a car. We've got to get out.'

'Yeah, but first you have to work out—'

'Maggie, if they're onto us here, they could kill us.'

'Just tell me what this means!'

'For Christ's sake, Maggie, there's no time.'

'Uri, I'm not leaving here until you work this out.'

Shaking his head he strode over to the machine, bent down to peer at the small bubble of text on the screen and repeated the riddle his father had hidden there. Then he said simply, 'All right, let's go.'

The nose-studded barista had appeared and was now murmuring in Hebrew to Uri, pointing to an exit at the back end of the café – and also, Maggie couldn't help noticing, widening her gorgeous brown eyes for his benefit. Apparently impervious to her charms, he thanked her, grabbed Maggie's wrist and made a dash into the dark.

They had already pushed open the fire door, to reveal a narrow, five-step basement staircase which would lead them back up to street level, when Maggie realized they had left the computer on, Guttman's avatar and his message still displayed. If they were being followed, their pursuers would simply have to stroll into the café, order themselves a latte and pull out a notebook.

She turned on her heel, feeling her wrist twist in Uri's grip. 'Let go of me. I've got to go back.'

'No way.'

'The computer's still on. They'll see everything!'

'Too bad. We're going,' he said, still striding upward, determined to get out onto the street.

'Get off me! Now!'

He refused to loosen his hold. She was being pulled up this tiny stone staircase whether she liked it or not. She began tugging at his arm, like a recalcitrant toddler refusing to be dragged to her first day at nursery. But he was stronger than she was. She hated herself even for imagining what she would do next, let alone actually doing it, but at that moment, she was certain she had no choice. She had to bend her head to do it, and to find the right angle onto his flesh, but once she had it was a single, quick movement. She simply bared her teeth and bit into his hand.

He yowled in pain, letting only the first note of it sound and smothering the rest. But it did the job: reflexively, he had released her and she dashed back away. Her eyes darted, struggling to locate in the haze of smoke the computer she had just used. When she finally saw the glow, she was appalled to see that someone else was now hunched over the screen, tapping on the keyboard.

She inched closer, staying in the shadows. Eventually she saw who was there: the nose-stud girl. Maggie exhaled her relief, marched towards the machine and, just as the woman was beginning to say how cool Second Life was, she hit the computer's off button.

'Hey—'

But Maggie was already gone, out the back entrance, up the stone stairs and into the alleyway. She stood, alone, looking left and right before she felt a hand grab her arm and tug her along first right, then left, then down a cobbled slope and eventually to a main street where a silver Mercedes was parked and ready. They got in.

'I swear if they don't kill you, I will.'

'Uri, I'm sorry. But I couldn't just leave it there, for anyone to—'

'Were they there?'

'Not that I could see.'

Uri shook his head, in furious disbelief at the maniac he had somehow landed up with.

'I'm sorry, I really am.'

'No, you're not.'

'Where are we going?'

'I don't know. Away from them, away from Jerusalem. We'll go back when it's clear.'

Maggie looked out of the window, watching the first glimmers of a blue, hazy light over the horizon. Jerusalem was barely waking up: all she had seen so far was the odd beggar. 'What about this message of your father's?'

'I don't know any more.'

'Come on. He said, "Go west, young man and make your way to the model city, close to the Mishkan", whatever that is. "You'll find what I left for you there, in the path of ancient warrens." So what do you think?'

Uri took his eyes off the road, to fix Maggie with a glare. 'Do you have any idea how much I hate my father right now? All these chickenshit games he's putting me through? As if it wasn't enough that all this madness has already killed my mother.'

'I know, Uri—'

'You know nothing, Maggie. Nothing! He had my mother killed, I'm running for my life and for what? What? For some fucking biblical relic that will prove that he and all his right-wing nutcase friends were right all along! He could never make me join him when he was alive, but somehow he has me working for him, like some fucking disciple, now that he's dead.'

'Is that where he's hidden it? In some right-wing nutcase place? On the West Bank?'

'No. It's in a much more obvious place.'

'You've worked it out already?'

'What's this whole thing about? It could only be in one place.'

'You mean it's on the Temple Mount.' Maggie smiled at the ingenuity of it. Of course he would bury the tablet there. Where else did title deeds for a house belong, except in the house itself?

'That's the Mishkan: the Temple, the palace. It refers to that whole area. Except whatever he's left is not on the Temple Mount. Jews hardly ever go there: too holy. He's hidden it underneath.'

'Underneath?'

'A few years ago, they excavated the tunnels that run alongside the Western Wall. My father and a few other archaeologists. Not the famous part of the Wall, where everyone prays and sticks those cutesy notes to God in the crevices. But a whole stretch of wall that was buried under the rest of the city. Under the Muslim Quarter, to be precise. Everyone went nuts.'

'You mean the Palestinians?'

'Of course. What did my father expect? The Arabs said the Jews were trying to undermine the foundations of the Dome of the Rock, you know the big building with the gold dome?'

'I know, thank you, Uri.'

'It's where they think Mohammed ascended to heaven. And here are the Jews tunnelling underneath. And then my dad and his friends make matters worse. They decide it's not enough that tourists can go into the tunnels. No, the tourists need an exit at the other end, rather than having to walk all the way back through the tunnels. So they build one. And it pops out right in the Muslim Quarter.'

'A provocation.'

'Exactly.'

'So that's what he means by "ancient warrens": the tunnels. "Go west", the Western Wall. Clever. And of course Jerusalem is the model city; it's the holiest place on earth. But what—'

'Oh fuck.'

Maggie could see Uri suddenly transfixed by his rear-view mirror. She looked over her shoulder and could see a car behind, its lights set to full beam. They had left the city behind now, descending instead on a mountain road that seemed to be unwinding. On either side were steep rocks, broken up only by the occasional car wreck – ruins of military vehicles, the marine had told her that day, which now felt ten years in the past – relics of the 1948 war that greeted the creation of the state of Israel.

'They're getting closer, Uri.'

'I know.'

'What the hell are we going to do?'

'I don't know. Let me think.'

He was being dazzled by the reflection in the mirror, which seemed to be filling the entire car with a searching yellow light.

Uri accelerated but the car behind caught up effortlessly. Despite Maggie shielding her eyes, the light was too bright to see who was in the car, even what kind of car it was.

'Can we turn off?'

'Not unless we want to go tumbling down the mountain.'

'Shit. Uri, we've got to do something.'

'I know, I know.'

After a few seconds, he spoke again. 'OK. At the next bend there is a lookout spot. I can pull in there. When I do, you have to open your door immediately and slip out of your side. And keep very low. And you have to do it the instant the car is turning into the spot. Don't wait for it to come to a complete stop. And then just run over the edge. It's low ground there for a while, like a ledge. OK?'

'Yes, but what about—'

'Don't worry about me. Once you're out, I'll be right behind you. Very low, you got that?'

'I've got it.'

'OK. Here it comes.'

Uri began to squeeze the brake. Maggie unbuckled her belt, which set off an immediate loud dinging. She waited for her cue.

Uri was looking in his rear-view mirror, then swerved into the space and yelled: 'Now! And keep low!'

Maggie pulled on the door handle, pushed it and ducked her way out of the car, tripping on the moving road, running in a crouch to the edge of the paved surface. Now, in one of those split-seconds where an enormous decision has to be made, she had to determine whether or not she truly trusted Uri. Instinct, in this half-light of dawn, told her this was a sheer drop and that to run off it was to guarantee death. Yet Uri had promised the view was deceptive, that the slope was gentle. Could she believe him? They had lived and breathed almost every one of the last forty-eight hours together. She had discovered his dead mother. She had told him about Africa. And just a few hours ago they had made love in a way both tender and fierce in its passion.

And yet, who was he? This veteran of Israeli intelligence who had struck her unconscious with a single blow, who had stolen a car and who had done God knows what else in his life. How could she trust such a man?

All this ran through her head during the long second in which she teetered on the edge, before she finally stepped off. The drop came – but it was a tiny one, no more than a couple of feet, like missing the bottom stair in the dark. Stumbling, she ran on until she was out of sight of the road.

As the sound of her breath quieted, she looked around to see that she was quite alone. A second later she heard a gunshot above her, from the road and knew, with an iron certainty that chilled her, that it was Uri who had been hit.

CHAPTER FIFTY-ONE

JERUSALEM, FRIDAY, 6.15AM

She held herself very still, wary even of her own breath. Her muscles were quaking, her face trembling. She could feel the tears trickling down her cheeks, but some instinct of self-preservation took over, forcing her feet to make no movement, determined that no one would hear so much as a crunch of a stone under her.

She stood like that for seconds that stretched into long minutes, her eyes closed so that she could concentrate on her ears. In the seconds after the gunshot, as she played back the memory of it now, she had heard a thud and the sound of footsteps on the gravel above. Then, a minute later, car doors slamming shut and an engine roaring away.

She had prayed then, as she prayed now, that she would soon hear something else: his footsteps coming towards her perhaps, or his voice calling out from the road above. The voice in her head was addressing God, the Father she claimed no longer to believe in, the God she had officially abandoned at convent school. She begged him, please, please, whatever else you do to me, don't let him be dead. Please, God, let him live.

How could she have allowed him to do that, letting her get

away first? How could she have been so stupid, so selfish? Of course, there was no plan. Uri had simply wanted to save her life: she would get out of the car and away, he would provide the cover for her escape. The pursuers would aim their guns at him, while she crept away, saving her own skin. She pictured his body, unmoving and bloody, on the gravelled road, and her own body convulsed at the thought of it. She knew she had to keep quiet, but it was no good: she was sobbing noisily now, for the man whom she had held in her arms, pulsing with life, just a few hours ago. She had held him and now she had lost him.

Still she did not move. Her survival instinct compelled her to stay here, on this ledge invisible from the road. She feared a trick: what if she climbed back up only to be ambushed by the men who had shot Uri? Maybe she had imagined the sound of a car departing; she was so tired, her head felt light. So she just stood where she was, her face soaking from the tears that were now streaming down it.

Eventually, she took one step forward, wincing against any sound she might make. Then another, then another, until she had a view, albeit restricted, of the road above. She could see nothing.

She took another few paces until she was at the edge of the ledge. Below her was the craggy, beige rock of the hillside. If anyone was on the road, they would surely be able to see her here. But she could see nothing – until a white car sped by. She ducked and it went on.

Silence. After a while she bobbed up and looked around. There was nothing on the road, nothing at the lookout spot. No cars, not even the Mercedes they had been driving. Above all, there was no Uri.

Maggie didn't know what to feel. She exhaled her relief that there was no corpse. Was it possible that Uri had somehow escaped, that the sound she had heard had been Uri, driving himself to safety?

But that, she knew, made no sense. He would have come back to get her. She knew what was more likely, her mind supplying the image: masked men picking up Uri's lifeless body, one taking the arms, the other the ankles, and swinging it into the boot of the Merc, then driving the car away.

She walked up onto the lookout spot and examined the ground. She could see tyre marks, but it was no good. She was no detective; she didn't know what she was looking at.

Maggie turned her back to the road, only now noticing the beauty of this view. The sky was a pale morning blue, the sun strong enough to light up this brittle, sandy landscape: the hills, stepped in terraces, punctuated by isolated olive trees. Hardy, unfussy, somehow stubborn, these trees seemed to Maggie like short, tanned men: tough and impatient.

Something in that view hardened her resolve. She would find that goddamned tablet if it was the last thing she did. She would do it for Uri's sake, and for the sake of his father and mother too. Whoever had done this to him, and to his parents, would not be allowed to get away with it. She would thwart them; she would find what they did not want her to find and she would expose them while she was at it. Yes, this peace process needed saving and yes, she was desperate to clear her name. But, at this moment, both of those feelings receded. She would do this for Uri.

And then she heard it, faint at first. She was struck, as she had been the first time, by the beauty of the melody, a haunting series of notes. And now it was a little louder, she could hear that it was not a recording or a car radio, but human voices singing, their sound carried on the breeze. She walked down to the edge of the ledge and saw that there was still no sheer drop, but rather a downward slope. She would have to make an initial jump of a few feet, and then she would just have to negotiate the hillside.

She did it, thanking Orli for the boots she was now wearing

instead of the shoes she had left at the ex-girlfriend's apartment. Still, though, she was not equipped for this. As she pushed towards the sound of the voices, her right foot slipped from under her, so that she landed on an ankle. A few paces later, she scratched her arm on a thistle, as she unthinkingly grabbed at the air to steady herself.

But soon she had threaded her way down from the road and had flat ground in view. And she could see the source of the song, though now it had given way to a much coarser chorus, a kind of football chant, to be sung by a crowd swaying in unison.

Hinei ma'tov u'ma'naim, shevet achim gam yachad . . .

It was the Arms Around Jerusalem protest, still going strong. Maggie had never been so glad to see a political demonstration in her life, never more grateful for the protesters' stamina in maintaining it around the clock, just as they had promised. Even now, not much after dawn, there was a group of activists, holding hands at the foot of this hill. Why they had decided this particular spot constituted the proper boundary of Jerusalem, she had no idea. But she was relieved they had.

'Are you journalist?' It was a woman wearing a vast pair of glasses, her arms extended to a teenage girl, perhaps her daughter, on one side and a rabbinic-looking man, Maggie's age, the fringes of his prayer shawl dangling, on the other.

'Oh no,' said Maggie, immediately and without forethought, exaggerating her Irish accent. 'I'm a visitor.'

'What, tourist?' *Turrrist.*

'Not quite, dear. I'm more of a pilgrim.' It was blatant, an impersonation of the nuns at school. But Maggie prayed it would work.

'Ah, you want Bethlehem?' The woman looked incredulous. 'You walking to Bethlehem?'

'Oh, no dear, perish the thought!'

Now the rabbi had stopped singing and was joining in the

conversation. 'You need to get to Bethlehem?' He positioned himself to give directions.

'No, actually, I'm on my way to Jerusalem. And it seems I've been tricked, I'm afraid.'

'Tricked?'

'By a taxi. Said he would take me there. He dropped me on the roadside there—' she pointed up the hill she had just descended, '—he said I should enjoy the view. Then, would you credit it, he only offs and leaves. With my coat and everything.'

'He was Jewish, this driver?'

Maggie was stumped. What was the right answer? Would it be an insult to accuse a Jew of this act of perfidy? Or would it be seen as a greater treachery to have hired a Palestinian driver in the first place?

'You know, I never asked him. But I do feel as if I've been terribly naive. I thought, this being the Holy Land and all—'

'Listen, lady.' It was the rabbi, now broken out of his place in the circle. 'Where do you need to get to?'

'Oh, I don't want to trouble a man of God like yourself.'

'No trouble, really. We have a driver.' And before she had had a chance to say another word, he had produced a walkie-talkie. 'Avram? *Bo rega.*' He looked at Maggie, briefly closing his eyes in a nod, as if to say, don't worry, it's all under control.

Within a few moments a car had arrived, a rugged, muddied SUV. Maggie sized it up and concluded that these rebels were supremely well organized. She didn't doubt that they had a fleet of such vehicles on hand, patrolling the battle lines not only of the Arms Around Jerusalem demo, but of the entire anti-Yariv campaign. If what she had read was right, much of the money would have been funnelled from Christian evangelicals in the States. Once again, she was reminded that, even if they were to calm things down and bring the parties back to the table, the peacemakers would face the most enormous obstacles.

Maggie thanked the rabbi and got in the car. A dark, burly man in shorts, with tanned, meaty forearms, was in the driver's seat. He raised his eyebrows in a question.

'Could you take me to the Old City please?'

Within a few minutes they were back on the main road, retracing the dawn journey she had made with Uri, winding steadily upward back to the centre of Jerusalem. She felt her ears pop.

Now the traffic was thicker, but hardly a regular urban rush hour. 'Shabbat, shabbat,' the driver said, gesturing to the view outside the windscreen. The city was emptying out for the sabbath, which would come with the darkness that evening.

And soon she could see it, as the car ascended Hativat Yerushalayim Street, the long, solid wall that marked the western boundary of the Old City. She was hardly looking, staring into space, thinking only of what might have happened to Uri. Had he really taken a bullet just so that she could break free? The heaviness on her chest, the sense of dread, almost broke her. Another mistake; another betrayal. Angrily, she forced herself to channel her emotions into an unbending determination: she would find the people who had shot Uri and she would do it by finding the tablet. She sensed she was getting close. The last testament of Abraham could not be very far away.

CHAPTER FIFTY-TWO

JERUSALEM, FRIDAY, 7.50AM

The car turned through the Jaffa Gate, stopping almost immediately in a small square, a paved plaza fringed by a souvenir shop selling the usual kitsch and a couple of rundown backpacker hostels. She would have to walk from here. Maggie thanked the driver, waved him off and took a good look. In front of her was the Swedish Christian Study Centre. Close by was the Christian Information Centre and next to that, the Christ Church Guest House. A distant memory of slide shows in Sister Frances's geography lessons rose to the surface. Maggie realized she had heard about such places long ago. These were all missions – missions to convert the Jews.

Straight ahead of her was what looked to be a central police station, complete with a tall communications mast sprouting multiple aerials. She began to walk towards it. She would report Uri missing, she would tell them about the shooting, they would send out patrol cars and find Uri and bring him back to her . . .

But then she stopped still. She would have to explain the stolen car and why they were being chased in the dead of night; why Uri was dressed in a stolen bellboy uniform. No one would believe a word of it. The police would immediately get on the phone to the consulate to check her out and she only had to imagine that call, as Davis, Miller and Sanchez were told that Maggie Costello had spent the night with Uri Guttman.

She stood there, frozen. If Uri was alive, he needed her help. But there was no one she could turn to, no one who would understand or believe what they now knew. Her only hope was the tablet. If she had that, she would have the answers: she would know who was behind these killings and who had Uri. If she could just find the tablet, she would have her own bargaining chip. Then all she had to do was decide how best to use it.

She looked around, trying to get her bearings. She had found this place almost suffocatingly intense as soon as she had arrived, but here in the Old City the sensation was heightened, as if all Jerusalem's fervour, its fevered history, was cooped up between these solid, sandy walls. No wonder people spoke of Jerusalem as if it were a form of mental illness.

She stopped a man with an oversized camera around his neck, wearing sandals and socks, and asked for the Western Wall. He pointed at an archway directly opposite the Jaffa Gate. This, she remembered, was the way to the *souk*.

It felt like plunging down a hillside, taking that steep, downward path that had been smoothed by millions of feet over hundreds if not thousands of years. It seemed different from the market she had seen twenty-four hours ago. It was still early; almost all the stalls were locked up behind green metal shutters, and, instead of the thick crowds of tourists and shoppers, there was just a boy pushing a handcart, occasionally jumping on the small tyre he kept loosely chained to the back that, when dragged along the ground, functioned as a makeshift brake.

She looked at the names of the shops, now visible thanks to the absence of people. She could imagine the older Guttman browsing here, visiting Sadi Barakat & Sons, Legally Authorized Dealers or the grandiosely named Oriental Museum, always on the lookout for some quirky item of ancient treasure. How he must have quaked when he came into Aweida's shop that day.

She passed a bearded man in full black robes. Was he a rabbi or an orthodox priest, maybe Greek or Russian? She had no idea and, in this city, any of those was possible. Coming from another direction, a gang of eight-year-old Arab boys and, walking around them, an old woman reading from a prayer book, muttering incantations, as if she couldn't afford to waste even a minute away from worship of the divine.

Finally Maggie saw a simple sign in English which appeared handwritten. *To the Western Wall*, it said, with an arrow indicating a right turn. She followed it, heading down some more steps until she saw another more formal sign, with a series of bullet points, all in English:

You are entering the Western Wall plaza.

Visitors with pacemakers should inform the security personnel . . .

There was an airport-style metal detector to go through, watched by a couple of Israeli police guards. A policewoman frisked her, all the while laughing and chatting with her colleagues, and then waved her through.

And now it stretched before her, a sloping, paved plaza already teeming with people and at one end of it the solid, enormous stones of the Western Wall. It seemed to belong to another world: its scale was not human. One stone was almost as tall as a man. The weeds sprouting from its cracks were small trees. And yet this dated from a temple built here some two and a half thousand years ago.

People were milling everywhere. Bearded men striding about as if they had trains to catch, others handing out skullcaps, while still a few more were smiling, like charity collectors hoping pedestrians might stop for a chat. She avoided eye contact, listening instead as a teenaged American boy allowed himself to be buttonholed.

'Er, Aaron.'

'Hi, Aaron. I'm Levi.' *Lay-vee.* Have you got somewhere to spend shabbes tonight?'

'Er, maybe. I'm not sure.'

'Do you wanna spend *shabbes* with a family, having chicken soup like at home? Maybe *daven* a little at the *Kotel*?' The last word was pronounced to rhyme with hotel, though with the emphasis on the first syllable. The driver had used the same word. *Kotel*. The Wall.

Now she could see more clearly the sets of white plastic garden chairs arrayed in front of the Wall. There was no pattern to them. Instead, there seemed to be a dozen different gatherings and services taking place at once. It was a scene of spiritual chaos, more like a railway terminal than any shrine she had ever been to.

Perhaps four fifths along the wall a partition emerged to bisect the crowd. It wasn't much, no different from the panels of fencing her father might have put up in their back garden. But on the left side of it, as you faced the giant stones, the crowd was much thicker. She walked closer, to work out what this division could mean.

Ah. Men on the left side, women on the right. There was another sign, addressed to the women. *You are entering an area of sanctity. Women should be in appropriate modest dress*. But it was the men whom she looked at. Even now, there were a good number of them, many draped in large black-and-white shawls, facing the Wall. Some let the shawls cover their heads, like boxers in hooded robes, readying for a fight. Others wore them over their shoulders. All seemed to be rocking back and forth on their heels or swaying from side to side, their eyes closed. Maggie tried to get nearer.

'Are you Jewish?' A matronly woman with a European accent. She was nodding and smiling.

'No, I'm not. But I am here to join these good people's prayers to the Lord,' she said, the voice of Sister Olivia from school in her head. The woman gestured towards the ladies' side of the partition and wandered off.

Maggie wondered how long she would be able to stay here before somebody moved her on. She had to find out where to go. She saw a policeman, armed, and asked for the Western Wall tunnels. He pointed at a small archway, apparently newly built into the long, but much lower, wall that ran perpendicular to the Kotel itself.

Outside was a group of maybe thirty men and women, kitted out with water bottles and video cameras. *Perfect.*

She loitered at the back, then followed them through the archway, her eyes down and fidgeting with her phone.

'All right, people. If we can all listen up. Thank you,' said the tour guide: American, late twenties, with a whiskery beard and bright, shining eyes. He clapped his hands three times and waited for silence. 'Great. Thanks. My name is Josh and I'm going to be your guide through this tour of the Western Wall tunnels – and this journey into the ancient heritage of the Jewish people. If you just follow me through here, we can begin.'

He led them into an underground cellar, a chamber whose shape was described by a vaulted arch. The stones were colder and greyer than the ones Maggie had grown used to in Jerusalem and there was a drone of fans, struggling to dispel the smell of dry, lightless must.

'OK, do we have everybody?' His voice was bouncing off the walls. 'All right. We're in a room the British explorer Charles Warren called the Donkey Stable. That may be because that was what this room was once used for – or perhaps it just looks that way.'

There was polite laughter from all those who were not framing up a shot on their camera phones. Maggie started scoping the walls, desperate to see if there was any kind of opening, a place where Shimon Guttman might have stashed his precious discovery.

'This gives us an opportunity to say a little about where we are. We are now very close to the area known as the Temple Mount. As you know, this is a very special place indeed. Our tradition holds that on this spot stood the Foundation Stone, from which the world was literally created five thousand seven hundred years ago. We also know it as Mount Moriah, where Abraham was asked by *Ha'shem*, by the Almighty, to sacrifice his son, Isaac. It's also where Jacob laid his head to rest, and had the dream of angels moving up and down between heaven and earth. And where he predicted that the House of God would be built.

'Sure enough, the Temple was constructed here many years later. And what you were looking at before, the Kotel, that was the western retaining wall of the temple. Which temple? Well, there were two. The First Temple was built by King Solomon nearly three thousand years ago and the Second was built by Ezra about five hundred years after that. When the Second Temple was destroyed by the Romans in the year 70, the only part that was left standing was the Western Wall.'

Maggie was keeping her place at the back, her eye scanning every crack between the white-grey stones. *You'll find what I left for you there, in the path of ancient warrens*, Guttman had said. Could that refer to something in this room?

'. . . most people don't realize is that the giant wall we just saw outside, with everyone praying, is not the entire Western Wall. It continued on, northward, for *four times* as long again. Trouble was, over the years, people built against it, and eventually *over* it. Building layer on layer of houses and foundations and support structures. Until we couldn't see much of the wall at all.

'But the good news is, we've been able to dig out a tunnel along the entire length of the wall. Now we can see all those layers of history – and see the beauty of the wall itself, a treasure that was hidden from the Jewish people for at least two millennia.'

While the men in shorts and women with sweaters tied around their waists ooh-ed and aah-ed, Maggie was trying to guide her eye like the beam of a flashlight. Was Abraham's tiny tablet hidden somewhere in here? She examined the ground, wondering if there was a trapdoor, a staircase perhaps, that might lead to a vault. But where?

'OK. We're going to follow that little light you can see there – and head down the Secret Passage.'

A teenage boy made a ghost sound. His sister sang the theme tune from *The Twilight Zone*.

The group walked in single file down a long corridor, beneath a low vaulted ceiling. There was no daylight now, just the orange glow of electric lights embedded at intervals along the ground. Maggie shivered, a product of shock and fatigue as much as the cold.

The guide was speaking again, his voice raised to be heard above the footsteps. The echo meant that, from her position at the back, Maggie had to strain to hear him.

'Legend has it that this was an underground walkway used by King David so that he could travel, unseen, from his palace, which would have been west of here, to the Temple Mount . . .'

Maggie looked above her and at the walls. Guttman surely wouldn't have left anything here. How would he have managed to hide it? Behind one of these stones? She began to worry. If he had loosened one of these ancient stones, and hidden the tablet behind, how on earth was she to find it? Where would she start?

The guide was answering a question. 'That's what I find so beautiful about being here, touching the very stones and breathing the very air that our ancestors would have touched and breathed. As we delve deeper, we can begin to reach the very roots of Jewish existence.' His eyes were shining, two dancing beams of light. 'We can touch our souls here.' He left a pause while he smiled wide enough to show all his teeth. 'OK, let's move on.'

Maggie was feeling twitchy. The light was too weak for a proper search and, if she was to stick with this group, there was too little time in each stop along the tour. She thought of Uri, cursing his father and his elaborate schemes. Leading them here was all very well, but not if they had no chance to find the tablet.

She suddenly became self-conscious. She glanced up to see a man gazing at her, then looking away. Had she been muttering? She was so tired it wouldn't have surprised her if, in her desperation, she had started thinking out loud. She could feel her cheeks grow hot.

The guide shepherded the group around a glass panel in the ground, which revealed they were in fact walking on a bridge, with a well-like hole directly below. 'This is only thirteen hundred years old,' he said, with a smile. 'Because this is not the original bridge, but one that was added later by the Muslims.'

They walked on, until they were under another vaulted ceiling. The smell of damp was getting stronger. They were, the guide explained, walking through a series of cisterns whose arches supported the houses built above. 'See the holes in the ceiling,' he said, as everyone looked up. 'They would drop a bucket from those, then pull it up, full of water.'

Maggie was barely listening, studying instead the two illuminated signs that had been placed down here: incongruously, they listed the foreign donors, the Schottensteins and Zuckermans, who had made these excavations possible. She scanned the names, looking for a Guttman or an Ehud Ramon or a Vladimir or a Jabotinsky, anything which might give her some clue. This place was so big, a maze of tunnels: how on earth was she meant to find anything here? She fully understood Uri's exasperation with his father: why couldn't he have been clearer?

The guide was calling them forward, to see what he introduced as Wilson's Arch. He pointed to a small opening, through which they could glimpse again the solid oblong stones of the Western Wall, no different from those they had seen outside. Most of their view was blocked, though, by a 'women's prayer area' that, even at this hour, was busy.

Enough of this, she decided. Tagging along in a tour party was never going to lead her to the tablet. She needed to search properly. And that meant alone. She walked, as quietly and unobtrusively as she could, away from the group and towards the first available opening.

It was a flight of newly-constructed metal stairs she had spotted when they came in. She went down, pressing her heel into each step to prevent her boots making the clacking noise that would give her away. At the bottom, she saw a deep rectangle that seemed to have been neatly carved out of the earth, with steps on each side. Some kind of bathing pool.

Go west, young man, and make your way to the model city, close to the Mishkan. You'll find what I left for you there, in the path of ancient warrens.

There was nothing here that connected this place to Guttman's clue. She moved forward, into a wider space, where a group of men in yellow hard hats were working: Arabs, Maggie couldn't help noticing. She remembered the note in the briefing material, noting the irony that the Jewish settlements on the West Bank, like Israel's security barrier or wall, which were so hated by the Arabs, were almost always built by Arab hands.

Facing her was the newly-exposed section of the Western Wall. She skim-read the sign: five tons each, finely cut, bevelled edges and neat borders, one longer than a bus, weighs in at five hundred and seventy tons, heavier than a 747 loaded with passengers and all their luggage. *Shit*. When was she going to see something that made sense?

She searched for an opening. There was only one and she took it, finding herself on a narrow path, faced on one side by an enormous arch that seemed to have been bricked up, filled in with a coarse, craggy rubble. Next to it was a sign: Warren's Gate.

Thank God for that. Guttman was not messing them around after all. Had not his clue spoken of the 'path of ancient warrens'? Both she and Uri had taken that to mean this warren of ancient tunnels, but Guttman had been far cleverer than that. He meant this place: not warrens at all, but Warren's. And here she was.

She looked up, down and around, confident that the hiding place was about to reveal itself. Yet all she could see was this wall of stone and brick, each piece apparently solid and unyielding. She began tapping and pulling, hoping to find a loose brick that might come away easily. None yielded.

Her confidence waning, she fell to her knees. She would work methodically, starting with the bottom line of stones. She began grabbing and tugging, the skin of her fingers scratching and tearing on the coarse brick. The wall was rock solid. Her hands moved frantically across the next line of stones, then the next. Nothing.

She stood up to look at the wall opposite. Perhaps the hiding place was here. She gazed high above and then below. Where in God's name had Guttman hidden it?

And then she saw him.

The same man she had made eye contact with during the tour, except now he was standing, alone, at the other end of this narrow pathway. Maggie registered no embarrassment, only recognition.

She had seen his face before. But where? Her mind was so addled with exhaustion, it was like wading through deep water to find the memory. It was recent, she knew that. Just the last few days. Was it at the hotel? At the consulate? No, she suddenly realized. Oh no. It was not there at all.

It had been at the nightclub in Tel Aviv where she and Uri had tracked down Baruch Kishon's son. Maggie had noticed him at the entrance, shortly after they had arrived. She had almost given him a sympathy smile: another thirtysomething, out of place in a club heaving with lithe and gorgeous kids. He had followed her then – and he had followed her now.

His purpose was beyond doubt. Whatever she was about to discover, he would want for himself, to pass on to God knows who. To the men who had killed Uri's mother, Kishon, Aweida and maybe even Uri. The men who would doubtless do the same to her, right here, right now, in this catacomb of age-old secrets.

CHAPTER FIFTY-THREE

JERUSALEM, FRIDAY, 8.21AM

Her legs made the decision before she did. She stood up and ran, rushing through a narrowing of the passageway, in which perhaps a dozen women were standing, each of them holding a prayer book. Their heads were covered with hats or crocheted snoods and their faces were pictures of intensity. As Maggie pushed past them, she could see they were all but touching a wall that was trickling with water, their lips nearly brushing it. Two other women, tourists probably, were standing apart from the rest. Maggie overheard them: 'The Foundation Stone is just through there, on the other side of the wall. Did you hear what they said? That those drops are God's tears.'

Maggie shoved them out of the way. She looked over her shoulder to see the stalker had now been joined by another man, a videocamera around his neck. They were getting closer. She picked up speed.

Now the pathway became a long, low, narrow tunnel. She ran on, hunched over. When she glanced back she saw them gaining on her, even as they ran in their own awkward crouch. In panic, she whirled around and dashed forward, only to smash her forehead on a metal rafter lodged in the ceiling. She gasped, then jumped as the wall on her left suddenly disappeared: an alcove, inside which was a wizened woman, dressed entirely in black, clutching a prayer book. Maggie felt dizzy.

Now the ground beneath her feet changed: a glass square looking down onto what might have been a cistern or a room below. The men were only about ten yards behind her.

Suddenly the tunnel passageway ended, opening out into another cistern. At last she could raise her head. She was desperate to find a way off the official path, so that she might give these men the slip. But there only seemed to be one opening each time. She would just have to stay ahead of them until she could break back out into the daylight. But how much longer would that be?

She was panting now, as she found herself in what looked like a corner of a long-buried Roman market. She faced two pillars, topped by a portico. Alongside it were two square slabs of stone, dumped on top of each other, as if the construction workers of two millennia past had simply downed tools and abandoned their task. She could hear heavy footsteps behind her. She looked for an exit but could see only one.

The path narrowed again, turning ninety degrees away from the Western Wall which had remained, until then, reliably on her right. Now, instead of the neat, regimented stones, she seemed to have entered some kind of underground gorge, a canyon of steep walls, as high as a cathedral, hugging her on both sides. They were wet and made up of solid, striated layers of colour, like the inside of a cake.

'Stop!' shouted one of her pursuers.

As she glanced over her shoulder, she thought she saw the second man, the one with the camera, draw a weapon and aim it at her. She yelped and ducked, but he could get no clear line of sight: the rocks twisted and turned too sharply.

At last she came to a set of narrow, metal stairs. She almost fell forward into them, and struggled to keep her balance. She clattered up them, breathing raggedly. Once at the top, she had to turn sideways just to get through, so tight was the gap. Behind her she heard a woman's scream: someone had just seen the gun.

And then the space opened out again, so that she was in what appeared to be a Roman vault. Once her eyes adjusted, she could see that it was in fact another pool, this one full of thick, stagnant water. She stood for a second, her lungs screaming to extract oxygen from this musty, humid air. Where did this pool lead? Maybe it came out somewhere outside, away from here. She stood at the edge, contemplating a dive. She had always been a good swimmer. Perhaps she could hold her breath . . .

But then she heard the footsteps, just a yard or two away and her instinct led her to turn away from the pool and scramble through the only opening instead. The second she had, she was flooded with relief. For now she could see daylight. Up a path, through a turnstile and she was out.

Gulping at the air, blinking at the sudden sunlight, she found that she had come out onto a narrow street, busy with people. Directly opposite her was a sign: Sanctuaries of the Flagellation and the Condemnation. And out of the sanctuary came a monk in a brown cassock with a rope around his waist. She was on the Via Dolorosa, Christ's route to the Crucifixion.

Maggie would have felt a moment's ancient Catholic comfort in the familiarity of it, if she had had the time. But she had no such luxury. Waiting for her at the exit were two men, their faces covered, who stepped forward and, calmly and with minimal exertion, grabbed her.

CHAPTER FIFTY-FOUR

JERUSALEM, FRIDAY, 8.32AM

Gloved hands gripped her wrists so hard it was as if they were made of steel rather than flesh and blood. She gasped but made no sound: other hands had already placed a small strip of material, like a rolled bandana, into her mouth. No one said anything.

They moved her backwards, off the street and back into the tunnels – away from public view. 'What are you doing? Who are you?' she tried to say through the gag. Knowing her words were useless, she added: 'And what have you done with Uri?'

Two of the men in front of her stepped forward, as if anticipating, and seeking to prevent, a violent reaction from her. They were right: instinctively, she tried to lash out. She attempted to move her arms, but they were now bound in what felt like tight plastic tape, the kind that comes on a new product, so strong it can be cut only with a sharp blade. She tried to scream but this only succeeded in making her retch on the material jammed into her mouth. Now she was panting even harder, her lungs forced to sate their craving for air through her nose. She could feel her heart thumping, driven not just by the exertions of the chase but by fear for her life.

The two men in front of her came closer, so that she could see the small portion of their faces that was not hidden. The eyes of the taller man, on her left, were dark, flat and glassy, like a pond frozen in winter. He looked as if even this, the sight of a woman surrounded by masked men, fighting for breath, bored him. Maggie looked at his partner, or rather looked *to* him, as if hoping to find some spark of the human. But what she saw chilled her. For the green eyes of this man did indeed betray an emotion; and that emotion was pleasure.

It was he who approached now with another strip of black material in his hands. As he moved his hands around the back of her head, his face just inches away from hers, she came to a cold, certain realization. He was the man who had assaulted her a few hundred yards away from here, in the back streets of the market. And now she understood, as the blindfold was tightened and the world fell into blackness, that she was as good as dead.

She felt a shove in the centre of her back and stumbled forward, someone catching her arm to prevent her falling to her right. She must be listing, like a drunk.

After a few minutes of staggering in this manner, maybe much less, maybe much more, she detected a change in the acoustics: no longer the echo of hard stone walls. And the cold dankness of the air was lifting, its mustiness less pronounced. Was she deceiving herself, or did she perceive, even through the blindfold, a change in the light?

They were stopping. She could hear other voices, further away. She imagined the world outside these tunnels and wondered if she would ever see it again.

There was some whispered talk; she strained to hear the language, but it was just out of reach. Then she was shoved forward again, her feet stumbling on the uneven surface. And then she was certain of the change. There was street noise: people, cars, footsteps. The colour of the dark under her blindfold altered, as if someone had let off fireworks in a night sky. And, the real giveaway, she felt warmth on her skin. The warmth of sunlight.

It made no sense, but she was relieved. They weren't going to kill her in those tunnels, then; she wouldn't have to rot in an abandoned cistern, the air echoing with women muttering endless psalms.

But she was only outside for a second or two. She felt the same metal hand that had gripped her wrists now grasp her neck from behind, and push it downward. He was pushing hard, as if trying to cantilever her entire body. She resisted, holding her back firm, refusing to be folded. She sensed the frustration in his hand as he pushed harder. Eventually he, or perhaps it was someone else, spoke, a male voice, behind her, uttering a single word: 'car'.

So that was it. They were shoving her into the back seat of a car. She gave way, glad for her little show of resistance. It wasn't much, but she felt she had achieved something. It had forced these men to break the silence they had maintained since they had cornered her just outside the tunnels. They hadn't wanted to speak, but they had just spoken. One word, admittedly, but it was a start. It had, in its own miniature way, been a negotiation. They had had to bend in order to win her co-operation. She may have been bound and gagged but, in mediation terms, she decided she had won the first round.

There seemed to be at least five people in this car: two men on either side of her, crammed in the back, and she could sense tension in the passenger seat by her right knee. They were still saying nothing to each other, but in the few seconds it had taken them to get in, she had heard a snatch of talk. It could have been people on the street, passers-by. Or it could have been the other members of the team of masked men who had hunted her down in the tunnels. Either way, there was no doubt what language she had heard. It was Arabic.

They drove for what she guessed was ten minutes. But it could have been half that or three times as long. It wasn't only that she couldn't check her watch or look at the clock in the car. Denied sight, her whole sense of time had been thrown off.

It sickened her that she was so close to these men, including, she felt certain, her assailant from the street market. Jammed into the back, her legs pressed against theirs, her knees couldn't help but touch theirs. Maybe his. She wanted to shove them away from her, hard, but her hands were tied. Her skin crawled.

Finally she felt the car slow down, then bump over a ridge, as if entering a driveway. She heard the driver's window wind down and then back up a moment later: perhaps he had had to show papers at some kind of checkpoint. Had she got the Arabic wrong? Was this in fact an Israeli team, taking her through the DCO to the West Bank? Were they going to do to her there what they would dare not do inside Israel proper?

The sound changed again. The car had gone down a ramp and now seemed to be indoors. Maybe they were in an underground car park. An image burst into her head, one that shocked her. She saw two bodies, dumped in the gloom of a subterranean garage, visible only in the bilious yellow of a fluorescent light. The two bodies, both dead, belonged to Uri and to her.

The car had stopped now, the engine off. She heard the rear doors open and the metal hand was on her back again, shoving her out. She didn't resist this time: she wanted to be out of that suffocating, confined space.

If it was a garage, they weren't in it for long. The car seemed to have parked right by a door. She was pushed through it, then up some stairs, guided by the man stuck to her right side. A few more paces forward and a door shut behind her.

'OK.'

She was so taken aback to hear a word spoken that she hardly listened or paid any attention to the voice that had spoken it. It was male, but more than that, she couldn't tell. What accent was it? She imagined it as Israeli and, playing the sound back in her head, it could have been. But then she tried the memory of it as Palestinian and it fitted that too. It could have been anybody, from anywhere, in any language.

A few seconds later she understood what the word meant. It was an instruction, a go-ahead. For now she felt a series of hands on her, some touching her legs, others moving, almost in caresses, around her back. She was confused. Unthinking, she cried out, only to hear the muffled choke of her voice against the gag. She felt herself retching again.

The hands were moving methodically, patting up and down each leg and down her arms, like an airport security check. *Of course,* she realized. They were searching her for the tablet. She felt them go into her trouser pockets, pulling out her mobile phone and the small wallet she carried. They would see her ID. The only time she had ever been as terrified as this was at a rogue roadblock in the Congo. Back then, the discovery of her identity was what she dreaded most: if they had known she was a diplomat, she would have been too valuable to let go. But it made no sense to fear that now: these people knew who she was.

There was a pause, in which she imagined some kind of silent consultation was taking place. Perhaps they had realized she had nothing, and they were debating whether to let her go. Perhaps this whole nightmare was about to . . .

But a second later, the hands were back. This time, though, there was no patting. Instead, they were rapid and determined, reaching immediately for their target.

They began with her shoes, removing them swiftly. Then she felt hands on the buckle of her belt, undoing it, then releasing the top button of her jeans, tugging down the zip and pulling her trousers clean off her. She cried out, a horrible, stifled, snotty roar.

Meanwhile another pair of hands was working on her top,

struggling to pull it off, obstructed by her bound wrists. There was a delay, until she could feel the plastic tape severed. Except her arms were not free. Each was now held tightly and lifted, so that another pair of hands could pull up her T-shirt and take it off.

She was now standing in only her underwear. She wanted to be tall, to overwhelm these men with the force of her rage, but she could feel a different urge rising in her – the desire to cower and shrink, to disappear from their gaze. Near-naked before them, and blind, she had never felt weaker.

And now the hands started again, touching her all over. Examining the small of her back, her armpits, running through her hair. There was a pause. *Still nothing.*

The voice spoke again. 'OK.'

Her bra came off first, not ripped off but unhooked slowly, a parody of a lover's touch that made Maggie's stomach churn. Once off, she could hear someone tearing at the material of the bra, as if expecting something to fall out of a hidden compartment.

Next they moved to the last thing left covering her, a pair of briefs that were not even hers but borrowed, along with everything else, from Orli.

And now two male hands were pulling them down, exposing her entirely. She tried to cover herself up, but the hands holding her wrists were too strong: she would have to stand there, uncovered.

She fought the urge to weep. She couldn't give them that victory. To deny them tears, that was her only resistance now. But it was so hard to hold them back. And then she felt the hand, from behind, pressing on her back.

It was the same action that had shoved her in the car, the hand trying to make her bend over at the waist. Is that what this was? Not a search, but a gang rape? Was this how it was going to end?

The shrinking humiliation was replaced by a hot torrent of

anger. She tried to punch out, her arms charged with a strength she hadn't felt before. She could tell that the man restraining her wrists had to work hard to keep hold of them.

At the same time, her legs moved in what was meant to be a kick. She got some movement on the right, but it was soon clamped down by another pair of hands. She wondered why they didn't bind her ankles.

She soon understood. Once they had crushed her rebellion, with men restraining each one of her limbs, she felt someone nudge her feet a few inches away from each other. That made possible the next manoeuvre. Two hands landed on her inner thighs, just below her buttocks, and with one clean shove, they pushed her legs apart. Then the same hands touched the buttocks themselves, parting them, too.

Now she could make no sound; the shock and shame were too great. She could only tremble as she felt her anus being forced open and an object pushed inside. Whether it was a finger or some kind of medical implement, she could not tell; all she could feel was the bolt of pain shooting deep inside her.

She could see the scene as if she was outside herself. She could picture it: her naked body presented to this group of masked men, her bottom in the air, her arsehole stretched open for their inspection. An involuntary spasm of protest made her muscles convulse. But she could barely move.

The object withdrew, roughly, and she screamed into her gag. But her pain was mixed with relief. For surely now this would be over.

She felt the hands turn her whole body around, so that now she was facing the men. They pushed her back, so that she felt herself land on some kind of surface, perhaps a table. Now they pulled her legs apart and through the blindfold she sensed a torchlight shone down at her; then she felt fingers probing inside her vagina. Her scream of outrage was grotesquely muffled by the gag. She wished tears would come, but her eyes were dry. As if this horror were too great for them to register.

There was a sound, of a door opening, of someone else entering the room.

'That's enough,' said a voice, just a few feet away. Amid the banging sound inside her own head, the pounding of her heart and the effort to swallow her tears, she couldn't make sense of the voice, couldn't even tell if it was the same man who had spoken before. Until he spoke again.

'Get her dressed.'

Now it came to her, unmistakable. She knew that voice all right. Because she knew that man.

CHAPTER FIFTY-FIVE

JERUSALEM, FRIDAY, 9.21AM

'They don't usually show people this part of the building, Maggie. It's a pity. Perhaps they should.'

As he spoke, she could feel multiple hands fussing over her, draping the T-shirt back over her head, placing her legs back into her jeans. They were working at speed, like stage hands making a rapid costume change before the next scene. They came to her face last, untying the gag – which triggered an instant spasm of coughing – and finally removing her blindfold. With that, they pushed her downward, into a hard, wooden chair.

In the time it took her to adjust to the light, the men in ski-masks had cleared the room. It was bare and featureless, the walls a dirty white; there were no windows and nothing on the walls. In front of her was a table. Perhaps this was the one the men had bent her over just a few moments earlier. And on the other side of it, sitting on a simple chair, just like hers, was him.

'I can only apologize for what happened just now, Maggie. Really. The strip-search, the body cavity thing. Horrible. Know what they call that in prisons back home? *Booty check*. How d'you like that? Anyway, like I say, I'm sorry. Wouldn't wish that on my worst enemy.'

Now that she could see him she felt dismayed by her own reaction. She thought she would want to rush at him, hands outstretched to squeeze at his neck, strangling his last breath. She expected she would long for acid to issue from her pores, until it dissolved him into nothing. But those feelings refused to come. They were subsumed by sheer disbelief, her dumbfounded incomprehension at the sight of this man here, in this place. They were overwhelmed by her confusion, which was total. 'What on earth are you doing?' was all she could manage to say.

'Let's not go too fast, Maggie. First I need to know the location of that tablet.'

'But, you? Why would you . . . ?'

'The question is, if you're not carrying it, if it's not hidden somewhere in the recesses of your body – and I have seen for myself that it isn't – where the hell is it?' He was raising his voice now, the way she had heard him do before.

'I don't know.'

'Oh, come on, Maggie. I know you've got it all worked out. You expect me to believe you don't know where it is?'

'And you expect me to talk to you, after what your thugs just did to me? I'll never say a fucking word to you again.' And then, a surprise to her as much as to him, she spat in his face.

'I like that, Maggie, you know I do. A girl with spunk. And you look good naked, too. That's what I'd call a killer combination.'

Maggie could say nothing. If her body was still reeling from the humiliation it had endured in this room, her mind was going through the very first convulsions of shock. Here was a man she had trusted, whom she had believed wanted the same things she wanted.

'Does this mean you were behind it all? All those killings?'

'It's our policy never to discuss the details of intelligence operations. You know that, Maggie.'

And he smiled. The knowing, complicit smile of one cynical political insider to another. The smile that Bruce Miller, senior counsellor to the President of the United States, had flashed a thousand times before.

CHAPTER FIFTY-SIX

JERUSALEM, FRIDAY, 9.34AM

'You had me followed?' Again she was disappointed by the weakness of her own question.

'We had you followed everywhere. You knew that.'

'But who's "we"? Who the hell are you working for?' It was as if the blood was finally reaching her brain. 'You're a traitor, that's what you are. You've betrayed your country. You've betrayed your own fucking president.'

'Maggie, can we skip the whole Irish outrage thing? You, Bono, that other asshole, what's his name, Bob Geldof? Every other do-gooding, bleeding heart coming on with that big, guilt-tripping accent. It's not going to work this time.' He was leaning back, pivoting the chair on its two hind legs, chewing his nicotine gum as energetically as ever. 'This is not some negotiation with a bunch of banana-munchers in Africa. You have something that I need. And you have no cards to play, Maggie. Not one. So tell me. Where is the fucking tablet?'

Negotiation. The mere mention of the word was enough to make her snap back into herself. She had always been good at what the shrinks call 'compartmentalization', shutting one aspect of her life out of another so that she could concentrate on the task at hand, and now, consciously, she forced herself to perform the trick again. To forget what had just happened, even her loathing of the monster opposite her, and do her job. To negotiate.

'I won't tell you a thing until you tell me what the hell is going on here.'

'Look, Maggie. I don't want to repeat myself. But you have no leverage here. I can force you to tell me what you know, if I have to.'

'Oh, really? The President's most trusted adviser personally directing the assault of a US citizen, a senior US diplomat – in an election year. That should play well in the polls.'

'No one's going to believe a word you say. A washed-up slut who can't keep her legs closed, banging first the Africans and then some Israeli. How do you think that'll look on the front page of the *Washington Post*?'

Maggie closed her eyes, involuntarily. She was proofing herself, like an animal instinctively hardening its hide against an incoming assault. She knew he was right. That her mistake in Africa, coupled with her relationship with Uri, could finish her off completely. That in a contest of credibility, which is what most political scandals came down to, she would lose to Bruce Miller every time.

'Yeah. And the soccer mums are going to just love a president whose main man watches while masked goons perform an anal probe of one of his female colleagues. You're already in the deepest shit imaginable. So why don't you talk to me and then maybe I'll talk to you?'

Miller eyed Maggie up, the suggestion of a smile on his lips. She could sense a poker player about to fold.

'Like I said, you got spunk, Costello. In a different life, I could imagine you and me getting on, if you know what I'm saying.'

Maggie kept her expression fixed. If a change in your opponent was about to come, you never wanted to make the slightest move that might divert him. Never break the spell.

'It's not that complicated, really.'

She wanted to exhale her relief: he was going to talk. But her face stayed frozen.

'We need a peace deal here, Maggie. And we were pretty fucking close. Then last weekend we hear there's some tablet floating around that could be Abraham's last will and testament—'

'How?'

'How what?'

'How did you hear?'

'Your boyfriend's dad. Guttman. He calls Baruch Kishon, the Israeli journalist, and tells him. Not the whole story, but enough of it. Mentions the trader Afif Aweida, mentions his pal Ahmed Nour. And, as luck would have it, NSA were listening in.'

'As luck would have it.'

'OK, it wasn't luck. We'd been bugging Kishon for years.'

'Kishon? Why the hell would you be bugging him?'

'You not been reading the files, Maggie? Kishon's the guy who broke the Tel Aviv connection story all those years ago.'

Maggie cursed Uri for not mentioning it. He must have known. It had been the biggest diplomatic rift between Israel and the US for decades: three CIA agents had been double-crossing the Agency, leaking secrets to the Israelis. To this day, the Israelis constantly demanded the spies' release from prison; even the most pliantly pro-Israel presidents repeatedly refused.

'Kishon still talks to them in jail. Campaigns for their release. We've been monitoring him ever since.'

'And so once you heard what Guttman had told him, you decided to kill him.'

'Oh, don't start fucking preaching to me, young lady. We knew immediately what was at stake here. The Arabs and the Israelis are about to do the business, which means doing the business on Jerusalem, split the fucking place down the middle, and now we've got God Almighty himself, or near as dammit, saying that no, it belongs to the Jews. The whole deal would be off.'

Maggie had to work hard to stay cool. *He had seen the text: he knew what it said.* She couldn't let him know that she hadn't and didn't. 'So you were frightened that the Israelis would walk away, because Abraham bequeathed the Temple Mount to them?'

'Or to the Muslims. It made no difference which one got it. Either way, the peace process would be over. We had to be sure neither of them got their hands on it.'

That allowed her a moment of relief: he was not ahead after all. Miller knew as little of the tablet's contents as she did. She would stay on the offensive. 'So it's been you all along. Killing Kishon, Ahmed Nour, Afif Aweida, Guttman, Guttman's *wife* – anyone who might know what's in the tablet and who might talk.' She didn't want to mention Uri; saying it might make it true.

'Don't get carried away, Costello. Guttman was killed by the Israeli secret service. The guy looked like he was about to pull a gun on Yariv, what were they supposed to do?'

'And that kibbutz in the north. The arson attack. That was you too?'

'Guttman was one of the main archaeologists of that site. We thought he might have hidden it there.'

Now it was Maggie's turn to say nothing. She stared at her wrists, red welts etched deep into both of them. She started shaking her head.

'What's that for?' Miller asked, irritated. She said nothing. Then, slamming his fist on the table, he shouted, 'Why are you shaking your fucking head?'

She looked up, glad she had needled him. 'Because I cannot believe how deeply, profoundly stupid you are.'

'How dare you—'

'You did all this because you worried that the release of the testament would derail the peace process? All this killing, of people on both sides?' There was a mirthless laugh in her voice. 'You did all this to *prevent* the breakdown in the peace process? Did you not think, for one second, that tit-for-tat killings, in the most delicate stage of negotiations, might actually fuck the peace talks up all by themselves? I mean, it beggars belief. What is it with you Americans? Like, Iraq poses a threat: so let's invade and make it a thousand times *more* of a threat! And now you've made the same mistake all over again.'

'You have no right to lecture me—'

'I have every right. I have been running around this country, risking my life, desperate to get to the bottom of whatever was causing all this violence, because I wanted to help save the peace process, because I actually believed in it. And now I find the real source of the trouble and of the violence that's been destroying everything, wasn't Hamas or Jihad or Fatah or the settlers or the Mossad or any of them. It was you!'

Miller had collected himself. 'I always knew you were naive, Maggie; it was part of your charm. But this is too much. You don't think these guys would have got started the moment they knew about the testament? Of course they would. There's been plenty of killing going on here all week that had nothing to do with us. Qalqilya. Gaza. The schoolbus in Netanya. If we'd done nothing, all that would still have happened, all by itself. Same with Hizbullah and the Iranians going batshit.' *Eye-ranians*. 'That's the real world, my girl. You're facing a disease that's 'bout to spread, you kill the first beast that gets it. Otherwise, it'll kill the whole herd.' It was the down-home, farm-boy shtick that Miller deployed to such good effect on the Sunday morning talk shows in Washington. It always intimidated the press, made them feel like soft-handed city boys.

'So that's what this was, eh? You derail the peace process a bit, before the lunatics derail it even more.'

'There are no good choices in this game, Maggie. You should know that by now.'

'And I suppose it was working. Until I came along and started poking around.'

'Oh, you don't need to worry about that.'

'Why? You'd have pulled it off, wiping out anyone who knew about the tablet. Abraham's secret would have remained a secret. But I waded in, didn't I, obsessing night and day to uncover what you had decided should stay hidden. What a bloody fool I am.'

'You want to ease up on yourself, Maggie.'

'Why should I do that?'

'Because you've done exactly what we wanted you to do – from the very beginning.'

CHAPTER FIFTY-SEVEN

JERUSALEM, FRIDAY, 9.41AM

Maggie stared at the ground. She needed to steady herself and this was the way she would do it. If she looked up, if she looked at him, she would lose her balance.

A shift had just taken place between them, they both knew that. Now she needed something from him as badly as he did from her. She was in a position of weakness. Had this been a negotiation about a border, or water, or even weekend access and custody of the house in the Hamptons, she would have known how to disguise the situation, how to conceal her neediness. But the most skilled negotiator becomes a dunce when negotiating on his own behalf. Maggie's colleagues told repeatedly the story of the UN mediator who, despite winning a Nobel peace prize, had tried and failed to land himself a pay rise.

'What the hell is that supposed to mean: I did exactly what you wanted me to do?'

Miller smiled. He knew as well as she did the mistake she had just made, revealing her need.

'Oh, come on, Maggie. Let's not dwell on this. We've got work to do. Believe it or not, we have a peace process to save.'

'Like you care.'

'You kidding? Are you fucking kidding?' The smile was gone now. 'What do you think we were doing here? This whole operation was about *saving* the peace talks. We knew they'd be deader than a turkey in November the second that tablet got out.' He gave Maggie a look of deep disgust. 'You just don't get it, do you? Not any of you smug East Coast, European, liberal elite assholes.' He leaned across the table, his eyes flashing. 'You love all the nice stuff, the talks, the meetings, the plans, the counterplans, the roadmaps, the UN resolutions, the ceremonies, the White House handshakes – you love all *that*. But d'you ever stop for one goddamned second and wonder how all that is possible? You ever wonder what drags a bloodthirsty bastard like Slobodan Milosevic to Dayton to sit down for one of your fucking peace treaties? Do you?

'Well, I'll tell ya. It's evil fuckers like me and my masked friends outside, that's what. Milosevic didn't do the deal because you flashed your pretty eyelashes at him. Just like your brethren in the IRA didn't sign on the dotted line because you or someone like you wiggled your ass in their direction. No, they did it because someone like me was threatening to drop a megaton of dynamite on their heads if they didn't. And not just threatening. Sometimes we did it, too.

'Sure, we let you guys get the credit and the peace prizes and the book deals and the interviews on Charlie Rose. Sure, let the *New York Times* suck your dick. I don't care. I'll be the son of the devil, I can take it. But don't fool yourself, missy. There'd be no peace unless there were guys like me ready to make war.'

Maggie took a deep breath. 'And that's what you were doing here? A bit of war so that we could make peace, that's what—'

'You're damn right, that's what we were doing. And it made sense, too. The two sides are still in the room—'

'Technically.'

'There's a back channel too, so they're talking, believe me. Besides technically's better than nothing. And nothing and nowhere is where we would have been if this bastard tablet had got out. I'm proud of what we did.'

'Did everyone know apart from me?'

Miller was quieter now, examining his own fingers. 'The opposite. This was need-to-know. Me and a small team recruited for the job. Ex-special forces.'

'The team who grabbed me in the street market. They did all the killing too?'

'I leave operational details to them and their commander.'

'And the rest of us were out of the loop? The Secretary of State? Sanchez?'

'All of them. Except you.'

'What the hell are you talking about?'

'You should feel proud.'

'Proud?'

'Of what you did. You nearly got us there. To the tablet. Just like we hoped.'

'I don't understand.'

'Oh come on, this ain't *Little House on the Prairie*. You know how it works. Why do you think we sent Bonham over there to get you?'

'To close the deal. The two sides were nearly there and you wanted me to close the deal.' Maggie's voice was wobbling.

'Yeah, whatever.'

'That's what Bonham said!'

'Course that's what he said,' Miller was staring hard at Maggie now. 'But come on, Maggie. You think the State Department's not crawling with people like you, skilled diplomats who couldn't do this job? Specialists on the Middle East conflict? Don't tell me you didn't wonder why, out of all the people we had, we had to have you. We needed you because of your – how can I put this delicately? – because of your unique expertise.'

Maggie could feel herself paling. 'What are you saying?'

'We needed someone to get close to Guttman Junior. If anyone knew where the old sonofabitch had hidden this tablet, it would be him.'

'You brought me here to, to . . .' She couldn't say the words.

'Well, let's face it, Maggie, you had the right resumé. You got close to that lunatic in Africa and we thought, given the right context, you'd do the same here. And you did. Like I said, you should be proud.'

A moment of puzzlement, followed by a strange feeling, one that Maggie had not known before, as if she was being crushed from the inside. So that's what this was about, that's what it had been about from the very beginning. Maggie heard again the voice of Judd Bonham, how he had recruited Maggie for this enterprise. Cancelling out the sin through repentance, he had said. He even mentioned redemption. *This is your chance.* He had spoken so softly, his voice sweet with reason. And yet he had been telling the opposite of the truth. He did not want her to come to Jerusalem to undo her mistake in Africa, but to repeat it. He, Miller and God knows who else had deployed her not because of her strengths – all that bullshit about the indispensable Maggie Costello, the great 'closer' – but because of this one weakness. All that praise; and she had believed every word of it.

She was nothing more than a honeytrap, that lowest form of espionage life, sent in to win the affection of Uri Guttman. The fact that she had succeeded only increased her nausea. What did that make her? Nothing more than a whore for the American government.

Instinct launched Maggie from her chair, where she had held herself throughout everything. She slapped Bruce Miller hard across the face. Feeling the sting, Miller put his hand to his cheek, then, with a smirk that oozed lechery, slapped her back. As she reeled, he pressed a button under the table, instantly bringing two masked men back into the room.

'OK, Maggie. This has gone on long enough. Not that I'm not enjoying myself. But you need to tell me where that tablet is.'

'I don't know,' she said, her words slurred by the blow to her face.

'That's not within a thousand miles of good enough, Maggie. Now, I think you know I got some boys here who've enjoyed getting acquainted with you. They might like the chance to get to know you a little better.'

'So now you're going to have the White House implicated in a rape.'

'We would be implicated in no such thing. We would issue a statement mourning the loss of a fine American, brutally assaulted and then murdered by terrorists. The United States wouldn't rest until your killers were brought to justice.'

Maggie could feel herself trembling, with rage, fear and a terrible sadness.

'Do I have your attention now, Miss Costello?'

CHAPTER FIFTY-EIGHT

JERUSALEM, FRIDAY, 9.52AM

It was as if she were raiding the emergency tank. She could feel herself digging deep into her own reserves – of restraint, of self-control, and of that mysterious inner drug she seemed able to generate when the moment truly demanded it, the one that could, as if by an act of sheer willpower, numb the pain.

She heard her voice talking, in the low calm it could find in a crisis. 'I don't know any more than you already know. You saw what I saw. The message from Shimon Guttman sent us to the Western Wall tunnels.'

'The message in the computer game?'

'Yes. He gave us nothing more specific. If he had, you'd know about it.'

Miller gave a tiny movement of his head, less than a nod, but it was enough. The two men in ski masks came closer, each taking an arm. They pulled Maggie up from her chair and, careful to synchronize their movements, performed an identical action – wrenching her arms until they were both flat and high against her back: a full nelson. She roared with pain, sending a jet of spittle across the room. That only made the men yank harder, tugging at her wrists to pull her arms higher. On her right side, she could feel the strain on the ball-joint where her arm met her shoulder. The pain was so intense she could see it: a bubbling redness in front of her eyes. She was sure they were about to pull her arms right out of their sockets.

And then it stopped and she was dropped back in the chair, limp as a child's doll.

Miller spoke again, his voice unchanged. As if he had merely paused to take a sip of water and was now picking up their conversation where they had left off. 'And you didn't see anything when you were in there this morning?'

It took a while for Maggie to open her eyes. The redness was still there, raging; the pain lived on, too, even through the relief of its ending. She could feel the memory of it still flooding her nervous system. When she finally forced her mouth to speak, all she could muster was a croak. 'You know I didn't. You searched me.'

Miller leaned forward. 'Not only that, but I've had people searching the entire tunnels area since you led us there. Under floodlights. And still nothing. Which means—'

'That the old man was not playing it straight. He said it was there, but it wasn't.'

'Or that Uri was tricking you. Sent you off chasing wild geese in those cellars, so that he could go and get his inheritance all by himself.'

'Maybe.' Even through the haze of agony and rage, Maggie was considering it. After all, she now understood, any kind of betrayal was possible. Uri could have faked the shooting on the road that morning, then headed off to collect the tablet alone. Maybe he realized who Maggie was before she had. He had served in Israeli intelligence; she had seen the way he had stolen a uniform and then a car. Perhaps all that was mere preparation for his ingenious dumping of her on the highway. Maybe he had Maggie's number from the start: a honeytrap, to be avoided. She was the only one who had not seen it.

Miller stared at her for a moment, then turned his mouth into an expression of regret. 'Just to be on the safe side, I think I should let the boys here see if they can't help you remember if there's anything else. Jog your memory.'

He gave another small nod and instantly the two men pulled her out of the chair. Except now they didn't stand her up, but threw her to the ground. The man on her right immediately came down on one knee beside her and put his arm around her neck. He had already begun to squeeze when she managed to choke out a few words, speaking them as soon as she thought them.

'Or maybe there's nothing to know.' She could barely hear her own voice.

'Excuse me?'

She tried to repeat the words but there was no air. The pressure on her windpipe was too great. She was being strangled.

Miller made a gesture and the pressure eased. The arm, though, stayed fixed around her neck.

'Say that again.'

'I said, maybe there's nothing to know.'

'What does that mean?'

'Maybe we couldn't find where Shimon Guttman hid the tablet because he hadn't yet hidden it.'

'Explain.'

Maggie tried to get up but she had no strength. She stayed there, on the ground, panting out the words. 'The messages Guttman left – the DVD, the one in Second Life – they were all done on Saturday. So was the call with Kishon.' She was gasping. 'But what if he hadn't finished doing what he needed to do? He *planned* to hide the tablet in the tunnels – and he would have done it. But events intervened: he got killed. He probably planned to do whatever he was going to do after the peace rally. He just never made it.'

Miller was listening closely. 'So where's the tablet now?'

'That's the whole point. I don't know. And if *I* don't know – when I've seen his last messages and had his son explain his childhood memories – that means nobody knows. And nobody will know.'

'The tablet will be lost.'

'Yes.'

Miller nodded slowly, not to her but to himself, as if he were weighing the pros and cons and had at last been persuaded. He got out of his chair and began to pace, circling around Maggie who remained a crumpled heap on the floor. Finally he delivered his verdict.

CHAPTER FIFTY-NINE

JERUSALEM, FRIDAY, 10.14AM

The driver took her the short distance to the hotel, but she didn't want to go in straightaway. She had seen so little daylight, she just wanted to absorb some of it now. She stood and looked around.

The entrance was busy, taxis parked with their engines running, guests coming in and out with multiple suitcases. More out than in, Maggie guessed: tourists were probably abandoning Jerusalem after the troubles of the last few days. If they only knew.

She could hear a megaphone blaring. She turned around to see a white estate car, covered in orange stickers and posters, driving slowly up King David Street: inside, someone was shouting slogans denouncing, it seemed, Yariv and his imminent surrender of Israel's patrimony. A minute later the car was joined by a van, this one blaring out a bland kind of Euro-pop. From the look of it, this was the peace camp, probably deriding Yariv for backing away from the negotiations.

She looked past the traffic lights, up the hill. The consulate's just up there, she thought, where this whole thing began. She remembered sitting there in the garden, just off the plane, wondering about the brothers in the monastery. That had been just five days ago, though it felt more like five years. She and Jim Davis had talked about 'closing the deal'. Maggie smiled bitterly.

She turned left, walking away from the hotel. Every part of her ached; her arms and neck especially. She imagined the bruises all over her body, even in those places you couldn't see. She yearned for a long soak in a hot bath and a deep sleep. But she was not ready for that now: her mind wouldn't let her rest.

She found instead a park, almost empty and looking unloved. The lawns were unkempt at the edges, the metal struts that supported a gazebo canopy in the middle had been allowed to rust. Maggie noticed that even the paving stones, and the benches, were made of that same golden Jerusalem stone: it was beautiful, but she reckoned people who lived here surely got tired of it. Like living in a town with a chocolate factory: visitors would love the smell, while the full-timers fast grew sick of it.

She sat on the bench and stared. When Miller told her she was free to go, that he had concluded she had nothing more to reveal, she had felt relief but no pleasure. It wasn't only the pain that still throbbed through her; nor the humiliation of having been exposed, even in her most intimate parts, like some kind of animal carcass; nor even what Miller had revealed was the true nature of her mission to Jerusalem. No, what Maggie felt was something she guessed most people would not grasp. Perhaps only another mediator would understand it: the gnawing anxiety that comes when the other side has given in too easily. Miller had folded too soon and she didn't know why.

She went over his words again and again, including the final statement he had delivered as he left the interrogation room. He warned her that if she tried to reveal what had happened, he would ensure that the *Washington Post* was briefed that poor Ms Costello had suffered a breakdown in Jerusalem, leaving her delusional and irrational, following a second affair while on duty. The authorities had given her a chance, after an earlier lapse had forced her to give up diplomatic work. But her curious weakness had thwarted their attempt to help. She couldn't seem to avoid developing intimate relations with those with whom she was meant to engage professionally, administration sources would say, speaking on condition of anonymity. If she tried to fight it, they had the tapes and photographs showing her with Uri, late at night, drinking, kissing . . .

She shuddered and stared at her feet, in boots she barely recognized. All the time she had done this job she had refused to let her gender be the decisive fact about her. Sure, she knew her womanhood was a factor in any negotiation, sometimes a disadvantage, usually an asset, so long as you knew how to play it. But it was only one element among many, alongside her Irishness or her relative youth. It was not all she was. But Miller had made her feel differently and it repelled her. He saw her not as an experienced mediator, a skilled reader of human dynamics and a reliable analyst of international relations, but as a whore. That's what it came down to. To him, her affair in Africa was the single most important line on her resumé. Along with her tits and her arse. She was there not for her savvy, or her intellect, or her years at assorted peace tables, but to get laid. Suddenly her manhandling in the souk felt like the least of it. She had been violated, she now understood, from the moment she took those tickets and got in the cab for Dulles Airport.

After Miller's little speech of warning, he had surprised her. His expression, the cocky, jabbing neck movements, gave way to something else, something she hadn't seen before. He leaned his head to one side and his eyes seemed to radiate sympathy. He held that look for a long time, before saying quietly, 'We have to do horrible things sometimes, really horrible things. But we do them for the right reason.'

What maddened her now, as she sat in this barren piece of parkland, was that she almost agreed with him. She was not some pacifist, incense-burning mung-bean merchant who thought all power was inherently evil and that we should all be nice to each other. She understood how the world worked. Specifically, she understood – better than anyone – how critical it was to keep this tablet out of the combatants' hands. Miller was right to do whatever it took to find it before they did. The President wanted to get re-elected and that meant he needed an Israeli-Palestinian peace deal. Who cared if his motives were shoddy? At least these two nations, who had been locked in a death embrace so long they could barely imagine life without the other, would finally get the accord they needed.

Maggie Costello would have signed up for all of that. She had been around the block enough times to know that peace settlements don't come about because of an outbreak of niceness or because some priest persuades the leaders to do the right thing or even because a passionate young brunette from Dublin tells them to stop killing each other. They do it because their interests or, more often, the interests of the great powers change. Suddenly the big boys have no use for war and so it ends.

So she knew how things were. If Miller or Davis or Bonham – and it pained her to think they were probably all involved in this – had ever come clean, explained the problem and why they needed her help, she would have agreed. She would have found her own way to do it. Instead they didn't trust her to know what the big boys knew. She was merely a tool to be deployed, a piece set down on the chessboard whose sole duty was to get fucked.

It was getting cold, or at least she was. Probably the tiredness. She would go back to the hotel, speak to no one and, once she had slept, she would go to the airport. Where would she go? She had no idea.

Once back in the cavernous lobby of the Citadel, she walked

with her head down, determined to make eye contact with no one. She realized it made no sense, but she felt as if everyone knew what had happened to her these last few hours and she couldn't bear to be seen.

'Miss Costello! Hello!' It was a clerk at reception, her ponytail swinging as she bounced up and down, waving a piece of paper, loudly calling across the lobby. 'Miss Costello, please!'

If only to shut her up, Maggie marched across the polished floor, hoping no one else had caught this little scene.

'Ah, Miss Costello. He said it was most urgent. You just missed him. He was here a minute ago, I told him—'

'Please, you'll have to slow down. Who said what was urgent?'

'The man who came here. I told him he could leave a voicemail message from the house phone but he refused. He wanted me to give you this.' She handed Maggie a piece of paper, torn from the hotel's message pad.

Meet me in an old moment. I know what we have to do. Vladimir Junior.

CHAPTER SIXTY

JERUSALEM, FRIDAY, TWO HOURS EARLIER

The throbbing was softened now, reduced to a rhythmic ache. He wondered if they had given him something, perhaps a jab in the thigh as they bundled him back into the Merc. Or maybe later. He wouldn't have noticed if they had.

He had come round half an hour ago. Or maybe it was an hour. It had taken him a while to realize that he was not staring into a darkened room, but was blindfolded. For several long minutes he thought he was staring at the underside of his own eyelids. Then he remembered the bullet and wondered, in earnest, if he was experiencing the consciousness of the dead.

Sensations returned only slowly, as if in succession. After the eyes came his arms, which told him they were immobile. He tried to remember: had he been shot there, too? Might he be paralysed? He did not panic. Instead he felt his heart plumb to the slow, low pressure deployed *in extremis*. It was as if the body went into emergency deep freeze, knowing it was now in a battle to survive. He knew all this, because he had experienced it once before.

Back then, the wound had been psychological. He had been in a tank across the Lebanese border when it was struck by a

Hizbullah roadside bomb. The driver and gunner had been killed instantly. As the commander, he should have been the most vulnerable: he was poking his head outside. But, perversely, that had saved him. He lowered himself back into the tank to see his two comrades slumped and still and knew instantly that he was sitting in a deathtrap. At that moment, when his heart should have raced with fear, his organs went instead into a mode altogether more frightening, for it was beyond regular terror. It was a still, slow calm; a prelude to death.

And he felt it again now. Coolly, he remembered the incident on the Jerusalem highway: it could only have lasted thirty seconds. He had seen the car behind, unmistakably following them. He had slowed down, swerving into the beauty spot lay-by, at an angle he hoped would allow Maggie to drop out unseen. In the instant, split-second he had had for a decision, that is what he had decided: that whatever happened to him, she should live.

Once Maggie was out and clear, he had attempted to spin the car around and repeat the manoeuvre, so that he too could bail out undetected. But the turn had proved impossible and by then the pursuers had caught up. He had taken no more than a step outside the car when the bullet had struck his leg. He had fallen, with none of the drama they showed in the movies, but rather like a puppet whose strings had been severed.

Now came a new signal, from his wrists. His neurological pathways, usually nanosecond fast, seemed to have reverted to the age of steam: the messages were reaching his brain so slowly. But the wrists were saying they could feel something, an abrasion that was not mere pain but external. A restraint. He was, he finally realized, bound. The blindness, the immobility, were not signs of the physical shutdown that might precede death, but of something less final. He had been shot and bundled in the car not as a corpse, but as a prisoner. His heart began to beat faster.

He began to struggle, to jiggle his wrists. He soon understood that they were not only bound to each other, but to the chair he was sitting on. He wanted to inspect his wound, but he could not touch it and, in the blackness, he could barely be certain which leg it was that had been struck.

Who had taken him? He pictured masked men, dressed in black; but that could have been a trick of the memory. He tried to remember what he had heard when they shoved him in the car. The name Daoud surfaced. He had heard someone call it, as if in a question, twice. It must have been a symptom of his delirium though, because in Uri's mind he heard the name, this Arabic name, called out in an accent that was distinctly American.

The thoughts were flowing more freely now. Uri wondered what Maggie had done. He guessed she had somehow found her way straight back to Jerusalem, to the tunnels. But where would she have even begun? His father's clue – was it really left inside some computer game, or was that also the fruit of his fevered imagination? – directed them only to the subterranean catacombs of the Western Wall, which covered a significant distance. Uri knew: he had refused his father's repeated requests to come back from New York and take the tour, but he had read about it. It took at least an hour to walk through.

In the dark like this, Uri at last had a chance that had not come since he took the phone call six days ago. The truth was, he had avoided it. But now he had little alternative but to think about his father. He had surprised him more in death than he ever had in life. Until this week, Uri would have described his father as predictable, the way all ideologues are predictable. He knew his views on everything. They were unbending and therefore, to Uri's mind, irretrievably dull. Uri had often wondered, only to himself and never out loud, of course, if that was why he had rejected his father's brand of hardline politics – on aesthetic rather than moral grounds. Had he become a left-winger simply to avoid being a bore like his dad?

Yet in the last few days, his father had proved him wrong. He had harboured many secrets, including one that had clearly given him the greatest thrill of his career – and they had cost him his life.

Of them all, the one that shocked most remained the one that he had heard first, courtesy of Maggie Costello. His father had traded archaeological know-how with the enemy, with a Palestinian, even giving him an Israeli codename, an anagram. What was it, Ehud Ramon? He might have been an arsehole, his father, but he was not stupid.

He heard a door unlock, followed by the sound of men. He knew what was coming and felt oddly armed against it. He would do what he had read survivors of all forms of brutality had done: he would stay within his own head.

He heard a voice with an American accent, the one he thought he had imagined in the car. 'OK, let's go to work.'

Next he could feel a bandage on his right leg being steadily unwound. Perhaps he was in hospital and he was about to be treated. Maybe these men were not torturers, but doctors.

He was about to speak, to ask for their help, when he felt fingers exploring the outside of his wound; he inhaled sharply at the sting. And then, a moment later, he felt a pain that made him howl as he had never howled before.

'Funny, ain't it, what one little finger can do?'

The pain stopped for a second.

'That's all it is, one little finger. All I have to do is push it right there, into this hole in your leg, and—'

Uri screamed at the agony. He had vowed to withstand their torture, not to let them see him suffer. But he could not hold back the pain. His wound was live and raw, every one of its nerve endings exposed.

'Get off me, you bastards, get off!'

At that, the red he had seen turned to white. The pain leapt in intensity and then disappeared, as if off the register. This blankness lasted only a few seconds, before he heard a voice that seemed to be far away.

'. . . in fact, if I kept on pressing, I'd probably be able to touch your bone. Like that.'

'What do you want? I don't know anything!'

Whiteness again, also for just a few short seconds. When it ended, Uri realized what was happening; that the agony was so excruciating, he was moving in and out of consciousness.

Now when the finger probed into his bullet wound, he prayed for oblivion to come. He waited through the pain, hoping for the relief of nothingness. Instead he heard himself scream again, as two fingers forced their way inside, widening the opening, pushing and prodding.

'Just tell us what you know.'

'You know what I know.'

Next he heard the wailing as if it were someone else. And suddenly a voice in some inner chamber of the self spoke to him. Now, it said. This is your chance; force yourself to do it. Detach yourself from the pain. *Stay inside your head.*

He tried to remember where his thoughts had been just before the men came in. He had been thinking of his father's ingenious codename, Ehud Ramon. Hold on to it, he thought; hold on. He repeated the name to himself, even as he felt his own body tremble from the agony. *Ehud Ramon. Ehud Ramon. Ehud, Ehud, Ehud . . .*

And then a memory surfaced that had lain buried for decades, a memory of the bedtime story he had loved as a child, the one he made his father read to him over and over, about a wonderfully naughty little boy. For a fleeting second, interrupting the red and white colours of his pain, Uri could picture the book cover: *My brother, Ehud*. What had his father said in that video message? *I have put it somewhere safe, somewhere only you and my brother could know.*

Of course, Uri thought, willing himself to stay on this train of thought and not to fall into the pits of hell below. Of course. It hadn't been a real brother that his father had spoken of. Rather he was referring to the fictitious brother in a story he assumed his son would immediately remember. And it was meant to lead him to another fictitious creation, the mythic Ehud Ramon.

The probing intensified now; they were using some kind of implement. And the questions kept on. Where is the tablet? Where is it? But Uri stayed in his head. What a typical Guttman rhetorical flourish, he thought. The professor had just seen the ancient, hand-chiselled words of Abraham, speaking of his two sons, Isaac, the father of the Jews and Ishmael, the father of the Muslims. Two brothers, Jew and Arab. 'My brother . . .' Shimon Guttman had said. If he could have, Uri would have smiled. His father, the fire-breathing, flint-hearted nationalist, was using that weariest cliché of the kumbaya-singing, hand-holding, soppy left – that Jews and Arabs are brothers.

Even here, with his body battered and his senses overloaded by the sharpest of torments, he felt a surge of admiration for his old man: it was a brilliant piece of cryptography. Was there a codebreaker in the world who would realize that when a fanatic hawk referred to 'my brother', the man he meant was none other than the stubborn Palestinian nationalist, Ahmed Nour?

CHAPTER SIXTY-ONE

JERUSALEM, FRIDAY, 11.50AM

Maggie stared at the message, her brow slowly smoothing into a smile. She only knew one Vladimir, and that was Vladimir Jabotinsky, mentor and pseudonym of Shimon Guttman. Vladimir Junior could only be one person. With a relief that flowed through her as a wave of exhaustion, she understood what Uri was telling her. That he was alive. Somehow he had survived the gunshot on the highway; somehow he had endured whatever agonies Miller's goons had inflicted on him. And now he was in 'an old moment'. She had to smile at that. He knew she would remember it, because they had talked about it: *the café that used to be Moment.*

When she opened the door, she saw him immediately, in the same seat she had found him in two days ago. Except now he was looking up, straight at her.

'You know,' she said, 'I normally insist on going somewhere new for a second date.'

He tried to smile, but only a wince would come. She sat beside him, planting a long kiss on his lips. She had been relieved when she got the note, but that was nothing next to her feelings now. She moved to hug him, stopping when he let out a yelp of pain.

He pointed at his leg, explaining that underneath these jeans was a thick bandage covering a bullet wound. He told her about the shooting and the interrogation, her face registering each new agony as he described it. And he told her how his tormentors, in the middle of their work, had received a phone call, one that made them stop. They had dressed him in new clothes and driven him to the centre of town, dumping him ten minutes from here. They left him with a warning: 'You saw what happened to your parents. If you don't keep your mouth shut, the same will happen to you.' He had been blindfolded throughout.

'Uri, did the men who . . . did they ever tell you who they were?'

'They didn't have to.'

'You guessed?'

'I guessed even before they spoke in English. They were speaking to each other in Arabic. Calling their leader Daoud, the whole thing. Their accents weren't bad. But they were like mine.' He tried to smile. 'They had intelligence-officer Arabic. You know, an accent learned in a classroom. Mine's the same. I wondered if they were Israelis at first. I spoke to them in Hebrew.' He shook his head. 'Not a word. So I worked it out. Later, when they were torturing me, they didn't even hide it. That's what frightened me the most.'

Maggie's eyebrows shaped themselves into a question.

'When they don't care if you know who they are, that can only mean one thing. That they're going to kill you. Their secret is going to be safe.'

When she described what had happened to her, trying hard not to spell out the physical details, his eyes held hers with a seriousness she hadn't seen before. His face registered fury and resolve but, above all, sorrow. Finally and quietly, he said: 'Are you OK?'

She tried to speak, to say that she was all right, but the words were caught in her throat. Her eyes were stinging too. She hadn't cried until this moment, not until Uri had asked her that question. He held her hand, squeezing it as if in compensation for the words she wasn't saying. And he kept holding it.

When she told him about Miller, keeping her voice low, his face showed only mild surprise. 'You do realize,' she said, 'that this goes all the way to the top.'

'Of course it does. Special forces don't just deploy themselves.'

And then she felt it again, that same unease she sensed when Miller had let her go. She reached into her pocket, pulling out the piece of paper from the hotel, with Uri's message on it. On the other side, she scribbled a question.

When did they let you go? What time did the phone call come?

Uri looked puzzled for a second, then wrote down a guess at the answer. Maggie looked at the clock on the wall in the café. It was hard to work out with any accuracy, but if Uri was right, he had been released just minutes after her. The phone call must have come from Miller. We're letting her go; now let him go, too.

Maggie pulled back the piece of paper. 'So, Uri, I need to eat. What do they have here? I need to have something hot.' As she spoke, she was writing furiously.

They set us free to follow us. They haven't given up. They want us to lead them to it.

'Well,' said Uri, reading Maggie's note and nodding. 'The eggs are not bad. And the coffee. They serve it in big cups. Almost like bowls.'

They carried on like that, chatting about nothing. They spoke about what had happened, knowing it would sound strange if they didn't. But of what they would do next, they said not a word. At least not out loud.

There were fewer cars on the road now: Shabbat was coming, Uri explained. Jerusalem was getting more and more orthodox these days which meant driving from Friday afternoon till sundown on Saturday was frowned upon. Another reason this place could make you crazy.

Uri hailed a cab, speaking to the driver who promptly cranked up the volume on the radio.

'OK, Vladimir Junior,' said Maggie. 'What's going on?' She made a dramatic face before quoting his message: '"I know what we have to do."'

Uri explained that he had worked it out as the pain had intensified; he was sure it came to him right then. They were torturing him for information he didn't have. But by the time they were ready to let him go, he had something. *My brother*, his father had said. Who else could he mean?

He had gone back to the internet café, logged on as his father once again and found that email Ahmed Nour's son or daughter had sent. *Who are you? And why were you contacting my father?* In their haste, Maggie and he had done nothing about it, assuming that Nour Junior knew as little about his father as Uri did about his.

This time Uri had replied and, not long afterwards, there had been a response. Uri had been careful to say little, just that he had information on the death of Ahmed Nour and was keen to share it. The two bereaved sons, Israeli and Palestinian, agreed to meet at the American Colony Hotel, just fractionally on the eastern, and therefore Arab, side of the invisible seam that divided Jerusalem. They would be there in just a few minutes.

Maggie nodded. She had stayed there once, the last time she had been here. Nearly ten years ago, but she remembered it: the place was a legend. Watering hole for visiting journalists, diplomats, unofficial would-be peacemakers, assorted do-gooders and spies for all she knew. They would sit in the shaded courtyard, sipping mint tea and trading gossip for hours. In the evening, you would see the news correspondents come in, the dust of Gaza on their shoes. After a day seeing Third-World poverty and often bloody violence, coming back to the Colony was like returning to a safe haven.

That's how it seemed now, too, as they paid the taxi and walked in. The cool stone floor of the lobby, the old-world portraits and drawings on the wall, the bowing welcome of the staff. 'Colony' was right; the place could have been air-dropped straight out of the 1920s. It came back to her now, a memory of the room she slept in nearly a decade earlier. Above the desk had been a black and white photograph of the British General Allenby, entering Jerusalem in 1917. Modern Israel might have been just outside, but in here you could find the Palestine of long ago.

Uri didn't linger. He headed through the lobby and down the stairs, limping heavily. It was hardly a precaution – he knew they were being followed – but he told Nour to meet them by the one place the Colony's guests rarely used. If there was anyone else but Nour's son around, they would know just how closely they were being pursued.

Sure enough, the swimming pool was desolate, surrounded by a few unused sunchairs. Even when the weather was good, no one really sunbathed in Jerusalem. Not that kind of city. There was only one person here.

When he saw Uri approach, followed a pace or two behind by Maggie, he stood up. Against the bright sunlight, Maggie couldn't make out much more than an outline at first. But as she got nearer, she could see that he was tall, with hair cut short, almost shaven. As her eyes adjusted, she registered that he was probably in his early thirties, with sharp, clear green eyes. He wore jeans and a loose T-shirt.

Uri offered a hand, which the Palestinian took hesitantly. Maggie remembered the famous Rabin-Arafat handshake on the White House lawn back in 1993, how awkward Rabin had seemed, his whole upper body clenched into a posture of reluctance. The media had made so much of it, but the world fraternity of mediators had given it a familiar nod: they saw similarly constipated body language all the time.

'I realize,' Uri began, 'that I don't even know your name.'

'It's Mustapha. And you're—'

'I'm Uri.' They were speaking over each other. Nervousness, Maggie decided, and unfamiliarity: Israelis and Palestinians might live yards away from each other but, she knew, they hardly ever did anything as simple as talk.

Each gestured for the other to continue. Then Uri remembered himself, dipping into his shoulder bag to produce the portable radio he had picked up that morning. He turned it up loud, before mouthing, by way of explanation, the single word: bugs. Then he began again, first introducing Maggie, then getting to business.

'Mustapha, thanks so much for coming here. I know it's not easy.'

'I'm lucky to have Jerusalem residency. Otherwise, from Ramallah, it would have been impossible.'

'Look, as you know, our fathers knew each other.' Uri went on to explain the discovery of the anagram and the coded emails. Then, taking a deep breath, as if girding himself, he explained everything else: the tablet, the videomessage from his father, the tunnels. How Uri knew they were close, but not close enough.

'And you think my father knew where this tablet was hidden?'

'Maybe. After my father, yours was the very first killed. Someone thought he knew something.'

Mustapha Nour, who had been holding Uri's gaze, now looked over at Maggie, as if for validation. She gave a small nod.

'You know,' he said finally, looking down at his fingers, 'I always stayed out of politics. That was my father's business.'

'I know the feeling,' said Uri.

'We went through his emails and notebooks. We didn't see anything about this. There was a lock on his phone, so we couldn't check that, but his assistant went through his computer thoroughly.'

'Did he talk to you, in the last few days? About some kind of discovery?'

'No. We didn't talk much about his work.'

Uri leaned back, exhaling noisily. Maggie could tell that he was about to give up; this had been his last good idea.

I have put it somewhere safe, somewhere only you and my brother could know.

A wheel began to turn slowly in Maggie's brain. She thought of how Shimon Guttman's messages had worked so far, urging Uri to remember things he already knew. *What did we do on that trip, Uri? I hope you remember that.* Perhaps, Maggie thought now, he had done the same with his 'brother', Ahmed Nour. He had passed on no new information to his Palestinian colleague. Nour merely had to remember something he already knew.

'Mustapha,' Maggie began, placing a hand on Uri's forearm, gently but firmly telling him to give her a moment. 'Did it come as a complete surprise to you that your father knew an Israeli?'

'Yes,' he said, looking up at her, the green eyes piercing. Maggie was disappointed, thinking of a new line of inquiry, when he spoke again. 'And no.'

'No?'

'Well, it did when I first heard from you,' he nodded towards Uri. 'But the more I thought about it, the more it kind of made sense. I mean, he knew a lot about Israel, my father. He was an expert in the languages of this region, including, by the way, the script those ancient tablets are written in. And of course he knew Hebrew. He knew a lot about the way this country worked.'

'Know your enemy.' It was Uri, speaking just before Maggie had a chance to stamp on his foot. She was nodding more energetically now, hoping that she could keep Mustapha's eyeline from straying over to Uri.

'So he was a real expert,' she said. 'Go on.'

'Well, it makes sense that he couldn't only have got that from books. I realize that he probably spent more time here than he ever said. And that maybe he had someone to show him around.'

'OK. Did he ever mention—'

'Like I know he went to the tunnels, under the Haram al-Sharif. Not many Palestinians have done that. But I know he did it, though he never said so publicly. He disagreed with them passionately. "They're a Zionist attempt to undermine the Muslim Quarter," he said.'

'But he went anyway.'

'He was curious.'

'He was an archaeologist,' Maggie said with a sympathetic smile.

'Always. So he wanted to see.'

Maggie imagined these two old men, from opposite ideological poles, one an ultra-Zionist, the other a Palestinian nationalist, tagging along with a tourist party through the ancient tunnels she had seen that morning. Was it possible? Could Shimon Guttman have acted as a guide to Ahmed Nour, showing him the hidden reaches of the Western Wall? Had Nour perhaps done the same for Guttman, ushering him through the buried places of the Palestinian past? No wonder Guttman had wanted to speak to Nour about the tablet. They might well have been the only two people in this divided land able to read what it said – and to understand its true meaning.

She let the silence hang a little longer. 'Mustapha, I know it's hard. But we really need you to think. Was there anywhere else, any other place, your father might have known of? That perhaps he had in common with Shimon Guttman?'

'I really can't think of anywhere.'

Maggie caught Uri's eye, full of resignation. *This is not working.* He began to get up.

'All right,' Maggie said. 'Let's try this. Can we tell you the exact message Shimon Guttman left behind? See what it means to you?'

Mustapha nodded.

Maggie repeated it word for word, from memory. '"Go west, young man, and make your way to the model city, close to the Mishkan. You'll find what I left for you there, in the path of ancient warrens."'

Mustapha asked Maggie to repeat it, slowly. He shut his eyes as he listened to her. Finally, he spoke. 'I think he has to mean the Haram al-Sharif, the exact place you went. Warrens are like tunnels, yes? And the model city. This is how we all speak of Jerusalem, Jews and Muslims.'

'Sure, but where?' Uri was showing his frustration.

'When he says "Go west", could that tell you the way to go through the tunnels?'

'There is only one way through and I've done it.' It was Maggie, her own exasperation no longer contained.

'I am sorry.'

'No,' said Maggie, remembering herself. 'It's not your fault. We just thought there was something you might know.'

They began to walk back into the hotel. Maggie and Uri kept their heads down until they were in the car park, for fear of being recognized. Once outside, under the covered driveway by the hotel entrance, Maggie realized that she had barely offered her condolences to Mustapha. Out of politeness, she asked after his late father, how many children he had left, how many grandchildren.

'And he was still working?'

'Yes,' he said, explaining about the dig at Beitin. 'But that was not his life's dream. His real dream, he will never see.' His eyes were glittering.

'And what was that, Mustapha?' Maggie was aware that her head was cocked to one side, an amateurish bit of body language to convey 'caring'.

'He wanted to build a Palestine Museum, a beautiful building full of art and sculpture, and all the archaeological remains he could collect. The history of Palestine in one place.'

Uri looked up, suddenly alert.

'Like the Israel Museum.'

'Yes. In fact, I remember him speaking about that place. He said that one day we should have something like this. In our part of Jerusalem. Something that would show the world what used to be here, so they could see it for themselves.'

Uri's eyes widened. 'He said that?'

'Yes.' Mustapha was smiling. 'A long time ago. "One day, Mustapha," he said, "we shall build what they have, to show the world the history of *our* Jerusalem. Not abstract, but there to see and to touch."'

'My father must have shown it to him,' Uri said quietly.

'Uri?'

He gave her a brief glance. 'I'll explain on the way. Mustapha, can you come with us?'

Within a minute, the three of them were in a taxi, heading west across the city. The smile barely left Uri's face, even when he was shaking his head, saying 'of course' to himself, again and again. When Maggie asked where the hell they were going, he looked at both Mustapha and her, his face breaking into a broad grin. 'Thanks to our two fathers, I think our journey is about to end.'

CHAPTER SIXTY-TWO

JERUSALEM, FRIDAY, 1.11PM

Uri kept his spirits high for most of the journey. Sitting in the front, alongside the driver, and against a pounding techno beat from the radio, he took delight in explaining his father's clue.

'You see, I read it too quickly. I assumed that 'Go west, young man' had to refer to the Western Wall. It was obvious. But why would my father go to all that trouble just to do something obvious? He meant go west across Jerusalem, to the west of the city. To the place that "my brother" – your father, Mustapha – would know. The clue was in the word *Mishkan*. It can refer to the Temple, but also this place, the Knesset.' Right on cue, they passed Israel's parliament.

'What about the rest? The path of ancient warrens?'

'Don't worry, Maggie. We'll see it when we get there. I'm sure of it.'

He then turned back towards the driver, asking to borrow his mobile phone. He had done the same thing the instant they had left the Colony, then, as now, speaking intently in Hebrew for a while, before smiling and hanging up. Maggie wondered whether he had just phoned Orli: perhaps she was not as ex a girlfriend as Uri had insisted.

She was about to inquire when Uri's face seemed to darken. He began drumming his fingers on the hard vinyl above the glove compartment, urging the driver to go faster. When Maggie asked him what was wrong, he came back with a single word: 'Shabbat.'

They pulled into a car park, one that was worryingly empty. Uri did his best to bolt out of the car, hobbling over to the ticket office which consisted of a series of windows, all of them closed. By the time Maggie and Mustapha had caught up, Uri was already gesticulating desperately to a security guard on the door. As he feared, the Israel Museum was closed for the sabbath.

After much pleading, the guard grudgingly passed Uri a cellphone, apparently already connected. Uri's voice changed instantly, suddenly lighter, full of warmth and humour. Maggie had no idea what he was saying, but she felt certain that Uri was speaking to a woman.

Sure enough, a few minutes later an attractive young woman carrying a walkie-talkie and with a name tag pinned to the front of her dark blue jacket, appeared at the gate. As she approached, Uri turned to Maggie and Mustapha and whispered: 'We're a TV crew from the BBC, OK? Maggie, you're the reporter.'

The woman had a quizzical look on her face, but it was not hostile and Maggie could only admire as she watched Uri go to work. He gave this girl, her hair pulled back into a ponytail, both barrels – the fixed eye contact and the occasional shake of the head, to get the long curls of hair out of his eyes, even the hand landing, as if inadvertently, on her forearm. It was a charm offensive that offended Maggie much less than it charmed the ponytail girl, at least if the sudden unlocking of bolts and creaking opening of the gate was anything to go by.

As they were ushered in, the guard shaking his head in jobsworth disbelief, the woman pointing at her watch as if to say 'just five minutes', Maggie gave Uri a bewildered look.

'Media relations officer,' Uri said. 'Told her we'd met a few years ago and how sad I was that she'd already forgotten me.'

'And did you meet her a few years ago?'

'I have no idea.'

Uri had played the film-maker, somehow persuading the young woman that he, Maggie and Mustapha were part of a documentary crew due to fly back to London tonight. They desperately needed to get one last shot. It was, Uri had explained, a long distance zoom, which is why there was no sign of a cameraman. He was, in fact, over there, Uri had said, pointing at the faraway trees just below En Kerem. The camera would begin with Maggie in shot, then pull out to show the whole, extraordinary panorama. Their colleague was in position now; the media relations officer could call him if she wanted. The whole thing would take just five minutes and they would be gone.

'And she bought that crap?'

'I think she liked that I still remembered her.'

They were walking through what seemed like a university campus, or a private garden. There were neat rows of shrubs, each lovingly irrigated by lines of black hosepipe. All around was playful modern sculpture, including a giant steel column, painted red, that revealed itself as an oversized dog-whistle. There were signs off the main path, directing visitors to galleries, the gift shop or the restaurant. She could understand why Nour, exhausted by the dust and grime of Ramallah, would have dreamed of such a place for Palestine.

Now they passed an enormous white structure, set in a square pool of shallow water. It was an extraordinary shape, like a sensuously moulded breast, its nipple in the dead centre, pointing skyward. The surface, Maggie could now see, consisted of a thousand tiny white bricks.

'Shrine of the Book,' Uri said briskly, marching forward. 'Where they keep the Dead Sea Scrolls. You know they were found in, how do you say that in English? An urn? So that's the shape of the lid.'

'So not a tit then,' Maggie said to no one in particular. But Mustapha, who was walking beside her, smiled.

'Here.' It was Uri who had led them upward, so that they were now standing on a raised stone platform, looking across at a sweeping view of Jerusalem. On her right, Maggie could see the various government buildings Uri had pointed out en route, even a running track. Opposite, and in the distance, was indeed a thick covering of trees: Maggie half-expected to spot a cameraman, waiting for their signal.

But that was not what Uri was looking at. Instead, like a passenger on deck pointing at the seas below, he was gesturing downward, leaning over the observation bar to what lay beneath.

And now Maggie saw it. Laid out on the ground below was a miniature city, its walls, its streets, its houses. Everything was perfect, down to the little red roofs and the rows of hand-crafted columns, the tiny trees and the minuscule bricks in each wall. There were courtyards, turrets, even a coliseum. She was confused: was this a model of ancient Rome? And what was this structure that loomed over all the rest, solid marble and three times taller than any other building, its entrance framed by four Corinthian columns, each one crowned in gold, leading to a roof that seemed to blaze with precious metal?

A heartbeat later and she understood. This was a model of ancient Jerusalem and *that* was the Temple, its dominating, all-encompassing vastness clear now in a way it had never been before. This was how the city would have looked two thousand years ago, when the Second Temple of the Jews still stood. Of course it was disorientating; the most obvious landmark of the Temple Mount – the gold Dome of the Rock – had not yet been built; it would come six centuries later. But how awesome this sight must have been to the people who lived here two millennia ago. How terrifying to gaze upon a building so high, its walls and colonnades stretching so far and so wide, rendering the rest of Jerusalem nothing more than its hinterland.

Go west, young man, and make your way to the model city . . .

Maggie wanted to laugh at the simplicity of it. Guttman had been both ingenious and obvious, so long as you knew where to look. He had, Maggie realized now, been thorough too. If 'my brother' Ahmed Nour had been alive, he might well have known to come here straight away. But if he was gone, there was an alternative path to this place, via Second Life. He had secured his treasure by both belt and braces.

Uri had already taken the stairs down, so that he was now at the same level as the model. As Maggie watched him walk around, searching, the scale suddenly became clear; most of this city barely reached the height of his knee.

'OK, Maggie,' he called up, his voice different. 'We'll need you here, I think. For the shot. Musta— Mark, if you can join me down here, we can work out the angle.'

There was a small, low rail surrounding the model, nothing more. Unless you counted the ring of craggy rock which formed a miniature moat around it. But both could be easily walked over, so long as you waded with care.

'Head there,' Uri said, pointing at one of the outer retaining walls of the vast Temple courtyard. Behind it was the back of the structure itself. Maggie realized what she was doing: this was the Western Wall and she was aiming for the very spot where she had walked, underground, that morning. They had searched around the Temple Mount in the real world. Now they would do the same here, in the model version.

'And take this,' he said, handing her the mobile he had borrowed from, and not returned to, the cab driver. 'I've called it already and it's on speaker. Leave it on and it'll be an open line between us.' He then added firmly, 'If anything happens, just do exactly what I say. Understand?' When Maggie asked what he meant, he shook his head: 'No time. As soon as they see what we're doing, they'll throw us out.'

She stepped as gingerly as she could over the barrier and then the moat. She felt like Gulliver in ankle boots, Alice in Wonderland treading her giantess feet between these dwarf dwellings and midget walls. The space between them was barely enough to stand in. As she tiptoed faster, she felt the crunch of what she feared was a portico entrance to some grand mansion.

She looked back to see Uri pointing at a particular spot on the wall. It was a staircase, side on, which ascended to a small opening. It was directly in line with the centre of the Temple and therefore with the Temple Mount itself. *Of course*. This was Warren's Gate, where she had been this morning, close to where she had seen the women crying, feeling the dampness of the wall: God's tears. Directly behind it, just a matter of yards away, the women had said, was the Rock itself, the Foundation Stone, the place where Abraham had been ready to kill his son. *You'll find what I left for you there, in the path of ancient warrens.*

She was now looming over this tiny staircase, close enough to examine each individually crafted step. It had been impossible to see from afar, the side wall of the staircase kept it in shadow. She crouched down to see the top of the stairs, the flat surface that led onto the gate. She touched it, but felt only dust. Even this, she thought, the model-makers had got right: the same Old City dust she had had on her feet that morning.

Maggie stayed low, scratching away at the dust, until she felt something. A gap, a line between the sidewall of the model staircase and what was meant to be its top landing. She dug in her nails, pulling away the dust. The space continued all around.

Maggie tugged harder now. There was movement, she could

feel it. Finally the small rectangle of ground gave way in her hand. She knew that, at long last, she had found it.

Suddenly, she heard the sound of a woman's screams, followed by the thundering noise of male footsteps, charging as if in an animal stampede. She had barely stood up to her full height when she heard a single word bellowed out at terrifying volume.

'FREEZE!'

Stationed all around the model city, surrounding it from every angle, were half a dozen men, all dressed in black, their faces covered in masks. And each one of them had an automatic weapon aimed at her head.

CHAPTER SIXTY-THREE

JERUSALEM, FRIDAY, 1.32PM

Her eyes searched for Uri, but could see no sign of him. Nor of Mustapha. She remained frozen to the spot.

'Put your hands in the air. Now!'

Maggie did as she was told, phone in one hand and the clay tablet in the other. Her heart was thumping, powered by the excitement, still coursing through her veins, at finding what she felt sure was the tablet and, now, by sheer mortal terror.

Then a familiar voice. 'Thank you, Maggie. You surpassed yourself.'

He had been the last to arrive, coming down the stairs only now to join his men on the same level as the model city. 'I'm grateful. Your country is grateful.' She had to move her eyes to the left to see him: Bruce Miller.

'So why don't we do this cool and calm. You just stay there, and one of my boys will approach and relieve you of the tablet. Try anything stupid and we'll blow your brains out.'

Maggie could barely think above the throb of her own blood. She was truly cornered; what option did she have but to surrender to Miller? After all she and Uri had been through, she had to face reality. He and his gang of torturers had won.

It was then she heard another voice, nearer than Miller's yet not as clear. It took her a second to realize where it was coming from.

'Maggie, it's Uri.' The mobile phone, on speaker, crackling away inside her own hand. 'Listen very carefully. Tell Miller there is a live camera on him right now, streaming pictures of this onto the internet.'

She looked around again; no sign of Uri. He must have seen the men coming and fled down the hillside, perhaps into the trees. And what was this lunacy about cameras and the internet? Blagging your way past some PR girl on the door of a museum was one thing. Trying to bullshit a henchman to the American president was madness.

Then she remembered the moment on the highway, the instant moment of judgment when she had had to decide whether she trusted Uri or not. She had trusted him – and she had been right.

'Now be a good little girl and give us the tablet. Otherwise my boys might want to finish what they started. Don't think they didn't enjoy inspecting that tidy little body a yours inside and out. But, gotta tell ya, they found it a little frustrating, being restricted to the use of their hands and all. Next time, what if they take turns banging you, front and rear, then find a hundred different ways to rub out your boyfriend? How's that sound?'

Uri's voice again. 'Tell him to call the consulate. Get them to look at www.uriguttman.com and tell him what they see.'

Maggie hesitated; a plan was forming in her head. This was a public place, exposed. Miller wouldn't want to take her by force. Not here, not if he could help it. That was why he hadn't yet pounced. She spoke again.

'Is that any way for Bruce Miller, Special Assistant to the President of the United States, to be talking?'

'I'm the Political Counsellor to the President, if you don't mind, young lady. Now give me that tablet.'

Maggie smiled. Nothing more important to a Washington man than his title.

Uri's voice crackled again: 'Maggie, what are you doing? Tell him about the camera! Tell him to call the consulate!'

Not yet.

'You mean this?' She held up the tablet, keeping it as straight and steady as she could. 'What could be so important about this little object that you've got six men aiming their guns at me, an innocent woman – Maggie Costello, negotiator for the United States State Department?'

'We've been over this, Maggie.'

'It's just a little bit of clay, Mr Miller. Not much bigger than a credit card. What could be so important about that?'

Uri was boiling over. *'Tell him!'*

'Are you bluffing, Costello? You playing for time, 'cause you been had? Is that some dummy tablet in your hand? 'Cause if it is, you ain't got nothing. No bargaining chip, no leverage, not a bean.'

'Oh, I've got the real thing here, Bruce Miller, believe me. The last will and testament of Abraham the patriarch. That's what you're looking for, isn't it?'

'Maggie!' Uri was getting desperate, but she wasn't done yet.

'And that's why Rachel Guttman had to die. And Baruch Kishon. And Afif Aweida and God knows who else. You got your men to kill those people, just because of this, didn't you?'

'Maggie, come on. You know why we had to take those people out. If we didn't get that tablet into safe hands, many more would die. Thousands, maybe even millions.'

'So you're not ashamed of killing those people, even though they were innocent? You're not ashamed of assaulting me and torturing Uri Guttman? Tell me honestly, Bruce Miller. Look me in the eye and tell me.'

'Ashamed? I'm proud of it.'

'All right. I'll give the tablet to you,' she said, doing her best to keep her voice steady. She had heard what she needed to hear. But the guns remained locked on her.

'But there's something you ought to know, Mr Miller. You've just made what could be your greatest ever TV appearance. There's a camera on you right now, relaying this whole conversation onto the internet. Call the consulate. Get someone to log on to www.uriguttman.com. Ask them to describe to you what they see. Go on. If I'm lying you'll soon find out and then you can do what the hell you like to me.'

She saw Miller pull out his mobile phone and whisper into it.

Uri spoke again. 'Tell him to wave for the camera.'

Maggie could hear the confidence in Uri's voice. 'Come on, Bruce Miller, Political Counsellor to the President of the United States of America, give us a wave,' she called out.

She heard two words of confirmation, from Miller's own mouth. They were said quietly, but their meaning was unmistakeable.

'Holy shit.'

God only knew how, but Uri had not been bluffing. He did indeed have Miller on camera; it had held steady on his face as he had identified himself and confessed everything.

'That's mighty clever, Miss Costello. I'll hand it to you. But with the greatest of respect, who cares about some no-name website? No one was watching that. It went into the ether and now it's vanished.'

'Not quite. We're recording this as it goes out. People will be able to play it again and again.' It was Uri's voice, except this time it was not coming through the phone. He was emerging from the hillside, climbing back up through the trees – with a small, hand-held video-camera at his eye. Walking beside him was Mustapha. Maggie could only smile at the sheer cheek of it.

'Right now, we've got the news editor over at Channel 2 looking at these pictures. And who was it you just phoned, Mustapha?'

'Al Jazeera. Ramallah bureau.'

'They're all watching this little scene. And before you get any ideas, Mr Miller, this is only a second camera. Getting what we call B-roll. The main camera is down there, safely hidden from view. You blast me now and my friend there will capture it in glorious Technicolor.'

Maggie could see Miller paling. He tried a smug smile, one of his characteristic TV expressions, but it came out crooked. Finally he stammered out some words. 'Who's going to believe this cock and bull story of yours?'

'No one would have believed it, Bruce,' Maggie conceded. 'Not until you confirmed every last detail just now. For which we are eternally grateful. You know, when this bit of video finds its way onto YouTube and CNN and ABC and all the rest, I don't think even you will be able to talk your way out of it.'

A mobile phone rang. Miller's. He answered, only to turn from pale to transparent. He swivelled around, showing his back to Uri's camera, though his voice was still audible.

'Yes, Mr President. I can hear you clearly, sir. I understand: you can see me too. I agree, technology is an incredible thing, sir.' He said nothing for a good half-minute, then spoke again. 'I will draft the letter of resignation immediately, sir. And yes, I will make clear that this was a rogue operation, wholly my own initiative. Goodbye, Mr President.'

Without another word, Miller gestured at the armed men. Their weapons still raised, they slowly withdrew back up the steps, away from the model, forming a kind of protective cordon around Miller's retreat. A few seconds later and they were gone.

Uri lowered his camera and walked over to Maggie. As they hugged, he pointed towards the trees. 'That's who I was calling from the car. An old cameraman friend of mine who lives in En Kerem. I told him to get in position, hide himself and aim his longest lens here. Oh, and to bring his smallest microwave transmitter with him. With the sound from your phone, I'd say it was my best work.'

Maggie suddenly broke off the hug, seized by a thought.

'Is that thing still on?'

Uri nodded.

It was the object in her hand that made her do it. It felt like an explosive, primed to go off at any moment. So many people had already been killed for it; she and Uri had been chased, beaten and shot for it. No one who held its secrets was safe.

'Point the camera at me,' she said to Uri. 'Right now.'

He brought the viewfinder to his eye, steadied himself, then gave her a thumbs up.

'My name is Maggie Costello. I'm a peace negotiator working for the United States government in Jerusalem. This,' she held up the tablet, just as Shimon Guttman had done in the video-message they had seen yesterday, 'this tablet is nearly four thousand years old. Over the course of the last week, Bruce Miller and an American covert-ops team have bugged, burgled and murdered their way across this country and beyond trying to get hold of it. You heard Mr Miller confess to that a moment ago. He wanted to keep the fact of this tablet's existence, and above all its contents, a secret. And here's why.'

At last she took a good look at the object she had peeled from its hiding place by the miniature Warren's Gate, gripping it tightly ever since. When she finally saw it up close, she was almost disappointed. It was so small, the characters etched on it so tiny. The whole thing was no bigger, and much slimmer, than a cigarette packet, hewn from rough, earthen clay. And yet her own government had been prepared to kill for it – along with any number of fanatics among both the Israelis and Palestinians. The words carved here, so many thousands of years ago, would have the power to unleash a war of wars, one that would never stay confined to those two sides. What if Abraham had given Mount Moriah to Ishmael but the Israelis refused to hand it over? The world's Muslims would insist they had been cheated of their birthright. The clash of civilizations would be made terrifyingly real. And if Abraham had bequeathed the Temple Mount to the Jews, would the Muslims simply give way, letting go of the site where Mohammed rose to the heavens? Whatever this small chunk of clay said, it could only spell victory for one side and disaster for the other.

As she turned it over, she looked for a small piece of tape on the bottom edge which she had noticed when she pulled the tablet from the ground. She had assumed it was part of the fixing that Shimon Guttman had cleverly devised to keep this treasure hidden in the shadows of the model city. But when she brought it up to her eye she saw that it was not just tape, though it was sticky on one side. It was instead a tiny clear plastic envelope, a small-scale version of the kind traffic wardens put on car windscreens to keep a parking ticket dry. Carefully, she peeled it away from the tablet. Then she removed from it a small white square of paper bearing three neat, if tiny, blocks of print. The first was in Hebrew, the second in Arabic and the third in English.

She skimmed the English paragraph and began to read aloud, into the camera.

'This is a tablet dictated to a scribe by Abraham the patriarch, shortly before his death in Hebron. It is in cuneiform script, in Old Babylonian language. The translation of his words reads thus:

> *'I Abraham, son of Terach, in front of the judges have attested thus. The land where I took my son, there to make a sacrifice of him to the Mighty Name, the Mountain of Moriah, this land has become*

a source of dissension between my two sons; let their names here be recorded as Isaac and Ishmael. So have I thus declared in front of the judges that the Mount shall be bequeathed as follows—'

She fell silent the instant the shot rang out. When she hit the ground, her hand stayed tightly wound around the tablet, clinging on to it, as if to life itself.

CHAPTER SIXTY-FOUR

JERUSALEM, FRIDAY, 1.44PM

The camera fell from his hand with a thud. Uri dashed over to her, crouching over her body to see where she had been hit. Less than a second later he heard a bullet whizzing past his own ear. Now he too fell flat, trying to lie on top of Maggie, to shield her body from the incoming fire.

He looked across and saw Mustapha, also prone on the ground. With a tiny movement of his finger, the Palestinian gestured for Uri to look upwards. There, directly above them, leaning over the parapet that overlooked the model city, were the barrels of several guns, firing into the trees opposite. Were these Miller's men, regrouped? Were they trying to kill the hidden cameraman, as if that would somehow save them and their boss?

There was a rustle from the trees and then a Hebrew cry of *'Al tira!'*

Don't shoot.

From above, Uri heard a response: *'Hadel esh!'*

Hold your fire.

He gradually raised himself up. Maggie was on the ground, deathly still.

Now, he could hear a clamour of Hebrew voices as more than a dozen men pounded down the steps: Israeli police. Their semi-automatic weapons were aimed squarely at two men standing on the hillside just below the model.

'Identify yourselves!' the police commander barked.

There was silence.

'Identify yourselves or we shoot!'

Were these Palestinians, their Hebrew learned in jail, come here to mount some suicide mission? If they hesitated even a second longer, Uri knew what would happen: they would be shot in the head, the only sure way to prevent them setting off a bomb.

But they wore no bulky clothes, the usual giveaway. They were dressed casually; truth be told, they looked Israeli.

'We are The Defenders of United Jerusalem,' the older of the pair said eventually in unaccented Hebrew. And now, as the police circled them, Uri could see clearly, perched on the back of each of their heads, a knitted kippa, or skullcap – the unambiguous badge of the Jewish settler movement.

'So they were after us as well.'

Uri wheeled round to see Maggie sitting up, rubbing her eyes.

'Maggie! You're alive!'

'I'm sorry about that. I didn't know I was such a wuss.'

'What are you talking about?'

'I'm meant to be a big tough diplomat. I'm not meant to faint the moment someone fires a gun.'

The police kept all three of them, Uri, Maggie and Mustapha, for several hours, asking each of them to give long, detailed statements. At their side throughout was a lawyer, Uri's brother-in-law, who insisted on his clients' right to keep their private property, including the clay tablet, private. After his intervention, the tablet stayed with them at all times. As for the tiny white square of paper, Maggie hid that deep in a pocket and never let it go.

When they emerged from the police station, it was to a scene Maggie and Uri had seen plenty of times on TV but which neither ever expected to experience directly. Hundreds of camera lenses were aimed at them, flashbulbs strobing, arc lights on full glare.

They had barely set foot outside the building when this vast crowd gave a collective roar, as dozens of photographers and reporters called out in unison: 'Maggie! Maggie! What did he say? Maggie, what did Abraham say? What does the tablet say?'

Uri and Mustapha flanked her on either side, each of them shoving people out of the way in order to get to the taxi that was waiting for them. The driver had to do two full circuits before he had shaken off the chasing vans and motor cycles, eventually reaching Maggie's hotel.

In the sanctuary of her room, Maggie switched on the television. She had some clue what to expect from her mobile phone, returned to her by the police with a flashing message announcing *Inbox Full.* She listened to the first few voice messages: BBC, NPR, CNN, Reuters, AP, the *New York Times,* all requesting an interview as soon as humanly possible. The *Daily Mail* in London offered a six-figure sum if she would tell them the exclusive story of a single woman's quest for the tablet of Abraham. There were also several messages from the White House.

Now when she clicked through the channels she kept catching sight of herself, holding the clay tablet up to Uri's camera. Fox News was playing, in an apparent loop, the tape of Bruce Miller confessing his multiple sins, culminating in the line, 'Ashamed? I'm proud of it.' Finally, Maggie settled on BBC World.

'We're joined now by Ernest Freundel of the British Museum here in London, one of the very few people in the world capable of reading the cuneiform text in which this crucial tablet was allegedly written. Dr Freundel, what do you make of this claim?'

'Well, ordinarily any report of this kind would be treated with the utmost scepticism. But I understand this tablet was found and translated by Professor Shimon Guttman, who was one of the greatest authorities on this subject. If he said it was authentic, then I am inclined to believe him.'

'And your reaction to the notion that this is the last will and testament of Abraham himself?'

'Well, there will be tests and so on. But Guttman was not a gullible man. One has also to say that if the Americans were going to such lengths to obtain this tablet, it does suggest that they at least were persuaded that it was real.'

'And an emotional moment for a scholar like yourself, Dr Freundel?'

'I cannot deny that I would give almost anything to have had the chance to see this tablet, or hold it, myself. Alas, I never had that chance. But it is of immeasurable significance.'

As Maggie perched on the end of the bed, Uri came over, clutching a laptop computer. He clicked through a series of websites: *Al-Ahram*, the *Washington Post*, the *Guardian*, the *Times of India* and *China Daily*. They were all covering the same story. Finally, he showed her the headline on the front page of the *Haaretz* site.

A world on tenterhooks; Israelis and Palestinians await the word of Abraham.

Underneath was a news account of that afternoon's events at the Israel Museum. It said that Israeli police had arrested settlers' leader Akiva Shapira, the suspected leader of The Defenders of United Jerusalem. What's more, the police spokesman added, they had gathered evidence that Uri Guttman and Maggie Costello had also been within the sights of a radical Islamist cell linked to the wanted militant Salim Nazzal.

Maggie clicked and clicked. There were endless columns and debates devoted to discussing what Abraham might or might not have said. There were cries on all sides that it must be a fake, especially, said the Israeli hawks, if Abraham gave the Temple Mount to the Muslims and especially, said the Palestinian hard-liners, if Abraham gave the Haram al-Sharif to the Jews. The blogosphere was replete with conspiracy theorists, insisting the timing of the tablet's release was just too neat to be real.

'You know, Maggie, you're going to have get the truth out, the full text of the testament. It can't wait.'

Maggie looked back at the TV. It now showed the British prime minister, standing in Downing Street, declaring that 'History is holding its breath'.

Maggie sighed. 'I know, Uri. I just need to work out who should be the one to say it.'

When she looked back on it, as she would many times in the years ahead, she would conclude that Bruce Miller's most valuable lapse was a single sentence: *There's a back channel too, so they're talking, believe me*. That's what he had said. Other people would probably have forgotten it, but not Maggie, nor any other mediator. Back channels were too intriguing to forget. Even under the duress of the body search and the battering from Miller's men, the reference had lodged in her head and stayed there.

Maybe it shouldn't have surprised her; it was common for even the bitterest enemies to keep a line of communication open, whether through some trusted business tycoon, a personal friend of a prime minister or a foreign government. Of course the Israelis and Palestinians would have maintained a way to keep talking.

She thought of it again now, as she lay on the hotel bed, allowing herself to drift off into a few minutes of exhausted sleep. She dreamed she was roaming the streets of Jerusalem not in her own body, but as the bra-topped avatar created by her sister in Second Life. She was floating above the golden Dome of the Rock, soaring high above the Western Wall. The men down below, in their beards, black coats and prayer shawls were looking up at her, their mouths agape . . .

She woke suddenly, her forehead clammy with sweat. Could it be? Was it possible? She grabbed at the computer and headed straight for Second Life, logging on again as Shimon Guttman's alter ego, Saeb Nastayib. She teleported straight back to the seminar room at Harvard University. *Please be there.*

Sure enough, there were the avatars she had seen before: Yaakov Yariv and Khalil al-Shafi. She approached, hit the *Chat* button and typed a simple message: *I have the information the world is waiting for.*

The reply did not come instantly, for reasons she would later understand. It turned out that both Yariv's office and al-Shafi's would dump 'sleeping' avatars in Second Life's Harvard seminar room, just to maintain a presence there. That way they could keep the channel open, ensuring that each side was available to the other twenty-four hours a day. Amir Tal, the personal aide to the Israeli prime minister, would check in hourly during the day and several times at night while his Palestinian counterpart would do the same. It had been al-Shafi's idea: he had read about internet simulations of the Middle East peace process while in jail and had logged on to one, taking the role of Khalil al-Shafi, soon after his release. All it needed, he realized, was a senior Israeli to join in and they would have their own back channel. No need for midnight flights to Oslo or clandestine weekends in Scandinavian wood cabins. This dialogue could take place in full daylight, with total deniability. If anyone asked what was going on, 'Yaakov Yariv' and 'Khalil al-Shafi' could say they were simply American students, playing a game.

The first reply came from al-Shafi. She asked him to telephone her, to verify that it was really him and, sure enough, she soon heard that familiar voice down the telephone. She arranged to meet his closest aide in an hour's time.

Then she made the same arrangement with Amir Tal.

They gathered in the plush, west Jerusalem home of an American businessman. Maggie was too tired for pleasantries and got straight to the point.

'As you know, I have the tablet. Today I was about to reveal the full text, on camera, because I feared that if I didn't, if something happened to me, the last testament of Abraham would be lost forever. But now it is safe.'

She explained that she would not yet show them the tablet – that would have to wait until the leaders themselves met. She produced instead Guttman's translation, reading the English out loud to the two men, then passing the paper so that the two of them could read the words again, in their own languages. They both paled in unison.

'Of course you'll have every chance to verify the authenticity of the tablet and this translation as soon as we move to the next stage,' Maggie said quietly, anxious to give them as much time as they needed to absorb what they had just read.

'And what is the next stage, Miss Costello?' the Palestinian asked.

Maggie explained that it was up to the two leaders to tell the world what Abraham had decided. It wasn't right for the announcement to come from her, an outsider. Instead they should call a joint press conference for the next day, straight after the Jewish sabbath. Uri Guttman and Mustapha Nour would be at their side, representing their late fathers, as the two leaders made the announcement.

Maggie watched the press conference on television. It would have been fun to be there, but she didn't want to create another media zoo like the one at the police station. Besides, in the background was where she belonged. For this to work, the words had to come from Yariv and al-Shafi, no one else.

She wondered how they would do it. Would Yariv go first, in Hebrew, then al-Shafi in Arabic, followed by an interpreter? Or would they do it the other way around? In the end, they came up with something much, much better.

Al-Shafi went first and he spoke in English, introducing this as the tablet dictated by Abraham the patriarch and then reading the text:

'I Abraham, son of Terach, in front of the judges have attested thus. The land where I took my son, there to make a sacrifice of him to the Mighty Name, the Mountain of Moriah, this land has become a source of dissension between my two sons.'

Then he paused and Yaakov Yariv took over, also in English:

'Let their names here be recorded as Isaac and Ishmael. So have I thus declared in front of the judges that the Mount shall be bequeathed as follows—'

Then the two men paused, veteran showmen the pair of them, before reading on, in unison, their voices chiming perfectly:

'That it shall be shared between my two sons and their descendants in a manner of their choosing. But that they be clear that it belongs to neither one of them, but to both, now and forever. That they be entrusted as its guardians and custodians, to protect it on behalf of the Mighty Name, the one Lord who is sovereign over everything and all of us. Sworn with the seal of Abraham, son of Terach, witnessed by his sons, in Hebron, this day.'

EPILOGUE

JERUSALEM, TWO DAYS LATER

She had all her papers on her lap, in a neat black portfolio case. Less was always more when it came to a negotiation, she believed: a blank note pad should really be enough. Only at the very last stage did you need sheaves of documents, usually maps. And they were not at that stage. Not yet, anyway.

She took a look at this room, at the large dark wooden table stretching out before her, its faded elegance typical of this building. The same vintage as the American Colony Hotel, she reckoned, a leftover of the grand imperial past and the delusions of nearly a century ago. She looked at her watch, again. She had got here twenty minutes early. Another five minutes and they would get started.

The sheer drama of the joint press conference had had an even more powerful effect than anyone had anticipated. Television is a sentimental medium and the sight of those two old warhorses joining together, incanting the words of their common ancestor, had proved irresistible. The news networks stayed in twenty-four-hour mode – all Abraham, all the time – wiping out the coverage of the earlier violence. The pundits began wondering if peace was in fact the Middle East's age-old destiny, a destiny of which it had been cruelly cheated. *Time* magazine put a renaissance image of Abraham on its cover above a single line: *The Peacemaker*.

A euphoric Amir Tal and his Palestinian counterpart had been on the phone just before midnight on Saturday, asking Maggie what she wanted in return for throwing their bosses an extraordinary political lifeline, allowing them to take credit for a discovery that would endow them both with enormous, enduring authority.

'Only that the two sides resume face-to-face talks immediately,' she had said. Not through officials: just the two leaders in a room with a single mediator.

The tablet meant there was now no excuse for failure to solve the last remaining question: the status of the Temple Mount. They should aim to have a final peace accord ready for signing within a week, one that their peoples would accept, one that would have the blessing of Abraham himself.

The two officials offered their provisional agreement. Maggie pressed home her advantage.

'And there's one last thing I want.'

'And what is that, Miss Costello?'

'Well, it relates to the identity of the mediator.'

That had been two days ago. She had spent the forty-eight hours since that phone call preparing herself. She had read every note, every minute, of the talks so far, every official document prepared by both sides, occasionally demanding translations of key texts used by the Israeli and Palestinian teams internally. She also bought herself some new clothes.

In between it all, she saw Uri. After she had watched the press conference on TV – and the moment when Mustapha and Uri had hugged before the cameras had been one of the highlights – they had met up at Someone to Run With, the late-night café where they had hammered away at the computer before fleeing, fearing pursuit from Miller's men. 'We're still the oldest people here,' she said and he smiled. Each asked the other about their plans and each shrugged. Uri said he had some things to sort out here in Jerusalem, his parents' house, his father's papers.

'Your father gave you one last surprise, didn't he?'

'You know, it's funny. The whole world is going crazy over this tablet. Everything it means. But for me the most amazing thing is that my dad did so much to keep it safe. Even though it says what it says.'

'He was a scholar.'

'Not just that. Remember what he told my mother, over and over? That this changes everything? Maybe it changed him.'

Hesitantly, Maggie steered the conversation round to Bruce Miller and why she had been sent to Jerusalem. She told Uri that Miller had wanted them to sleep together, that she had been – she hesitated before the word – a honeytrap. She told him how ashamed it made her, that she felt sickened by it.

He listened hard, unsmiling. 'But you didn't know you were a trap, did you, Maggie? It wasn't your fault. You can't be a trap if you don't know you're a trap. And it's my fault for walking into you. Besides, you're much rarer than honey.'

They hugged, a long, tight hug, and then shyly, like teenagers at summer camp, they exchanged email addresses. Neither had a physical address they could be sure of. When Maggie began to say goodbye, he placed a finger over her lips. 'Not goodbye,' he said. '*L'hitraot*. It means "Until we see each other again". And we will. Soon.' And then they kissed, until both of them knew that promise was not vain.

Now a distant grandfather clock struck ten, the clock no doubt a parting gift of the British who had built this Government House when they ruled Palestine. Maggie could hear a sudden surge of noise outside: the sound of several cars pulling up, and a press ruck, questions being shouted, bulbs flashing. A minute or two later, and the same thing all over again. Maggie straightened her papers one last time.

Then, the sound of footsteps down two corridors. From opposite directions she could see the leader of the Israelis and the leader of the Palestinians walking, each man alone, towards this room. She took a deep breath.

She shook both their hands, then invited them to shake hands with each other and gestured for them to take their seats.

'Thank you, gentlemen,' Maggie Costello said, aiming a warm smile at both of them.

The smile was genuine. It was the smile of a woman who, at long last, was back where she belonged.

She cleared her throat. 'Shall we begin?'

ACKNOWLEDGMENTS

They say writing is a lonely business, but it's not completely true. Writers rely on people who are willing to share their time and wisdom – and I am delighted to have a chance to thank some of them here.

John Curtis, Keeper of the Department of the Ancient Near East at the British Museum, and one of the very first to sound the alarm at the looting of Iraq's heritage following the invasion in 2003, patiently explained the full extent of that tragic series of events. His colleague at the Museum, Irving Finkel, was kind enough to tutor me in the customs of the Abrahamic period and the rarefied field of old Babylonian cuneiform writing, a subject in which he may well be the world's leading authority. The sample of cuneiform that appears in this book was his handiwork, while some of Shimon Guttman's experiences as a scholar echo those of Dr Finkel. I am greatly indebted to him for both his learning and his energetic backing for this project.

Insight into the extraordinary international trade in stolen antiquities came via Karen Sanig of London lawyers Mishcon de Reya, along with former Detective Sergeant Richard Ellis, the founder of Scotland Yard's Art and Antiquities Squad. I hugely admire their determination to fight a crime that seeks to deprive civilization of some of its greatest treasures. I'm also grateful to Dr Rupert L Chapman III, formerly Executive Secretary of the Palestine Exploration Foundation and to Edward Fox, whose book *Palestine Twilight* explains so well the political charge generated by archaeology in the Middle East. The staff of BA Cargo at Heathrow and of HM Revenue and Customs could not have been more helpful.

I was introduced to Second Life by my *Guardian* colleagues Aleks Krotoski and Victor Keegan, Vic generously playing Virgil as he guided me through the depths of that mysterious underworld. Once again Tom Cordiner and Steven Thurgood were ready to share their limitless wisdom on matters computing.

On the Middle East itself, I owe a debt to the hundreds of people, Israeli and Palestinian, I have met while studying or writing about this region over two decades. Many of their stories inform this one. Particular thanks are due to Dr Meron Medzini; Aryeh Banner of the Western Wall Heritage Foundation; Chris Stevens of the US State Department; Doug Krikler; and my old friend, Marshall Yam, who offered a pivotal thought just as I was first shaping this story. Both of my parents, Michael and Sara Freedland, along with my father-in-law Michael Peters, read an early draft, giving valuable advice along the way.

At HarperCollins, Jane Johnson is the kind of editor every writer would kill for: eagle-eyed, enthusiastic, demanding and with a maddeningly consistent habit of being right. She and Sarah Hodgson form a dauntingly capable team.

Three individuals deserve special thanks. Jonathan Cummings is not only able to ferret out the most obscure nugget of information at lightning speed, he has also become a cherished comrade and co-conspirator. Jonny Geller is the godfather to this entire project, having believed in it from the very beginning, nudging it along with regular doses of sage advice. I've said it before and I'll say it again: he's the best agent in the business, a model friend – and none of this would have happened without him.

Finally, my wife Sarah. Her enthusiasm and excitement for this story never flagged, even when work on it kept me chained to the desk for too many hours. She read the manuscript with insight and care, suggesting multiple improvements. She is a source of constant encouragement, laughter and love. Like this book, my story has a heroine – and it is her.